Belgravia

ABOUT THE AUTHOR

Educated at Ampleforth and Magdalene College, Cambridge, Julian Fellowes is a multi-award-winning actor, writer, director, and producer. As creator, sole writer, and executive producer of the hit television series *Downton Abbey*, Fellowes has won three Emmy Awards.

Fellowes received the Academy Award for Best Original Screenplay for *Gosford Park* (2002). His work was also honored by the Writer's Guild of America, the New York Film Critics' Circle, and the National Society of Film Critics for Best Screenplay. Other writing credits for film include *Piccadilly Jim* (2004), *Vanity Fair* (2004), *Young Victoria* (2009), *The Tourist* (2010), *Romeo & Juliet* (2013), and the upcoming three-part drama *Doctor Thorne* for ITV. Fellowes also directed the award-winning films *Separate Lies* and *From Time to Time*. Fellowes wrote the books for the Tony-nominated stage production of *Mary Poppins* and *School of Rock—The Musical*, which opened on Broadway in December 2015 and is written and produced by Andrew Lloyd Webber.

Fellowes has authored two novels: the international bestsellers *Snobs* (2005) and *Past Imperfect* (2008/2009).

Julian Fellowes became a life peer in 2011. He lives in Dorset and London with his wife, Emma.

EDITORIAL CONSULTANT: IMOGEN EDWARDS-JONES

An international bestselling author, columnist, and scriptwriter, Imogen Edwards-Jones is probably best known for the Babylon series of books, which sold over one million copies in the UK and went on to inspire the BBC1 hit TV series *Hotel Babylon*. She lives with her husband and two children in west London.

HISTORICAL CONSULTANT: LINDY WOODHEAD

Lindy Woodhead is the author of two acclaimed books, *War Paint: Madame Helena Rubinstein and Miss Elizabeth Arden, Their Lives, Their Times, Their Rivalry* (2003) and *Shopping, Seduction & Mr. Selfridge* (2007), which was adapted by Andrew Davies into the hugely successful Sunday night drama series *Mr. Selfridge*. Made by ITV Studios and coproduced with Masterpiece-PBS in the United States, Season One of *Mr. Selfridge* opened in January 2013 to an audience of 8.5 million. In June 2016, the Goodman Theatre, Chicago, will stage the world premiere of the musical based on *War Paint*. Married with two sons, Lindy divides her time between Oxfordshire and London and is a Fellow of the Royal Society of Arts.

JULIAN FELLOWES

Belgravia

Editorial consultant
Imogen Edwards-Jones

Historical consultant
Lindy Woodhead

GRAND CENTRAL
PUBLISHING

New York   Boston

Grand Central Publishing
Hachette Book Group
1290 Avenue of the Americas, New York, NY 10104
grandcentralpublishing.com
twitter.com/grandcentralpub

JULIAN FELLOWES'S is an unregistered trademark of Julian Fellowes and is
used by Grand Central Publishing under license.

BELGRAVIA is a registered trademark of The Orion Publishing Group Limited.

First published as a complete volume in Great Britain in 2016 by Weidenfeld & Nicolson,
first published in serial form as Julian Fellowes's BELGRAVIA, an imprint of The Orion
Publishing Group Ltd, Carmelite House, 50 Victoria Embankment, London EC4Y 0DZ.

First U.S. Edition: July 2016

Grand Central Publishing is a division of Hachette Book Group, Inc. The Grand
Central Publishing name and logo is a trademark of Hachette Book Group, Inc.

The publisher is not responsible for websites (or their content)
that are not owned by the publisher.

The Hachette Speakers Bureau provides a wide range of authors for speaking events.
To find out more, go to www.hachettespeakersbureau.com or call (866) 376-6591.

Imogen Edwards-Jones acted as an editorial consultant on the
writing of Julian Fellowes's *Belgravia*.

Lindy Woodhead acted as a historical consultant on the writing of
Julian Fellowes's *Belgravia*.

Library of Congress Cataloging-in-Publication Data has been applied for.

ISBNs: 978-1-4555-4116-4 (hardcover), 978-1-4555-4194-2 (large print),
978-1-4555-4119-5 (ebook), 978-1-4789-4153-8 (audiobook, downloadable),
978-1-4789-4148-4 (audiobook, cd)

Printed in the United States of America

RRD-C

10 9 8 7 6 5 4 3 2 1

To my wife, Emma,
without whom
nothing in my life
would be quite possible.

CONTENTS

.1.

Dancing into Battle

The past, as we have been told so many times, is a foreign country where things are done differently. This may be true—indeed it patently *is* true when it comes to morals or customs, the role of women, aristocratic government, and a million other elements of our daily lives. But there are similarities, too. Ambition, envy, rage, greed, kindness, selflessness, and, above all, love have always been as powerful in motivating choices as they are today. This is a story of people who lived two centuries ago, and yet much of what they desired, much of what they resented, and the passions raging in their hearts were only too like the dramas being played out in our own ways, in our own time...

It did not look like a city on the brink of war; still less like the capital of a country that had been torn from one kingdom and annexed by another barely three months before. Brussels in June 1815 could have been *en fête*, with busy, colorful stalls in the markets and brightly painted, open carriages bowling down the wide thoroughfares, ferrying their cargoes of great ladies and their daughters to pressing social engagements. No one would have guessed that the emperor Napoléon was on the march and might encamp by the edge of the town at any moment.

None of which was of much interest to Sophia Trenchard as she pushed through the crowds in a determined manner that rather belied her eighteen years. Like any well-brought-up young woman, especially in an alien land, she was accompanied by her maid, Jane Croft, who, at twenty-two, was four years older than her mistress. Although if either of them could be said to be protecting the other from a bruising encounter with a fellow pedestrian, it would be Sophia, who looked ready for anything. She was pretty, very pretty even, in that classic blonde, blue-eyed English way, but the cut-glass set of her mouth made it clear that this particular girl would not need Mama's permission to embark on an adventure. "Do hurry, or he'll have left for luncheon and our journey will have been wasted." She was at that period of her life that almost everyone must pass through, when childhood is done with and a faux maturity, untrammeled by experience, gives one a sense that anything is possible until the arrival of real adulthood proves conclusively that it is not.

"I'm going as fast as I can, miss," murmured Jane, and, as if to prove her words, a hurrying Hussar pushed her backward without even pausing to learn if she was hurt. "It's like a battleground here." Jane was not a beauty, like her young mistress, but she had a spirited face, strong and ruddy, if more suited to country lanes than city streets.

She was quite determined in her way, and her young mistress liked her for it. "Don't be so feeble." Sophia had almost reached her destination, turning off the main street into a yard that might once have been a cattle market but which had now been commandeered by the army for what looked like a supply depot. Large carts unloaded cases and sacks and crates that were being carried to surrounding warehouses, and there seemed to be a constant stream of officers from every regiment, conferring and sometimes quarreling as they moved around in groups. The arrival of a striking young woman and her maid naturally attracted some attention, and the conversation, for a moment, was quelled and almost ceased. "Please don't trouble yourselves," said Sophia, looking around calmly. "I'm here to see my father, Mr. Trenchard."

A young man stepped forward. "Do you know the way, Miss Trenchard?"

"I do. Thank you." She walked toward a slightly more important-looking entrance to the main building, and, followed by the trembling Jane, she climbed the stairs to the first floor. Here she found more officers apparently waiting to be admitted, but this was a discipline to which Sophia was not prepared to submit. She pushed open the door. "You stay here," she said. Jane dropped back, rather enjoying the curiosity of the men.

The room Sophia entered was a large one, light and commodious, with a handsome desk in smooth mahogany and other furniture in keeping with the style, but it was a setting for commerce rather than Society, a place of work, not play. In one corner, a portly man in his early forties was lecturing a brilliantly uniformed officer. "Who the devil is come to interrupt me!" He spun around, but at the sight of his daughter his mood changed and an endearing smile lit up his angry red face. "Well?" he said. But she looked at the officer. Her father nodded. "Captain Cooper, you must excuse me."

"That's all very well, Trenchard—"

"Trenchard?"

"*Mr.* Trenchard. But we must have the flour by tonight. My commanding officer made me promise not to return without it."

"And I promise to do my level best, Captain." The officer was clearly irritated but he was obliged to accept this, since he was not going to get anything better. With a nod he retired, and the father was alone with his girl. "Have you got it?" His excitement was palpable. There was something charming in his enthusiasm, this plump, balding master of business who was suddenly as excited as a child on Christmas Eve.

Very slowly, squeezing the last drop out of the moment, Sophia opened her reticule and carefully removed some squares of white pasteboard. "I have three," she said, savoring her triumph, "one for you, one for Mama, and one for me."

He almost tore them from her hand. If he had been without food and water for a month, he could not have been more anxious. The copperplate printing was simple and elegant.

Miss Sophia Trenchard

THE DUCHESS OF RICHMOND.
At Home.

23 Rue de la Blanchisserie
Thursday, 15th June, 1815

Carriages   Dancing
Three o'clock   Ten o'clock

He stared at the card. "I suppose Lord Bellasis will be dining there?"

"She is his aunt."

"Of course."

"There won't be a dinner. Not a proper one. Just the family and a few people who are staying with them."

"They always say there's no dinner, but there usually is."

"You didn't expect to be asked?"

He'd dreamed, but he hadn't expected it. "No, no. I am content."

"Edmund says there's to be a supper sometime after midnight."

"Don't call him Edmund to anyone but me." Still, his mood was gleeful again, his momentary disappointment already swept aside by the thought of what lay in store for them. "You must go back to your mother. She'll need every minute to prepare."

Sophia was too young and too full of unearned confidence to be quite aware of the enormity of what she had achieved. Besides which, she was more practical in these things than her starstruck papa. "It's too late to have anything made."

"But not too late to have things brought up to standard."

"She won't want to go."

"She will, because she must."

Sophia started toward the door, but then another thought struck her. "When shall we tell her?" she asked, staring at her father. He was caught out by the question and started to fiddle with the gold fobs on his watch chain. It was an odd moment. Things were just as they had been a moment before, and yet somehow the tone and substance had changed. It would have been clear to any outside observer that the subject they were discussing was suddenly more serious than the choice of clothes for the Duchess's ball.

Trenchard was very definite in his response. "Not yet. It must all be properly managed. We should take our lead from him. Now go. And send that blithering idiot back in." His daughter did as she was told and slipped out of the room, but James Trenchard was still curiously preoccupied in her absence. There was shouting from the street below, and he wandered over to the window to look down on an officer and a trader arguing. Then the door opened and Captain Cooper entered. Trenchard nodded to him. It was time for business as usual.

Sophia was right. Her mother did not want to go to the ball. "We've only been asked because somebody's let her down."

"What difference does that make?"

"It's so silly." Mrs. Trenchard shook her head. "We won't know a soul there."

"Papa will know people."

There were times when Anne Trenchard was irritated by her children. They knew little of life, for all their condescension. They had been spoiled from childhood, indulged by their father, until they both took their good fortune for granted and scarcely gave it a thought. They knew nothing of the journey their parents had made to reach their present position, while their mother remembered every tiny, stone-strewn step. "He will know some officers who come to his place of work to give him orders. They, in their turn, will be astonished to find they are sharing a ballroom with the man who supplies their men with bread and ale."

"I hope you won't talk like this to Lord Bellasis."

Mrs. Trenchard's face softened slightly. "My dear"—she took her daughter's hand in hers—"beware of castles in the air."

Sophia snatched her fingers back. "Of course, you won't believe him capable of honorable intentions."

"On the contrary, I am sure Lord Bellasis is an honorable man. He is certainly a very pleasant one."

"Well, then."

"But he is the eldest son of an earl, my child, with all the responsibilities such a position entails. He cannot choose his wife only to suit his heart. I am not angry. You're both young and good-looking, and you have enjoyed a little flirtation that has harmed neither of you. So far." Her emphasis on the last two words was a clear indication of where she was headed. "But it must end before there is any damaging talk, Sophia, or you will be the one to suffer, not he."

"And it doesn't tell you anything? That he has secured us invitations to his aunt's ball?"

"It tells me that you are a lovely girl and he wishes to please you. He could not have managed such a thing in London, but in Brussels everything is colored by war, and so the normal rules do not apply."

This last irritated Sophia more than ever. "You mean that by the normal rules we are not acceptable as company for the Duchess's friends?"

Mrs. Trenchard was, in her way, quite as strong as her daughter. "That is exactly what I mean, and you know it to be true."

"Papa would not agree."

"Your father has successfully traveled a long way, longer than most people could even imagine, and so he does not see the natural barriers that will prevent him going much further. Be content with who we are. Your father has done very well in the world. It is something for you to be proud of."

The door opened and Mrs. Trenchard's maid came in, carrying a dress for the evening. "Am I too early, ma'am?"

"No, no, Ellis. Come in. We were finished, weren't we?"

"If you say so, Mama." Sophia left the room, but the set of her chin did not mark her as one of the vanquished.

It was obvious from the way that Ellis went about her duties in pointed silence that she was burning with curiosity as to what the row had been about, but Anne let her dangle for a few minutes before she spoke, waiting while Ellis unfastened her afternoon dress, allowing her to slip it away from her shoulders.

"We have been invited to the Duchess of Richmond's ball on the fifteenth."

"Never!" Mary Ellis was usually more than adept at keeping her feelings concealed, but this amazing information had caught her off guard. She recovered quickly. "That is to say, we should make a decision on your gown, ma'am. I'll need time to prepare it, if it's to be just so."

"What about the dark blue silk? It hasn't been out too much this season. Maybe you could find some black lace for the neck and sleeves to give it a bit of a lift." Anne Trenchard was a practical woman but not entirely devoid of vanity. She had maintained her figure, and with her neat profile and auburn hair she could certainly be called handsome. She just did not let her awareness of it make her a fool.

Ellis knelt to hold open a straw-colored taffeta evening dress for her mistress to step into. "And jewels, ma'am?"

"I hadn't really thought. I'll wear what I've got, I suppose." She turned to allow the maid to start fastening the frock with gilded pins down the back. She had been firm with Sophia, but she didn't regret it. Sophia lived in a dream, like her father, and dreams could get people into trouble if they were not careful. Almost in spite of herself, Anne smiled. She'd said that James had come a long way, but sometimes she doubted that even Sophia knew quite how far.

"I expect Lord Bellasis arranged the tickets for the ball?" Ellis glanced up from her position at Anne Trenchard's feet, changing her mistress's slippers.

She could see at once that her the question had annoyed Mrs. Trenchard. Why should a maid wonder aloud at how they had been included on such an Olympian guest list? Or why they were invited to anything, for that matter. She chose not to answer and ignored the question. But it made her ponder the strangeness of their lives in Brussels and how things had altered for them since James had caught the eye of the great Duke of Wellington. It was true that no matter the shortages, whatever the ferocity of the fighting, however the countryside had been laid bare, James could always conjure up supplies from somewhere. The Duke called him "the Magician," and so he was, or seemed to be. But his success had only fanned his overweening ambition to scale the unscalable heights of Society, and his social climbing was getting worse. James Trenchard, son of a market trader, whom Anne's own father had forbidden her to marry, thought it the most natural thing in the world that they should be entertained by a duchess. She would have called his ambitions ridiculous, except that they had the uncanny habit of coming true.

Anne was much better educated than her husband—as the daughter of a schoolteacher she was bound to be—and when they met, she was a catch dizzyingly high above him, but she knew well enough that he had far outpaced her now. Indeed, she had begun to wonder how much further she could hope to keep up with his fantastical ascent; or, when the children were grown, whether she should retire to a simple country cottage and leave him to battle his way up the mountain alone.

Ellis was naturally aware that her mistress's silence meant she had spoken out of turn. She thought about saying something flattering to work her way back in, but then decided to remain quiet and let the storm blow itself out.

The door opened and James looked around it. "She's told you, then? He's done it."

Anne glanced at her maid. "Thank you, Ellis. If you could come back in a little while?"

Ellis retreated. James could not resist a smile. "You tell me off for having ideas above my station, yet the way you dismiss your maid puts me in mind of the Duchess herself."

Anne bristled. "I hope not."

"Why? What have you got against her?"

"I have nothing against her, for the simple reason that I do not know her, and nor do you." Anne was keen to inject a note of reality into this absurd and dangerous nonsense. "Which is why we should not allow ourselves to be foisted on the wretched woman, taking up places in her crowded ballroom that would more properly have been given to her own acquaintance."

But James was too excited to be talked down. "You don't mean that?"

"I do, but I know you won't listen."

She was right. She could not hope to dampen his joy. "What a chance it is, Annie! You know the Duke will be there? Two dukes, for that matter. My commander and our hostess's husband."

"I suppose."

"And reigning princes, too." He stopped, full to bursting with the excitement of it all. "James Trenchard, who started at a stall in Covent Garden, must get himself ready to dance with a princess."

"You will not ask any of them to dance. You would only embarrass us both."

"We'll see."

"I mean it. It's bad enough that you encourage Sophia."

James frowned. "You don't believe it, but the boy is sincere. I'm sure of it."

Anne shook her head impatiently. "You are nothing of the sort. Lord Bellasis may even think he's sincere, but he's out of her reach. He is not his own master, and nothing proper can come of it."

There was a rattle in the streets, and she went to investigate. The windows of her bedroom overlooked a wide and busy thoroughfare. Below, some soldiers in scarlet uniforms, the sun bouncing off their gold braid, were marching past. How strange, she thought, with evidence of imminent fighting all around, that we should be discussing a ball.

"I don't know as much." James would not give up his fancies easily.

Anne turned back toward the room. Her husband had assumed an expression like a cornered four-year-old. "Well, I do. And if she comes to any harm through this nonsense, I will hold you personally responsible."

"Very well."

"As for blackmailing the poor young man into begging his aunt for invitations, it is all so unspeakably humiliating."

James had had enough. "You won't spoil it. I won't allow you to."

"I don't need to spoil it. It will spoil itself."

That was the end. He stormed off to change for dinner, and she rang the bell for Ellis's return.

Anne was unhappy with herself. She did not like to quarrel, and yet there was something about the whole episode she felt undermined by. She liked her life. They were rich now, successful, sought after in the trading community of London, and yet James insisted on wrecking things by always wanting more. She must be pushed into an endless series of rooms where they were not liked or appreciated. She would be forced to make conversation with men and women who secretly—or not so secretly—despised them. And all of this when, if James would only allow it, they could have lived in an atmosphere of comfort and respect. But even as she thought these things, she knew she couldn't stop her husband. No one could. That was the nature of the man.

So much has been written about the Duchess of Richmond's ball over the years that it has assumed the splendor and majesty of the coronation pageant of a mediaeval queen. It has figured in every type of fiction, and each visual representation of the evening has been grander than the one that went before. Henry O'Neil's painting of 1868 has the ball taking place in a vast and crowded palace, lined with huge marble columns, packed with seemingly hundreds of guests weeping in sorrow and terror and looking more glamorous than a chorus line at Drury Lane. Like so many iconic moments of history, the reality was quite different.

The Richmonds had arrived in Brussels partly as a cost-cutting exercise, to keep living expenses down by spending a few years abroad, and partly as a show of solidarity with their great friend the Duke of Wellington, who had made his headquarters there. Richmond himself, a former soldier, was to be given the task of organizing the defense of Brussels, should the worst happen and the enemy invade. He accepted. He knew the work would be largely administrative, but it was a job that needed to be done, and it would give him the satisfaction of feeling that he was part of the war effort and not simply an idle onlooker. As he knew well enough, there were plenty of those in the city.

The palaces of Brussels were in limited supply, and most were already spoken for, and so finally they settled on a house formerly occupied by a fashionable coachbuilder. It was on the rue de la Blanchisserie, literally "the street of the laundry," causing Wellington to christen the Richmonds' new home the Wash House, a joke the Duchess enjoyed rather less than her husband. What we would call the coachbuilder's showroom was a large, barnlike structure to the left of the front door, reached through a small office where customers had once discussed upholstery and other optional extras but that the memoirs of the Richmonds' third daughter, Lady Georgiana Lennox, transmogrified into an "ante-room." The space where the coaches had been placed on display was wallpapered with roses on trellis, and the room was deemed sufficient for a ball.

The Duchess of Richmond had taken her whole family with her to the Continent, and the girls especially were aching for some excitement, and so a party was planned. Then, at the beginning of June, Napoléon, who had escaped from his exile on Elba earlier that year, left Paris and came looking for the allied forces. The Duchess had asked Wellington whether it was quite in order for her to continue with her pleasure scheme, and she was assured that it was. Indeed, it was the Duke's express wish that the ball should go ahead, as a demonstration of English sangfroid, to show plainly that even the ladies were not much disturbed by the thought of the French emperor on the march and declined to put off their entertainment. But of course, that was all very well…

"I hope this isn't a mistake," said the Duchess for the twentieth time in an hour as she cast a searching glance in the looking glass. She was quite pleased with what she saw: a handsome woman in early middle age dressed in pale cream silk and still capable of turning heads. Her diamonds were superb, even if there was some discussion among her friends as to whether the originals had been replaced by paste replicas as part of the economy drive.

"It's too late for that sort of talk." The Duke of Richmond was half amused to find himself in this situation. They had seen Brussels as something of an escape from the world, but to their surprise the world had come with them. And now his wife was giving a party with a guest roll that could scarcely be rivaled in London, just as the town was bracing itself for the sound of French cannons. "That was a very good dinner. I shan't be able to eat the supper when it comes."

"You will."

"I can hear a carriage. We should go downstairs." He was an agreeable man, the Duke, a warm and affectionate parent adored by his children and strong enough in himself to take on one of the daughters of the notorious Duchess of Gordon, whose antics had kept Scotland in gossip for years. He was aware there were plenty at the time who thought he could have made an easier choice and probably lived an easier life, but, all in all, he was not sorry. His wife was extravagant—there was no arguing with that—but she was good-natured, good-looking, and clever. He was glad he had chosen her.

There were a few early arrivals in the small drawing room, Georgiana's anteroom, through which the guests were obliged to pass on their way to the ballroom. The florists had done well, with huge arrangements of pale pink roses and white lilies, all with their stamens neatly clipped to spare the women from the stain of pollen, backed with high foliage in shades of green, lending the coachbuilder's apartments a grandeur that they lacked in daylight, and the shimmering glow of the many candelabra cast the proceedings in a subtly flattering light.

The Duchess's nephew, Edmund, Viscount Bellasis, was talking to Georgiana. They walked over together to her parents. "Who are these people that Edmund has forced you to invite? Why don't we know them?"

Lord Bellasis cut in. "You will know them after tonight."

"You're not very forthcoming," said Georgiana.

The Duchess had her own suspicions, and she was rather regretting her generosity. "I hope your mother is not going to be cross with me." She had given him the tickets without a thought, but a moment's reflection had convinced her that her sister was going to be very cross indeed.

As if on cue, the chamberlain's voice rang out: "Mr. and Mrs. James Trenchard. Miss Sophia Trenchard."

The Duke looked toward the door. "You've not invited the Magician?" His wife looked bewildered. "Wellington's main supplier. What's he doing here?"

The Duchess turned severely to her nephew. "The Duke of Wellington's victualler? I have invited a merchant supplier to my ball?"

Lord Bellasis was not so easily defeated. "My dear aunt, you've invited one of the Duke's most loyal and efficient helpers in his fight for victory. I should have thought any loyal Britisher would be proud to receive Mr. Trenchard in their house."

"You have tricked me, Edmund. And I do not like to be made a fool of." But the young man had already gone to greet the new arrivals. She stared at her husband.

He was rather amused by her fury. "Don't glare at me, my dear. I didn't invite them. You did. And you have to admit, she's good-looking." At least that was true. Sophia had never looked lovelier.

There was no time to say more before the Trenchards were upon them. Anne spoke first. "This is good of you, Duchess."

"Not at all, Mrs. Trenchard. I gather you have been very kind to my nephew."

"It's always a pleasure to see Lord Bellasis." Anne's choice had been a good one. She cut a dignified figure in the blue silk, and Ellis had found some fine lace to trim it. Her diamonds might not have rivaled many in the room, but they were perfectly respectable.

The Duchess could feel herself becoming slightly mollified. "It is hard for the young men, so far from home," she said, pleasantly enough.

James had been struggling with his certainty that the Duchess should have been addressed as "Your Grace." Even though his wife had spoken and no one seemed to have taken offense, yet still he could not be sure. He opened his mouth—

"Well, if it isn't the Magician." Richmond beamed quite jovially. If he was surprised to find this tradesman in his drawing room, you could not have told it. "Do you remember we made some plans in the event of the reservists being called to arms?"

"I recall it very well, Your—your schedule, I mean. Duke." He spoke the last word as quite a separate entity, having nothing to do with the rest of their conversation. To James, it felt like suddenly lobbing a pebble into a silent pool. The ripples of its oddness seemed to engulf him for a few awkward moments. But he was reassured by a gentle smile and a nod from Anne, and no one else seemed disturbed, which was a relief.

Anne took over. "May I present my daughter, Sophia?" Sophia curtsied to the Duchess, who looked her up and down as if she were buying a haunch of venison for dinner, which naturally she would never do. She could see that the girl was pretty, and quite graceful in her way, but one look at the father reminded her again only too clearly that the thing was out of the question. She dreaded her sister learning of this evening and accusing her of encouraging it. But surely Edmund couldn't be serious? He was a sensible boy and had never given a minute's trouble.

"Miss Trenchard, I wonder if you would let me escort you into the ballroom?" Edmund attempted to maintain a cool manner as he made his offer, but he could not deceive his aunt, who was far too experienced in the ways of the world to be distracted by his dumb show of indifference. In fact, the Duchess's heart sank as she saw how the girl slipped her arm through his and they went off together, chatting in low whispers as if they already owned each other.

"Major Thomas Harris." A rather handsome young man made a slight bow to his hosts as Edmund called his name.

"Harris! I didn't expect to see you here."

"I must have some fun, you know," said the young officer, smiling at Sophia. She laughed, as if they were all so comfortable to be part of the same crowd. Then she and Edmund walked on toward the ballroom, watched by his anxious aunt. They made a pretty couple, she was forced to admit, Sophia's blonde beauty somehow emphasized by Edmund's dark curls and chiseled features, his hard mouth smiling above his cleft chin. She caught her husband's eye. They both knew the situation was almost out of control. Perhaps it was out of control already.

"Mr. James and Lady Frances Wedderburn-Webster," announced the chamberlain, and the Duke stepped forward to greet the next arrivals. "Lady Frances, how lovely you look." He caught his wife's worried glance after the young lovers. Surely there was nothing more the Richmonds could do to manage the matter? But the Duke saw the care on his wife's face and leaned in toward her. "I'll speak to him later. He'll see sense. He always has before now." She nodded. That was the thing to do. Sort it out later, when the ball was over and the girl was gone. There was a stir at the door, and the ringing voice of the chamberlain sang out: "His Royal Highness, the Prince of Orange." A pleasant-looking young man approached the host and hostess, and the Duchess, her back as straight as a ramrod, plunged into a deep Court curtsy.

The Duke of Wellington did not arrive much before midnight, but he was cool enough about it when he did. To James Trenchard's intense delight, the Duke looked around the ballroom and, on spotting him, walked over. "What brings the Magician here tonight?"

"Her Grace invited us."

"Did she, indeed? Good for you. Has the evening proved enjoyable so far?"

James nodded. "Oh yes, Your Grace. But there is a good deal of talk about the advance of Bonaparte."

"And is there, by Jove? Do I understand this charming lady is Mrs. Trenchard?" He was very collected, no doubt about it.

Even Anne's nerve failed her when it came to addressing him as Duke. "Your Grace's calm is very reassuring."

"That's what it's supposed to be." He laughed gently, turning to an officer nearby. "Ponsonby, are you acquainted with the Magician?"

"Certainly, Duke. I spend a good deal of time outside Mr. Trenchard's office, waiting to plead the cause of my men." But he smiled.

"Mrs. Trenchard, may I present Sir William Ponsonby? Ponsonby, this is the Magician's wife."

Ponsonby bowed slightly. "I hope he is kinder to you than he is to me."

She smiled too, but before she could reply they were joined by the Richmonds' daughter, Georgiana. "The room is buzzing with rumors."

Wellington nodded sagely. "So I understand."

"But are they true?" She was a good-looking girl, Georgiana Lennox, with a clear, open face, and her anxiety only served to underline the sincerity of her question and the threat that hovered over them all.

For the first time, the Duke's expression was almost grave as he looked into her upturned eyes. "I'm afraid they are, Lady Georgiana. It looks as if we'll be off tomorrow."

"How terrible." She turned to watch the couples whirling around the dance floor, most of the young men in their dress uniforms as they chattered and laughed with their partners. How many would survive the coming struggle?

"What a heavy burden you must carry." Anne Trenchard was also looking at the men. She sighed. "Some of these young men will die in the days ahead, and if we are to win this war, even you cannot prevent it. I do not envy you."

Wellington was, if anything, agreeably surprised at this from the wife of his supplier, a woman of whom he had barely been aware before this evening. Not everyone could understand that it wasn't all glory. "Thank you for that thought, madam."

At this moment, they were interrupted by a blast from a score of bagpipes, and the dancers fled the floor to give way to a troop of the Gordon Highlanders. This was the Duchess's *coup de théâtre*, which she had begged from their senior officer, citing her Gordon blood as her excuse. Since the Highlanders had originally been raised by her late father twenty years before, there wasn't much chance for the commander to refuse, and so he was pleased to grant the Duchess's request. History does not record his true opinion of being obliged to lend his men to play the centerpiece of a ball on the eve of a battle that would decide the fate of Europe. At any rate, their display was heartwarming for the Scots who were present and entertaining for their English neighbors, but the foreigners were openly bewildered. Anne Trenchard watched as the Prince of Orange looked quizzically at his aide, screwing up his eyes at the noise. But the men started to reel, and soon the passion and power of their dancing overcame the doubters, inflaming the company until even the bewildered princes of old Germany began to respond, cheering and clapping.

Anne turned to her husband. "It seems so hard that they will be engaging the enemy before the month is out."

"The month?" James gave a bitter laugh. "The week, more like."

Even as he spoke, the door burst open, and a young officer who had not stopped to scrape the mud from his boots tore into the ballroom, searching it until he had found his commander, the Prince of Orange. He bowed, producing an envelope, which at once drew the attention of all the company. The Prince nodded and stood, walking across to the Duke. He presented him with the message, but the Duke slipped it into a pocket of his waistcoat unread as the chamberlain announced supper.

Anne smiled in spite of her foreboding. "You must admire his control. It may be a death warrant for his own army, but he'd rather take a chance than show the slightest sign of worry."

James nodded. "He isn't easily rattled, that's for sure." But he saw that his wife's brow had furrowed. Among the throng headed for the supper room, Sophia was still walking with Viscount Bellasis.

Anne struggled to keep her impatience from showing. "Tell her to eat her supper with us, or at any rate with someone else."

James shook his head. "You tell her. I won't."

Anne nodded and walked across to the young couple. "You mustn't let Sophia monopolize you, Lord Bellasis. You will have many friends in the room who would be glad of the chance to hear your news."

But the young man smiled. "Never fear, Mrs. Trenchard. I am where I want to be."

Anne's voice grew a little more determined. She hit her left palm with her folded fan. "That is all very well, my lord. But Sophia has a reputation to protect, and the generosity of your attentions may be putting it at risk."

It was too much to hope that Sophia would stay silent. "Mama, don't worry. I wish you would give me credit for a little sense."

"I wish I could." Anne was losing patience with her foolish, love-struck, ambitious daughter. But she sensed a few of the couples looking at them and dropped back rather than be seen arguing with her child.

Somewhat against her husband's wishes, she chose a quiet side table, sitting among some officers and their wives as they watched the more glittering company at the center. Wellington was placed between Lady Georgiana Lennox and a ravishing creature in a low-cut evening gown of midnight blue embroidered with silver thread. Naturally, she wore exquisite diamonds. She laughed carefully, showing a set of dazzlingly white teeth, then looked at the Duke with a sort of sideways glance through her dark lashes. It was obvious that Lady Georgiana was finding the competition rather tiring. "Who is the woman on the Duke's right?" Anne asked her husband.

"Lady Frances Wedderburn-Webster."

"Of course. She came in just after us. She seems very confident of the Duke's interest."

"She has every reason to be." James gave her a slight wink, and Anne looked at the beauty with more curiosity. Not for the first time, she wondered how the threat of war, the near presence of death, seemed to heighten the possibilities of life. Many couples in this very room were risking their reputations and even future happiness to gain some satisfaction before the call to arms pulled them apart.

There was a stir at the doorway and she looked across the room. The messenger they had seen earlier was back, still in his muddy riding boots, and once more he approached the Prince of Orange. They spoke for a moment, whereupon the Prince rose and crossed to Wellington, then bent and whispered in his ear. By this time, the attention of the assembly had been well and truly caught, and the general conversation began to subside. Wellington stood up. He spoke for a moment to the Duke of Richmond, and they had started to leave the room, when he stopped. To the Trenchards' amazement, he glanced around and came toward their table, much to the excitement of everyone seated at it.

"You. Magician. Can you come with us?"

James jumped to his feet, abandoning his supper on the instant. Both of the other men were tall, and he seemed to be like a little plump joker between two kings—which was what he was, really, as Anne was obliged to acknowledge.

The man opposite her at the table could not hide his admiration. "Your husband is obviously in the Duke's confidence, madam."

"So it would appear." But she did feel rather proud of him for once, which was a nice sensation.

When they opened the door of the dressing room, a startled valet, disturbed in the act of laying out a nightshirt, looked up to find himself staring into the face of the Supreme Commander. "May we have the room for a moment?" said Wellington, and the valet almost gasped as he made good his escape. "Have you got a decent map of the area?"

Richmond muttered that he had and, pulling a large volume from the shelves, opened it to show Brussels and the surrounding countryside. Wellington was starting to reveal the rage he had concealed so successfully in the supper room earlier. "Napoléon has humbugged me, by God. Orange has had a second message, this one from Baron Rebecque. Bonaparte's pushed up the Charleroi to Brussels Road, and he's getting nearer." He leaned over the page. "I've given orders for the army to concentrate at Quatre Bras, but we shall not stop him there."

"You may. You have some hours before daylight." Richmond did not believe his own words any more than the great Duke.

"If I do not, I shall have to fight him here."

James craned over the map. The Duke's thumbnail rested at a small village named Waterloo. It seemed oddly unreal that one minute after quietly eating his supper in a nondescript corner he was in the Duke of Richmond's dressing room, alone with him and the Commander-in-Chief at the center of events that would change all their lives.

And then Wellington acknowledged him for the first time since they had arrived. "I shall need your help, Magician. You understand? We will be first at Quatre Bras, and then, almost certainly, at..." He paused to check the name on the map. "Waterloo. Rather a strange name to qualify for immortality."

"If anyone can make it immortal, you can, Your Grace." In James's comparatively simple set of values, a little toadying seldom went amiss.

"But do you have enough information?" Wellington was a professional soldier, not a bungling amateur, and James admired him for it.

"I do. Don't worry. We will not fail for lack of supplies."

Wellington looked at him. He almost smiled. "You're a bright man, Trenchard. You must use your talents well when the wars are done. I believe you have the potential to go far."

"Your Grace is very kind."

"But you mustn't be distracted by the gewgaws of Society. You're cleverer than that, or should be, and worth much more than most of those peacocks in the ballroom. Don't forget it." He seemed almost to hear a voice telling him the hour had come. "Enough. We must get ready."

When they emerged, the company was already in turmoil, and it was at once clear that the word had spread. The flower-filled rooms that had been so fragrant and elegant when the evening began were filled with scenes of heartrending good-byes. Mothers and young girls were weeping openly, clinging to their sons and brothers, their husbands and their sweethearts, and abandoning all pretence of calm. To James's amazement, the band was still playing and, even more astonishingly, some couples continued to dance, although how they could, surrounded by consternation and grief, was hard to understand.

Anne came to him before he had found her in the throng. "We should leave," he said. "I must go straight to the depot. I'll put you and Sophia into the carriage and then I'll walk."

She nodded. "Is it the final struggle?"

"Who knows? I think so. We've promised ourselves every skirmish was the last battle for so many years now, but this time I really believe it is. Where's Sophia?"

They found her in the hall, weeping in the arms of Lord Bellasis. Anne thanked the chaos and rout that surrounded them for concealing their folly and indiscretion. Bellasis whispered in Sophia's ear and then handed her over to her mother. "Take care of her."

"I usually do," said Anne, a little irritated by his presumption. But his own sorrow at parting protected him from her tone. With a last glance at the object of his affections, he hurried out with a group of fellow officers. James had retrieved the shawls and wraps, and now they found themselves caught in the crowd, pushing for the door. The Duchess was nowhere to be seen. Anne gave up searching and resolved to write to her in the morning, although she gave the Duchess credit by assuming she would not be much concerned by the social niceties at such a moment.

At last they were in the outer hall, through the open door, and then outside in the street. There was a crush here, too, but less so than in the house. Some officers were already mounted. Anne spied Bellasis in the melee. His servant had brought his horse and held it as his master mounted. Anne watched as, for a second, Bellasis seemed to scan the multitude searching for someone, but if it was Sophia she did not catch his attention. It was exactly at this moment that Anne heard a gasp behind her. Her daughter was staring at the group of soldiers below them. "What is it?" Anne did not recognize any of the men. But Sophia could only shake her head, though whether in sorrow or horror was difficult to determine. "You knew he must go." Anne slipped an arm around her daughter's shoulders.

"It's not that." Sophia could only fix her gaze on one group of the uniformed men. They started to move off. She shuddered and let out a sob that seemed to be torn from the roots of her soul.

"My dear, you must control yourself." Anne looked around, trying to make sure there were no witnesses to this moment. Her daughter was beyond control or command. She was shaking now, like someone with an ague, trembling and sweating, tears pouring down her cheeks. Anne took charge. "Come with me. Quickly. We must get back before you're recognized."

Together, she and her husband dragged the shivering girl down the line of waiting coaches until they found their own and pushed her into it. James hurried away, but it was an hour before the vehicle escaped from the pack of carriages and Anne and Sophia were able to make their way home.

Sophia did not leave her room the following day, but it made no matter as the whole of Brussels was on tenterhooks and nobody noticed her absence. Would the invasion sweep through the town? Was every young woman in danger? The citizens were torn. Should they hope for victory and bury their valuables to save them from the returning troops, or would it be defeat and must they run? Anne spent most of the day in contemplation and prayer. James had not come home. His man went down to the depot taking a change of clothes and a basket of food, although she almost smiled at her folly in sending supplies to the chief supplier.

Then news of the engagement at Quatre Bras started to filter through. The Duke of Brunswick was dead, shot through the heart. Anne thought of the dark, raffishly handsome man she'd seen waltzing with the Duchess only the night before. There would be more such news before it was over. She looked around the drawing room of their rented villa. It was nice enough: a little grand for her taste, not grand enough for James's, with dark furniture and white curtains of silk moiré finished off with heavily draped and fringed pelmets above. She picked up her embroidery and put it down again. How could she sew when, within a few miles, men she knew were fighting for their lives? She did the same with a book. But she couldn't even pretend to concentrate on a fictional story when so savage a tale was being played out near enough for them to hear the cannons boom. Her son, Oliver, came in and threw himself into a chair. "Why aren't you at school?"

"They've sent us home." She nodded. Of course they had. The teachers must be making their own plans for escape. "Any news from my father?"

"No, but he is not in any danger."

"Why is Sophia in bed?"

"She's not feeling well."

"Is it about Lord Bellasis?"

Anne looked at him. How do the young know these things? He was sixteen. He'd never been in anything that could remotely be called Society. "Of course not," she said. But the boy only smiled.

It was Tuesday morning before Anne saw her husband again. She was breakfasting in her room, though up and dressed, when he opened her door, looking as if he had been through the mud and dust of a battlefield himself. Her greeting was simple enough. "Thank God," she said.

"We've done it. Boney's on the run. But not everyone is safe."

"So I imagine, poor souls."

"The Duke of Brunswick is dead."

"I heard."

"Lord Hay, Sir William Ponsonby—"

"Oh." She thought of the gently smiling man who had teased her about her husband's firmness. "How sad. I hear that some of them died still in the dress uniforms they'd worn for the ball."

"That's true."

"We should pray for them. I feel our presence there that night gives us some sort of connection to them all, poor fellows."

"Indeed. But there is another casualty you will not have to imagine a link with." She looked at him expectantly. "Viscount Bellasis has been killed."

"Oh no." Her hand flew to her face. "Are they sure?" Her stomach lurched. Why, exactly? It was hard to say. Did she think there was a chance that Sophia had been right, and now the girl's

great chance was lost? No. She knew that for a fantasy, but still...
How terrible.

"I went there yesterday. Out to the battlefield. And a very
awful sight it was, too."

"Why did you go?"

"Business. Why do I ever do anything?" He regretted his caus-
tic tone of voice. "I heard Bellasis was on the list of fatalities, and I
asked to see his body. It was him, so yes, I'm sure. How is Sophia?"

"A shadow of herself since the ball, no doubt dreading the very
news that we must now take to her." Anne sighed. "I suppose she
should be told before she hears it from someone else."

"I'll tell her." She was surprised. This was not the sort of duty
James volunteered for as a rule.

"I think it must be me. I am her mother."

"No. I'll tell her. You can go to her afterward. Where is she?"

"In the garden."

He strode out as Anne pondered their exchange. So this was
where Sophia's folly would end: not in scandal, thankfully, but in
sorrow. The girl had dreamed her dreams, and James had encouraged her to do so, but now they must turn to dust. They'd never
know if Sophia was right and Bellasis had honorable plans or if she,
Anne, was nearer the mark and Sophia was only ever a charming
doll to be played with while they were stationed in Brussels. She
moved over to sit in the window seat. The garden below was laid
out in the formal manner that was still admired in the Nether-
lands, even though it had been abandoned by the English. Beside a
graveled path, Sophia sat on a bench, a book unopened at her side,
when her father came out of the house. James talked as he drew
near and sat next to his daughter, taking her hand. Anne wondered how he'd choose the words. It looked as if he would not be
hurried, and he spoke for a while, quite gently, before Sophia suddenly flinched as if she had been struck. At that, James took her
into his arms and she started to sob. Anne could at least be glad
that her husband had been as kind as he knew how to be when he
told the dreadful tidings.

Later, Anne would ask herself how she could have been so sure this was the end of Sophia's story. But then, as she told herself, who would learn better than she that hindsight is a prism that alters everything? She stood. It was time for her to go down and comfort her daughter, who had woken from a beautiful reverie into a cruel world.

—.2.—

A Chance Encounter

1841. The carriage came to a halt. It hardly seemed a moment since she had climbed into it. But then the journey from Eaton Place to Belgrave Square was not worth taking out a carriage for and, if she'd had her way, she would have walked. Of course, in such matters she did not have her way. Ever. A moment later the postilion was down and the door had been opened. He held out his arm for her to steady herself as she negotiated the carriage steps. Anne took a breath to calm her nerves and stood. The house awaiting her was one of the splendid classical "wedding-cake" variety that had been going up for the previous twenty years in the recently christened Belgravia, but it contained few secrets for Anne Trenchard. Her husband had spent the previous quarter of a century building these private palaces, in squares and avenues and crescents, housing the rich of nineteenth-century England, working with the Cubitt brothers and making his own fortune into the bargain.

Two women were admitted into the house ahead of her, and the footman stood waiting expectantly, holding the door open. There was nothing for it but to walk up the steps and into the cavernous hall where a maid was in attendance to take her shawl, but Anne kept her bonnet firmly in place. She had grown used to being entertained by people she scarcely knew, and today was no exception. Her hostess's father-in-law, the late Duke of Bedford, had been a client of the Cubitts, and her husband, James, had done a lot of work on Russell Square and Tavistock Square for him. Of course, these days, James liked to present himself as a gentleman who just happened to be in the Cubitt offices by chance, and sometimes it worked. He had successfully made friends, or at least friendly acquaintances, of the Duke and his son, Lord Tavistock. As it happened, his wife, Lady Tavistock, had always been a superior figure in the background, leading another life as one of the young Queen's ladies of the bedchamber, and she and Anne had hardly spoken more than a few civil words over the years, but it was enough, in James's mind, to build on. In time the old Duke had died, and when the new Duke wanted James's help to develop the Russells' London holdings still further, James had dropped the hint that Anne would like to experience the Duchess's much talked-about innovation of "afternoon tea," and an invitation had been forthcoming.

It was not exactly that Anne Trenchard disapproved of her husband's social mountaineering. At any rate, she'd grown used to it. She saw the pleasure it brought him—or rather, the pleasure he thought it brought him—and she did not begrudge him his dreams. She simply did not share them, any more now than she had in Brussels almost thirty years before. She knew well enough that the women who welcomed her into their houses did so under orders from their husbands, and that these orders were given in case James could be useful. Having issued the precious cards, to balls and luncheons and dinners and now the new "tea," they would use his gratitude for their own ends until it became clear to Anne, if not to James, that they were governing him by means of his snobbery. Her husband had placed a bit in his own mouth and put the reins into the hands of men who cared nothing for him and only for the profits he could guide them to. In all this, Anne's job was to change her clothes four or five times a day, sit in large drawing rooms with unwelcoming women, and come home again. She had grown used to this way of life. She was no longer unnerved by the footmen or the splendor that seemed to be increasingly lavish with every year that passed, but nor was she impressed by it. She saw this life for what it was: a different way of doing things. With a sigh she climbed the great staircase with its gilded handrail beneath a full-length Thomas Lawrence portrait of her hostess in the fashions of the Regency. Anne wondered if the picture was a copy, made to impress their London callers while the original sat happily ensconced at Woburn.

She reached the landing and made her way into another predictably large drawing room, this one lined in pale blue damask, with a high painted ceiling and gilded doors. A great many women sat about on chairs and sofas and ottomans, balancing plates and cups and frequently losing control of both. A smattering of gentlemen, point-device in their outfits and obviously creatures of leisure, sat gossiping among the ladies. One looked up at her entrance in recognition, but Anne saw an empty chair at the edge of the gathering and made for it, passing an old lady who started to lunge for a sandwich plate that was sliding away from her and down her voluminous skirts when Anne caught it. The stranger beamed. "Well saved." She took a bite. "It is not that I dislike a light nuncheon of cakes and tea to carry one through to dinner, but why can't we sit at a table?"

Anne had reached her chair and, given her neighbor's relatively friendly opening, considered herself entitled to sit upon it. "I think the point is that one isn't trapped. We can all move about and talk to whom we like."

"Well, I like to talk to you."

Their rather anxious hostess hurried over. "Mrs. Trenchard, how kind of you to look in." It did not sound as if Anne was expected to stay very long, but this was not bad news as far as Anne was concerned.

"I'm delighted to be here."

"Aren't you going to introduce us?" This came from the old lady Anne had rescued, but the Duchess showed a marked reluctance to carry out her duties. Then, with a crisp smile, she realized she had to.

"May I present Mrs. James Trenchard." Anne nodded and waited. "The Dowager Duchess of Richmond." She said the name with tremendous finality, as if that must bring all reasonable conjecture on the subject to an end. There was a silence. She looked to Anne for a suitably overawed response, but the name had given her guest something of a shock, if a pang of nostalgia and sadness can be called a shock. Before Anne could make any observation that might rescue the moment, their hostess was gushing on. "Now you must let me introduce you to Mrs. Carver and Mrs. Shute." Clearly she had corralled a section of more obscure ladies whom she intended to keep out of the hair of the great and the good. But the old lady was not having it.

"Don't snatch her away yet. I know Mrs. Trenchard." The old lady screwed up her features in concentration as she studied the face opposite.

Anne nodded. "You have a wonderful memory, Duchess, since I would have thought I was changed past all recognition, but you're right. We have met. I attended your ball. In Brussels, before Waterloo."

The Duchess of Bedford was astonished. "You were at the famous ball, Mrs. Trenchard?"

"I was."

"But I thought you had only lately—" She stopped herself just in time. "I must see if everyone has what they want. Please excuse me." She hurried away, leaving the other two to examine each other more carefully. At last the old Duchess spoke. "I remember you well."

"I'm impressed, if you do."

"Of course, we didn't really know each other, did we?" In the wrinkled face before her, Anne could still see the traces of the queen of Brussels, who had ordered things just as she saw fit.

"No, we didn't. My husband and I were wished upon you, and I thought it very kind that we were allowed in."

"I remember. My late nephew was in love with your daughter."

Anne nodded. "He may have been. At least, she was in love with him."

"No, I think he was. I certainly thought so at the time. The Duke and I had a great discussion about it, after the ball was over."

"I'm sure you did." They both knew what they were talking about, these two, but what was the point in raking it up now?

"We should leave the subject. My sister's over there. It will unsettle her, even after so many years." Anne looked across the room to see a stately figure of a woman, dressed in a frock of violet lace over gray silk, who did not look much older than Anne herself. "There is less than ten years between us, which is surprising, I know."

"Did you ever tell her about Sophia?"

"It's all so long ago. What does it matter now? Our concerns died with him." She paused, realizing she had given herself away. "Where is your beautiful daughter now? For you see, I recall she was a beauty. What became of her?"

Anne winced inside. The question still hurt every time. "Like Lord Bellasis, Sophia is dead." She always used a brisk and efficient-sounding tone to impart this information, in an attempt to avoid the sentimentality that her words usually provoked. "Not many months after the ball."

"So she never married?"

"No. She never married."

"I'm sorry. Funnily enough, I can remember her quite clearly. Do you have other children?"

"Oh yes. A son, Oliver, but..." It was Anne's turn to give herself away.

"Sophia was the child of your heart."

Anne sighed. It never got easier, no matter how many years had passed. "I know one is always supposed to support the fiction that we love all our children equally, but I find it hard."

The Duchess cackled. "I don't even try. I am very fond of some of my children, on reasonably good terms with most of the rest, but I have two that I positively dislike."

"How many are there?"

"Fourteen."

Anne smiled. "Heavens. So the Richmond dukedom is safe." The old Duchess laughed again. But she took Anne's hand and squeezed it. Funnily enough, Anne did not resent her. They had both played a part, according to their own lights, in that long-ago story. "I remember some of your daughters that night. One of them seemed to be a great favorite of the Duke of Wellington."

"She still is. Georgiana. She's Lady de Ros now, but if he hadn't already been married, I doubt he'd have stood a chance. I must go. I've been here too long and I will pay for it." She got to her feet with some difficulty, making heavy use of her stick. "I have enjoyed our talk, Mrs. Trenchard, a nice reminder of more exciting times. But I suppose this is the advantage of the pick-up, put-down tea. We may go when we want." She had something more to say before she left. "I wish you and your family well, my dear. Whatever sides we may once have been on."

"I say the same to you, Duchess." Anne had risen, and she stood watching as the ancient peeress made her careful way to the door. She looked around. There were women here she knew, some of whom nodded in her direction with a show of politeness, but she also knew the limits of their interest and made no attempt to take advantage of it. She smiled back without making a move to join them. The large drawing room opened into a smaller one, hung with pale gray damask, and beyond was a picture gallery, or rather a room for displaying pictures. Anne strolled into it, admiring the paintings on show. There was a fine Turner hanging over the marble chimneypiece. She wondered idly how long she must stay when a voice startled her.

"You had a great deal to say to my sister." She turned to find the woman the Duchess had pointed out as the mother of Lord Bellasis. Anne wondered if she had imagined this moment. Probably. The Countess of Brockenhurst stood, holding a cup of tea resting in a matching saucer. "And now I think I may know why. Our hostess tells me you were at the famous ball."

"I was, Lady Brockenhurst."

"You have the advantage of me." Lady Brockenhurst had made her way to a group of chairs standing empty near a large window looking out over the leafy garden of Belgrave Square. Anne could see a nursemaid with her two charges playing sedately on the central lawn. "Will you tell me your name, since there is no one here to make the introduction?"

"I am Mrs. Trenchard. Mrs. James Trenchard."

The Countess stared at her. "I was right, then. It is you."

"I'm very flattered if you've heard of me."

"Certainly I have." She gave no clue as to whether this was a good thing or a bad. A footman arrived with a plate of tiny egg sandwiches. "I'm afraid these are too delicious to resist," said Lady Brockenhurst as she took three and a little plate to carry them. "I find it strange to eat at this time, don't you? I suppose we will still want our dinner when it comes." Anne smiled but said nothing. She had a sense that she was to be questioned, and she was not wrong. "Tell me about the ball."

"Surely you must have talked of it enough with the Duchess?"

But Lady Brockenhurst was not to be deflected. "Why were you in Brussels? How did you know my sister and her husband?"

"We didn't. Not in that way. Mr. Trenchard was the Duke of Wellington's head of supplies. He knew the Duke of Richmond a little in his capacity as chief of the defense of Brussels, but that is all."

"Forgive me, my dear, but it does not entirely explain your presence at his wife's reception." The Countess of Brockenhurst had clearly been a very pretty woman, when her gray hair was still blonde and her lined skin smooth. She had a catlike face with small, vivid features, defined and alert, a cupid's bow of a mouth and a sharp, pizzicato manner of speaking that must have seemed very beguiling in her youth. She was not unlike her sister, and she had the same imperious air, but there was a sorrow behind her blue-gray eyes that made her both more sympathetic and yet more distant than the Duchess of Richmond. Anne, of course, knew the reason for her grief but was naturally reluctant to refer to it. "I'm curious. I had always heard tell of you both as the Duke of Wellington's victualler and his wife. Seeing you here, I wondered if I was misinformed and your circumstance was rather different from the version I'd been given."

This was rude and insulting, and Anne was well aware she should be offended. Anyone else would have been. But was Lady Brockenhurst wrong? "No. The report was accurate enough. It was strange we were among the guests that night in 1815, but our life has changed in the interim. Things have gone well for Mr. Trenchard since the war ended."

"Obviously. Is he still supplying foodstuffs to his customers? He must be very good at it."

Anne wasn't sure how much more of this she was expected to put up with. "No, he left that and went into partnership with Mr. Cubitt and his brother. When we returned from Brussels, after the battle, the Cubitts needed to find investors, and Mr. Trenchard decided to help them."

"The great Mr. Thomas Cubitt? Heavens. I assume he was no longer a ship's carpenter by that stage?"

Anne decided to let this play itself out. "He was in development by then, and he and his brother, William, were raising funds to build the London Institution in Finsbury Circus when they met Mr. Trenchard. He offered to help and they went into business together."

"I remember when it opened. We thought it magnificent." Was she smirking? It was hard to tell if Lady Brockenhurst was genuinely impressed or was somehow toying with Anne for her own purposes.

"After that, they worked together on the new Tavistock Square—"

"For the father-in-law of our hostess."

"There were a few of them, as it happens, but the late Duke of Bedford was the main investor, yes."

Lady Brockenhurst nodded. "I remember well that was a great success. And then I suppose Belgravia followed for the Marquess of Westminster, who must be richer than Croesus, thanks to the Cubitts, and, I see now, your husband. How well things have gone for you. I expect you're tired of houses such as this. Mr. Trenchard has clearly been responsible for so many of them."

"It's nice to see the places lived in, when the scaffolding and dust have gone." Anne was trying to make the conversation more normal, but Lady Brockenhurst was having none of it.

"What a story," she said. "You are a creature of the New Age, Mrs. Trenchard." She laughed for a moment and then remembered herself. "I hope I don't offend you."

"Not in the least." Anne was fully aware she was being provoked, presumably because Lady Brockenhurst knew all about her son's dalliance with Sophia. There could be no other reason. Anne decided to bring matters to a head and wrong-foot her questioner. "You're right that Mr. Trenchard's later triumphs do not explain our presence at the ball that night. An army victualler does not usually have the chance to write his name on a duchess's dance card, but we were friendly with a favorite of your sister's and he contrived to get us invited. It seems shameless, but a city on the brink of war is not governed by quite the same rules as a Mayfair drawing room in peacetime."

"I'm sure it is not. Who was this favorite? Might I have known him?"

Anne was almost relieved that at last they had reached their destination. Even so, she was unsure quite how to manage it.

"Come, Mrs. Trenchard, don't be bashful. Please."

There was no point in lying, since clearly Lady Brockenhurst was fully aware of what she was going to say. "You knew him very well. It was Lord Bellasis."

The name hung in the air between them like a ghostly dagger in a fable. It could never be said that Lady Brockenhurst lost her composure, since she would not lose that before she breathed her last, but she had not quite prepared for the sound of his name being spoken aloud by this woman whom she knew so well in her imaginings but not at all in fact. She needed a moment to catch her breath. There was a silence as she slowly sipped her tea. Anne felt a sudden surge of pity for this sad, cold woman, as unbending with herself as with anyone else. "Lady Brockenhurst—"

"Did you know my son well?"

Anne nodded. "In truth—"

At this moment their hostess arrived. "Mrs. Trenchard, would you like—"

"Forgive me, my dear, but Mrs. Trenchard and I are talking." The dismissal could not have been more final if the Duchess had been a naughty housemaid still brushing up the cinders of a fire when the family returned to the room after dinner. Without a word, she simply nodded and withdrew. Lady Brockenhurst waited until they were alone again. "You were saying?"

"Only that my daughter knew Lord Bellasis better than we did. Brussels was quite a hothouse at that time, filled with young officers and the daughters of many of the older commanders. As well as the men and women who had come out from London to join in the fun."

"Like my sister and her husband."

"Exactly. I suppose, looking back, there was a sense that nobody knew what was coming: the triumph of Napoleon, the enslavement of England, or the reverse and a British victory. It sounds wrong, but the uncertainty created an atmosphere that was heady and exciting."

The other woman nodded as she spoke. "And above all else, the knowledge must have hung in the air that some of those smiling, handsome young men, taking salutes on the parade ground, pouring the wine at picnics, or waltzing with the daughters of their officer, would not be coming home." Lady Brockenhurst's tone was even, but a slight tremble in the sound of her voice betrayed her emotion.

How well Anne understood. "Yes."

"I suppose they enjoyed it. The girls who were there, like your daughter, I mean. The danger, the glamour; because danger is glamorous when you're young. Where is she now?"

Again. Twice in one afternoon. "Sophia died."

Lady Brockenhurst gasped. "Now, that I did *not* know," confirming that she had known everything else. Obviously she and the Duchess of Richmond had discussed the whole story, countless times for all Anne knew, which would explain her manner until this moment.

Anne nodded. "It was quite soon after the battle, less than a year, in fact, so a long time ago now."

"I am very sorry." For the first time Lady Brockenhurst spoke with something like genuine warmth. "Everyone always claims to know what you're going through, but I do. And I know that it never goes away."

Anne stared at her, this haughty matron who had expended so much effort putting Anne in her place. Who had brought so much anger into the room with her. And yet the knowledge that Anne, too, had lost a child, that the wicked girl of Lady Brockenhurst's bitter ruminations was dead, had somehow altered things between them. Anne smiled. "Oddly, I find that comforting. They say misery loves company, and perhaps it does."

"And you remember seeing Edmund at the ball?" Lady Brockenhurst had dispensed with rage, and now her eagerness to hear something of her lost son was almost uncomfortable.

The question could be answered honestly. "Very well. And not just from the ball. He would come to our house with other young people. He was very popular. Charming, good-looking, and funny as could be—"

"Oh yes. All that and more."

"Do you have other children?" The moment she said it, Anne could have bitten off her tongue. She remembered very well that Bellasis had been an only child. He'd often talked about it. "I'm so sorry. I remember now that you don't. Please forgive me."

"You're right. When we go, there will be nothing left of us." Lady Brockenhurst smoothed the silk of her skirts, glancing into the empty chimneypiece. "Not a trace."

For a second, Anne thought Lady Brockenhurst might cry, but she decided to continue just the same. Why not comfort this bereaved mother, if she could? Where was the harm? "You must be very proud of Lord Bellasis. He was an excellent young man, and we were so fond of him. Sometimes we would get up a little ball of our own, with six or seven couples, and I would play the piano. It seems strange to say it now, but those days before the battle were happy ones. At any rate, for me."

"I'm sure." Lady Brockenhurst stood. "I'm going now, Mrs. Trenchard. But I have enjoyed our talk. Rather more than I anticipated."

"Who told you I'd be here?" Anne stared at her calmly.

Lady Brockenhurst shook her head. "No one. I asked our hostess who was talking to my sister and she told me your name. I was curious. I have talked *about* you and your daughter so many times that it seemed a shame to miss the chance of talking *to* you.

But anyway, I see now I have been wrong. If anything, it's been a treat for me to discuss Edmund with someone who knew him. You've made me feel I have seen him again, dancing and flirting and enjoying himself in his last hours, and I like to think of that. I *will* think of that. So thank you." She glided away between the chattering groups, stately in her progress, the colors of half mourning moving through the gaily brilliant crowd.

Seeing her gone, the Duchess of Bedford returned. "Heavens. I must say I had no need to worry about you, Mrs. Trenchard. You are clearly among friends." Her words were more amiable than her tone.

"Not friends exactly, but we have memories in common. And now I must also take my leave. I am so pleased I came. Thank you."

"Come again. And next time you can tell me all about the famous gathering before the battle."

But Anne was conscious that somehow to discuss that long-ago evening with someone who had no investment in it would not satisfy her. It had been cathartic to talk about it with the old Duchess, and even with her more astringent sister, as they both had their links to that night. But it would not do to dissect it with a stranger. Ten minutes later, she was in her carriage.

Eaton Square may have been larger than Belgrave Square, but the houses were a shade less magnificent, and although James had been determined to occupy one of the splendid piles in the latter, he had yielded to his wife's wishes and settled for something a little smaller. That said, the houses in Eaton Square were grand enough, but Anne was not unhappy there. Indeed, she liked it, and she had worked hard to make the rooms pretty and pleasant, even if they were not as stately as James would have chosen. "I have a taste for splendor," he used to say, but it was a taste Anne did not share. Still, she walked through the cool, gray entrance hall, smiling at the footman who had let her in, and continued up the staircase without any sense of resisting her surroundings. "Is the master at home?" she asked the man, but no, it seemed James had not returned. He would probably race in, just in time to change, and she would have to leave their discussion until the end of the evening. For a discussion there must be.

They were dining alone with their son, Oliver, and his wife, Susan, who lived with them, and the evening passed easily enough. She told them of the Duchess of Bedford's tea party as they sat in the large dining room on the ground floor. A butler in his late forties, Turton, was serving them with the help of two footmen, which seemed to Anne rather excessive for a family dinner of four persons, but it was how James liked things to be done, and she did not really mind. It was a pleasing room, if a little cold, ennobled by a screen of columns at one end, separating the sideboard from the rest of the chamber. There was a good chimneypiece of Carrara marble and, above it, a portrait of her husband by David Wilkie that James was proud of, even if Wilkie might not have been. It was painted the year before he produced his famous picture of the young Queen at her first Council meeting, which James was sure must have put up Wilkie's price. That said, he did not look his best. Anne's dachshund, Agnes, was sitting by her chair, eyes raised upward in optimism. Anne slipped her a tiny piece of meat.

"You only encourage her to beg," said James. But she didn't really care.

Their daughter-in-law, Susan, was complaining. This was so ordinary a state of affairs that it was hard to concentrate, and Anne had to force herself to listen to this evening's litany of woe. The problem seemed to be that she had not been taken to the Duchess of Bedford's tea party. "But you weren't invited," said Anne, reasonably enough.

"What difference does that make?" Susan was almost in tears. "Women all over London simply reply saying they would be delighted to accept and that they will be bringing their daughters."

"You're not my daughter." As soon as she had said it, Anne knew this was a mistake, since it gave the moral high ground to Susan on a platter. The younger woman's lip quivered. Across the table their son put his knife and fork down noisily.

"She is your *daughter-in-law*, which would mean the same

as 'daughter' in any other house." There was something harsh in Oliver's voice that was more pronounced when he was angry, and he was angry now.

"Of course." Anne turned to help herself to more sauce, deliberately making things normal again. "I just don't think I would be justified in taking someone, anyone, to the house of a woman I barely know."

"A duchess you barely know, and I don't know at all." Apparently Susan had recovered. Enough to fight her corner, anyway. Anne glanced at the opaque faces of the servants. They would soon be enjoying this down in the servants' hall, but, like the professionals they were, they gave no hint of having heard the exchange.

"I didn't see you in the office today, Oliver." Mercifully, James found his son's wife as tiresome as Anne did, even though he and Susan shared so many ambitions as far as the beau monde was concerned.

"I wasn't there."

"Why not?"

"I went to inspect the work in Chapel Street. I wonder we have made the houses so small. Haven't we surrendered a healthy share of profits?"

Anne looked at her husband. However misguided James might be when dazzled by the glare of high Society, he certainly knew his business. "When you develop an area as we have done, you must build for the whole picture. You can't only have palaces. You must house the supporters of the princes who live in the palaces. Their clerks and managers and upper servants. Then there must be a mews for their coaches and coachmen. They all take space, but it is space well used."

Susan's petulant voice reentered the fray. "Have you given any more thought to where we might live, Father?" Anne watched her daughter-in-law. She was a good-looking woman, no doubt about it, with her clear complexion, green eyes, and auburn hair. She had an excellent figure and she dressed well. If only she could ever be satisfied.

The issue of where the young couple should live was an old and tired one. James had offered various options as Belgravia was going up, but his ideas and theirs never seemed to match. They wanted something similar to the house in Eaton Square, while James believed they should cut their coat according to their cloth and start more modestly. In the end, Susan preferred to share a house that suited her pretensions rather than lower her standards, and so a kind of ritual had been achieved. From time to time, James would make suggestions. And Susan would turn them down.

James smiled blandly. "I'd be happy to give you the pick of anything empty in Chester Row."

Susan wrinkled her nose slightly but softened her reaction with a laugh. "Aren't they a little poky?"

Oliver snorted. "Susan's right. They're far too small for entertaining, and I suppose I have a position to keep up, as your son."

James helped himself to another lamb chop. "They're less poky than the first house I shared with your mother." Anne laughed, which only served to annoy Oliver more.

"I have been brought up very differently from the way you two began your lives. Maybe I do have grander expectations, but you have given them to me." Of course there was truth in this. Why else had James insisted on Charterhouse and Cambridge, if he had not wanted Oliver to grow up thinking like a gentleman? In fact, his son's marriage to Susan Miller, the daughter of a successful merchant like himself, had been a disappointment to James, who had hoped for something higher. Still, she was an only child, and there would be a considerable inheritance when the time came. That's if Miller didn't change his mind and cut her out. James noticed that Susan's father was becoming more reluctant to hand over money to his daughter in the way he had done when the pair were first married. "She's such a fool with it," he'd said to James once, after a liquid luncheon, and it was difficult not to agree.

"Well, well. We'll see what can be done." James laid down his cutlery and the footmen stepped in to remove the plates. "Cubitt's had an interesting idea to do something with the Isle of Dogs."

"The Isle of Dogs? Is there anything there?" Anne smiled her thanks to the footman as her plate was taken. Naturally, James was far too important for any such thing.

"The opening of the West India Docks and the East India Docks have made a hell of a difference—" He stopped, catching Anne's expression, and started again. "Have made a terrific difference. Ramshackle buildings are going up every day, but Cubitt thinks we can build a solid community if we give respectable people—not just workers, but management—somewhere decent to live. It's exciting."

"Will Oliver be part of this?" Susan kept her tone bright.

"We'll have to see."

"Of course I won't," said Oliver curtly. "When was I ever brought in to anything interesting?"

"We seem to be failing on every count tonight." James helped himself to another glass of wine from the decanter he kept by his place. It was an inescapable truth that Oliver was a disappointment to him, and the younger man suspected it. It did not make for a comfortable relationship.

Agnes was beginning to whine, and so Anne picked her up, hiding her in the folds of her skirt. "We'll be at Glanville for most of next month," she said, in an effort to lighten the atmosphere. "I hope you'll come down when you can. Susan, perhaps you can stay for a few days?" There was a silence. Glanville was their house in Somerset, an Elizabethan manor of great beauty that Anne had rescued from the brink of collapse. It was the one place which, before his marriage, Oliver had enjoyed above all others. But Susan had different ideas.

"We will if we can." She smiled briskly. "It's such a ways." He knew that, in addition to something splendid in London, Susan had her heart set on an estate near enough to the city to make the journey in no more than a few hours. Preferably with a large and modern house equipped with every convenience. The ancient, mottled, golden stone of Glanville, with its mullioned windows and uneven, gleaming floors, held no appeal for her. But Anne was undeterred. She would not give up the house or the estate—and James did not expect her to. She would try to encourage her son and his wife to appreciate its charms, but in the end, if Oliver didn't want it, then she must find her own heir elsewhere. Which she was fully prepared to do.

Anne had been right about the servants' pleasure in their account of the upstairs conversation. Billy and Morris, the two footmen who had served at dinner, kept the table in the servants' hall in stitches with their telling of it. That was until Mr. Turton came in. He paused on the threshold. "I hope there is no disrespect on display in this room."

"No, Mr. Turton," said Billy, but one of the maids started to giggle.

"Mr. and Mrs. Trenchard pay our wages, and for that they are entitled to be treated with dignity."

"Yes, Mr. Turton."

The giggles had subsided by now as Turton took his place at the table and the servants' dinner began. The butler lowered his voice as he spoke to the housekeeper, Mrs. Frant, who sat in her usual place beside him. "Of course, they're not what they like to pretend, and it is only the more obvious when they're alone."

Mrs. Frant was a more forgiving person. "They're respectable, polite, and honest to deal with, Mr. Turton. I've known far worse in households headed by a coronet." She helped herself to some horseradish sauce.

But the butler shook his head. "My sympathy is with Mr. Oliver. They've brought him up as a gentleman, but now they seem to resent him for wanting to be one." Turton had no problems with the social system then operating, only with his own place in it.

A sharp-faced woman in the black garb of a lady's maid spoke up from farther down the table. "Why shouldn't Mrs. Oliver have a house where she can entertain? She's brought enough money to the table. I think it's unjust and illogical of Mr. Trenchard to try to force them into a rabbit hutch when we all know he wants to be thought of as the head of a great family. Where's the sense in that?"

"Illogical? That's a big word, Miss Speer," said Billy, but she ignored him.

"It was Mrs. Trenchard who provoked Mrs. Oliver at dinner," said Morris.

"She's as bad as he is," said Miss Speer, helping herself to a large slice of bread and butter from the plate before her.

Mrs. Frant had more to add on the subject. "Well, I'm sorry to say it, Miss Speer, and I'm glad if you think her a good employer, but I find Mrs. Oliver very hard to please. You'd think she was an Infanta of Spain with all her airs and graces. But I've never had any trouble with Mrs. Trenchard. She's straightforward in what she wants and I've no reason to complain." The housekeeper was warming to her defense of their employers. "As to the younger pair—wanting houses and estates that are bigger and grander than his parents', what's he done to earn them? That's what I'd like to know."

"Gentlemen don't 'earn' their houses, Mrs. Frant. They inherit them."

"We don't see these things in the same way, Mr. Turton, so we'll have to agree to differ."

Miss Ellis, Mrs. Trenchard's maid, seated on Turton's left, did not appear to disagree with the butler. "I think Mr. Turton's right. Mr. Oliver only wants to live properly, and why shouldn't he? I commend his efforts to better himself. But we must feel some sympathy for the master. It's hard to get the trick of it in a single generation."

Turton nodded, as if his point had been proved. "I quite agree with you there, Miss Ellis." And then the conversation turned to other topics.

"Of course you can't tell her! What are you talking about?" James Trenchard was having the greatest difficulty keeping his temper. He was in his wife's bedroom where he generally slept, even though he was careful to have his own bedroom and dressing room farther down the landing, as he had read this was customary for aristocratic couples.

The room in question was another tall and airy chamber, painted pale pink, with flowered silk curtains. Her husband's rooms could have been the private apartments of the Emperor himself, but, as with all the rooms Anne had arranged for her own use, her bedroom was pretty rather than splendid. At this moment, she was in bed and they were alone. "But haven't I a duty to her?"

"What duty? You say yourself she was very rude."

Anne nodded. "Yes, but it was more complicated than that. The whole situation was so peculiar. She knew exactly who I was and that her son had been in love with our daughter. Why shouldn't she know? Her sister had no reason to keep it secret."

"Then why didn't she just say so honestly?"

"I know and I agree. But perhaps she was trying to learn what kind of person I was before she would admit the connection."

"It doesn't sound as if she has admitted it yet."

"She would have disapproved of it, fiercely, if she'd known at the time. We can be sure of that much."

"All the more reason to keep her in the dark."

James pulled off his silk dressing gown and flung it angrily over a chair.

Anne closed her book and put it carefully on the little Sheraton table by her bed. She picked up the snuffer. "But when she said, 'There will be nothing left of us . . .' If you'd been there, you'd have been as touched as I was. I promise."

"You have taken leave of your reason if you think we should tell her. What can come of it? The ruin of Sophia's reputation, the end of our chances as we label ourselves creatures of scandal—"

Anne could feel her temper starting to rise. "That's what you don't like. The idea that Lady Somebody will turn up her nose at you because you had a daughter who was no better than she ought to be."

He was indignant. "I see. And you like the idea that Sophia should be remembered as a harlot?"

This silenced her for a moment. Then she spoke, more calmly this time. "It's a risk, of course, but I would ask her to keep it to herself. Of course I know I couldn't force her to, but I don't think we have the right to keep it from her that she has a grandson."

"We've kept it from them for more than a quarter of a century."

"But we didn't know them. Now we do. Or at least, I know her."

James had climbed in beside his wife and blown out his candle. He lay down with his back to her. "I forbid it. I will not have our daughter's memory defaced. Certainly not by her own mother. And get that dog off the bed." Anne could see there was no point in arguing any further, so she gently snuffed out the candle on her side, settled down under the bedclothes, and lifted Agnes into the crook of her arm. But sleep was a long time in coming.

The family had returned to England before Sophia told them. The aftermath of the battle consumed James's efforts for some weeks, but at last he had brought them all back to London, to a house in Kennington that was an improvement on their previous abode but hardly a fashion leader. He continued to supply foodstuffs to the army, but catering to an army in peacetime was not the same as dealing with the drama of war, and it was increasingly clear to Anne that he was bored with the work, bored with the world he was operating in, bored with its lack of possibilities. Then he started to notice the renewed activity of London's builders. The victory over Napoléon and the peace that followed had stoked a new confidence in the country's future. The figure of the French emperor had loomed over them all, more perhaps than they had recognized, for twenty years, and now he was gone to a faraway island in the South Atlantic, and this time he would not be back. Europe was free, and it was time to look ahead. And so the day dawned when James came into the house flushed with excitement. Anne was in the kitchen, supervising the stores cupboard with her cook. There was no need for this. Their life and income had overtaken the way they used to do things, as James never tired of pointing out, and seeing his wife in an apron checking groceries was never very pleasing to him, especially as he was still flying high from their experiences in Brussels. On this particular evening, however, nothing could spoil his humor.

"I have met an extraordinary man," he said.

"Oh?" Anne stared at the label on the flour. She was sure it was wrong.

"A man who is going to rebuild London." Anne didn't know it then but he was right. Thomas Cubitt, a former ship's carpenter, had devised a new method for managing a building project. He undertook to deal with, and employ, all the different trades involved: bricklayers, plasterers, tilers, plumbers, carpenters, stonemasons, painters. Those responsible for the commission would only ever have to deal with Cubitt and his brother, William. Everything else would be done for them.

James paused. "Isn't it brilliant?"

Anne could see that there was considerable appeal in this system, and it might have a bright future, but was it worth throwing over a perfectly established career when James knew nothing about it? Still, she soon learned that he wouldn't be shaken. "He's building a new home for the London Institution at Finsbury Circus. He wants help with the funding and dealing with the suppliers."

"Which you have been doing all your working life."

"Exactly!" And so it began. James Trenchard the developer was born, and everything would have been as merry as a marriage bell if Sophia had not dropped her bombshell barely a month later.

She came into her mother's room one morning and sat on the bed. Anne was at her glass as Ellis finished her hair. The girl waited in near silence until the work was done. Anne knew something was coming, something big, but she wasn't eager to begin it. At last, however, she accepted the inevitable. "Thank you, Ellis, you may go." The maid was curious, naturally; if anything, more curious than the mother, but she picked up some linen for the laundry and closed the door behind her.

"What is it?"

Sophia stared at her. Then she spoke in a kind of gushing sigh. "I'm going to have a child." Once, as a young girl, Anne had been kicked in the stomach by a pony, and she was reminded of that sensation when she heard the words.

"When?" It seemed an oddly practical question, given the circumstance, but she didn't see the point in screaming and writhing on the floor, even if it had considerable appeal.

"The end of February. I think."

"Don't you know?"

"The end of February."

Anne counted backward in her mind. "Do I have Lord Bellasis to thank for this?" Sophia nodded. "You stupid, stupid fool." The girl nodded again. She was putting up no resistance. "How did it happen?"

"I thought we were married."

Anne almost burst out laughing. What tomfoolery had her daughter been put through? "I take it you weren't."

"No."

"No, of course you weren't. Nor ever likely to be." How could her child have been so absurd as to think Bellasis would really marry her? She felt a sudden wave of fury at James. He had encouraged this. He'd convinced the girl that impossible things were possible. "Tell me everything."

It was hardly an unfamiliar story. Bellasis had professed his love and persuaded Sophia that he wished to marry her before he went back into action. At the news of Napoleon's march on Brussels, he had come to her, begging her to let him arrange a marriage that would be clandestine at first, but which he promised he would reveal to his parents when he felt the time was right. Either way, she would have proof of the ceremony if anything happened to him, and she could claim the protection of the Brockenhursts if she needed it.

"But didn't you know you should have had your father's permission for it to be legal? You're eighteen." She said this to provoke more self-flagellation from Sophia, but instead the girl just looked at her for a moment.

"Papa gave his permission."

That brought a second pony kick. Her husband had helped a man to seduce his own daughter? She felt so angry that if James had walked through the door at that moment, she would have scratched his eyeballs out of their sockets. "Your father *knew*?"

"He knew that Edmund wanted to marry me before he went back to the fighting, and he gave his permission." Sophia took another deep breath. In a way it was a relief to reveal it. She was tired of carrying the burden alone. "Edmund said he'd found a parson to marry us, which he did, in one of the army chapels they had erected. Afterward the man wrote out a letter certifying it and...that's when it happened."

"I assume the marriage was false?"

Sophia nodded. "I never suspected it, not for a moment. Edmund spoke of his love and our future, right up until the moment we were leaving his aunt's ball on the night of the battle."

"So when did you find out?"

The girl got up and walked over to the window. Below, her father was climbing into a carriage. She was glad he would be out of the house, giving her mother some time to calm down and think up a plan. "As we came out of the Richmonds' house into the street, there was a group of officers on horseback, all in the uniforms of the Fifty-second Light Infantry, the Oxfordshires, Edmund's own regiment..."

"And?"

"One of them was the 'churchman' who married us. So there you have it." She sighed wearily. "He was a soldier, a friend of Edmund's, who had turned his collar around to deceive me."

"Did he say anything?"

"He never saw me. Or if he did, he pretended he had not. I wasn't close and, of course, once I'd recognized him I shrank back."

Anne nodded. The scene when they had left the ball together suddenly made sense. "Now I understand what put you in such a state that night. I thought it was simply Lord Bellasis leaving for the battle."

"The moment I saw the man I knew I'd been taken in. I was not loved. I was not heading for a golden future. I was a stupid young woman who had been treated as a streetwalker, tricked and used, and no doubt I would have been thrown aside into the gutter where Edmund thought I belonged, if he had lived." Her face seemed so mature in the daylight, the bitterness in her speech adding ten years to her age.

"When did you know you were carrying a child?"

"Hard to say. I suspected it a month later, but I wouldn't admit it until any further denial was pointless. Edmund was dead, and for a time, like a madwoman, I pretended nothing had changed. I didn't know what I was doing. I was at my wit's end. I confess I have taken some foolish remedies, and paid a gypsy five pounds for what I am quite sure was sugar water. But they all failed. I am still *enceinte*."

"What have you told your father?"

"He knows I was deceived. I told him that morning in Brussels when he brought me the news of Edmund's death. But he thinks I got away with it."

"We must make a plan." Anne Trenchard was a practical woman, and one of her chief virtues was that she did not linger over a disaster but sought, almost immediately, to remedy what could be remedied and to accept what could not. Her daughter must be spirited away from London. She would have an illness or a relation in the north who needed caring for. They would have a story ready before the day was finished. Sophia must be four months gone at least, and now that Anne concentrated on it, the girl's figure was thickening. Not noticeably so, yet, but it wouldn't be long. They had no time to lose.

Anne was not kind to James when he returned that evening and found himself alone with his wife in his study. "And you never thought to consult me? When a rich viscount proposed a secret marriage that no one must know of, performed by a parson no one could vouch for, with a beautiful eighteen-year-old from an entirely unsuitable background, you never thought to talk to *anyone* about what his motives might possibly be?" She was trying hard not to shout.

James nodded. He had gone over it often enough in his own mind. "It sounds so obvious when you say it, but Bellasis seemed a nice young man and genuinely fond of her—"

"You think he would have confided in you that he was hoping to seduce your daughter if it could possibly be managed?"

"I suppose not."

She almost spat at him. "When you gave your permission, she was ruined."

He winced. "Please, Anne. Do you think I don't regret it?"

"I assume you regret it even more now."

In time, Anne came to be sorry she had blamed her husband so entirely for Sophia's fall. Because when the girl died in childbirth, he remembered the charge and saw her death as his own fault, his punishment for his vanity and ambition and self-importance. It didn't seem to cure him of any of these failings, but the guilt never left him, nonetheless.

There had been no indication of what was coming, but then, as the doctor said at the time, there seldom was. Anne and Sophia had gone up to Derbyshire and taken a modest house on the edge of Bakewell, as Mrs. Casson and her married daughter, Mrs. Blake, a Waterloo widow. They had no friends or acquaintances in the area, but anyway they saw no one. And they lived simply. Neither of them took their maids with them, and Ellis and Croft went on to board wages until their mistresses returned. If they were curious, Anne never knew. At any rate, they were too professional to show it.

It wasn't an unhappy time. Their life up there was pleasant enough, reading, taking walks in the park at Chatsworth. They made inquiries and enlisted the help of a highly regarded physician, Doctor Smiley, and he'd been pleased with Sophia's progress. Anne came to suspect that he knew the truth, or at least that they were not who they pretended to be, but he was too well mannered to be openly curious.

Before they left London, they had arranged that James would find the child a suitable home. Even Sophia knew she couldn't hope to keep it. The baby must be properly looked after, given a name, educated, but brought up with no awareness of his or her real identity. None of them wanted Sophia's name to be dragged through the mud, and Anne knew her husband also feared that his own attempts at self-betterment would be dashed by a public scandal. If it had been their son who had fathered a bastard, it might be different, but for a daughter it was a crime with no possible forgiveness. James had acted swiftly, and with the help of the company spies found a clergyman, Benjamin Pope, who lived in Surrey. He was born a gentleman but the living was a poor one and so the extra money would be welcome. More to the point, the couple was childless and sad to be so. Sophia accepted the situation, when it was explained to her—not without a pang, but she accepted it. Armed with this, James made the final arrangements, and Mr. Pope agreed to adopt the baby as the "child of his late cousin." The Popes would get a generous additional income, which would allow them to live reasonably well, while the child would be educated and a progress report would be sent regularly to Mr. Trenchard's office for his private perusal.

Meanwhile, Dr. Smiley enrolled an experienced midwife, made every preparation, and came to the house to supervise the birth. And it should have been fine. Except when it was done and the boy was safely born, the doctor simply could not stop the bleeding. Anne had never seen so much blood, and there was nothing for her to do but hold Sophia's hand and assure her that everything would soon be mended and that nothing was wrong. She never forgot how she had just sat there, lying and lying, on and on, until her little girl was dead.

She couldn't look at the baby for weeks, this boy who had killed her daughter. Dr. Smiley found a wet nurse and a nursemaid and between them they made sure he survived, but still Anne could not look at him. She'd employed a cook and a housemaid when they first arrived, so life went on, with empty days parsed by uneaten meals, but still she could not set eyes on the child. Until one evening Dr. Smiley came to her in the little parlor where she sat by the fire, staring blankly at the book in her hands, and said gently that all she had left of Sophia was her son. Then Anne did allow herself to be coaxed into holding the baby, and having held him, she could hardly bear to let him go.

Anne often wondered if she had only learned to love the boy sooner, would she have tried to change the plan and insisted on bringing him up herself? But she doubted James would have allowed it, and since the arrangements were fixed, it would have been hard to renege on them. At last the house in Bakewell was closed and Anne traveled south with the nurse, who traveled on to Surrey to deliver the baby to his new home. The nurse was paid off and life returned to normal. Normal, that is, without Sophia. There was a tearful good-bye to Croft, whose services were no longer needed. Anne gave her a bonus as a farewell, but she was interested that the maid never showed any curiosity as to why her young mistress had died. Maybe she had guessed the truth. It would be hard to hide a pregnancy from a lady's maid.

So the years passed. The original plan had been for Charles to be trained for the cloth, and this had continued as a goal while he grew through his teens, but he had early displayed a talent for mathematics, and as he neared the end of boyhood he announced that he wanted to try his luck in the City. It was impossible for James not to feel flattered by this development, as he reasoned it must be his own blood coming out in the lad, but still they had not met him. They could only judge the young man by the reports sent from the Reverend Mr. Pope. In truth, James longed to help his grandson, but he was unsure how to do so without opening the Pandora's box that a revelation of his origins was bound to prove. And so they hung back, paying him a modest allowance that Mr. Pope explained to Charles was a gift from well-wishers, living for the letters that Pope would send, four times a year, as regularly as clockwork. The boy had been happy. They were sure of that. At least, they had no reason to think otherwise. On their instruction, he had been told that his father had died in battle and his mother in childbirth and that therefore he was adopted, but that was all. He seemed to have accepted it, and the Popes had grown fond of him so there was no cause for concern, but still, as Anne would say to herself night after night as she lay in the dark, he was their grandchild and yet they did not know him.

And now Lady Brockenhurst had entered the picture and complicated things further. Anne might not know Charles Pope, but at least she knew of his existence. She knew that her daughter had not vanished from the earth leaving no trace behind. Lady Brock-enhurst had almost wept when she talked of their having no heir, while she, Anne, could have told her that her child had fathered a healthy and promising son. She had known James would forbid it, of course. Partly for motives she did not respect, but partly to protect the good name of their dead daughter, and that she could not simply dismiss. Hour after hour she lay with James snoring beside her, unable to resolve what she should do, until at last she slipped into a fretful sleep, waking early and unrefreshed.

It took a month of uneasy rest and sorrow before Anne decided on a course of action. She did not like Lady Brockenhurst. She did not even know her, but she couldn't bear the responsibility of the secret. She was only too aware that, had their positions been reversed and she'd discovered Lady Brockenhurst had kept such a story from her she would never have forgiven her. So, one day, she sat at the pretty desk in her little sitting room on the second floor and wrote: "Dear Lady Brockenhurst, I should like to call on you at a time that is convenient. I would be grateful if you could find a moment when we might be alone." It wasn't hard to learn which house in Belgrave Square they occupied, since her husband had built it. She folded the paper, sealed it with a wafer, wrote the address, and went out herself to give it to the carrier. It would have taken her maid ten minutes to deliver her message to the door, but Anne was not anxious to have all her business discussed below stairs.

She did not have long to wait. The following morning there was a note on the breakfast tray that Ellis laid across her lap. She picked it up.

"It was brought by hand, ma'am. A footman delivered it this morning."

"Did he say anything?"

"No. Just handed it in and left." Naturally the question only whetted Ellis's appetite, but Anne had no intention of giving any clues. She took up the little silver paper knife that had been laid on the tray and opened the envelope. A small sheet of thick, cream paper, embossed with a capital *B* under an earl's coronet, contained a short message. "Come at four o'clock today. We will be alone for half an hour. CB"

Anne did not order a carriage. Lady Brockenhurst probably would not approve but she wanted no witnesses. It was a nice enough day, and the walk would be a short one. More tellingly, she did not even ring for help with her cape and bonnet, but simply went up to her room at twenty minutes to the hour and slipped them on herself. Then she descended the stairs and left. The footman in the hall held the door for her, so the excursion could not be a complete secret, but what could be in her life these days? With prying eyes upon them from the moment they woke?

Outside, she regretted for a moment not bringing Agnes for the walk, but then she decided it would only complicate matters, and she set off. The sky was looking a little darker than in the morning, but she turned left and walked until she came to Belgrave Place, then left again, and in less than a quarter of an hour since she had quit her own front door she was standing before Brockenhurst House. It was a large building, straddling the corner between Upper Belgrave Street and Chapel Street, one of the three freestanding palaces at the corners of the square. She hesitated but then she saw that a footman, lounging near the gate at the entrance, was watching her. She straightened her back and walked up to the front door. Before she could pull the bell, the door swung open and another liveried footman invited her in.

"Mrs. James Trenchard," she said.

"Her ladyship is expecting you," replied the man in the curious neutral tone, implying neither approval nor disapproval, that the experienced servant always masters. "Her ladyship is in the drawing room. If you would like to follow me." Anne removed her cape and gave it over for him to lay on one of the gilded sofas in the hall, and then followed the man up the broad green marble staircase. They reached the top, and the servant opened one of the double doors and announced, "Mrs. Trenchard," before closing it and leaving Anne to negotiate her way across the wide expanse of colorful Savonnerie carpet to where the Countess sat by the fire. She nodded.

"Come in, Mrs. Trenchard, and sit by me. I hope you do not mind a fire in summer. I'm afraid I am always cold." It was as near to a friendly greeting as Anne suspected she was capable of. She took a seat on a damask-covered Louis XV *bergère* opposite her hostess. There was a portrait over the chimneypiece of a beauty in the style of the century before, with high-piled, powdered hair, lace *décolleté*, and panniers. With a slight surprise, she realized the picture was of Lady Brockenhurst. "It was painted by Beechey," said her hostess with a chuckle. "On my marriage in 1792. I was seventeen. They said it was quite a good likeness at the time, but no one could tell that now."

"I knew it was you."

"You surprise me." She sat, patiently waiting. After all, it was Anne who had requested the interview.

There was no getting around it. The moment had arrived. "Lady Brockenhurst, it seems that I am in possession of a secret that I have sworn to my husband never to reveal, and indeed he would be very angry if he knew that I was here today..." She paused. Somehow she could not make herself frame the words.

Lady Brockenhurst had no desire to be drawn into the complexities of the Trenchard marriage. Instead she said simply, "Yes?" Despite herself, Anne was impressed. There was something very powerful in her hostess's composure. She must by now have deduced that something momentous was about to be revealed, but she could have been entertaining the vicar's wife for all that it showed on her face.

"The other day, you said that when you and your husband go, there will be nothing left of you."

"I did."

"Well, that's not quite true."

Lady Brockenhurst stiffened almost imperceptibly. At least Anne had her full attention.

"Before she died, Sophia was delivered of a child, a boy, Lord Bellasis's son." At that moment, the large double doors of the drawing room flew open and two footmen arrived bearing trays of tea. They proceeded to put up a table, cover it with a cloth, and lay out everything, much as the Duchess of Bedford's servants had done.

Lady Brockenhurst smiled. "I liked it more than I knew at the time, and I have taken to staging an imitation of my own every day at some point after four. I'm sure it will catch on." Anne acknowledged this, and together they chatted about the merits of eating as well as drinking tea until the men had completed their work. "Thank you, Peter. We will manage by ourselves today." To Anne it felt as if an age had passed, as if she were physically older by the time the men left.

Lady Brockenhurst poured them both a cup and handed one to Anne. "Where is he now, this boy?" She betrayed neither excitement nor revulsion. In fact, she gave away nothing. As was her habit.

"In London, and the 'boy' is a man. He was twenty-five last February. He works in the City."

"What is he like? Do you know him well?"

"We don't know him at all. My husband placed him, soon after his birth, in the care of a clergyman named Pope. He goes under the name of Charles Pope now. We have never thought it would be useful to make his origins public knowledge. He himself knows nothing."

"You must protect the memory of your daughter, poor child. Of course I can see that. We must try not to blame her when she is to be pitied. You said yourself the atmosphere in Brussels before the battle was such that anyone could lose their reason for a moment."

If this was supposed to be a defense of Sophia, it was not effective. "I do not blame her, and she didn't lose her reason," said Anne firmly. "She believed she was married to Lord Bellasis. He tricked her into thinking that a marriage had taken place."

This was not at all what Lady Brockenhurst had been expecting. She drew herself up. "I *beg* your pardon?"

"He tricked her. He bamboozled her. He told her he had arranged for them to be married, then he persuaded a fellow officer to pretend to be a clergyman, and Sophia did not find out the truth until it was too late."

"I don't believe you." Lady Brockenhurst spoke with absolute, unchallengeable conviction.

Anne was quite as firm. She spoke calmly, putting down her cup as she did so. "Of course that is your privilege, but I am telling you the truth. It was only when we left the ball, immediately before Lord Bellasis rode away to join his regiment, that Sophia recognized his partner in her undoing. The so-called parson was laughing and joking with his fellow officers, as far from a churchman as anyone could be. She almost fainted."

Lady Brockenhurst had also placed her cup firmly back on its saucer and now she stood. "I see how it is. Your daughter was scheming to catch my wretched son in her net, no doubt encouraged by her parents—"

Anne cut in sharply. "Now it is *my* turn to be incredulous."

But Lady Brockenhurst continued on her path, warming to her subject as she spoke. "When she heard that he was dead and his seduction had been for nothing, she concocted a story that would give her some excuse if the worst happened, and it did."

Anne was bristling now, furious at this cold and heartless woman, furious at the dead Lord Bellasis, furious at herself for being so blind. "You mean, Lord Bellasis was incapable of such behavior?"

"I most certainly do. He could never have conceived of the very idea." Lady Brockenhurst was getting carried away with her performance. She had become Indignation on a monument. She did not value Anne's type, and so she could not see or judge the woman clearly. But Anne Trenchard was quite as much a fighter as she.

"Wasn't his godfather Lord Berkeley?"

Anne could see at once the name was a slap across Lady Brockenhurst's face. She almost flinched. "How did you know that?"

"Because Lord Bellasis spoke of him. He told me that when Lord Berkeley died in 1810, his eldest son was disallowed the use of his titles because his father had not truly married his mother before the boy's birth, as she thought. It came out later that he'd gotten a friend to pose as a priest, so he might lure the unsuspecting girl into bed. They did marry later but they could not legitimize the child. You know all this to be true." Lady Brockenhurst was silent. "I beg you not to tell me Lord Bellasis could never have conceived of any such idea."

After a pause to regroup, Lady Brockenhurst recovered her style. Gliding smoothly over to the chimneypiece, she tugged at the embroidered bell rope, talking as she went. "I will only say this. My son was seduced by an unscrupulous and ambitious girl, aided for all I know by her equally ambitious parents. She wanted to use the chaos of war to bring about a union that would advance her beyond even her father's dreams. But she failed. My son took her as his mistress. I do not deny it, but so what? He was a young man, and she was a pretty slut who threw herself at his head. And I won't apologize for that because I do not care. Ah, Peter. Please take Mrs. Trenchard down. She is leaving." She spoke to the footman who had come in answer to the bell. He waited in the doorway.

Anne could not, of course, reply in front of him, but she was too angry to speak anyway, just nodding to her enemy to avoid giving the servant any clue as to what had really taken place. She started for the door, but Lady Brockenhurst had not quite finished. "Funny. I thought you had some sentimental tale to tell me of my son. A happy story from his last days on earth. You spoke so well of him when we first met."

Anne stopped. "I spoke of him as I knew him before that night. We did have fun with him. I wasn't lying. And I didn't want to hurt you. But I was wrong. You were bound to know the truth eventually. I should have been more honest. If it's any consolation, no one was more surprised than I to learn what he was capable of." She hesitated at the door. The footman had gone ahead of her along the gallery, and they were alone again for a moment. "Will you keep our secret?" She hated to ask but she had to. "Can I have your word of honor?"

"Of course you may have my word." The Countess's smile

would have frozen water. "Why would I publicize my late son's degradation?" With that, Anne had to accept that she'd allowed Lady Brockenhurst the final say on the matter. She swept out of the room, down the staircase, and into the street before she allowed herself to stop and take full account of her shaking fury.

·3·

Family Ties

Lymington Park was not the oldest seat of the Bellasis dynasty, but it was unquestionably the grandest. They had begun their career among the landed gentry in a modest manor house in Leicestershire, but marriage to an heiress in the early seventeenth century had brought the Hampshire estate as a welcome dowry, and the family had been glad to move south. A desperate appeal for funds from King Charles I, in the heat of the Civil War, had brought the promise of an earldom, and the pledge was made good by the decapitated King's son, when he returned in glory at the Restoration. Although it was the second Earl who decided that the existing house was no longer appropriate to their station, and a large Palladian palace, designed by William Kent, was proposed. This was to be funded by some sensible investment in the early days of Empire, but a sudden downturn meant it never happened, and in the event it was the present Earl's grandfather who had employed the architect George Steuart in the 1780s to design a new and grander envelope to be built around the original hall. The result could not be described as cozy or even comfortable, but it spoke of tradition and high office, and as Peregrine Bellasis, fifth Earl of Brockenhurst, strode through the great hall, or sat in his library with its fine books and his dogs round his feet, or climbed the staircase lined with portraits of his ancestors, he felt it was a suitable setting as the background to a noble life. His wife, Caroline, knew how to manage such a place, or rather how to assemble the right team to manage it, and while her own enthusiasm for the house, like all her enthusiasms, had slipped into the grave with the body of her son, she knew how to make a decent show and take command of the county.

But this morning, her thoughts were on other matters. She thanked her maid, Dawson, as the woman placed the breakfast tray across her knees as Caroline watched a group of fallow deer move softly across the park outside her windows. She smiled, and the strangeness of the sensation seemed to freeze her for a moment. "Is everything all right, m'lady?" Dawson looked concerned.

Caroline nodded. "Quite. Thank you. I'll ring when I'm ready to dress." The maid nodded and left. Lady Brockenhurst poured her coffee carefully. Why did her heart feel lighter? Was it so remarkable? That a little harpy had tried to blackmail her dead son? That this was the reason for the existence of the boy she had no doubt, and yet... She closed her eyes. Edmund had loved Lymington. Even as a child, he had known every inch of the estate. He could have been left in any part of it blindfolded and found his way back unaided. But he would not have been unaided, since every keeper, every tenant, every worker had taken the child to their heart. Caroline knew well enough that she was not loved, and nor was her husband. They were respected. In a way. But no more than that. The local people thought them chilly and unfeeling, hard and even harsh, but they had given birth to a prodigy. That was how she thought of Edmund: a prodigy, a golden child who was loved by everyone he knew. At least, that was how he had come to seem as the empty, lonely years stumbled on, until, with the varnishing patina of history, she came to believe that she, of all people, had given birth to the perfect son. They'd wanted more children, of course. But in the end, and after three stillbirths, only Edmund was left to occupy the nurseries on the second floor; yet he was enough. That was what she told herself, and it was the truth. He was enough. As he grew, the tenants and the villagers looked forward to the day he would inherit. She knew that, and told it against herself. He was their hope for a better future, and maybe he would have given them one. But now they had only Peregrine to endure and John to look forward to; an old man with no interest in life to be followed by a greedy, selfish peacock who would care no more for them than if they were stones in the road. How sad.

Still, this morning Caroline felt different. She looked around the room, which was lined in pale green striped silk, with a tall gilt looking glass above the chimneypiece and a set of engravings on the walls, wondering quite what was making her feel unlike her usual self. Then, with a kind of surprise, she realized she felt happy, as if the sensation were so lost to her that it took a while for her to identify it. But it was true. She was happy to think her child had left a son. It wouldn't change anything. The title, the estates, the London house, everything else, would still be John's, but Edmund had left a son, and might they not come to know this man? Might they not find him and help him? After all, they would not be the first noble family to boast a love child. The late King's bastards were all received at Court by the young Queen. Surely they could lift him from obscurity? Surely there must be some property outside the entail? Her imagination was beginning to spill over into a myriad of possibilities. Didn't that tiresome woman say the boy had been brought up by a clergyman, in a respectable household, and not by herself and her vulgar husband? With any luck, he would favor his father and not his mother. He might even be a sort of gentleman. Of course she knew she had given her word that she would say and do nothing to reveal the truth, but was it necessary to keep one's word if it were given to someone like Mrs. Trenchard? She wriggled. Caroline Brockenhurst was a cold woman and a snobbish one—she would have admitted as much—but she was not dishonest or dishonorable. She knew she could not break her oath and turn herself into a liar. There must be some other way through the maze.

Lord Brockenhurst was still in the dining room when she came down, engrossed in his copy of the *Times*. "It's beginning to look as if Peel might win the election," he said without looking up. "It seems Melbourne's on the way out. She won't like that."

"I believe the Prince favors Sir Robert Peel."

Her husband grunted. "He would. He's a German."

Lady Brockenhurst had no interest in going on with this. "You haven't forgotten Stephen and Grace will be here for luncheon?"

"Are they bringing John?"

"I think so. He's been staying with them."

"Drat." Her husband did not look up from the page. "I suppose they want money."

"Thank you, Jenkins." Lady Brockenhurst smiled at the butler standing to attention by the sideboard. He nodded and left. "Really, Peregrine, are we to have no secrets at all?"

"You don't have to worry about Jenkins. He knows more about this family than I ever will." It was true that Jenkins was a child of Lymington. A tenant farmer's son who had joined the household as a hall boy at thirteen and never left, he had climbed through the ranks over the years until he reached the dizzying throne of butler. His loyalty to the Bellasis clan was unshakable.

"I do not worry about him. I simply think it rude to test him. Whether we like it or not, Stephen is your brother and your heir and should be treated with respect, at least in public."

"But not in private, by God. Besides, he's only my heir if he outlives me, and I'll make damn sure he doesn't."

"Famous last words." But she sat with her husband, chatting away, engaging him with talk of the estate, more friendly than she had been in months or even years, perhaps because she felt so guilty about the things she was not saying.

In the end, the Honorable and Reverend Stephen Bellasis came with his family early, not long after midday. The excuse he gave at luncheon was that he wanted to take a turn in the gardens before they ate, but Peregrine was convinced they'd come before time simply to annoy him. At any rate, neither of the Brockenhursts were there to receive their relatives when they arrived.

Shorter than his elder brother and substantially heavier, Stephen Bellasis had inherited none of the Brockenhurst charm that had made Peregrine so attractive in his youth, to say nothing of the late Lord Bellasis, who could turn heads in a ballroom with his dark, masculine beauty. By contrast, Stephen's bald pate was struggling to hold on to the few gray strands of hair he carefully combed across it every morning, while below his oddly lush, long, gray mustache, his chin was soft and weak.

He was followed into the great hall by his wife, Grace. The eldest of five sisters, Grace was the daughter of a Gloucestershire baronet, and she had grown up hoping for better things than a fat and impecunious younger son. But she'd overestimated her own value in the marriage market and, with her pale brown eyes and thin lips, Grace, as her mother had repeatedly told her, was very much second son material. Her birth and her education might have meant the young Grace would set her sights high and aim at a great position, but her looks and her modest dowry had ensured that she could not hope to achieve one.

As she stood taking off her cape, bonnet, and gloves and handing them over to the footman, she gazed at the huge bowl of lilacs on the table at the bottom of the wide, shallow, stone stairs. Grace inhaled their sweet scent. She loved lilacs, and a large display of them at home would have pleased her immensely. But the hall in the vicarage was too small for anything quite so grand.

John Bellasis marched past his mother. She was always so slow, and he was impatient for a glass of something. Handing his cane to the man, he walked straight into the dining room, approaching the collection of cut-glass decanters on the silver salver to the right of the large marble fireplace. Before Jenkins could catch up with him, he had picked one up and was pouring himself a large slug of brandy, which he knocked back in one. "Thank you, Jenkins," he said, turning to face the butler. "You can give me another."

Jenkins, hurrying after him across the room, reached for a small, unopened bottle. "Soda, sir?" he replied.

"Yes."

Jenkins didn't blink. He was used to Master John. He refilled the glass with brandy, this time mixed with soda, and held it out on a small silver tray. John took it and walked back to rejoin his parents, who were disposed about the drawing room on the other side of the hall. They broke off their conversation as he came in.

"There you are," said Grace. "We wondered what had become of you."

"I can tell you what will become of me," he answered, bringing his forehead to rest against a cool pane of glass as he stared out across the park. "If I can't lay my hands on some funding."

"Well, that didn't take long," said Lord Brockenhurst. "I thought we might get to the pudding before you started asking for money." He was standing in the doorway with his wife.

"Where have you been?" said Stephen.

"We were at Lower Farm," said Caroline briskly, walking in past her husband. She gave a swift, cool kiss to Grace as the other woman rose to greet her. "John? You were saying?"

"I'm serious," said John. "There is nothing else for it." He turned around to meet his aunt's eye.

"Nothing else for what?" asked Peregrine, his hands behind his back as he stood warming himself by the fireplace. Although it was a pleasant and sunny June day outside, there was a large, well-stoked blaze. Caroline liked to keep every room as hot as an orchid house.

"I have a tailor's bill to pay and the rent on Albany." John shook his head, his hands gesturing surprise, as if he were entirely blameless and these expenses had been foisted on him by an unreasonable stranger.

"Albany? Doesn't your mother pay that?" his uncle asked in mock bemusement. "And *more* tailor's bills?"

"I don't know how a man in my position can get through the Season without any clothes," John replied with a shrug, taking a sip of his drink.

Grace nodded. "It's not fair to expect him to look like a raga-muffin. Especially not now."

Caroline looked up. "Why? What's happening now?"

Grace smiled. "That is our reason for coming—"

"Your *other* reason for coming," said Peregrine.

"Go on." Caroline was impatient to hear.

"John has an understanding with Lady Maria Grey."

Perhaps to his surprise, Peregrine was pleased with the news. "Lord Templemore's daughter?"

Stephen nodded. It pleased him to score a point. "Her father's dead. The present Earl is her brother."

"She is still Lord Templemore's daughter."

But Peregrine was smiling as he spoke. He found he was almost enthusiastic. "That's very good, John. Well done, and congratulations."

John was rather irritated by his uncle's obvious amazement. "Please don't sound so surprised. Why shouldn't I marry Maria Grey?"

"No reason. No reason. It's a good match. I say again, well done, and I mean it."

Stephen snorted. "It's a good match for her. The Templemores have no money to speak of, and she's marrying the future Earl of Brockenhurst, after all." He could never resist a dig at his brother and sister-in-law's childlessness.

Peregrine looked at him but did not reply. He had never been fond of his brother Stephen, even when they were boys. Perhaps it was his florid, pink-cheeked face. Or the fact that he had cried a great deal as a child and demanded endless attention. There had been a sister after the boys, but Lady Alice was not quite six when she was carried off by whooping cough. As a result, Stephen, who was only two years younger than his brother, had become the baby of the family, a role their mother had very much indulged. John took another sip from his glass.

"What's that you're drinking?" Peregrine stared at his nephew.

"Brandy, sir." John was quite unapologetic.

"Were you cold?"

"Not particularly."

Peregrine laughed. He did not like John much, but he preferred him to his father. At least he had nerve. He looked back at Stephen with ill-concealed distaste. "Why were you here so early?"

"How are you these days?" replied the Reverend from his armchair, ignoring the question. He had one knee crossed over the other and was swinging his right foot. "The damp weather not affecting you?"

His brother shook his head. "It seems warm to me."

"Everything all right at Lower Farm?"

"Checking up on your future concern?" asked Peregrine.

"Not at all," said Stephen. "Is it a crime to be interested?"

"It's nice to see you, my dear," lied Caroline, sitting down near Grace. She found the endless fencing of the siblings tiresome and pointless.

"That's good of you." Grace was a woman whose cup was always half empty. "I was wondering if you have anything you could give me for the church fete. I'm looking for embroidery, handkerchiefs, little cushions, that sort of thing." She drew her fingertips together to make a steeple. "I'm afraid the need is very great." She paused. "We have so many requests for help. The old, the crippled, young widows with children and no one left to earn. It's enough to break your heart."

Caroline nodded. "What about fallen women?"

Grace looked blank. "Fallen women?"

"Mothers who never had a husband."

"Oh, I see." Grace frowned as if Caroline had committed some kind of solecism. "We usually prefer to leave them to the Parish."

"Do they apply to you for help?"

"Sometimes." The subject was making Grace uncomfortable. "But we try to resist sentimentality. How else are other girls to learn, if not from the sad example of the fallen ones?" She returned to safer shores and started to elaborate on her plans for the bazaar.

As the Countess listened to Grace discussing proposals for games and tents and coconut shies, she could not help but think about Sophia Trenchard, pregnant at eighteen. If she had stood, wringing her hands and weeping, in front of that stony-faced committee, would Grace have turned her down, too? Probably. And would she herself have been more merciful, if Sophia had come to the family for help? "I'll find some things that might be useful," she replied eventually.

"Thank you," said Grace. "The committee will be so grateful."

Luncheon was served in the dining room with four footmen and Jenkins in attendance. It was a far cry from the huge shooting and hunting parties of the old days. They had hardly entertained since Edmund's death. But even when there was no one but family present, Peregrine was a stickler for the rules. There were six courses—consommé, pike quenelles, quail, mutton chops with onion custard, a lemon ice, and a currant pudding—which seemed excessive in a way, but Caroline knew that her brother-in-law would only complain if he was given the slightest excuse to do so.

While they drank the consommé, Grace, fortified by the Countess's uncharacteristic willingness to provide her with help for her sale, decided to entertain them with family news. "Emma is to have another child."

"How lovely. I shall write to her." Caroline nodded.

Emma was five years older than her brother, John. She was a pleasant woman, far nicer than the rest of her family, and even Caroline was pleased to hear a good report of her. She had married a local landowner, Sir Hugo Scott, Bart., and they lived the blameless and unimaginative life that was her destiny. Emma's first child, a daughter named Constance, had been born a gratifying nine months after the marriage, and thereafter Emma had produced a baby every year. This new one would make five. So far, she had three healthy daughters but only one son.

"We think it's due in the autumn, although Emma is not quite sure." Grace took a quick sip of consommé. "Hugo is hoping for a boy this time. An heir and a spare, he keeps saying. An heir and a spare." She laughed rather merrily, but as she put her spoon back into the soup she caught the look on Caroline's face and fell silent.

Caroline was not in fact angry. She was bored. She'd lost count of the number of times Grace or Stephen had regaled her with stories of their numerous boisterous grandchildren. She wasn't sure if they meant to be hurtful or if they were just profoundly tactless. Peregrine always thought they were being deliberately unpleasant, but Caroline was more inclined to blame their stupidity. She was convinced Grace was too slow-witted to be that studiedly malevolent.

The footmen cleared the plates in silence. They were used to his lordship not making much of an effort when it came to small talk around the luncheon table, or in fact at any time, and in his brother's company he was always particularly taciturn. Having put considerable energy in his youth into revitalizing the estate, he had lost his taste for it when his son died, and in his later years he was more inclined to spend the time alone in his library.

"So," began Stephen, taking a mouthful of claret, "I was wondering, dear brother, if I might have a little word in private after luncheon."

"A private word?" queried Peregrine, leaning back in his chair. "We all know what that means. You want to talk about money."

"Well." Stephen cleared his throat. His pale, sweating face shone brightly in the sunshine that poured in through the windows. He fingered his bands as if to loosen them. "We don't want to bore the ladies." His voice was faltering. How he hated being in this position. His brother knew exactly what he wanted, what he needed, and to think it was only due to timing, to chance, to bad luck that he was in this spot. How else could anyone describe his being born a mere two years later than the handsome and once popular Peregrine? Why should he be forced into this humiliating situation?

"Well, you don't mind boring me." Peregrine helped himself to some port and sent the decanter on around.

"If we could just—"

"Come on. Out with it."

"What my father is asking for is a loan against my future inheritance," said John, staring at his uncle.

Peregrine snorted. "Your inheritance, or his?"

John clearly did not think his father would outlive his uncle, and nor did anyone else in the room. "Our inheritance," he said smoothly. Peregrine had to admit the young man was well groomed, well dressed, and looked every inch the heir he intended to be. He just didn't like him.

"He wants *another* loan against his inheritance."

"Very well. Another loan." John held his uncle's stare. He was not easy to outface.

Peregrine sipped his port. "I think my little brother has chipped away at his prospects quite substantially already."

Stephen hated being called "little." He was sixty-six years old. He had two living children and soon to be five grandchildren. He was seething. "You will agree that the family's honor demands we keep up appearances. It is our duty to do so."

"I wouldn't agree at all," said Peregrine. "You must live decently, I grant you, as a country vicar should. But more than that, any kind of show in a man of the cloth the public neither expects nor approves of. One has to ask oneself what you are spending the money on."

"On nothing of which you would disapprove." Stephen was skating on thin ice. Peregrine would disapprove very much if he knew what the money was intended for. "You've released funds in the past."

"Many times. Too many." Peregrine shook his head. So this was why his brother had suggested luncheon in the first place, as if he hadn't known it.

Things were getting awkward, and Caroline decided to take control of the situation. "Tell me some more about Maria Grey." She sounded quite surprised in a way. "I thought she'd only just been presented."

Grace helped herself to a mutton chop. "No, no. That was the year before last. She is quite out by now. She's twenty-one."

"Twenty-one." Caroline looked a little wistful. "How time flies by. I'm surprised Lady Templemore has said nothing to me." She and Maria's mother had been friendly acquaintances for years.

"Perhaps she was waiting until things were quite settled." Grace smiled.

"And they are settled now. They have an understanding." Consciously or unconsciously, Lady Brockenhurst's tone told the table she thought the idea of this mismatch an unlikely one.

Grace's smile became more firm as she put down her knife and fork. "There are one or two details to clarify, but after that we'll announce it properly."

Caroline thought of the pretty, intelligent girl she knew and of her pompous, pushy nephew, and then, inevitably, about her own beautiful son lying stone-cold in the ground.

"So you see, we, I mean John, needs funds," said Stephen, glancing appreciatively across at his wife. She had been right to play that card. Surely Peregrine could not really refuse the money. Imagine how badly that might reflect on the family if Peregrine kept his own heir in penury. Particularly as the Countesses were bound to discuss it between themselves almost immediately.

At last, after the currant pudding and the lemon ices had been consumed, the coffee drunk in the drawing room, the gardens toured, Stephen, John, and Grace left. They had secured enough cash to pay their tailors, as well as the other debts that Stephen had failed to mention. Peregrine retired to his library.

It was with a heavy heart that he sat down next to the fire in his large leather armchair, attempting to read some Pliny. He preferred the Elder to the Younger, as he liked dealing in the facts of history and science; but this afternoon the words didn't dance off the page but rather half swam before his eyes. He'd read the same paragraph three times when Caroline walked through the door.

"You were quiet at luncheon. What's the matter?" she said.

Peregrine closed the volume and sat in silence for a moment. He stared around the room at the line of portraits above the mahogany bookcases, stern-looking men in periwigs, women laced into their satin dresses, his forebears, his family, who had lent their blood to him, the last of his immediate line. Then he looked back at his wife. "Why does my brother, a man who never said or did anything of the slightest value, live to see his children married and his grandchildren gathered round his chair?"

"Oh, my dear." Caroline sat down next to him and put her hand on his thin knee.

"I'm sorry," said Peregrine, shaking his head as his face flushed. "I'm being a silly old man. But sometimes I can't help railing at the injustice of it all."

"And you think I don't?"

He sighed. "Do you ever wonder what he would be like now? Married, of course, and rather fatter than when we knew him. With clever sons and pretty daughters."

"Perhaps he'd have had clever daughters and pretty sons."

"The point is, he's not here. Our son, Edmund, is gone, and God knows I don't understand why it had to happen to us." Peregrine Brockenhurst suffered from the Englishman's lack of ease when it came to discussing his emotions, that could at times be more poignant than fluency. He took hold of his wife's hand and squeezed it. His pale blue eyes were watering. "I am sorry, my dear, I'm being very foolish." He looked at his wife with something like tenderness. "I suppose I can't help wondering what is the point of it all." But then he laughed drily, pulling himself together. "Don't listen to me," he said. "I must stop drinking port. Port always makes me miserable."

Caroline stroked the back of his hand. It would have been so easy to tell him the truth, tell him that he had a grandson, an heir to his blood if not to his position. But she did not know all the facts. Had Anne Trenchard been speaking the truth? She needed to investigate. And she had promised that woman to stay silent. In her defense, Caroline was a person who usually kept her promises.

No amount of valerian seemed to help Anne's terrible headache. She felt as if her skull were being cut in two with a steel knife. She knew the cause and, while she was not prone to histrionics, she recognized that her lonely walk home to Eaton Square after her interview with Lady Brockenhurst was one of the most difficult of her life.

She had been shaking so much when she arrived back at number 110 that when she knocked on her own front door she failed to offer any form of explanation for the state she was in. Billy had been terribly puzzled when he answered. What was his mistress doing out on her own, shivering like a jelly? Where was Quirk, the coachman? It was all very confusing and provided them with plenty to discuss down in the servants' hall as they waited to be fed later that night. But no one was more confused than Anne as she wandered slowly upstairs to her rooms.

"It was like she was in a daze," said her maid, Ellis, as she sat down at the table that evening. "Just hugging that dog and rocking in her chair."

The years had not been overly kind to Ellis. After the heady days of Waterloo, when the streets of Brussels teemed with handsome soldiers who liked nothing more than a bit of chat with a pretty lady's maid, she'd found the move to London a little too sedate for her liking. She would talk about her friend Jane Croft, Miss Sophia's maid in the old days, who was doing well for herself as a housekeeper in the country now, and Ellis was always threatening to go off and try something similar. But, truth be told, she knew she'd be a fool to leave. She hankered after employment in a more illustrious household, and it bothered her that she did not work for a family with a title, but the Trenchards paid their servants more than most of the aristocrats she'd ever heard of, and the food they served below stairs was significantly better than anywhere else she'd come across. Mrs. Babbage had a proper budget and she served meat at nearly every meal.

"She's not wrong," agreed Billy, rubbing his hands together as he inhaled the smell of stewed beef and potatoes from the large copper pot in the middle of the table. "I mean, who's ever heard of a mistress walking about the streets alone like that? She was off doing something she didn't want the master finding out about, that's for sure."

"Do you think she's got a fancy man?" giggled one of the housemaids.

"Mercy, go to your room!"

Mrs. Frant stood in the doorway, hands on hips, dressed in a black high-necked shirt and black skirt, a pale green cameo pinned at her throat. She had only been working for the Trenchards for three years, but she had been in service long enough to know it was a job worth keeping, and so she suffered no nonsense below stairs.

"I'm sorry, Mrs. Frant. I was only—"

"You were only going upstairs with no dinner, and if I hear one more word you'll be out without a reference tomorrow."

The girl sniffed but did not attempt any further defense. As she scuttled away, Mrs. Frant took her place.

"Now, we will converse in a genteel fashion, but we will not make our employers the subject of our conversation."

"All the same, Mrs. Frant"—Ellis was anxious to show that she did not consider herself under the housekeeper's command—"it is quite unlike the mistress to have such a head it needs valerian. I've not seen her so unwell since she and Miss Sophia went to visit that ailing cousin of hers in Derbyshire." The two women exchanged a rather piercing look.

In lieu of any explanation, all James Trenchard could do was speculate as to why his wife had taken to her bed and why she had asked for her supper to be sent up on a tray. He assumed it had something to do with Charles Pope and his refusal to allow Anne to share the young man's existence with Lady Brockenhurst, and while he had not changed his mind on this, still he was anxious to get back on good terms with his wife as soon as he could decently manage it. So when he came across the card among the letters delivered in the last post inviting her to a reception at Kew Gardens, he decided he would take it up there and then, in the hope that it might lift her spirits. She was very fond of gardening and an enthusiastic supporter of Kew, as he knew well.

"I could come, too," he suggested merrily as he watched her turn the card over in her hands. She was propped up against her pillows and looking generally wan, but she was interested. He could tell.

"All the way out to Kew?" replied Anne. "You barely walk the length of the gardens at Glanville if you can avoid it." But she was smiling.

"Susan might like to go."

"Susan dislikes flowers and can't see beauty in anything that doesn't glitter in Mr. Asprey's window. She made me take her to see the new shop last week. I could hardly drag her back into the carriage."

"I can imagine," nodded James, smiling. "That reminds me. After our dinner conversation the other night, I've been wondering if I might try to get Oliver a little more advanced in the business. He's pootling around on the edge of it at the moment, and maybe he needs some direction. I have a meeting with William Cubitt tomorrow about the Isle of Dogs project, and if Oliver does want to be involved, as he implied, I thought I could try to sell the idea."

"But do you think he really meant it?" said Anne. "It doesn't sound like Oliver's sort of thing at all."

"Perhaps he should be a little less choosy about what interests him." James didn't mean to snap, but the disdain with which Oliver treated the idea of trade and hard work annoyed him.

"Well, I suppose it can't hurt," said Anne. "You might as well ask."

It was not quite the reaction that James had hoped for. It would be quite an imposition to ask William Cubitt to give his son a larger stake in the business, a business in which Oliver had so far shown little aptitude or interest. For all their lucrative partnership, it was a bold move.

Anne could see his concern and she felt the same, but somehow she could not summon up much fight. She had always prided herself on her ability to judge a situation; she could read people well and kept her cards close to her chest. She wasn't one of these foolish women who become indiscreet after one glass of Champagne. So what had she been thinking when she told the truth to Lady Brockenhurst? Had she been intimidated by the Countess? Or had she simply been carrying the burden on her own for too long? The fact remained, she'd told a secret of unimaginable magnitude, a secret that could cause them unlimited damage, to a total stranger, a woman she knew little or nothing about, and in doing so she had given Lady Brockenhurst the ammunition to bring down Anne's entire family. The question was, would she use it? She rang for Ellis to take Agnes for her evening walk.

The following day James disappeared early. He would normally look in on his wife before he left, but she had slept so badly she'd taken a draught in the middle of the night and would probably not rise until noon. Even so, he was not overly concerned. Whatever it was, she'd get over it. He was far more worried about seeing William Cubitt. He had to get to his office and finish his morning's business; their meeting was at twelve.

Cubitt had chosen the Athenaeum for their encounter, and James was determined to arrive early so he might have a look around. He'd heard that the club had relaxed their membership rules a little of late—they were in need of funds—and he had applied to join. James wasn't a member of any gentlemen's club, and it galled him.

Arriving at 107 Pall Mall, he admired the impressive columns outside the front of the building, he even crossed the road in order to see the homage to the Parthenon frieze at the top of the façade. It was hard to believe that Decimus Burton was only twenty-four years old when he designed the place.

When James walked inside and handed over his gloves and cane to the waiting steward, he was anxiously wondering whom he might ask about his application. It had been a while now, and he'd heard nothing. Perhaps he'd been turned down? But wouldn't they have told him? It really was so tiresome. He looked around enviously at the vast hall with its magnificent imperial staircase, dividing at the first landing to sweep on upward on either side of that great space.

"James!" said William, leaping out of a chair to greet his friend. "Good to see you." Slim, with a full head of gray hair, William Cubitt had a kind and clever face, with large intelligent eyes that he half closed when he was listening intently. "Did you see the new Reform Club on your way here? Isn't it beautiful? Clever chap, that Charles Barry. I am not sure about the politics of the place," he added, raising an eyebrow. "Full of liberals, and all of them bent on making trouble, but it's a fine achievement nevertheless." Having built Covent Garden, Fishmongers' Hall, the portico for Euston Station. and much else besides, Cubitt invariably remarked on details that few people noticed. "Did you take in the nine-bay treatment of the front? Very bold," he enthused. "And the scale of it. It puts the poor little Travellers Club into the shade. Now, would you like anything to drink? Shall we go up to the library?"

The library of the club, a huge chamber occupying most of the first floor, lined in bookcases housing the club's splendid collection, only made James fidget in his anxiety to be part of this place. By what right did they keep him out? It was with the greatest difficulty that he forced himself to concentrate on what was being said, but at last he calmed down, and, over a glass of Madeira, he and Cubitt caught up on the plans, the ideas, and the changes William had in mind for "Cubitt Town." "I'll change the name," he said, sitting back in his seat. "But that's what it's called at the moment."

"So the plan is to expand the docks, create local businesses, and build houses for those working there nearby?"

"Exactly. There's pottery, brick production, cement. All dirty stuff, but it has to be made, and I want to be the person to make it," Cubitt remarked. "But we want houses for the bookmakers and clerks, too, and hopefully we can persuade some of the management to make their homes there, if we can create sufficiently salubrious areas. In short, we want to reinvent the place entirely and rebuild it as a whole community."

"There's a lot of work to be done," said James.

"There certainly is. We'll have to drain the land first, of course, but we know well enough how to do that after building Belgravia, and I have high hopes that it will make us proud in the end."

"Do you think there might be an opening for Oliver? It's just the sort of thing he'd love to be part of." James struggled for a casual tone.

"Oliver?"

"My son." James could feel his voice falter.

"Oh, that Oliver." For a moment, the atmosphere was rather flat. "It may be that he is taking time to settle into the business, but I have never thought he was very interested in architecture," said William. "Or building, come to that. I am not saying I object to his working for us, you understand, only that the demands of an enormous project like this might be rather more than he would be willing to undertake."

"No, he's keen to be involved," insisted James, trying to quell his embarrassment and thinking of Anne's comments all the while. "He's tremendously interested. But sometimes he's not good at . . . expressing himself."

"I see." William Cubitt could not be said to look convinced.

James had known William and his elder brother, Thomas, for almost twenty years, and in that time they had become close; not just as business partners but as friends. The trio had made a lot of money together and they all had reason to rejoice, but this was the first time James had asked either of the brothers for anything resembling a favor, and he was not enjoying it. He rubbed his right temple. Actually, that was not quite right. The first favor had been to get them to take on Oliver at all. Obviously, the young man had made no very favorable impression and here James was, pushing his luck.

William half-closed his eyes. To be honest, he was a little taken aback; he had not been expecting this request. He'd known Oliver since he was not much more than a boy, and in all his time working in the company the man had never asked him a single question about the development of Bloomsbury or Belgravia, or any of his previous contracts. He had done his work in the offices. Sort of. But seemingly without enthusiasm or even interest. That said, William was fond of James Trenchard. The man was clever, tenacious, hardworking, and completely reliable. He could be pompous at times, and his relentless social ambitions made him a little ridiculous, but then everyone had their weaknesses.

"Very well. I shall look for a way to involve him," said Cubitt. "I think it is important for families to work together. My brother and I have done so for years, so why shouldn't you and your son? We'll take him out of the office and put him on-site. We're always in need of good managers. Tell him to come and see me on Monday, and we'll get him started on the Isle of Dogs project. You have my word on it."

He extended his hand and James took it with a smile. But he felt less confident about the outcome than he might have wished.

Once recovered, it would have taken nothing short of typhus to stop Anne from attending the gathering at Kew. The gardens had been thrown open to the public only the year before, in 1840, largely due to the enthusiasm of the Duke of Devonshire who, as President of the Royal Horticultural Society, was at the very heart of the project. He was supported in this by the interest in gardening throughout the land. It seemed gardening was the perfect fashion for every class of Englishman in the 1840s. Anne Trenchard had been a major contributor to the funds, which no doubt accounted for her inclusion on their list. Despite her worries over Lady Brockenhurst and her usual social reticence when she was operating under orders from James, this was one occasion Anne was genuinely excited about.

Gardening wasn't so much a hobby for Anne; it was her passion, her obsession. She'd started taking an interest in all things horticultural just after Sophia's death, and she had found it therapeutic as she tended and studied the flowers that seemed to grant her a measure of peace. James had unwittingly encouraged her when he stumbled upon an extremely rare and expensive book one afternoon in Bloomsbury, Thomas Fairchild's *The City Gardener*, published in 1722, and he'd continued to add to her gardening library ever since.

But it was the purchase of Glanville back in 1825 that had really fanned her enthusiasm. There was something about this dilapidated Elizabethan manor house that she simply adored, and she was never happier than when she was in deep discussion with Hooper, her head gardener. Together they replanted the orchards, organized a fine kitchen garden that now provided food for the house and the entire estate, and essentially re-created the overgrown terraces, taking both from the open fashions of the previous century and also reviving the original shapes and knot gardens of the house's own period. She'd even had a greenhouse built, in which she managed to grow quince and peaches. The latter were few but fragrant and perfectly formed, and she'd had Hooper enter them into the Royal Horticultural Society Show in Chiswick the previous year.

She'd naturally made many acquaintances among the gardening fraternity over the years, and among them was Joseph Paxton, a talented beginner when she first met him, with extraordinary and almost revolutionary ideas. She had been very excited when he told her he'd been asked to work in the Duke of Devonshire's gardens at his villa on the edge of London, Chiswick House. She was subsequently even more pleased when Paxton had moved on to Chatsworth, the Duke's great palace in Derbyshire, where he'd been responsible for overseeing the construction of a three-hundred-foot conservatory. Of course, Anne did not know the Duke personally, but as President of the Royal Horticultural Society, he was clearly as passionate about gardens as Anne herself.

It was Paxton she hoped to meet that day at Kew. She'd come armed with questions about her quince trees, as he knew everything there was to know about growing under glass. The gardens were busy when she arrived. Hundreds of ladies in pretty pastel shades wearing bonnets and carrying parasols were strolling around the lawns, admiring the new beds and pathways, designed to cope with the ever-increasing enthusiasm of the crowds who would pour out of London whenever the sun shone. Anne was on her way to the Orangery when she found the man she was looking for. "Mr. Paxton. I was rather hoping I might see you here." She put out her hand to take his.

"Mrs. Trenchard." He nodded, grinning broadly. "How are you? And how are your prizewinning peaches?"

"What a memory," said Anne, and soon they were discussing the intricacies of quinces and how hard it was to get them to fruit in such an unkind climate, and quite what the judges would be expecting to find if she were to enter them into the RHS show. In fact, they were so engaged that neither of them saw the two distinguished-looking figures approach.

"There you are, Paxton," declared the Duke of Devonshire. "I've been looking everywhere for you." A tall, elegant man with dark hair, a long nose, and large almond eyes, he radiated good humor. "Have you heard the news?"

"What news is that, Your Grace?" replied Paxton.

"They've taken all the citrus out of the Orangery." Clearly this was amazing news. "Can you believe it? Too dark in there, apparently. Built at the wrong angle. They didn't have the advantage of your planning." He smiled as he turned pleasantly to Anne, clearly waiting for an introduction. It was at this moment that Anne noticed the Duke's companion, who was staring at her from beneath her bonnet.

"Your Grace, Your Ladyship," said Paxton, taking a step back. "May I present a very keen gardener and well-known member of the Society, Mrs. Trenchard."

"A pleasure, Mrs. Trenchard," replied the Duke with a courteous nod. "I have heard your name before now. Not least from Paxton here." He looked back at the woman by his side. "May I—"

"Mrs. Trenchard and I have met before," said Lady Brockenhurst, her eyes expressionless.

"Excellent!" declared the Duke, frowning slightly as he looked from one to the other. He did not quite understand how his friend Lady Brockenhurst could know this woman, but he was happy that she did. "Shall we go and see what they have done with the conservatory?" Leading the way, he set off at a brisk pace, Paxton and the two women following in his wake. The Duke could not know it, but his proud companion was in the grip of an excitement that had closed its fist around her heart. This was her chance.

"Mrs. Trenchard," she said. "That man we were talking about the other day—"

Anne's heart was in her mouth. What should she say for the best? Then again, the secret was out. Why pretend otherwise? "Charles Pope?" She spoke a little hoarsely, and no wonder.

"The very one. Charles Pope." Lady Brockenhurst nodded.

"What about him?" Anne looked about at the family groups, at men writing notes on pocket pads, women attempting to control their children, and, not for the first time in such a case, she wondered how they could all be living their lives as if nothing extraordinary were happening within a few feet of them.

"I have forgotten where he lives, this Mr. Pope." Paxton was watching them by now. Something in the tone of their voices transmitted to him that he was witnessing a kind of revelation, that secrets were being asked and told. Anne saw his curiosity and longed to quench it. "I am not sure of the address."

"What about his parents?"

For a moment Anne thought she might just walk away, excuse herself to the others, plead a headache, even faint. But Lady Brockenhurst was not having any of that. "I remember the father was a clergyman."

"The Reverend Benjamin Pope."

"There we are. That didn't hurt too much, did it?" Lady Brockenhurst's cold smile could have frozen snow. "And the county?"

"Surrey. But that's really all I can tell you." Anne was desperate to get away from this woman who held their fate in the palm of her hand. "Charles Pope is the son of the Reverend Benjamin Pope who lives in Surrey. It is enough."

And so it proved.

It did not take long for Caroline Brockenhurst to track down her grandson. Like all her kind, she had many friends and relations among the clergy, and there were plenty who were willing to help her find this young man who, she soon learned, was apparently making something of a name for himself in the City. She discovered that he was ambitious; that he had plans. He had bought a mill in Manchester, and he was looking for a regular supply of raw cotton to expand his production, perhaps in the Indian subcontinent or elsewhere. Either way, he was a dynamic fellow, full of ideas and enterprise. All he needed was a little more investment. That, at any rate, is what her inquiries had yielded.

When Lady Brockenhurst knocked on the door of Charles Pope's office she felt surprisingly calm. She had been quite matter-of-fact when she'd spoken to her coachman, Hutchinson, instructing him to drive to the address on Bishopsgate. She'd told him to wait and that half an hour should be sufficient. In her mind, it was to be a brief meeting. She had not thought through the details or rehearsed what she would say. It was almost as if she did not dare to believe that the Trenchard woman's story was actually true. After all, why should it be?

"The *Countess of Brockenhurst*? She's here already?" The young man leaped out of his chair as the clerk opened the door and announced the name. She was there, standing in the doorway, facing him.

For a moment, Caroline could not move. She stood staring at his face: his dark curls, his blue eyes, his fine nose, his chiseled mouth. It was the face of her son, Edmund reborn, more humorous perhaps, heartier certainly, but her own darling Edmund.

"I am looking for a Mr. Charles Pope," she said, knowing full well she was staring him in the face.

"I am Charles Pope,' he said, and smiled, walking toward her. "Do please come in." He paused and frowned. "Are you all right, Lady Brockenhurst? You look as if you've seen a ghost."

It was her own fault, really, she thought, as he helped her to a seat opposite his desk. She should have considered the matter properly instead of making an appointment on the spur of the moment, on the pretext of investing in his venture. It would have been easier if Peregrine had been here. Then again, she might have wept, and she had done enough of that to last her a lifetime. She had also needed to be sure. He offered her a glass of water and she took it. She had not fainted exactly, but her legs had certainly buckled with the shock. Of course Edmund's son might very easily resemble Edmund. Why hadn't she thought of that, and prepared for it?

"So," she said eventually, "tell me a little bit about where you are from."

"Where I'm from?" The young man looked bewildered. He'd presumed he was going to talk to the Countess about his business venture. How she'd heard about him and his cotton mill he was not entirely sure. It seemed odd for a great lady to take an interest in such things, but he knew she was well connected and was certainly rich enough to be able to invest in his mill. "It is not a very interesting story," he continued. "I am from Surrey, the son of a vicar."

"I see." She was placing herself in an awkward position. What comment could she possibly make? How would she explain any prior knowledge of his circumstance? But he took her question at face value, without wondering as to her motives.

"Well, actually, my real father was dead before my birth. So his cousin, the Reverend Benjamin Pope, brought me up. I think of him as my father, but sadly he is also gone now."

"I'm sorry." Caroline almost winced with the pain his words brought her. She sat opposite her grandson and listened intently. It seemed so strange he should think of an obscure country vicar as his father. If he only knew who his real father had been! She longed to ask him question after question, mainly to hear more of the sound of his voice, but what was there to say? It was as if she were frightened that if she brought this meeting to an end, she might wake up tomorrow to find that he, Charles Pope, no longer existed, had never existed, and it had all been a dream. Because this young man was everything she could ever have hoped for in a grandson.

Eventually, after she'd promised to invest a significant amount of money in his plan, it was time for her to leave. She walked to the door and then she halted. "Mr. Pope," she said. "I am giving an At Home on Thursday. I generally receive on the second Thursday of every month during the Season, and I wondered if you might like to come."

"Me?" If he had been bewildered earlier, he was astonished now.

"It starts at ten. We will have dined, but there will be some supper at midnight, so there's no need to eat beforehand, if you don't want to."

Charles was not in any real sense a member of Society, but he knew enough about it to realize that this was a very great compliment indeed. Why on earth should he be the recipient of such an honor?

"I don't fully understand—"

"Mr. Pope, I am asking you to a party on Thursday. Is it so very puzzling?"

He was not devoid of a sense of adventure. No doubt everything would be explained eventually. "I should be delighted, m'lady," he said.

When the liveried footman arrived at Eaton Square with the card inviting Mr. and Mrs. Trenchard to a soirée given by the Countess of Brockenhurst, it did not remain a secret for long. Anne had hoped to wait until James came home to discuss it with him. She had no desire whatsoever to go to that woman's house. And why indeed had they been asked? Lady Brockenhurst had made her feelings perfectly clear at Kew Gardens. The Countess was haughty, unpleasant, and Anne wanted to have nothing more to do with her. Still, it would be a difficult invitation for James to refuse. The Brockenhursts were just the sort of people her husband wanted so passionately to spend his time with. Before she could consider the matter further, there was a knock on her door.

"Mother?" Susan walked in, a pretty smile on her pretty face, her intentions as transparent as glass. She bent to stroke the little dog, which was always a giveaway. "Am I to understand that you've been invited to dinner by the Countess of Brockenhurst?" she asked with a shake of her curls. Presumably this last was to give a sense of girlishness, to which her mother-in-law was impervious.

"Not to dinner. To a reception after dinner, although I daresay there will be something to eat later on," replied Anne. "But I'm not sure we'll go." She smiled and waited for Susan to act. The poor girl was so entirely predictable.

"Not go?"

"We hardly know her. And it's difficult to get up much enthusiasm for something that begins so late in the evening."

Susan's face twisted in a kind of small agony. "But surely..."

"What is it you're trying to ask, my dear?"

"I just thought that we might be...included in the invitation."

"But you're not."

"Please don't make me beg. After all, Oliver and I are living in the same house as you. Shouldn't we be part of the Society you keep? Would it be so terribly difficult to ask?"

"You mean you're determined we should go."

"Father thinks you should." Susan had recovered herself. This was a good argument. James would not allow her to refuse, and Anne knew she'd never hear the end of it if she did not ask for Oliver and his wife to accompany them. It was simply not worth the atmosphere in the house.

So that evening Anne sat down at her *secrétaire,* picked up her pen, and wrote a reply to Lady Brockenhurst requesting in the politest of terms that their son and his wife, Susan, might be allowed to attend the evening with them. As she picked up the wax to seal the envelope she knew that her request would be thought of as forward, and possibly vulgar, but also that Lady Brockenhurst would not refuse.

However, what Anne did not expect was the message that came with the reply. When she received it, she dropped the letter. Her heart was beating so fast she could barely breathe. She had to read it again. There, along with another At Home card in the name of Mr. and Mrs. Oliver Trenchard, was a note, which simply stated:

"I have also invited Mr. Charles Pope to join us."

·4·

At Home in Belgrave Square

It was almost ten o'clock. Anne Trenchard's hands were trembling and her stomach was knotted with excitement. She stared at herself in the glass, silently willing Ellis to hurry up and put the finishing touches to her hair. She was wearing a tiara and she could feel some of the pins pricking her scalp. She would have a headache before the evening was over. That much she knew.

She glanced across at the gilt clock on her chimneypiece. Two rather sulky-looking cherubs held up the face between them. Belgrave Square was less than five minutes away by carriage. It would be impolite to arrive much before half past, but she wasn't sure she could wait that long.

It was rare for Anne to feel any kind of enthusiasm when it came to social engagements. But then again, it was rarer still to meet one's own grandson for the first time in twenty-five years.

Could Lady Brockenhurst's letter be true? Anne couldn't quite bring herself to believe it. What would he look like, she wondered, adjusting her diamond *collier de chien*. He used to have pale blue eyes, just like Sophia's, but then all babies are born with blue eyes so perhaps they'd changed. She remembered his scent, warm and sweet with milk, his sturdy little legs and dimpled knees and the strong grip of his tiny hand. She also remembered all the emotions she had gone through: the anger and the terrible, painful sadness when he had been taken from her. How one small, helpless human being could provoke such feelings was beyond understanding. She lifted Agnes from her attendant position at her mistress's feet. There was something comforting in her unqualified love, or was it just a need to be fed that kept her faithful? Guilty at doubting her, Anne kissed the dog's nose.

"Are you ready?" asked James, poking his balding head around the door. "Susan and Oliver are in the hall."

"We don't want to be the first there." But Anne smiled at her husband's ebullience; there was nothing he enjoyed more than a grand evening out, and few came more grand than an At Home at Brockenhurst House.

"We won't be. There'll have been a crowd for dinner." Which was true enough. They were in the second tier of *invités*. She knew James would have sold his soul to be on the list of the dining guests, but he was too excited to let that spoil things now. It was odd the way he appeared, in his eagerness to be received in Brockenhurst House, to have forgotten the very real connection between the families. Apparently they were to conduct themselves as if there were no link, there was no child. Of course he was in for an awakening if Charles Pope were present, but there was no point in disturbing him now. She stood. "Very well. Ellis, could you fetch my fan, please? The Duvelleroy."

Despite James's generous allowance, Anne had little interest in fashion, but fans were one of her few extravagances. Indeed, she had quite a collection. The Duvelleroy was one of the best. Hand-painted and exquisitely made, she kept it for special occasions. Ellis slipped it into her hand. It featured a painted image of the new French royal family, brought to the throne by a revolution a decade before. She stared at the plump, elderly King. How long would he hold on to that troubled, slippery crown, she wondered? But then, how long would she be able to keep her own secret? How long would they continue to enjoy fortune's favor before it all came crashing down around their ears?

James's impatience broke into her musings. "We mustn't let the horses catch a chill." She nodded, and clutching the fan to her bosom, she tried to control her nerves as she followed her husband's jaunty gait toward the staircase. How she hoped, she prayed, he might understand what she had done in breaking her silence. There had been no other choice, she told herself. Maybe, in time, he would forgive her. She had been wrong to think he had put Sophia and Bellasis out of his mind, which she realized as they reached the foot of the stair. "Don't forget." He laid his hand lightly on her sleeve. "You are not to mention anything about the other business. I absolutely forbid it." She nodded but her heart sank. Surely at the first moment of being introduced to Mr. Pope he would know that the cat was out of the bag. For the hundredth time she was torn between anger and a tingle of anticipation.

Anne noticed she wasn't the only one who was excited. Susan was considerably more animated than usual. Her auburn hair was swept up, and she wore a becoming pearl *parure* of necklace, bracelet, and earrings. More to the point, her habitually sour mouth bore a smile. At last she had succeeded in storming the citadel, and she was clearly going to make the most of it. She'd spent three days with her dressmaker putting the finishing touches to her costume. It might have been a little too *jeune fille* for a young matron, but she did look pretty. Anne had to admit it.

"How lovely your hair looks," she said pleasantly. She was determined to get the evening off on the right foot, but she had chosen badly. Susan was wearing diamond stars in her hair, and they did look nice, but her face clouded. "I have no tiara," she said. "Or I would have worn it."

"We must remedy that," said James with a laugh. "Now, all aboard." And he led the way out onto the pavement, where the carriage waited by the curb. Anne chose to ignore her daughter-in-law's remark. There really was nothing more tiresome than Susan's constant scrutiny. How much money had Anne spent at the milliner? How many sapphires were in that brooch? It was one of the things that Anne found most difficult about sharing a house with her son and his increasingly acquisitive wife.

In the end it only took a few minutes, after they'd mounted and descended from the carriage, for the two pairs of Trenchards to arrive at Brockenhurst House on the corner of Belgrave Square. A footman opened the door, directing them past the gilded sofas in the hall, across the black and white marble floor to the magnificent green malachite staircase lined with more motionless footmen. As they climbed up toward the drawing room, they could already hear the animated conversation of the other guests.

"I wonder how many they had to dine before us?" Susan whispered to her husband as she gathered up her skirts.

"It certainly sounds like a houseful."

Anne needn't have worried they would be too early. The drawing room was already crowded when they walked through the double doors. Among the haze of pale silks and the noisy rustle of taffeta, Anne could make out a few familiar figures, but the majority were unknown to her. As they waited for the butler to announce them, she scanned the room again, peering through groups and couples deep in conversation, in the hope of seeing his face. But which face? She smiled to herself as she realized she was sure she would know him when she had nothing to go on. She was convinced that there would be some telltale detail—the shape of his chin, those fine, long brows of Sophia's—that would help her recognize her own, even across a crowded room.

"How good of you to come," said the Countess, approaching from beside a large fragrant vase of pale pink lilies.

"Lady Brockenhurst."

Anne knew her reply had sounded a little startled. She'd been so intent on the arrival of Charles Pope, she was unable to think about anything else. Lady Brockenhurst caught the anxious look in her guest's eyes as they darted around the room, this woman who had kept their grandson's existence a secret for so long. Now it was her turn to be in the dark. It took all of Caroline's willpower not to appear triumphant.

"What beautiful flowers." Anne attempted to recover herself. What she really wanted to do was take this difficult woman by the arm and fire questions at her. Is he really coming? What is he like? How on earth did you find him? Instead she added, "And what a heavenly scent."

"They came up from Lymington this morning." Lady Brockenhurst was also happy to play her part. "I don't believe I've met your husband."

"Lady Brockenhurst," said Anne, stepping to one side, "may I present Mr. Trenchard."

He was not what the Countess had expected. He was worse.

Not that she had ever considered what he might look like. She knew he was in trade, so she had not hoped for much, but he was smaller than she'd thought, and certainly rounder. Over the years, she had heard much from her sister about Sophia's beauty, so she could only suppose the girl had inherited her qualities from her mother's side.

"Lady Brockenhurst, it is very gracious of you to invite us to your charming home." James made a sort of half bow, as ungainly as it was inappropriate.

Anne's smile stiffened. Her husband simply could not help himself. There was something about his genuflecting, his obsequiousness, that still, even after so many years, telegraphed to anyone present that he, and therefore she, did not belong in the drawing rooms of Belgravia.

"Not at all," replied Lady Brockenhurst. "I doubt the house holds any surprises for you, Mr. Trenchard. Since you built it."

James laughed a little too enthusiastically. "May I present my son, Mr. Oliver Trenchard, and his wife."

Susan pushed forward and bowed her head. "Countess," she said, making Anne wince at the vulgarity. "What a beautiful drawing room."

Lady Brockenhurst nodded back. "Mrs. Trenchard," she said carefully, not letting either approval or disapproval color her tone. The girl was rather pretty; her pale blue dress and matching ribbons contrasted cleverly with her thick auburn hair. But it was the husband who piqued her interest. So this was Sophia's younger brother: too young to have attended the Duchess of Richmond's ball, but certainly old enough to have known her son.

"Tell me, Mr. Trenchard," she said. "Do you share the same interests as your father?"

"Oliver works for me," interrupted James, before catching the look on his daughter-in-law's face. "Or should I say *with* me," he corrected. "We've begun on a new project, developing the Isle of Dogs."

Lady Brockenhurst looked blank. "The Isle of Dogs?"

"In east London."

"East London?" The Countess looked increasingly puzzled. It was as if they were discussing some recently discovered civilization on the other side of Zanzibar. James did not notice.

"We're creating a new embankment, with business properties and workers' cottages and even houses for management, and so on. And we're expanding the docks. The ships have run out of room." Anne tried to catch his eye; could he please stop talking business? But still he continued. "They need new places to load and unload, with all the trade coming in from around the world. The farther the Empire expands, the more—"

"I see." Lady Brockenhurst smiled tightly. "How exciting you make it sound. But will you excuse me?" And on the pretext of another introduction, Lady Brockenhurst drifted away, leaving Anne, James, Oliver, and Susan standing at the entrance to the room, ignored by the rest of the company. Alone.

"What sort of person has all their fires lit in high summer?" mumbled Susan, flapping her fan. "It's stifling in here. Oliver, let's move through."

James made as if to leave with his son and daughter-in-law, but Anne touched his arm, indicating he should remain. He looked at her quizzically. "I'd rather stay here," she said. "To watch the arrivals. There may be someone we know who can lend us face." She glanced toward the door. Just as she spoke, an exquisite girl with fair ringlets and the palest skin arrived, escorted by her equally attractive mother.

"The Countess of Templemore," announced the butler. "And Lady Maria Grey."

Lady Templemore was dressed in a blue watered silk frock with a lace collar, her wide skirts draped over a horsehair crinoline. But it was the daughter who caught the attention of the room. Her pale cream dress draped beautifully across shoulders that were as smooth and as faultless as one of Lord Elgin's marbles. Her blonde hair was parted down the middle, piled high at the back, and set off with two large "spaniel curls" that framed her pretty, heart-shaped face to perfection. Anne watched the pair as they made their way through the guests toward the smaller drawing room beyond.

"Mr. Trenchard?" James turned abruptly to find a puffed-up looking character squeezed into a frock coat standing in front of him. The newcomer had a large, shiny face, a lengthy gray mustache, and a long nose that was crisscrossed with broken veins like the twigs on a tree. Here was a man clearly fond of late nights and plenty of port wine. "I am Stephen Bellasis."

"Sir."

"The Reverend Mr. Bellasis is the brother of our host," said Anne firmly. There was not much she didn't know about the Brockenhurst family.

Grace stood stiffly behind her husband. Her pale brown eyes appeared a little distant as she stared blankly across the company. Her mouth was set straight and her maroon silk dress had clearly seen better days.

"Mrs. Bellasis." James nodded. "May I present my wife, Mrs. Trenchard." Anne nodded politely. Grace glanced over, taking in Anne and her gown. She managed a small smile that didn't quite reach her eyes.

"I gather you're Cubitt's man," said Bellasis, standing with one foot in front of the other. "Responsible for turning the streets of London into a white colonnade overnight."

"It has taken a little longer than that." James was used to this criticism. He'd had it hurled at him many times before in the drawing rooms of London and had lost count of how often he'd had to chortle through the charge of smothering the capital in "wedding cakes." "What we do seems to be popular, Reverend."

"Riot is popular, sir. Revolution is popular. What sort of a test is that?"

"Are you not an admirer of Brockenhurst House?"

"The size of the rooms and their height are well enough. But I can't say I prefer it to my parents' London house."

"And where was that?"

"Hertford Street, in Mayfair."

James nodded. "I suppose the new houses are more suited to entertaining."

"So that's how you've made your fortune? Out of people's desire to show off?" Grace knew that Stephen was simply angry that this odd little man should have so much more money than they did, but he would never be honest enough as to say it, even to himself.

James was silenced by this, but Anne took charge. "Heavens, the rooms are filling up."

For once, Grace was prepared to help. "We understand from Lady Brockenhurst that you knew our nephew, Lord Bellasis."

"We did," confirmed James, grateful for the rescue. "We knew him well. But I'm afraid it is a long time ago now."

"And you were at the famous ball?"

"If you mean the Duchess of Richmond's ball, then yes, we were."

"How very interesting. It seems the stuff of legend these days, doesn't it?" Grace smiled. She had done enough to repair the damage done by her husband's rudeness.

Anne nodded. "Legend and tragedy. It is so terrible to think of poor Lord Bellasis, indeed to think of all those gallant young men who left the ballroom to die."

Stephen had begun to repent his impertinence. Why had he crossed the room to insult this man when he might be useful? "You're quite right, of course. The loss of Edmund was a terrible business for this family. Now there's only my son, John, between us and extinction, in the male line at least. That's him over there, talking to the pretty girl in blue."

James glanced across the room to see the man engaged in an animated conversation with Susan. She was touching the rim of a champagne glass with her index finger and laughing as she looked up at him through her lashes.

"And that pretty girl in blue is my daughter-in-law," added James, watching as John leaned over and briefly touched Susan's hand. "He seems to be keeping her entertained."

"John is about to announce his engagement." Presumably

Grace said this to calm any suggestions of impropriety, but naturally it had the opposite effect.

Anne could not help smiling. She only hoped that the poor girl, whoever she might be, had an inkling that she was taking on a ladies' man. "How exciting for you," she said.

"May we know the name of his intended?" asked James, eager to demonstrate his familiarity with this elevated company.

"Lady Maria Grey." Grace glanced toward the other drawing room. "The daughter of the late Earl of Templemore." She smiled with the satisfaction that everything was settled.

"That is good news," said James, enviously. "Isn't it? Anne?"

If anything, Anne felt rather sorry for that charming girl she had seen arriving earlier. She seemed too good for this coxcomb. But she did not reply. She was too distracted by the arrival of a young man who had suddenly appeared at the doorway. Tall, dark, with pale blue eyes and well-shaped brows. It had to be him. He was the image of Edmund Bellasis. He could have been his father's twin. Her mouth went dry and her knuckles turned white as she gripped her glass. He stood on the threshold, apparently nervous of entering the party, scanning the room and clearly looking for someone.

Lady Brockenhurst moved toward him with unhurried grace, declining two conversations en route in order to greet her guest. Anne watched the evident relief on the young man's face when his hostess finally came into view. And then they turned and began to walk toward her. How was she to react? What was she to say? She had imagined this scenario so many times, not just since the arrival of Lady Brockenhurst's letter but for years before that. How would it be when they met?

"Mrs. Trenchard," began Lady Brockenhurst as she swept toward her like a galleon in full sail. There was the whiff of victory in her voice. She could not contain it. "May I present a new acquaintance." She paused. "Mr. Charles Pope."

But Mr. Pope's reaction was not at all as expected. Instead he looked beyond Anne to where James stood, his mouth open like a codfish. "Mr. Trenchard," said the young man. "What are you doing here?"

"Mr. Pope," blurted James, and dropped his glass.

The loud smash brought all conversation at the party to a momentary halt as everyone turned and stared at the group gathered near the door. At the center of it was James, hot, bothered, mortified, and completely at sea as his cheeks turned puce and his earlobes redder still.

Naturally, the first to recover was Lady Brockenhurst. "Well, this is amusing," she said as the conversation in the room resumed and two footmen rallied around in a whirlwind of soft-shoed efficiency, sweeping up the glass on the parquet floor. "There I was, thinking that Mr. Pope is my secret only to find you're well acquainted, Mr. Trenchard. How funny." She laughed. "Have you known each other long?"

James hesitated. "No. Not long."

"A while," said Charles at exactly the same moment.

"Not long? A while?" Lady Brockenhurst repeated, looking from one to the other.

Anne turned to face her husband. Not since Sophia had announced her pregnancy, all those years ago, had she felt such a kick in the gut. Here it was again. Somehow this time it was even more devastating. Decades of sitting through turgid dinners and vapid receptions, men and women talking down to her and barely trying to conceal their disdain, had made Anne adept at hiding her feelings, but the expression on her face at that moment was something James had never seen in more than forty years of marriage. The sense of betrayal, injustice, the fury at the duplicity of the one man she thought she could trust, were there to be plainly read in her sensitive gray eyes.

"Yes, dear, do tell us," she said, when she could speak. "How long have you known Mr. Pope?"

James tried to make everything sound as normal as possible. He had met the man when he started working in the City. Charles's father was an old friend and had asked James to give the boy some advice on how he should manage things when he decided to move to London. James had been impressed with the young chap, and when he heard of his plan to take over a mill in Manchester he felt he could be useful, in that and in helping to source new suppliers of raw cotton.

"Where does one buy cotton now?" said Lady Brockenhurst, joining in James's valiant efforts to make the conversation seem ordinary. "America, I suppose."

"I would prefer to get it from India if I can," said Charles.

"And I've traded with India in the past"—James was more relaxed now, back in his right space—"I know something of the place, so it seemed only natural that I should try to lend a hand." He almost laughed, as if to demonstrate the ease with which the pair of them had fallen into a kind of friendship.

"And did you?" said Anne.

"Did I what?"

"Lend a hand." Her voice was as cold as steel.

"Oh, very much so," said Charles, missing all the darts and currents that flowed to and fro. "I had trained in accountancy in Guildford and had begun to work in business there, so naturally enough I thought myself ready for anything, but when I got to London it didn't take me long to realize I was playing a very different game. Mr. Trenchard's intervention rescued me and helped me get my business up and running. I couldn't have managed it without his help. It is the same venture you're interested in, Lady Brockenhurst."

"In what way are you 'interested'?" Anne turned to look at her hostess.

But Caroline was not so easily caught. "Isn't London a tiny place?" She clapped her hands with glee.

"Forgive me, but I don't quite understand." Anne was finding it harder than ever to control her rage. "Are you and Mr. Trenchard...?" She was literally at a loss for words.

"In business together?" Charles added helpfully. "We are, in a way, I'm glad to say."

"And for how long has this been going on?"

"Nine or ten months, I should think. But Mr. Trenchard was a good friend of my father's for years."

James cut in. "Mr. Pope's father asked for my help for his son not long before he died. He was an old friend, and so naturally I took his request very seriously, and I was glad to do so."

But Lady Brockenhurst had other plans. She took hold of Charles by the elbow and moved him on. She had her grandson by her side, Edmund's child, and nothing was going to spoil this moment. "Mr. Pope," she said pleasantly, "you must come and meet Lord Brockenhurst."

The Trenchards were left alone. For a moment, she just stared at him. "Anne, I—" James was at his most coaxing.

"I can't talk to you," she whispered as she started to turn away.

"But *you* knew he was going to be here," said James. "Why didn't you tell me?" Anne stopped in her tracks. She couldn't lie. Unlike her husband, apparently. He continued, warming to his argument. "You were expecting to see him. You were surprised that I knew him, I understand that, but you were expecting him to be here. In other words, you have disobeyed my instructions and told our hostess everything."

"Keep your voice down," Anne hissed as a couple of guests turned to look in their direction.

"I thought we had an agreement." James's neck was beginning to turn crimson again.

"You are in no position to lecture me on any given topic," said Anne as she walked off. "You work with our grandson and you tell me nothing."

"I don't work with him. Not exactly. I invested in his business. I gave him advice. Don't you think Sophia would have wanted that?"

"Mr. Trenchard! There you are! I have been looking for you," came the smooth voice of the Reverend Mr. Bellasis. "Do please let me introduce you to my son, Mr. John Bellasis."

James was bewildered. What was the significance of Charles Pope's presence here? And why was Stephen Bellasis making such an effort to present his son to him? Did everyone know he was Sophia's father? That he and Lord Brockenhurst shared a bastard grandson? His heart was racing as John stepped forward, right hand outstretched.

On the other side of the drawing room, Lady Brockenhurst was ushering Charles around the party. It was almost as if she couldn't help showing him off, and had she been a less controlled person she might have called for silence and announced his presence to the whole room. Instead she was parading him like a champion as the young man stood, smiling and nodding affably, while she fired name after name at him. For those who knew Lady Brockenhurst well, it was an odd display; she was not usually one of those women who promote favorites, who find lame ducks and sell them to the world as swans. Mr. Pope seemed a nice enough fellow for a tradesman, and nobody wished him ill, but what was Lady Brockenhurst doing extolling the virtues of this obscure cotton merchant?

Short of leaving the party, there was little Anne could do except circulate, making small talk and biding her time until she was allowed to go home. To walk out would cause gossip, and gossip was the last thing the Trenchards needed now.

She watched Lady Brockenhurst introduce Charles to the great names of London. What a handsome man he was—so self-possessed, so accomplished, and seemingly so patient and kind. The Reverend Mr. Pope and his wife had obviously given him manners as well as an education. How Sophia would have loved him. Anne glowed a little with pride, but then she checked herself. What had she to be proud about? She, the grandmother who gave him up for adoption. . . .

Meanwhile, John was desperate to extricate himself from the company of this absurd little man who insisted on explaining to him—at length—the intricacies of his business dealings in the East End. Of course John was interested in money per se, there could be no doubt about that, but the effort of earning it held no fascination for him. How fortunate, then, he'd concluded long ago, that he was heir presumptive to a significant fortune. His father might be fascinated by any man capable of making money because he himself was so *incapable* of doing it, but for John things were rather different. All he really had to do was wait. And while he waited, who could blame him if he wanted to amuse himself? John's favorite diversion was not gambling. He had seen the misery that particular vice had inflicted on his papa; rather, it was the company of women—the prettier, the better. Outside of Society, this was relatively simple, if expensive, to arrange. But when it came to respectable ladies, then he inclined toward the married brigade. Bored wives were most likely to give in, and having done so, they were in no position to ask for more than he cared to give. The threat of scandal and ruin was enough to keep the strongest women firmly in their place.

He had not let his imminent betrothal to Maria Grey alter his behavior much. She was beautiful and he was glad of that. But, if he was honest, she was proving to be rather more demanding, and even, he hesitated at the word, more *intellectual* than he had previously noticed. He was beginning to suspect that she found him...again, could *boring* really be the term he was looking for? It was an odd conceit. A chit of a girl found him, John Bellasis, one of the most eligible men in London, a shade too dull for her taste? In the light of this, and even though Maria was in the room and so he might get into trouble at any moment, still he could not ignore the more obvious charms of Susan Trenchard.

She saw him lurking as she talked brightly to some diplomat from a country of which she had never heard. He winked at her, and of course she knew enough to disapprove, but it was hard to demonstrate disapproval and she started to giggle. Her companion was puzzled at first and then offended when he caught sight of John hovering behind them. Without much ado, he excused himself and walked away.

"We meet again." John stepped closer.

"Really, Mr. Bellasis." Susan smiled, the ribbons in her hair shivering with delight. "Now you've made me offend nice Baron Whatever-his-name-was. Honestly, and I was on my best behavior, too."

"I bet your behavior's always pretty good, worse luck." He laughed. "Quickly!" he said suddenly, and pulled her through the door into a card room that was much emptier than the drawing room they had left. "That terrible bore was coming toward us, and it took me half an hour to shake him off the last time."

Susan followed his gaze. "That bore is my father-in-law," she said.

"Poor you." He laughed and, despite herself, so did she.

"I know your type. You're just the sort of man who makes me say things I don't want to say at all."

"And I hope I can make you *do* things you don't want to *do* at all." He stared into her eyes as he spoke, and it started to dawn on her that she was getting into very deep waters indeed. John wondered if he should make any further advance. He was inclined to think he'd done enough for one evening. She was a very pretty woman, and she didn't seem unassailable, but there was no rush. She had made no more than a glancing reference to her husband during the time they had spent talking together, so he could safely classify her as a bored wife. But they had better separate now. There was no point in causing talk before anything had really happened.

Maria Grey was wandering slightly aimlessly through the rooms. She saw her mother conversing with my great-aunt, and rather than join them for the usual discussion of how strange it was that she had grown so much since they last met, she decided to occupy herself for a moment admiring the Beechey portrait of the young Countess of Brockenhurst above the fireplace. But it was not long before she was overcome by the roaring heat and sought refuge on the terrace.

"I'm sorry," she spoke as she stepped out into the cool air of the June night. "I didn't mean to disturb you."

Charles Pope looked around at the sound of her footstep. He had been staring pensively over the white stone balustrade and into the square. "Not at all," he answered. "I'm afraid it is I who am disturbing you. If you would rather be alone...?"

"No."

"I suspect your mother would rather you were alone. Or at least not alone with a strange man to whom you haven't been introduced." But he looked amused as he said it.

Maria was rather intrigued by him. "My mother is deep in

conversation with my great-aunt who will not release her without a fight."

This time he laughed. "Then perhaps we had better introduce ourselves. Charles Pope." He held out his hand and she took it.

"Maria Grey." She smiled.

There was a pause while they both turned their attention to the square below. The pavements were almost empty, but the roads were lined with carriages, the horses occasionally pawing the ground, the familiar scraping of their metal hooves against stone just audible from where they stood.

"So why are you hiding out here?" she asked eventually.

"Is it that obvious?"

She found herself studying this man's face, and there was no denying he was attractive. The more so because, unlike John, he didn't appear to be aware of it. "I felt so sorry for you when you were being paraded around by our hostess. How do you know them? Are you related?"

Charles shook his head. "Heavens, no." He looked at her, this pretty girl who seemed so confident in what was, to him, an unsettlingly alien environment. "This isn't my natural habitat at all. I am a very ordinary sort of fellow."

She seemed quite unfazed by his revelation. "Well, Lady Brockenhurst doesn't seem to agree with you. I've never seen her so animated. She is not a woman known for her enthusiasms."

"You're right that she's taken an interest in me, although I couldn't tell you why. She wants to invest in a venture I'm working on."

Now this really was extraordinary. She almost gasped. "Lady Brockenhurst wants to invest in a *business venture?*" If he had told her that their hostess wanted to walk on the moon, she could not have sounded more astonished.

He shrugged. "I know. I don't understand it, either, but she seems very enthused by the whole idea."

"What is the idea?"

"I have bought a mill in Manchester. Now I need a better supply of raw cotton, and for that I must have some more funding. I also have a mortgage on the mill, and I believe it would pay me to lower that and increase my debt to Lady Brockenhurst, if she is willing. She will be the one to gain in the end. I'm sure of it."

"Of course you are." She was touched by his obvious desire to create a good impression.

He saw her amusement. Was he being very gauche? Of what possible interest were his business dealings to this beautiful young woman? Hadn't he been told never to discuss money? Least of all with a lady? "I don't know why I said that. Now I seem to have told you everything there is to know about me."

"Not quite." She studied him. "I thought Indian cotton production was in terrible disarray. I heard the shipping was too expensive to be worth it. Haven't most of the mills gone over to American cotton?"

Now it was his turn to be astonished. "How on earth do you know that?"

"India interests me." She smiled. It felt good to have surprised him. "I have an uncle who served there as Governor of Bombay. Unfortunately, I was too young to visit him during his term, but he is full of the country's woes and strengths to this day. He still reads the Indian newspapers, even if they are three months old when he gets them." She laughed, and he wondered at the evenness and whiteness of her teeth.

Charles nodded. "I've never been, but I believe it is a country with a great future."

"Within the Empire." Did she say this approvingly? He couldn't decide.

"Within the Empire for now, but not forever," he said. "What is your uncle's name?"

"Lord Clare. He was there from 1831 to 1835. He used to bring back silks that were the finest I have ever seen, and precious stones that were simply stunning. Did you know they have wells where you climb down more than a thousand steps before you get to the water? And there are cities where the skies are full of kites? And temples made of gold. I've heard they don't bury their dead as we do. They burn them, or float them down the river. I've always wanted to go to India." Charles looked into her clear blue eyes, admiring the softness of her lips and the curve of her determined chin. He had never met anyone quite so charming. "Do you know which part of India you'll be dealing with?" she continued, quite aware of his gaze and yet uncertain what to do with it.

"I am not sure just yet. The north, I think...."

"Oh." Her enthusiasm brought color to her cheeks, and he thought he had never in his life seen anyone lovelier. "Then, if I were you, I should be sure to visit the Taj Mahal in Agra." She almost sighed at the thought. "It's said to be the most beautiful monument to love ever built. A Mughal emperor was so struck down with grief on the death of his favorite wife that he ordered its construction. I'm afraid he had several wives, which of course we disapprove of terribly." She laughed and he laughed with her. "But she was his favorite. The marble is supposed to change color—from a blush pink in the morning, to a milky white in the evening, to gold when lit by the moon. The legend is that the shade reflects the mood of any woman who sees it."

Charles Pope was transfixed. The way she moved, the way she spoke, her wit, the alluring way she did not seem to be aware of her own beauty. "What about the men who see it?" he said. "What does it tell us about them?"

"That when they lose the right woman, they find her harder to replace than they expected."

They were still laughing when they heard a voice. "Maria?"

The girl turned around. "Mama."

Lady Templemore stood, silhouetted, in the doorway. "They're calling us to supper," she said, looking Charles up and down. It was obvious he did not meet with her approval. "It is time we went and found John. I've hardly spoken to him all evening."

And a moment later they were gone. Charles stood gazing at the spot where Maria had been standing, his reverie broken only when Lady Brockenhurst found him on the balcony and insisted he accompany her to the supper, which was just being served.

The guests crowded into the dining room, where a collection of small round tables were now dressed with linen cloths, silver candelabra, and exquisitely decorated plates and cut-glass decanters. Charles had never seen anything so lavish. He knew that things were done well in Society, and he'd heard that Lady Brockenhurst was known for her entertaining, but he had never expected anything quite on this scale.

"Mr. Pope," she said, indicating the seat right next to her. "You will come and sit by me." There were only four other places at the table. He looked frantically around the room. Surely the hostess would want someone else to sit in the place of honor? He felt himself flush. She patted the seat with her closed fan and smiled up at him. There was little else he could do but accept. Footmen were circulating the room as guests arrived and left, and soon Charles was dipping his spoon into a plate of iced soup. This was followed by cold salmon mousse, then quail, a little venison, pineapple, ices, and finally candied fruits: These were all served in the new fashion, *à la russe*, with the footmen bringing each course and standing to the left of the guests to allow them to help themselves. And all the while Lady Brockenhurst was delightful, including Charles in as many of her conversations as she could, even interrupting her passing husband at one point so he could hear about Charles's plans.

"What on earth is my sister-in-law up to?" complained Stephen Bellasis to his son, who was seated on the other side of Anne Trenchard. She was consequently drawn into the conversation without the slightest desire to be so. "Why is she making such a fuss of that dull man?"

John shook his head. "I can't understand it."

"There are at least three dukes in the room, but when they look across at the seat to the right hand of our dear hostess, they see it occupied by...by whom, exactly? Who is he?" Stephen was finding time to wrestle with a rather bloody quail as he spoke.

John turned to his neighbor. "I think Mrs. Trenchard will know the answer. Doesn't he work for your husband, Mrs. Trenchard?" Anne was quite surprised, as Mr. Bellasis had not given the slightest clue before this that he knew who she was.

She shook her head. "No, he doesn't work for him. He works for himself. They know each other. They may have some common interest. But that's all."

"So you can't explain Lady Brockenhurst's fascination?"

"I'm afraid not."

Anne looked over to the table. Caroline Brockenhurst was playing a dangerous game. Even John Bellasis had noticed the attention she was paying her grandson, and Anne was worried. Did Lord Brockenhurst know? If not, how long would it be before he did, if his wife was prepared to be this indiscreet? How long would it take for the secret to get out? How long before Sophia's reputation lay in tatters and all they had worked for was in ruins at their feet? She caught her husband's eye. He was sitting opposite her, flanked by Oliver and the tiresome Grace. He caught her eye, nodding at the perilous situation evolving in front of them.

"I believe your aunt is interested in one of Mr. Pope's enterprises," Anne suggested eventually, abandoning her own quail and wishing she had held on to the salmon mousse. At least it was soft enough to swallow. As it was, she could barely eat a thing.

"I have business with the local butcher," said John indignantly. "But I don't invite him to the supper table."

"I don't think Mr. Pope is quite the local butcher," replied Anne as diplomatically as she could.

"Don't you?" said John, as he stared across the room at Susan and smiled. She had been so angry to miss the last chair at that table and was trying to be content with a group of politicians who were ignoring her. But now, after John's smile, she felt ready to burst into song.

It was almost time to leave before Anne managed a private word with their hostess. Even then she had to catch her on the landing of the main stair and pull her into the columned recess of a window. "What are you doing?" she whispered.

"I am getting to know the grandson you concealed from me for a quarter of a century."

"But why so publicly? Can't you see that half the room is asking who this strange young man could possibly be?"

The Countess smiled coolly. "Of course. That must worry you.'

And then Anne saw the trap she had walked into. Lady Brockenhurst had promised that Charles's identity would remain a secret, and she was honor bound to keep her word, but she hadn't the slightest aversion to others guessing the truth. Her son had enjoyed an affair in Brussels before he died. What did that say about him that Society was not bound to forgive? Nothing. He'd had a fling before he was married. There could be few men in these crowded drawing rooms who had not done the same. The illegitimate offspring of a gentleman might not be quite as easily absorbed into Society as they had been a century before, but there was still nothing new to it. And if someone did venture an opinion, Mrs. Trenchard would surely not expect Lady Brockenhurst to lie? She might not volunteer the information, but she could hardly be expected to deny it. "You want them to guess," said Anne, as the scales fell from her eyes. "You want them to guess, and you wanted us to witness it."

Caroline Brockenhurst looked at her. She no longer disliked this woman as much as she had at first. Anne had led her to Charles, and for that she ought to be grateful, or at least forgiving. She glanced into the hall. "I think the Cathcarts are leaving," she said. "Will you forgive me if I go down to say good-bye?" And she glided away, descending the stairs so smoothly she could have been skimming over the surface of the steps.

The ride back to Eaton Square felt like an eternity. All of the passengers in the carriage were so full of the evening's events that no one said a word. The coachman, Albert Quirk, was a man more usually interested in the changing elements and the strength of the cognac he kept in his flask than the vagaries of the family he served, but this evening he could not help but notice the mood. "If that's what they're like when they've been out at a party," he said much later to Mrs. Frant as he sat drinking a large mug of tea at the servants' hall table, "they'd be better off staying at home. Don't you agree, Miss Ellis?" But the maid said nothing as she continued to sew on a missing button.

"You'll get nothing out of Miss Ellis," snorted Mrs. Frant sourly.

"Which is just as it should be in a lady's maid," said Mr. Quirk. He rather approved of Miss Ellis.

James had decided that attack was the best form of defense. Caught out in his secret dealings with Charles, he decided to blame the whole fiasco on his wife. If she'd kept their secret, none of it would have happened. Which was of course true, except that it conveniently absolved him of leading a double life, knowing his grandson, enjoying his company, and leaving his wife in the dark.

Anne could hardly look at him. It felt to her as if the husband she had known and loved had been spirited away by wicked fairies and a hostile being put in his place.

Oliver was just as angry with his own wife, but for more traditional reasons. She had ignored him all evening, flirting continually with John Bellasis, who had barely deigned to notice Oliver. He was furious with his father, too. Who was this Pope fellow, anyway? And why did his father's face light up when he entered the room?

As for Susan, she was torn between depression at the dreariness of the family she had married into and wonder at the world she'd dreamed about for so long and had at last been allowed to see. Those drawing rooms and staircases, those gilded galleries and eating chambers, all vast and magnificent and packed with a glittering assembly whose names read like a journey through English history...and then there was John Bellasis. She glanced across at Oliver. She could see he was spoiling for a fight, but she didn't care. She studied his doughy, petulant face and thought with longing of that other face, that very different face, she had been looking into until only a few minutes before. She knew her husband was angry, but that was because he was not used to the ways of the *ton*. No one else there would grudge a respectable married woman the odd flirtation, an amusing evening in the company of a witty, handsome stranger. She paused as she thought about the word. Would he always be a stranger? Was that all she was destined to know of Mr. John Bellasis? The coach drew to a halt. They had arrived.

"Thank you, William. I can manage from here. You may go." Oliver loved to talk to the servants as if he were in some play at the Haymarket Theatre. But Billy was used to it, and he quite enjoyed valeting. Even for Mr. Oliver. It made a change from cleaning the silver and waiting at table, and he was sure he could get a job as a proper valet when he was ready to leave. That would be a step in the right direction, and no mistake.

"Very good, sir. Would you like to be woken in the morning?"

"Come at nine. I'll be late for work, but I think I can be forgiven that after the night I've just been through."

Naturally, Billy would have loved some more detail, but Mr. Oliver was already in his dressing gown so he'd missed his chance. He might try to raise the subject the next day. With a slight bow of the head he retreated, closing the door softly behind him. Oliver waited for a few moments, indulging his irritation at everything: Susan, Charles Pope, his stupid valet who wasn't a real valet anyway, just a footman. Then, when he'd decided that Billy must have left the gallery, he slipped out of his dressing room and pushed into Susan's bedroom without knocking.

"Oh!" said Susan. He had succeeded in startling her. "I thought you'd gone to bed."

"What a terrible evening." He spat out the words as if he'd released a bung from a barrel, which, in a way, he had.

"I thought it was fun. You can hardly complain about the people who were there. There must have been half the Cabinet in the room, and I'm sure I saw the Marchioness of Abercorn talking to one of the Foreign Office ministers. At least I think it was her, only she was so much more beautiful than the portrait they engraved in—"

"The evening was damnable! And you made it more so!"

Susan took a deep breath. It was going to be one of those nights. She was acutely aware of her maid, Speer, hovering, frozen, by the door. She was keeping still so they would forget she was there. Susan knew that well enough. "You may go, Speer," she said, keeping her voice even and light. "I shall ring for you in a little while." The disappointed maid withdrew. Susan turned to Oliver. "Now, what is this about?"

"You'd know if you hadn't spent the entire evening staring into the eyes of that scented degenerate."

"Did Mr. Bellasis wear scent? I hadn't noticed." But his comment interested her as it was clear from her husband's phrasing that John was not the main cause of his anger.

"Behave like a slut and you'll be treated as one. You don't have carte blanche, you know. Just because you're barren, it doesn't give you an open ticket."

Susan was silent for a moment, gathering her thoughts. This was becoming rather more unpleasant than she had bargained for. She looked at Oliver calmly. "You should go to bed. You're tired."

He regretted what he'd said. She knew him well enough to see that. But, being Oliver, he couldn't apologize. Not possibly. Instead, he changed his tone. "Who is this man Pope? Where has he come from? And why is Father investing in his business? When did he ever invest in my business?"

"You don't have a business."

"Then when did he ever invest in *me*? And why was Lady Brockenhurst guiding him around the room the whole time like a show pony? How did he manage that? When she barely spoke a civil word to either of us all evening." There was a catch in his voice, and for a moment Susan wondered whether he was actually crying.

Oliver began to pace the room again. Susan watched, thinking over her own experience of Brockenhurst House. She really had enjoyed herself. John had been very entertaining. He'd made her feel attractive, more attractive than she'd felt for years, and she'd enjoyed the sensation. "I liked the Reverend Mr.—" She looked at her husband quizzically. Her mind had gone blank. "Bellasis. Of course. Mr. Bellasis's father. They seemed a nice family." She was trying to bring her long and very public conversation with John back to more neutral territory. Hopefully, Oliver was sufficiently taken up with his rage against Mr. Pope to accept her unspoken explanation for her behavior.

"You know who he is? I mean, apart from that man's father."

"Do I?" She wasn't sure where this was taking them.

"The Reverend Mr. Bellasis?"

Oliver looked at his wife. Did she really not know who the man was? He had not been completely idle with his time since his father's rise, and he understood the truth behind the legend of most of the senior aristocratic families, but he thought he had taken Susan along with him. Surely she had some clue? "He is Lord Brockenhurst's younger brother. He is his heir, or more probably his son, John, will inherit, since Lord Brockenhurst looks considerably healthier than his younger sibling."

"John Bellasis will be the next…?" Susan was slipping away, down some sugar-covered slope in her dreams, lost in her own fantasy.

"The next Earl of Brockenhurst. Yes." Oliver nodded. "The present Earl's only son died at Waterloo. There is no one else."

It was creeping toward three o'clock when Lady Brockenhurst finally sat down at her glass, taking off her diamond earrings, while her maid, Dawson, removed the pins from her hair.

"It sounded as if everyone was having a wonderful time, your ladyship." Dawson removed the last pins carefully and lifted off the heavy tiara. Caroline shook her head. She enjoyed wearing her jewels; she had a taste for magnificence, but it was a relief when they came off and she was free. She scratched her scalp and smiled.

"I think it did go well," she declared brightly.

There was a light tap at the door. Lord Brockenhurst's head appeared. "May I come in?"

His wife answered. "Please."

He entered the room, slipping into a nearby armchair. "What a relief when they've gone."

"We were saying how well it went."

"I suppose. But there are only so many times in an evening one can inquire after somebody else's health, or delight in the news of the Queen's pregnancy, or ask how they're going to spend the summer. Who was that fellow in the cotton trade? And what was he doing there?"

Caroline scrutinized her husband's face in the glass. Had he guessed? Could he not see how alike Charles was to her beautiful Edmund? Those eyes. Those long fingers. The way he laughed. The boy was pure Bellasis. Wasn't it obvious? "You mean Mr. Pope?"

"Pope? Was that the name?" Peregrine smoothed down his mustache and winced a little. His shoes were pinching. "Yes," he mused, gazing at one of his wife's watercolors of Lymington Park. "I thought him a nice chap, and more interesting than the women you stuck me with at supper, but I still don't understand why he was standing in our drawing room."

"I've taken an interest in him."

"But why?"

"Well..." Caroline paused, and so did Dawson. The maid held one brush in her right hand, another in her left, her head cocked to one side in anticipation. It was one of the most interesting aspects of her job, helping her ladyship undress after an evening in Society. Tongues were always loosened by a little wine, and the tidbits she picked up were good currency for discussion in the servants' hall. "You see..."

Then Caroline caught Dawson's eye and stopped herself. There was nothing she wanted more than to tell her husband the truth, but she had given her word. Did that apply to husbands and wives, she wondered? Weren't they breaking a commandment by keeping secrets from each other? Didn't the Bible say so? But even if that were true, Caroline could see that it wouldn't be quite right to launch Charles socially on a tidal wave of servants' gossip. Dawson might be discreet as a rule, but you could never count on a maid's discretion. She could just as easily spread it all through Belgravia before the butcher's boy arrived with the bacon joint at five. The servants really were worse than the rats, the way they went from house to house, passing on God knows what to whomever they pleased. She knew how much they talked downstairs, even those who were loyal. No. She couldn't tell her husband now, whether or not she did later. So Caroline did what she always did when things became complicated: She changed the subject.

"Maria Grey has grown up to be a pretty girl," she said. "She used to be so serious, her head always in a book. Now she looks enchanting."

"Hmm," agreed Peregrine. "Lucky John. I hope he deserves her." He slipped off his shoes, attempting to summon the energy to go to bed.

"She seems to have taken her father's death in her stride."

"Terrible business."

Dawson picked up a hairbrush again and went on disentangling Lady Brockenhurst's tresses. She'd heard this story before, how Lord Templemore had fallen from his horse and smashed his head against a rock while out hunting. "Lady Templemore was full of praise for Reggie."

"Reggie?"

"Her son. She was telling me that he is more or less running the estate. And he's only twenty. She says their agent is a good man, but even so."

Peregrine grunted. "He'll need more than a good agent if he's to keep it safe from the bailiffs. I gather his father left it weighted down with debt like a sack of stones."

Caroline sighed sympathetically. "They had new dresses on tonight, mother and daughter. I did rather wonder at it. But then, I suppose they knew John was coming, and it doesn't do to look impoverished. Certainly not in front of one's intended."

Peregrine placed his head in his hands, overcome by a sudden wave of sadness. There was something about the arrival of summer, so much hope in the air, so many people whirling from gala to gala, every one of them filled with plans to escape the heat of the city. And watching John tonight, flirting with the pretty daughter-in-law of the curious Mr. Trenchard…what was he? Thirty-two or -three? There wasn't much in it. Edmund would have been forty-eight by now, a man still in the prime of his life. But he wouldn't be escaping to the north coast of France or the mountains around the Italian lakes. He was trapped in his tomb, like all those gallant young men who had died on that morning in June so long ago. Peregrine had hoped the move to the new house in Belgrave Square, with its splendid rooms for entertaining, would have given them both a new lease on life, a new energy. But somehow, tonight, he felt the opposite had happened, that the sight of the frivolity, the clothes, the chatter, the diamonds, had only served to illustrate the folly of human life, which must always end in a cold and lonely grave. He heaved himself to his feet and started for the door. "Better turn in. Busy day tomorrow."

Caroline could feel his sadness; it hung in the room like a cloud. She longed to tell him the news, now that she was sure. Edmund had a son. We have someone we can love again.

"My dear." He looked back. She paused. "Sleep well. Maybe things will look different in the morning."

James Trenchard was dreading tomorrow. And the day after, for that matter. He was dreading however long it took for the scandal to break. It was like a clock slowly ticking toward doomsday, he concluded, as he lay in bed staring at the intricate white cornice above him. It felt like some soldier's grenade waiting to go off. No wonder he couldn't sleep. He'd been stretched out for an hour, listening to the silence. He knew Anne was not asleep either. She lay next to him, her back toward him, rigid. He could sense her tension.

They had come home in silence. James disappeared into his dressing room while Anne took the dog out and then retired to her own apartment. She was not especially talkative as a rule, but even Ellis had been surprised by the silence. The maid's gentle invitations to discuss Lady Brockenhurst's party were not taken up, and as soon as she could, Ellis finished her work and left. By the time James appeared, Anne was already in bed, the covers pulled tightly around her, pretending to be asleep, with her dog curled up in her arms. Standing in his bare feet, dressed in his nightshirt, he was on the point of leaving the room and going back to his own splendid bedroom—something he had only done a handful of times in their forty years of marriage. Instead, he climbed into bed, blew out his candle, and rested on his back with his eyes wide open. There was no point in avoiding the collision that must come, since each blamed the other for their misery. They were seething, furious at the other's underhand, duplicitous behavior.

"Charles must know," he said eventually, unable to keep his counsel any longer.

"He does not!" Anne sat up in bed, startling Agnes out of her sleep.

She could see her husband's profile, illuminated by the gaslight from the street. Sometimes she regretted the absolute darkness of the nighttime city of her youth. This ubiquitous dim half-light seemed to keep the world in a perpetual dusk. But London was safer now, of course, and that must be a good thing.

James hadn't finished. "She placed him next to her at dinner. On her right. Everyone noticed. The rest of the Bellasis family certainly noticed. It was as good as putting it in the *Times*. She must have meant to draw attention to him, and why would she do that if she didn't want it to get out? If he doesn't know the truth yet, he will in a matter of days if not hours."

"How long have you been in contact with him?"

James did not even pay her the courtesy of a response. "How do you know she hasn't already told him? What other reason could there be for him to receive an invitation? He has to know. People like Charles Pope do not get asked to intimate suppers in Belgrave Square to tear a pheasant with half the peerage. People like Charles Pope do not sit next to the Countess of Brockenhurst. People like Charles Pope do not *know* the Countess of Brockenhurst. In the ordinary way of things, the Countess of Brockenhurst would not even give Charles Pope the time of day, *let alone invite him to sit next to her at dinner!*" James was up now, too, his words getting louder and louder as he turned to face his wife.

"Keep your voice down!" hissed Anne. Oliver and Susan were directly above them. Cubitt may have put shells in the ceilings of these houses to prevent the noise from traveling between floors, but they weren't that thick.

"As for this nonsense about her investing in his business—"

"Why is it nonsense? You've invested in it. You've been backing him for months." Her tone was not reassuring.

"I am a man. Lady Brockenhurst doesn't have any money. At least, none she could invest without her husband's permission. And why would he give it if he didn't know the reason for her interest? It's all nonsense and blather, and it will result in the ruin of the Trenchards!" It was no accident that James had done so well in the lawless, free-flowing atmosphere of wartime Brussels. When he needed to play rough and tough, he did. He was still the son of a market trader, more than capable of fighting his corner. And now he had been backed into one. Everything that he'd earned and struggled for was about to be undone by his wife. His own wife, of all people.

"I simply could not let her go on thinking that she and her husband were the last of their line." Anne smoothed the sheets around her.

"Why not? They've spent the last twenty-five years thinking it. Surely they're used to it by now!" His face was starting to go red again. Now that he had released his fury, he could not get it back under control. "And what has changed? Charles Pope can't make the smallest claim against the family. He has no rights. He is a bastard, though he may not thank you for throwing the fact into the face of the public!"

"They have a grandson. They needed to know it."

"Is that why we were invited, then?" he asked. "Is it?" But

Anne stayed silent. She had made her point. "So we could watch her parade Charles in front of us, unable to speak to him? Was that her revenge?"

"You have been able to speak to him. You are old friends by now." Her voice was like ice.

"Of course, we already know his presence there was no surprise to you."

In a way, it was almost a relief to admit it. "Yes," answered Anne. "Yes, I did know he was going to be there. And if you think I'm going to listen to one word of reproof, you have another think coming. You're as much to blame as I am."

"Me?" Trenchard leaped out of bed. "What have *I* done?"

"You have been in contact with our grandson, you've met him, you are even working with him, and you never saw fit to tell me, your wife, the mother of the woman who bore him." Her voice was cracking now. She could hear it, and however much she wished to sound strong and resolute, the tears kept pushing through. "You've spoken to him. You've touched him. And you never told me. I have been living in ignorance for more than twenty years, wondering every day what he must look like, what he must sound like, and you knew him without telling me. Not an hour has gone by when I did not regret my decision to hand him over to a strange family. I gave away our beautiful grandson because you were afraid it might mean fewer invitations to dinner if we brought him up. And now you deceive me in this hateful and hurtful way!"

Of course, in this tirade, Anne had conveniently forgotten that she had been glad of the plan to be rid of the unloved baby when he'd first arrived and Sophia was dead. James thought of reminding her, but he decided against it. He was probably wise. He watched her tears glinting as they poured down her cheeks. Her hands were tugging at the sheets. "Lady Brockenhurst's ignorance was no excuse for the cruelty of keeping the secret. It was time she knew. She had to know."

There was no point in saying any more. James understood that but he couldn't resist one final jibe. "Your sentimentality will bring the roof down on our heads. When our daughter's name is dragged through the mud, when she is spoken of as loose and fallen, when all the doors that we have worked so hard to open are closed to us, then you will only have yourself to blame."

With that, James Trenchard turned over, placing his back firmly toward his sobbing wife, and closed his eyes.

— ·5· —

The Assignation

Susan Trenchard lay in bed listening to the church bells of All Saints, Isleworth. Every now and then she could hear the noises of the river: watermen calling to each other, the splash of an oar. She looked around the room. It was decorated like a bedchamber in a great house rather than a lodging, with heavy brocade curtains, a classical chimneypiece, and a fine four-poster which she found so comfortable. Another woman might have been alarmed to discover that John Bellasis kept a small house in Isleworth with a single room for eating, a large and luxuriously appointed bedroom, and more or less nothing else beyond a service area and presumably a room for the near-silent man who ministered to them. Again, the fact that the servant had asked no questions when they arrived but simply produced a delicious luncheon before ushering them into a bedroom where the curtains had been drawn and the fire lit might have implied that he knew the form for this type of encounter a little too thoroughly for comfort. But Susan was too content, too satisfied—indeed, more satisfied than she had been in years—to pick holes in her present happiness. She stretched.

"You should probably get dressed." John stood at the foot of the bed, buttoning his trousers. "I'm dining in town, and you should be back in time to change."

"Do we have to?"

Susan propped herself up in the bed. Her auburn hair snaked in curls over her smooth white shoulders. She bit her plump bottom lip as she looked up at John. In this mood, she really was quite irresistible, and she knew it. John walked over and sat down next to her, running his index finger down the side of her neck, tracing the curve of her collarbone, while Susan closed her eyes. He cupped her chin and kissed her.

What an extraordinary proposition Susan Trenchard had turned out to be. Their meeting at his aunt's soirée had been quite fortuitous and entirely unplanned, but she was his best discovery this Season. He really believed she would keep him entertained for weeks.

He had Susan's maid, Speer, to thank for the ease of their adventure. For a wiry, miserable-looking woman she was prepared to be remarkably complicit in her mistress's seduction. Not that Susan had really needed much encouragement, especially when faced with someone as proficient in the bedroom arts as John. He'd always had a sharp eye for a woman who was likely to stray. Her boredom and lack of affection for her husband had been obvious to him as soon as he'd approached her that evening at Brockenhurst House. All he'd had to do was flatter her a little, tell her how pretty she was, frown with interest at her opinions, and slowly but surely he knew he would be able to prise her away from the weak-looking Oliver Trenchard. In the end, women really were very simple creatures, he thought now, looking into her pale blue eyes. They might tremble with indecision, affect shock and dismay at the very idea, but he knew these for the stages they felt obliged to go through. From the moment she'd laughed at his jokes, he knew he could have her whenever he wanted.

He'd followed up that first encounter in Belgrave Square with a letter. For discretion's sake, he had sent it by post, for the price of a new Penny Red stamp. In it he declared, in the most florid and romantic of terms, how much he had enjoyed their conversation and how rare a beauty he thought she was. It was impossible to get her out of his head, he'd enthused, smiling as he imagined her reading his words.

He'd suggested they meet for tea at Morley's Hotel in Trafalgar Square. It was a well-frequented establishment, but not usually by anyone with whom John was closely acquainted. The invitation had been something of a test. If Susan was the sort of woman who could manufacture an excuse to travel across London and meet him in the middle of the day, then she was a woman who was free with the truth, capable of duplicity, and therefore worth pursuing. He barely managed to contain his feelings of triumph as she walked through the glass revolving door of the hotel, accompanied by Speer.

Of course it must be said that in most of this John was entirely mistaken. He thought so much of his powers of seduction that it never occurred to him that Susan Trenchard had no need to be seduced. The truth was that when she learned of John's dazzling prospects, coupled with the very real attraction she'd felt for him at their first meeting, Susan had decided that she would be first John's mistress and then, if things went well, she would decide how far things might progress. He should have known that the mere fact she'd brought her maid into the secret—as she must have done by getting her to accompany her to the hotel—meant that she was an active, and not a passive, participant in the plan. Susan knew well enough that no one would question a wife leaving the house with her maid. There were plenty of legitimate reasons for her to be traveling around London or elsewhere shopping, lunching, visiting, as long as she was accompanied by a maid. Bringing Speer into her confidence had ensured the success of Susan's scheme. She would certainly allow John to give himself the credit for turning her head and luring her into sin—all men like to feel they are leading the dance—but the truth was that if Susan had not made the decision to go astray, it would not be happening.

On the day in question, she told Oliver she was meeting an old school-friend up from the country and taking in an exhibition at the National Gallery. Oliver had not even bothered to ask the name of the woman she was meeting. He just seemed to be glad that she was keeping herself busy.

Speer very tactfully disappeared as soon as they entered the foyer of the hotel, leaving her mistress to approach John on her own. He was sitting in a corner, next to the grand piano, with a flourishing potted palm just behind him. He was more attractive than she remembered, much more attractive than her wretched husband. As she wove her way through the chairs and tables, she found, to her surprise, that now the moment had actually arrived, she felt a little nervous. It wasn't the prospect of an affair. She had known for a year or two that she would fall into one sooner or later, so unsatisfactory had the occasional fumblings with Oliver become. And she was barren—something that had caused her a good deal of heartbreak in the past but which had its uses now. She allowed herself a smile. Her nervousness must be all that remained of her girlish modesty, a fragment that had somehow survived her hardening into the woman she'd become. She kept her head down to avoid eye contact with the groups of ladies who were sitting together, drinking tea. Morley's was not the sort of hotel that any of her close circle would frequent, John had been right in that at least, but one could never be too careful. The capital was a small place, and a reputation could be ruined in one afternoon.

She sat down swiftly with her back to the room and gave John a look. Well versed in these matters, or so he thought, John took it on himself to put her at ease, which she allowed. Susan knew well enough that he would need the thrill of conquering a virtuous woman for him to enjoy the experience fully, and the fact was she wanted him to enjoy himself very much indeed. Her blushing modesty played its part, and sure enough, it was not long before he started to suggest that they might meet again, but this time in slightly different circumstances.

The truth was, Oliver Trenchard was not enough of a husband for Susan. For the first five years of their marriage they had tried, unsuccessfully, to conceive, but after that Oliver had all but left her alone. She did not entirely blame him. Once it became clear there would be no child, they did not like each other enough for the thought of their coupling to be enticing to either of them. It was not something they discussed, unless it was a casual insult during an argument, or they might save it for a particularly tight-lipped conversation in her dressing room after dinner, most especially if Oliver had been drinking too much.

But what she had come to realize was that, as a childless wife, she had lost her hold on her husband, and she would never achieve much control over her parents-in-law. From this it followed that, if she wasn't careful, she might end up with nothing. Even her father had lost interest in her. She might have blamed her own extravagance for this, at least in part, but instead she chose to put it down to his disappointment at her inability to be a mother. He would have no descendants, and she wasn't sure he could forgive her for that, while the Trenchards would no doubt have been glad if some disease had carried her off, allowing Oliver to find another wife who would fill the nurseries in Eaton Square. It was perhaps the realization of this bitter truth that inclined Susan to believe it was time to forge her own path if she was ever to know any fulfilment at all. Naturally, this journey took time—to travel from optimism through disillusionment to a determination to find her own life—and it was just as these ideas had fully formed that she met John Bellasis.

So when, that afternoon, John suggested a trip to Isleworth where he kept "some rooms that allow me to escape the hurly-burly of London," Susan had made a poor pretense at hesitation. All she had to do was fashion an excuse to visit Isleworth for the day. She'd decided not to lie about her destination, as she might be seen by someone and there was no need to risk being caught out. In the end, she decided to say she was thinking of purchasing an orchard and she wanted to look at what was on offer. Many of the great London houses had orchards there, to supply them with fresh fruit through the late summer and autumn, and while Oliver grumbled that it would be he who would be doing the buying, he had raised no objections. To complete her image of innocence, she would travel with Speer and arrange where the maid would wait until Susan was ready to leave.

And that was exactly what they had done. The Bridge Inn, a little way along the river from John's lodgings, would be where Speer would wait from three o'clock onward. Once that was settled, she strolled away, leaving the assistant coachman in total ignorance. Even the servants had been told about the garden purchase, as it would give Susan the excuse for many such visits in the future.

"I was thinking I might give my horse a rest and come back with you." John stroked her cheek with his thumb.

"Wouldn't that be lovely?" she replied with a sleepy stretch. "If only we could."

"Can't we?" He was rather surprised.

She gave him a languid smile, promising more to come in better times. "I'm traveling with my maid in my husband's carriage."

John could not understand the problem at first. Why couldn't they put the maid up on the box with the coachman and ride happily back to town? He didn't much care if he was seen with a pretty married woman in her husband's carriage. But, when he thought about it, even he could see it would matter a great deal for Susan to be recognized, and her face made it clear this was not going to happen. For a second, he almost glimpsed that she was as strong as he was, and quite as much in control of events, but then the vision was gone, and all he saw was a laughing woman lying back on the pillows with her eyes half shut, madly in love with him. This he felt comfortable with, and did not push the point further.

With a sigh, implying as she meant it to that her most fervent wish would be for them to stay together for always, she got out of bed and slipped on her chemise. She walked barefoot to the window, dragging her feet across the luxurious Turkish carpet, and picked up her corset.

"Speer is waiting for me at the Bridge Inn." She pursed her lips coyly. "So I need some help with this."

John raised his eyebrows and made a show of sighing, too. She laughed and he joined her, although in truth he did find the complexities of women's fashions terribly tiresome. "Do I have to lace it?"

"No. That's only for comedies in the theater. The laces are tied, but the hooks down the front can be stubborn." It took him over five minutes to fasten the beastly hooks, only for her to ask for help doing up the fiddly little buttons all the way down the back of her dress. It was getting increasingly hot in the room, and his fingers were sweating as he fumbled at the yellow silk.

"Next time," he suggested smoothly, "it might be an idea if you were to wear something a little less...complicated."

"I can hardly walk the streets in a dressing gown. Even for you. And you didn't make such a fuss when you were helping me to undress." Once again, he had a sneaking suspicion that she was mocking him; somehow he was doing her bidding and not, as he had thought, the other way around. But again he dismissed it.

"Shall we meet in London next time?" suggested John as he checked his pocket watch. "Or at least somewhere a little closer?"

Susan nodded. "What a difference these new railways will make."

"In what way?"

She smiled. "I only meant we could meet in a faraway place and be back in time for tea. They say it won't take much more than an hour or two to get to Brighton, and only five or six hours to travel to York. The prospect of it makes me feel quite breathless."

He wasn't so sure. "I don't see why everything has to keep changing. I'm perfectly happy with the way things are."

"Well, I wouldn't change anything about the afternoon we've just enjoyed." She pumped up his vanity just as he liked it pumped up. Which of course she knew. "And now I really must be gone." She kissed him once more, letting her tongue touch his lips before she drew back, a promise for the next time. "Don't make me wait too long," she whispered into his ear, and before he could respond she was through the door and on her way down to the hall, where the silent servant waited to see her out. It was clearly a routine that held no surprises for him.

Susan's only challenge was to get from John's rooms to the Bridge Inn. After that, she would have her maid and her carriage and she'd be as sedate and proper as any matron in the town. She wore a thicker veil than usual, so nobody who glimpsed her could be quite sure, but her nerve held and she walked calmly back to the hotel and safety. Speer was waiting demurely, with an empty tea-cup in front of her. She stood as Susan approached. "I've been for a walk, ma'am."

"I'm glad. I should hate to think of you cramped up in a public house all afternoon."

"I went to see an agent, and he has given me some descriptions of garden properties that are for sale." She produced the selling sheets for three or four orchards and kitchen garden properties. "I thought they might come in useful."

Susan said nothing as she took the papers, folded them carefully, and put them into her reticule. Her alibi was rock solid.

Is there such a thing as a losing streak? Stephen Bellasis wondered idly as he saw his counters being swept away again by the dealer. Everyone talks of a winning streak, a lucky streak, but what of an *unlucky* streak? Because if it were a streak, then it must come to an end, but his losing never seemed to end. He had already lost a good deal that afternoon. A small fortune, in fact. As his son was entertaining himself in Isleworth, Stephen was already a thousand pounds down at Jessop's Club, just off Kinnerton Street.

Jessop's was not one of those clubs ambitious men aspired to join; it was one of those places wastrels ended up. Fetid, filthy, and strung out over four floors, the club was composed of a series of dingy rooms in which disparate gamblers were served low-grade alcohol while they frittered away any money they had left, or any money they had managed to beg, borrow, or steal from others. This was another side of Belgravia.

A few years before, Stephen had been a member of Crockford's in St. James's, where the great and the good would go for a little supper and a lot of fun. But William Crockford was a wily man who'd studied the histories and the members of the country's great families, and he knew how much they were worth. He knew to whom he should extend a long line of credit and to whom he should not. Needless to say, the Honorable and Reverend Stephen Bellasis did not last long at Crockford's. Somehow he convinced himself that one had no need for a fancy French chef and smart company to accompany one's gaming and began to inhabit less lofty establishments. He grew increasingly fond of the Victoria Sporting Club on Wellington Street, where the members talked not about gambling but "gaming," and he placed bets for runners at Ascot or Epsom. Unfortunately, he seemed to be as lucky with horses as he was with cards.

But how he loved that feeling of victory! It would not take much, just a whiff of a win, a few pounds on a winner, and he'd be off again. Sometimes to enjoy the sedate charms of the Argyll Rooms, where he'd celebrate in his own inimitable style—with a bottle of port and the chance of a fumble under the skirts of a pretty dancer. At other times, he would be more daring, drifting east to the Rookery around Seven Dials, where even the police would not go if it could possibly be avoided. Like a man risking his life on a whim, he would drink in the bars he found there, chatting with thieves and prostitutes, occasionally letting the night take a frightening turn, wondering whether the morning would find him dead in the gutter with a knife in his side, or back in his own bed, next to the wife who gave him no pleasure.

Today, however, victory was nowhere to be seen. He was not untalented at whist, if there was a game he could play to some effect, and he often made back some of his losses, he thought, as he sat shuffling the cards. But somehow, on this afternoon, nothing was working. Lady Luck had most definitely deserted him, and he was beginning to regret being quite so cavalier with his money.

In fact, Stephen was not only regretful, he was terrified. A thousand pounds was a large sum of money, and he had no way of paying, unless somehow he could make it back. As he continued to lose, the poorly lit room became increasingly claustrophobic. The temperature in the dark-paneled basement was stifling, and he tugged at the collar that encased his clammy neck. He never wore his clergyman's bands to play, but the thick neckerchief he had replaced them with seemed to choke him in its folds. The gin he'd swallowed was not helping either, nor the constant fumes from Count Sikorsky's pipe. Stephen felt he could barely breathe.

There were three other players seated around the sticky card table, two of them acquaintances of Stephen's. There was Oleg Sikorsky, the aging Russian aristocrat with a crumbling estate in the Crimea he could no longer afford to visit. Sikorsky talked endlessly about the good old days in St. Petersburg, sipping champagne on the Fontanka, while he slowly worked his way through his grandmother's fortune, a venerable lady who, if he was to be believed, had once had the ear of Tsar Alexander I. Next to him was Captain Black, an officer in the Grenadier Guards and a friend of John's. He was new to the table, having picked up the gambling bug from his men. He had an agile mind and was good at remembering tricks, but he was also prone to rash moves and flamboyant gestures that rarely resulted in a large win, though he was doing well enough this afternoon, God knew. The fourth player was a Mr. Schmitt, a bear of a man whose skull had apparently been damaged by a hammer during a fight at some point in his misspent youth. Oddly, he'd survived the attack, the evidence of which was a frightening indentation in his forehead. Schmitt had gone on to found a successful moneylending business, which was why he was here. For not only did he enjoy gambling, he also facilitated the habits of others. And today he'd been very generous to Stephen. In short, his generosity meant that Stephen now owed Schmitt one thousand pounds.

"I think I might fold now," declared Oleg, puffing on his unsavory pipe. "I need to rest. I'm going to the theater this evening."

"You can't fold!" protested Stephen, his heart starting to race as he reached for the last of his gin. "You're my partner! We're about to have a winning streak!"

"Winning streak?" Schmitt snorted. He placed his heavy forearms on the table and stared at Stephen. "You mean like the Spanish Armada?"

"I am sorry, Bellasis"—Count Sikorsky rubbed his bespectacled face—"but I have no choice. I'm out of funds and I already owe Mr. Schmitt from last week."

"Two hundred guineas," said Schmitt. "Plus the three hundred for today. When will you pay?"

"We mustn't bore the others," said the Count, clearly reluctant to share details of the state he was in.

"When will you pay?" said Schmitt.

"Friday. And now I really must go." Oleg nodded.

"Well, if you're off, Oleg," said Black, "I may as well make tracks myself. It is not often a chap finds himself seven hundred pounds up on the day." He laughed, and scraping his wooden chair across the stone floor he rose rather unsteadily to his feet. They had been sitting around the table for the past three hours, and it took a while before the blood started to circulate through his limbs. "I am not sure I've ever had quite such a success before." He gathered up his money, pushing the pile of large notes into a bundle. "Bad luck," he said, patting Stephen on the back. "See you next week?"

"No!" said Stephen loudly. There was a trace of panic in his voice, which they could all hear. As if to save a situation that was already lost, Stephen let out a bold laugh. "Please, no!" He put his hand in the air, waving it jocularly, trying to take control. "Come on, can't we play one more round? Surely? It'll only take twenty minutes. Oleg, you can go straight to the theater from here. Black, you can't just leave the table, you have to give a chap a chance to win back some of his money!" He looked from one man to the next, his small dark eyes pleading. "Just one more round. It's not much to ask..."

Stephen's voice trailed off. He was aware of how pathetic he sounded but he couldn't stop himself. He had to do something. They were getting up now, leaving the table, leaving him here in the dark basement with Schmitt. And there was no telling what the man might do. Stephen had owed him money in the past, but it had never been as large a sum as this, and he'd always managed to pay Schmitt back.

He remained seated as Captain Black and Count Sikorsky ascended the staircase, their feet on the wooden steps sounding unnaturally loud in the echoing space. The wax from the cheap brass candelabra slowly dripped onto the table in front of him.

"So, your lordship," said Schmitt sarcastically, getting out of his chair and stretching his large frame.

"Yes?" Stephen shook his head defiantly. He was not going to be intimidated by this frightful man. He had connections, he reminded himself, friends in high places.

"There remains the question of one thousand pounds."

Stephen winced, waiting for the man to crack his knuckles or hammer his fist down on the table. But Schmitt did neither. Instead, he paced the stone floor, his hobnailed boots clicking as he went.

"We are both gentlemen," began Schmitt. Stephen resisted the temptation to point out that perhaps Schmitt, as a moneylender with a dented head, was not. "I am also a pleasant fellow, and I'm prepared to be reasonable."

"Thank you." Stephen's reply was barely audible.

"So you have two days to get the money. Two days to deliver it to me." He paused, and with a sudden gesture smashed the empty gin bottle on the table right in front of Stephen, shattering the glass. Stephen leaped out of his seat. "Two days," Schmitt hissed, his odd-shaped skull bearing down on Stephen, the broken bottle still in his hand. "Two days," he repeated, bringing the jagged glass edge closer and closer to Stephen's neck.

Stephen ran out of there as quickly as a small, fat man full of gin possibly could, and he kept on running until he reached the corner of Sloane Street. It was only then, while he stood, panting and huffing, leaning against a wall for support, that he realized something else was wrong. Two ladies taking a late-afternoon stroll avoided him. A man drew near and then quickly crossed the road. He ran his fingertips over his face. It felt wet. He took out his handkerchief and dabbed at his skin. It came away covered in blood. A nearby shopwindow told him that there were cuts all over his face, from tiny splinters of shattered glass.

The next day things looked a little better. Or at least Stephen's face did, as he checked himself in the glass. It was only a few small cuts, he told himself, nothing too bad, nothing too remarkable— which was fortunate, as he was about to go, cap in hand again, to his brother. The last thing he needed was to look remotely disordered.

Downstairs in the bleak dining room of their Harley Street home, the atmosphere between Stephen and Grace was frosty.

Neither of them really enjoyed living there. The house had been a wedding present from Grace's mother, but, like most things associated with Grace, it was now a little faded and shabby around the edges. With so many developments and so much building in the capital, it sometimes seemed to him that one day Harley Street would be left behind. And the house itself was narrow, dark, and always cold. No matter the weather outside, there was still a chill in the air; whether this was to do with Grace's parsimony when it came to lighting fires or whether it was the lack of staff to keep those fires lit, the net result was the same. Guests had a tendency to shiver as they crossed the threshold. Not that they entertained much. Grace occasionally had some ladies up from the parish, or from one of her charitable committees, but usually Stephen dined out and Grace ate alone.

They survived with a skeleton staff: a cook and a kitchen maid, a butler who doubled as valet, a head housemaid who dressed Grace, and two other maids who seemed to leave with numbing regularity. Grace told herself this was because of the low wages they offered, but she'd come to suspect that Stephen might be behind several of the hurried departures. The truth was, they couldn't really afford a London life, and if they'd had any sense they would have sold the house years ago and been content in Hampshire, saving the money they had to spend on their curates. But then they had no sense. Or Stephen had no sense, thought Grace wryly; no sense, no ambition, and, heaven knew, no intention of performing his parish duties, light as they were. She ate her unappetizing breakfast. Grace always prided herself on not having breakfast in bed like the other married ladies she knew, but today she rather regretted it. At least her bedroom was warm. She picked up the envelope on the table.

She did not raise her eyes from her daughter's letter when her husband arrived downstairs. She knew he'd been out gambling the day before and that he'd probably lost. She could tell by the way he sighed when he sat down. If he'd won, he would have clapped his hands and rubbed his palms together as he walked into the room. There would have been a spring in his step. Instead, he could barely be bothered to eat. He lifted the lid of the chafing dish and stared down at the dried-out scrambled eggs.

"Emma is well," said Grace, eventually, lifting her eyes to his face and stiffening with shock. "Good God, what happened to you?"

"Nothing, nothing. A window broke when I was standing near it. How are the children?" He helped himself to a sliver of luke-warm bacon.

"She says Freddie has a cough."

"Good, good." He slumped into his chair.

"Why is it good?" Grace looked down the length of the dark table. "Why is it good if the boy is not well?"

Stephen looked at her for a moment. "I was thinking I might visit my brother today."

"Does this have something to do with how you spent yesterday afternoon?" Grace said, rising from her chair.

"It wasn't one of my best." He spoke without lifting his eyes, as if he were voicing some inner thought without reference to his wife.

To Grace, this did not bode well. As a rule Stephen never admitted to defeat or failure of any kind. In fact, he would seldom admit to gambling. "Exactly how bad was it?" she asked, thinking there wasn't much left in her depleted jewelry box that they could sell. Thank heaven she'd already paid John's rent on his rooms in Albany, though why he wouldn't live with them in Harley Street she simply could not understand.

"Nothing to worry about." Stephen had regained control of himself, and now he smiled blandly at his wife. "I'll sort it all out this afternoon."

"Sort out your face first."

When Stephen arrived at the house in Belgrave Square he paused before making his presence known. Standing on the wide paved street, staring up the steps at the shiny black door flanked by white Doric columns, he shook his head at the iniquity of it all, singing the same refrain as always in his head. Why, by some

fault of birth, did Peregrine get to live in such splendid surroundings, while he had to contend with his own cramped and grubby
house? No wonder he gambled, Stephen thought. Who wouldn't
gamble when life had dealt them such a bitter blow? Was it any
wonder he sought comfort in the embrace of women with loose
morals? Was it his fault if he was addicted to the thrill and danger
of the game?

Stephen knocked on the door. It was answered by a young liveried footman who ushered him into the library to wait for his
brother.

"What an unexpected pleasure!" declared Peregrine, walking
in some five unhurried minutes later. "I was just about to head out
to White's."

"Then I'm glad to have caught you," said Stephen. He was not
quite sure how to open the conversation, even though he knew
only too well that his brother already expected what was coming.

"Whatever's happened to your face?" Peregrine stared at the
spattering of small scabs across Stephen's cheeks.

"I had a bad experience at the barber's," replied Stephen. It
seemed better than the broken window, but they both knew it was
untrue.

"Remind me never to use the fellow." Peregrine chortled, sitting down at his desk. "So, to what do I owe this honor?"

They both knew he was teasing. Stephen only ever wanted
money from him, but Peregrine needed to hear his brother say it
out loud. If he was going to give him anything, he demanded that
the maximum humiliation should precede it.

"It seems I'm in a spot of bother," began Stephen, bowing his
head. He hoped if he displayed remorse, or made a show of gen-
uflection a little in front of his brother, Peregrine might be more
generous.

"How much bother?"

"One thousand pounds' worth of bother."

'A *thousand* pounds?' Peregrine was genuinely shocked. Everyone enjoyed a flutter now and again. His old friend the Duke of
Wellington was easily capable of dropping more than a thousand

in one night playing whist at Crockford's, but he could afford to do so. Really, Stephen had lost a thousand pounds? He raised his eyebrows. He had not been expecting such an enormous sum. Quite apart from the fact that he had already given his brother almost as much quite recently, after luncheon at Lymington.

"I wouldn't normally ask..."

"Yes, but the thing is you *do* normally ask," interrupted Peregrine. "In fact you ask continually. I cannot remember when you last came to my house *without* asking for money." He paused. "No."

"No?" Stephen was confused.

"No. I won't give it to you. Is that clear enough?" Was Stephen hearing correctly? "Not this time."

"What?" Stephen was incredulous. The feigned humility drained out of his face to be replaced by simple fury. "But you have to! You have to! I'm your brother, and I need it! I must have it!"

"You should have thought of that before you gambled it away. You played with money you did not have, and this is the result."

"I didn't gamble it away! That wasn't what happened at all!" Stephen's plump hands were clenched into fists. This was not the outcome he had imagined. His brain was whirring. If he hadn't gambled, what was his excuse? What could he say had happened to the money?

"We both know that is a lie." Peregrine felt quite calm. His brother was intolerable, devoid of the slightest trace of responsibility, a disgrace to his blood. Why should he keep financing the wastage of his life?

"How dare you accuse me of lying?" Stephen puffed himself up. "I am a man of the cloth!"

"I say you are lying because it's the truth." Peregrine shook his head. "I will not pay any more of your debts. You have a decent income from your inheritance and the Church, or you should have, and your wife provides you with additional funds. You must simply learn to live within your means."

"Live within my means!" Stephen was ready to explode. "How

dare you? Who do you think you are? Just because you're two years older than me you take the title, the house, the estates, and all the money—"

"Not quite all."

"Do you ever think how unfair it is? Do you?" Stephen was spluttering. "And you have the audacity to tell me to live within my means?"

"Life is not fair," agreed Peregrine. "I will grant you that. But it is the system into which we were both born. Nobody ever told you to expect any more than you were given. There are many men who would think it a fine thing to be a cleric living in a large rectory, without having to do a stroke of work from January to December."

"Well, one day John will inherit." Stephen raised his chin triumphantly. "My son, not yours, will have everything."

This was a low blow, but Peregrine decided to rise above it. "And when he does I would remind you that, by definition, you will be dead and so it will be too late for him to take over the funding of his father's vices."

Stephen stood staring, his teeth gritted and his scabbed face bright pink. He was so angry he was at a loss for words. "Well, well," he said at last. "Good day to you, brother!" He marched out, slamming the door hard enough to make a little sprinkle of plaster fall from the wall.

Outside, on the landing, Stephen stopped for a moment. He had no idea what to do next. Peregrine had not followed him out of the room. He had not run after him and pushed a collection of notes into his hand. What was he supposed to do? He had no way of paying his debts. As for Schmitt, even the thought of him made Stephen shiver. He paced up and down, wondering if he should go back inside and beg, tell his brother how sorry he was, appeal to his better nature. He needed a plan. Should he stay? Or should he go? He tugged at his chin, deep in thought.

The sound of laughter rang out, a woman's laughter. He looked across the gleaming stairwell. It was coming from Caroline's sitting room. Had she heard their argument, he wondered? Was she laughing at him? She was definitely laughing. Was she delighting in his downfall? Stephen crossed the gallery, toward the door. There she was, that hateful woman, giggling away, and was that a man's voice he could hear? Who could possibly be entertaining Lady Brockenhurst so much? He knelt down to put his ear right next to the keyhole. Then the door opened.

"My God! Stephen! You nearly gave me a heart attack!" Caroline clutched her chest in shock. "What on earth are you doing down there?"

"Nothing," said Stephen, standing up with some difficulty, his eyes narrowing. Who was that dark-haired fellow? He looked familiar. The young man's cheeks were flushed, as if he'd been caught out. Caroline was still looking at him. "I was just..." His voice trailed off.

"Do you remember Mr. Pope? He was here the other evening," said Caroline, taking a step back and proudly presenting her guest.

"Yes, I do," nodded Stephen. He remembered the fellow, all right. This was the young man who had been seated next to her in the place of honor. He was the man she had paraded around the party. He was working at something with that pompous fool Trenchard. And now here he was again.

"Charles has just been telling me all about his plans. He has a cotton mill in Manchester." She was beaming.

It seemed very strange to Stephen. "Are you interested in Mancunian cotton mills?" he said.

"Lady Brockenhurst has given her patronage to my efforts." Charles smiled, as if this explained anything.

"She has?" Stephen looked from one to the other.

The Countess nodded. "Yes," she said. But she did not elaborate. Instead, she ushered Charles toward the head of the stairs. "And I have delayed him quite long enough." She laughed lightly, sweeping past Stephen to follow Charles down the stairs. "I have so enjoyed our conversation, Mr. Pope. I look forward to our next meeting." In the hall, the waiting footman gave Charles his coat and held the door as he left. Caroline glanced up, but rather than rejoin her brother-in-law, she walked into the dining room and closed the door. It was some minutes before Stephen came down. He had the nagging suspicion that what he had just witnessed and his need for money could somehow be combined to his advantage, but he had not yet formulated how.

When Charles Pope walked out of Brockenhurst House into the bright sunshine of Belgrave Square, he was excited. His meeting with the Countess had gone well, and she had promised him more money than he could possibly have hoped for, double the amount she had originally proposed. Of course the burning question was why? But then why had Mr. Trenchard been so generous in advancing the deposit for the mill in the first place, on such advantageous terms? Now his new patroness would allow him to establish his cotton sources in India and expand the business in a way that he'd thought would take another decade. Again, why? It was very puzzling. He felt truly honored to have been invited to Lady Brockenhurst's house, and she had made him feel welcome. But he could not help wondering what he could possibly have done to deserve such good fortune.

"Someone looks terribly pleased with himself."

Charles spun around and squinted into the sun. "You?"

"Me?" The girl smiled.

"Lady Maria Grey, if I am not mistaken?" He had asked after her at the party, pointing her out to their hostess, and so he knew her rank. It was a blow. If he had hoped she was within his grasp, he knew at once that she was not. Still, it was good to see her again. He couldn't deny it.

"The very one. And you are Mr. Pope." She was wearing a tight, buttoned, dark blue jacket over her wide petticoats and a bonnet trimmed with flowers of the same color. He thought he had never set eyes on a lovelier sight. "And why, may I inquire, are you so full of the joys of spring?" She laughed pleasantly.

"Just business. You'd find it very dull," said Charles.

"You don't know that. Why do men always presume that women are only interested in gossip and fashion?" They stared at each other. There was a slight cough. Charles turned to see a woman in black. She must be Lady Maria's maid, he thought. Of course. She'd never be allowed out unchaperoned.

"Forgive me," replied Charles, bringing his hands together as if in supplication. "I meant no offense. I simply didn't think the financing of a cotton supply would be particularly diverting."

"I shall be the judge of that, Mr. Pope." She smiled. "So, tell me some more about your mill and your cotton, and if I find the subject tiresome, I shall stifle a yawn behind my gloved hand and then you'll realize that you have failed. How would that be?" She cocked her head to one side.

Charles smiled. Maria Grey was unlike any woman he'd met. She was beautiful and charming, certainly, but also forthright, challenging, and possibly rather stubborn. "I will endeavor to meet the challenge," replied Charles. "Are you on your way somewhere?"

"I'm going to the new London Library; I was thinking I might join. Mr. Carlyle is a friend of Mama's, and he waxes lyrical over its merits, which, according to him, are vastly superior to those of the library at the British Museum, although I find that hard to believe. Ryan is accompanying me."

She nodded at the woman with her, but Miss Ryan did not seem very comfortable with the way things were progressing. At last she spoke. "M'lady—"

"What is it?" But the maid was silent, so Maria took her to one side. She returned in a moment, smiling. "She thinks Mama will disapprove of our being seen walking and talking together."

"Will she?"

"Probably." But this answer did not seem to indicate that the proposed adventure was not going to happen. "Where are you headed?"

"I was on my way back to my office."

"And where might that be?"

"Bishopsgate. In the City."

"Then we shall walk with you for part of the journey. The library is at forty-nine Pall Mall, so we won't take you out of your way. And while we go, you shall explain to us the world of cotton and exactly what you're planning to do in India, in as entertaining a manner as possible. Then we shall part and continue about our business."

And so, for the next half an hour, as the three of them walked through the Green Park, Charles Pope explained the intricacies of the cotton trade. He talked about how he planned to expand, and after that about a new loom that had an automatic braking system that would shut down as soon as the threads broke. And all the time Maria was watching his excitement and listening to the fervor in his voice and enjoying the way his lips moved. By the time they reached the corner of the Green Park and Piccadilly, Maria knew almost everything there was to know about the harvesting, supplying, and weaving of cotton.

"You win!" she declared, spinning her lilac parasol on her shoulder.

"Win what?" Charles was confused.

"I did not have to stifle a single yawn. You were both informative and amusing. Bravo!" She laughed, clapping her gloved hands. He made a bow. "I should love to come and see your offices for myself one day," she said.

"I'm afraid if your mama did not think we should walk together"—he looked across at Ryan, who was standing with a stony face—"I'd find it hard to believe that she would think a visit to Bishopsgate quite the—"

"Nonsense. You say Lady Brockenhurst has taken an interest in your company, so why shouldn't I come and see it for myself?"

"I don't see the connection." Charles frowned.

But Maria had spoken without thinking. Now she stumbled over her reply. "I'm . . . engaged to her nephew."

"Ah." How foolish he was to feel disappointed. To feel worse than disappointed, as if he had lost a pearl of great price. What was he thinking? That someone as beautiful and clever as Maria Grey would have no suitors? Of course she was engaged. And anyway, she was the daughter of a noble family and he was a nobody, the son of no one. But still all he could say was, "Ah."

"Perhaps Lady Brockenhurst and I could visit you together," continued Maria a little too brightly.

"Nothing would give me more pleasure." Charles Pope smiled and raised his hat. "To work," he declared, then he bid them good day, turned, and walked off up Piccadilly.

John Bellasis was in Mr. Pimm's Chop House at number 3 Poultry, sipping a tankard of ale, when his father marched through the door and sat down opposite him. John had been visiting a broker friend who had an office around the corner in Old Jewry, as he did most Tuesdays. He was already working out ways to expand and invest his future fortune. It was important to be seen to go through the motions, he told himself, so that those to whom he currently owed money would have confidence they might eventually be paid.

"There you are," announced Stephen.

"Good day, Father. How did you know where to find me?"

"You're always here," said Stephen, leaning in. "So." He slapped his hands hard on the table. "He said no."

"Who?" John put down his pint and pushed away his plate of well-chewed mutton bones.

"Your uncle, of course." Stephen tugged at his bands. "What am I to do?" He knew his tone was becoming shrill, but he was panicking. "I only have two days . . . or rather, one day now."

"How much did you ask him for?" John didn't need to guess the reason for his father's distress. It was always about money and bad debts.

"A thousand pounds." Stephen looked down at John's plate to see if there was anything worth picking at. His fingers hovered over the bones but eventually plumped for a cold buttered carrot. "I owe Schmitt."

"Schmitt? That brute!" John raised his eyebrows and sighed. "Then you had better pay him."

"I know." Stephen nodded, chewing the carrot. "Can you think of anyone who could help me?"

"You mean a moneylender?"

"Of course I mean a moneylender. If I could borrow from them to pay Schmitt, that would give me a few days to negotiate a loan, or something. There'll be an interest payment, but if I can borrow even five hundred then I might be able to buy myself some extra time."

"I know a few. But I am not sure you could get that amount of cash so quickly. Why can't you go to a bank?" John drummed his manicured fingers on the table. "They know who we are, they know the family has a fortune and that eventually it will come to me. Couldn't you borrow against that?"

"I've tried before." Stephen was holding nothing back. "They think my brother is too healthy and the wait will be a long one."

John shrugged. "I do know a Polish chap, Emile Kruchinsky, who lives near the East End. He could get you the money in time."

"What does he charge?"

"Fifty percent."

"*Fifty!*" Stephen puffed his cheeks out as he watched the waitress bend over to clear the small wooden booth opposite. Her plump backside swayed left and right as she wiped the table. "That's a bit steep."

"It's the going rate for emergencies," replied John. "They have you over a barrel and they know it. Is there really nothing left to sell?"

"Only Harley Street, and that's mortgaged to the hilt. I doubt we'd walk away with a penny piece."

"Then you must convince the bank or visit the Pole," John said, and sniffed.

"Do you know whom I saw in Belgrave Square today, at your uncle's house?" Stephen said, frowning. "That man, Charles Pope."

"Trenchard's protégé? The one who was at the party?" John looked confused. "Why was he there again?"

"Who knows?" nodded Stephen. "But he was. He and your aunt were laughing away, in her private sitting room of all places. I caught them as he came out. It seemed very rum to me. The boy blushed when I saw him. He really blushed."

"You don't suppose they were enjoying an assignation?" John joked.

"Good gracious, no." Stephen chuckled as he leaned back into the banquette. "But there is something going on there, let me tell you. She's investing in his business."

"She is?" John sat up. Now that money had been mentioned, he was suddenly interested. "Why would she take an interest in any business, let alone business with an unknown man from nowhere?"

"Exactly," agreed his father. "And they were very friendly, for two people who have just met. Do you remember the way she paraded him around the rooms at her soirée? It was almost unseemly. A woman in her position, and such a young man...."

"Who is he? Does anyone know anything about his background? There must be something we can turn up."

"Not that I can tell. I don't like the look of him myself, and I certainly don't like the hold he has over my Lady Brockenhurst. She's making a fool of herself."

"Do you know how much she's invested?"

"Well, young Mr. Pope looked exceptionally pleased with himself when he left," mused Stephen. "So I imagine it must be a good sum. Why on earth is she giving money to a stranger when my dear brother will not even help out his own flesh and blood?"

"Exactly." John nodded. They both sat at the wooden table in silence for a moment, contemplating the injustice of the situation.

"We need to discover who this man is," said Stephen eventually.

"I think I may be able to help you," said John.

"How?" Stephen looked at his son across the table.

"I'm quite friendly with the younger Mrs. Trenchard," John ventured. "She told me that her father-in-law has known Pope for a while."

His father was looking at him. "How friendly?"

"I bumped into her at the National Gallery and we had some tea."

"Indeed?" Stephen knew his son only too well.

John shook his head. "It was all perfectly respectable. She was there with her maid. I could ask her what else she knows."

"The maid?"

"I meant Mrs. Trenchard, but perhaps that's not a bad idea.

Servants always find out everything. And whatever is going on with this Charles Pope, I want to know about it. All we have to go on is that he's a business friend of that clodhopper James Trenchard, and now, suddenly, my fastidious aunt is throwing money at him, money that should one day, given a cold breeze in the right direction, be ours. Is it so unreasonable that we should want to know why?"

Stephen nodded vigorously. "The answer must lie with the Trenchards."

"And when we unravel that, we can trace the connection with my aunt."

Stephen nodded again. "There has to be some history between them. Between Mr. Pope and Caroline, or possibly between him and Peregrine. And if we find it out, then maybe, as Caroline is being so free with her finances at the moment, she'll pay to keep that information secret."

"Are you suggesting we blackmail my aunt?" John looked at his father. For once, he was almost shocked.

"I most certainly am. And you will start us off by learning the secrets of the Trenchard household." Stephen's right leg began to bounce up and down under the table. This could be the answer to all his prayers.

Two days later, John walked into the Horse and Groom public house in Groom Place. It might have been only a few minutes' walk from Eaton Square and the grand houses of Belgravia, but it was a different world.

He had managed to arrange a brief meeting with Speer on the pavement opposite the Trenchards'. On the pretext of planning another rendezvous with Susan, he'd picked the maid's brains as to where the members of the Trenchard household enjoyed spending their hours off. Of course she knew he was up to something, and, for a moment, he'd contemplated asking her to do a little digging on his behalf, but he suspected she and Susan shared most of their conversations and he did not want Susan privy to too much of his business quite yet. She was delightful, of course, but the speed with which she had fallen into bed made him wary. She was clearly not a cautious woman, and he was not sure how far he could trust her. Eventually, the maid suggested that if he wanted some inside help, he should start with Mr. Turton, the butler, and he always drank at the Horse and Groom around the corner. John was surprised at first. The butler was usually the best paid and therefore the most loyal in a household. But he decided Speer must know what she was talking about.

As he walked into the public house, the smell of spilled beer and damp sawdust was overwhelming. John was well used to some of the seamier parts of town, but even he found the Horse and Groom a little too much for his taste.

He ordered himself a pint of beer and stood in the corner with his back to the wall, waiting. Speer had told him that Mr. Turton always looked in for a quick one at around five, and sure enough, on the dot of five, when the clock over the bar was actually striking, a tall, slim, gray-faced man wearing a black coat and shiny black shoes walked through the door. He looked quite out of place in this establishment, yet as he pulled up a chair the barman walked over with a bottle of gin and poured from it into a small glass without a single word being exchanged. Turton nodded. He may not have been an ebullient sort of fellow, but he was obviously a regular here and a creature of habit.

"Mr. Turton, isn't it?" asked John.

Turton knocked back the glass of gin then looked up at him. "Might be." Close up, he looked weary. "Do I know you?"

"No," said John, sitting down opposite him. "But I understand we might be able to do business."

"You and me?" Turton was slightly unnerved. He was in the habit of selling on the odd side of beef, rolling out some good cheese, or a few nice bottles of claret that nobody would ever notice. He and the cook, Mrs. Babbage, had an understanding. She would overorder slightly, nothing too drastic—some extra pheasants to be sent up from Glanville, a touch more mutton than they would need, and he would sell on the extras. He was well known in the pub; he'd sit there from five to six of an afternoon and do a little business of his own. Naturally, he gave Mrs. Babbage a cut. Not perhaps as much as she deserved, but he was the one taking the risk; all she had to do was make a deliberate mistake with the orders and nobody could ever build a charge on that. He'd worked for the Trenchards for almost twenty-five years, joined them not long after their daughter died, so they trusted him. The only person he really had to keep an eye on was Mrs. Frant. She was an irritating busybody, always poking her nose in. He and Mrs. Babbage had a good thing going, and he was determined that the housekeeper wouldn't get the chance to destroy it. Now he checked John up and down, taking in the expensive clothes and the gold chain of a pocket watch. He did not look like a man in need of a haunch of ham.

"I doubt you and I would have much business in common, sir," he said.

"Oh," said John, "but that's where you are wrong." He took a sip of his ale. "I am looking for some help in a private matter, and you could be just the right man for the job. There would be a small reward, of course."

"How small?"

John smiled. "That rather depends on the results."

Which got Turton's attention. It was all very well selling a cut of beef here and there, but some proper money, a nest egg, that would be very welcome indeed. So he allowed this young gentleman to buy him another gin while he listened carefully to what he was after.

Forty minutes later, the two of them walked out of the Horse and Groom and headed back toward Eaton Square. Turton asked John to wait for him at the corner of the mews. He would be back in a few minutes. He had the perfect person, he said: someone else who had worked in the household for years, and who was always partial to extra money. "She's a woman who knows what's good for her," he said before he disappeared around the corner. "You mark my words."

John stood on the street, underneath a gas lamp, with his collar turned up and his hat pulled down. This was all too close to the

Trenchards' home for comfort. He wished the man would hurry up. The last thing he needed was to bump into Susan, or Trenchard himself for that matter.

Eventually, Turton returned with a stout-looking party by his side. She was wearing a black bonnet and an expensive maroon lace shawl. "Sir," Turton said, his hand outstretched. "This is Miss Ellis. Mrs. Trenchard's maid. She's been working in the household for thirty years. What she doesn't know about the comings and goings of this family isn't worth worrying about." It was irritating to Turton that he couldn't manage this commission without the help of Miss Ellis, but he knew he couldn't. He and Mr. Trenchard got along well enough, but they were not confidants by any stretch of the imagination, while Miss Ellis...She and Mrs. Trenchard were as thick as thieves. It was a wonder that the mistress never suspected that all Ellis needed to betray her secrets was a sufficient offer, and now, with any luck, they were going to get one.

"Ah, Miss Ellis." John nodded slowly. He was annoyed that Speer hadn't steered him toward Ellis in the first place. He suspected Speer resented Ellis's superiority within the household, and in this he was quite right. Now he would have to pay enough money to keep them both happy, which was tedious, but Turton was correct. A valet or a maid could winkle out a family's secrets quicker than anyone. He had heard tell that half the major powers paid valets and maids to spy for them. He smiled at Ellis, who was waiting in silence. "I wonder if we might be able to come to some arrangement?"

.6.

A Spy in Our Midst

James Trenchard was sitting at a particularly fine Empire desk with ormolu mounts in his office in the Gray's Inn Road. On the first floor, above a firm of solicitors and at the top of a sweeping staircase, it was a large paneled room with some serious pictures and impressive furniture. Without ever saying it, James had a sort of vision of himself as a gentleman businessman. Most of his contemporaries would have thought of this phrase as an oxymoron, but that was his view and he liked his surroundings to reflect it. There were drawings of Cubitt Town on display, carefully arranged to advantage on a round table in a corner of the room, and a beautiful portrait of Sophia hung above the fireplace. Painted during their stay in Brussels, it captured his daughter at her most beguiling; youthful and confident, staring straight at the onlooker, she was wearing a cream dress with her hair arranged in the style of that time. It was a good likeness, very good really, and a vivid reminder of the girl he knew. Probably for this reason, Anne refused to hang it in Eaton Square as it made her too sad, but James liked to look on his darling lost daughter; he liked to remember her in moments of rather uncharacteristic quiet solitude.

Today, however, he found himself contemplating the letter on his desk. It had been delivered when his secretary was with him, but he wanted to read it in private. Now, he turned it over and over in his plump hands, scrutinizing the florid script and the thick cream paper. He did not need to open it to know who sent it, as he had received an identical letter to tell him he was on the application list for the Athenaeum. This would be the answer, from

Edward Magrath, the secretary of the club. He held his breath—he so desperately wanted to be accepted, he scarcely dared to read it. He knew the Athenaeum was not most people's idea of a fashionable club. The food was notoriously bad, and in Society it was seen as a London stopping place for an assortment of clerics and academics. But it was still a place for gentlemen to meet, no one could deny it; with the difference that, under their slightly revolutionary rules the club also admitted men of eminence in science, literature, or the arts. They even had members in public service, without significant birth or educational requirements.

This policy made the membership far more diverse than the clubs of St. James's. That was how William Cubitt had been accepted, and hadn't James helped him and his brother to build half of fashionable London? Wasn't that a public service? William had put him up for membership months ago, and when they'd heard nothing, James had pestered him to chase the nomination. He knew he wasn't ideal member material, even given their more liberal rules—to be the son of a market stall trader was not the sort of lineage much admired by the bastions of the Establishment, but would God be so cruel as to deny him? He knew he would never have a chance of joining White's or Boodle's or Brooks's, or any of the other really smart places, but didn't he deserve this? Besides, he'd heard that the club needed cash, which he had, and plenty of it. Of course there was a risk he would be snubbed and sneered at, and Anne would never understand what such a place could give him that his home did not, but still, he needed that sense of belonging to the Great World, and if all he had to offer was money, then so be it. Let money be enough.

In fairness to him, there was a part of James, if a small part admittedly, that knew his ambitions were nonsense. That the grudging approval of fools and dandies would add nothing of real value to his life, and yet...he could not control his secret passion for acceptance. It was the engine that drove him, and he must travel as far and as fast as he could.

The door opened and his secretary came in. "Mr. Pope is outside, sir. He would like the honor of an interview."

"Would he? Then bring him in."

"I hope I don't disturb you, Mr. Trenchard," said Charles, walking briskly round the door, "but your clerk said you were in, and I have some news." His smile was as warm and his manner as charming as ever.

"Of course." James nodded, putting the letter down on his desk. He stood to shake the young man's hand, wondering at the pleasure it gave him just to look upon his grandson. "Won't you sit down?"

"I won't, if you don't mind. I'm too excited."

"Oh?"

"Lady Brockenhurst has been kind enough to write and tell me how much she and her husband wish to invest. And I believe I have all the money I need." He was obviously near to bursting, but he restrained himself. He was a fine young fellow, no doubt about it.

"Nobody has all the money they need." James smiled, but he was very torn. Seeing the chap so full of energy and enthusiasm, his dreams on the verge of coming true, he found it hard to be anything but pleased. Still, he couldn't delude himself. The strangeness of the case—a great lady in high Society investing a fortune in the business interests of an obscure nobody—was bound to draw comment, and combined with the inexplicable attentions Lady Brockenhurst had showered on Charles in public the other night, it could not be long before someone put two and two together.

Charles hadn't finished. "With your investment, sir, and hers, it means I have all I need to pay off the mortgage, fund the new looms, retool the factory, and generally improve our output. I can plan my visit to India, organize the supplies of raw cotton, appoint an agent out there, and then sit back and watch as our production moves to the forefront of the industry. Not that I will sit back, of course," he added with a laugh.

"Of course not." James smiled, too. Inwardly, he was cursing that he had not undertaken to fund the venture fully in the first place, thereby removing the need for the Countess to intervene.

He could easily have done it, but he'd thought it would make things too smooth for Charles, that the boy ought to learn something about doing business in the modern world, but now he could have kicked himself. Then again, Lady Brockenhurst would have found some other way into Charles's life. Once she knew who he was, nothing would have kept her away for long. Why oh why had Anne felt she had to tell her? But even as he asked himself this same question for the thousandth time, he understood they were on the path of no return. Their fall would not be long in coming now. "Well"—he chuckled pleasantly—"I confess I'm a little surprised. When I heard the other night that the Countess was taking an interest in your endeavors, I asked myself how likely that was, and I suppose I doubted that she would make good on her promise. But she has. I was wrong, and I am heartily glad I was wrong."

Charles nodded eagerly. "I'm going to stock up on raw cotton as and when I can get it, until I have enough for a year's production. That done, I'll sail for India and put the last piece of the puzzle in place. Then I believe I shall be all set."

"All set, indeed. And you still have no clue as to the reason for Lady Brockenhurst's interest? She never said anything about why she wanted to help? It seems so odd."

"I agree." Charles shook his head in disbelief. "She likes me. She 'approves' of me, whatever that means. She asks me to her house. But she's never explained how she came to hear of me in the first place."

"Well, well. One mustn't look a gift horse in the mouth."

"No. And I'll find out the truth one day. She did say that I reminded her of someone she was once fond of. But that can't be the real reason, can it?" He raised his eyebrows at the very idea.

"I shouldn't have thought so. There must be more to it than that." What a good liar I am, thought James. I did not suspect it of myself, but clearly I can look into a man's eyes and lie to him as easily as I can write my own name. We learn about ourselves with every day that passes.

Absentmindedly, he picked up the letter from the desk and opened it. It was indeed from Edward Magrath. He skimmed the first couple of paragraphs to the last sentence and there it was: "And we take great pleasure in accepting you as a member of the Athenaeum." He smiled, but rather wryly, as he wondered how long it would be before they came to him and asked for his resignation.

"Good news, sir?" Charles was watching him from his position in front of the chimneypiece.

"I've joined the Athenaeum," he said, dropping the letter onto the desk.

What a bitter irony it was—just as he had finally transformed himself into an insider, of a sort at least, it was all about to come crashing down around him. Caroline Brockenhurst would never keep her word now. Or if she did, others would guess the truth. She must have told her husband for a start, for him to agree to the investment. In this he was quite wrong, as it happens. She had only to tell Lord Brockenhurst that she wished them to support young Pope and he was happy to let her lead the way, as he had always been in every undertaking. But James was right. If the news did get out it would be all around London in a day, and then Sophia would be branded a slut, and he, James Trenchard, would be the father of a strumpet. Anne's pity for the Countess would be their undoing.

With the sword of Damocles hanging over his head, James Trenchard decided he might as well make the most of this moment, as it was sure not to last. So he invited Charles to luncheon at his new club, by way of celebration, and they headed out into the bright sunshine. As he sat by his grandson's side in the carriage, Quirk at the reins, on the way to Pall Mall, James could not help thinking that this might have been one of the happiest days of his life. After all, here he was, about to enter the hallowed halls of what would certainly be the smartest club he would ever have a chance of belonging to, with Sophia's son by his side. At that thought, he allowed himself a smile.

Walking into the grand hall with its splendid staircase dominating the space, its marble floors, its statues, its white and gilded columns, James's heart beat a shade faster. The stateliness that had been so threatening before, when he had come as a guest of William Cubitt, suddenly seemed transformed into the welcome of an old friend.

"Excuse me, sir," came the voice of an officious-looking man dressed entirely in black save for a white shirt. With his pale gray hair and sharp blue eyes, he reminded James of Robespierre. "May I help you, sir?"

"My name is Trenchard," said James as he fumbled in his pocket for the letter. "James Trenchard." He flapped the paper in the man's face. His confidence seemed suddenly to have deserted him. "I am a new member here."

"Ah yes, Mr. Trenchard." The man smiled and bowed politely. "Welcome to the club. Will you be taking luncheon with us today?"

"Absolutely," confirmed James, rubbing his hands together.

"With Mr. Cubitt, sir?"

"Mr. Cubitt? No." James was confused. Why did they think William would be there?

The club servant was very important. He frowned slightly, to demonstrate a slight dismay. "It is customary for a new member's first luncheon to be with the person who proposed him, sir."

His superiority was becoming hard to take. "Is it a rule?" asked James, his smile hardening on his lips.

"It is not a rule, sir. Just a custom."

James felt that old familiar knot of anger starting to form in his chest. In one way all he wanted was to be mistaken for a member of this society, but in another he wished that he could grind the lot of them to dust. "Then it is a custom we must set aside for today. I am here with my"—he paused and gave a quick cough—"with my guest, Mr. Pope."

"Of course, sir. Would you like to go straight into the dining room, or would you like to sit in one of the drawing rooms first?"

James was regaining control. "I think we'll eat straightaway. Thank you." He smiled at Charles, back at the center of his own life.

They were escorted through the hall, past the staircase, and into the dining room beyond. With large sash windows overlooking the lush green of Waterloo Gardens, the room was airy and spacious, and by the time they had been shown to a table in the right-hand corner and asked if they would like anything to drink, James was beginning to feel quite mellow.

He ordered two glasses of champagne and laid the large white linen napkin across his lap. This really was delightful, a long-held dream come true, and as the waiter poured the wine James took in the rest of the room: the groups of men lunching together, the large vases of flowers, the paintings of racehorses hanging in a row along a side wall. Why must all gentlemen pretend to be interested in horses, he wondered vaguely, picking up his glass.

"Your good health, and the good health of your new venture." He tried to clink Charles's glass before he remembered he should not and drew his own back. Did Charles notice his mistake? If he did, he didn't show it. Of course, thought James, my grandson is too much of a gentleman to care about such things. For a moment, he almost envied the younger man. "I am very proud of you," he said, and it was true. His grandson was the man that James so wanted to be but felt, deep inside, he never would be. Cool, unflustered, relaxed in these surroundings, Charles might be a little unsure in the arcane chambers of Brockenhurst House, but not here, where many prominent men worked for their living. James wondered if he should just tell him the truth. Soon the news would be out and he would know it anyway. Wouldn't it be better to tell him who he was, here and now, in this pleasant, peaceful atmosphere, and not let him pick it up as gossip at a party?

"It takes a certain type of man to get this sort of venture off the ground as quickly as you have: a chap who is focused and determined, who works hard, with a keen sense of reality. I can see a lot of myself in you."

"High praise, Mr. Trenchard," replied Charles with a laugh, bringing James back to the present with something of a bump. Of course he couldn't tell the boy now before the secret was out. Maybe no one would guess. Maybe Lady Brockenhurst would go mad. Or die. Maybe there would be another war with France. Anything could happen.

"I mean it. Very well done," James added hastily before his emotions got the better of him. "And in business terms," he continued as brusquely as he could, pulling out some papers from the inside pocket of his coat, "I think the profits, despite the initial outlay, could be immense. Nor do I suppose you'll have too long to wait. People need cotton, it's a fact." He smoothed down the papers. "And if you study this column closely..."

"Excuse me, sir." James looked up. Standing in front of him was the same man who'd welcomed them into the club. "I'm very sorry, Mr. Trenchard, but business papers are not allowed in any part of the building. And that *is* a rule. I am afraid," he added, in case his rudeness had been excessive.

"Of course." James's ears went puce. Was he not to be allowed one moment of dignity in front of his grandson, or must his humiliation be total?

"That was my fault," said Charles. "I asked Mr. Trenchard to show me. I am not a member, so I hope I may be forgiven my ignorance."

"Thank you, sir." The club servant was gone. James watched the young man sitting opposite him. With a jolt, he realized this fellow would never know the insecurity that had bedeviled his grandfather's life. He would not feel undermined by others' ease with Society's laws; he would never find himself at sea in a social gathering.

"They're very officious, I must say," said Charles. "They should be proud of any member who has some business papers to show." Trenchard looked down at the table. Charles was defending him. Naturally, that must mean he felt sorry for his patron, but he also felt enough affection to want to spare his feelings. There was a good deal of comfort in that thought, and then the first course arrived and they both tucked in and the rest of the luncheon passed without incident. They ate salmon and partridge and apple snowballs, followed by a slice of cheddar and a cube of quince jelly. I'm eating luncheon with my own grandson, thought

James, and his heart danced in his chest until he thought it might break open his waistcoat.

"I didn't think that was bad, did you?" He finished the small glass of port they had ordered with the cheese. "Given the reputation the kitchens here enjoy."

"I thought it was excellent, sir." Charles's face was serious. "But I'm afraid I must go. I shouldn't have been away for as long as this."

James pushed back his chair and stood. "Then we will walk out together."

They ambled into the hall, only to be met by an extremely irate Oliver Trenchard. "Oliver? How did you know where I was?"

"They told me at your office. I've been here for twenty minutes."

"Why didn't you ask them to come and get me?"

"Because they told me the time you arrived, and I couldn't believe you would take an hour and a half for *luncheon*. When did you become a member?" His petulance was embarrassing. What a poor specimen he made next to his secret nephew, thought James as he patiently waited for Oliver to regain control of his temper.

"I apologize if I've wasted your time," he said. "Mr. Pope and I were celebrating some good news."

"Mr. Pope?" Oliver's head swung around. Wrath had clouded his vision, and he had failed to notice the young man standing nearby. "Mr. Pope? Why are *you* here?" Oliver could hardly contain himself.

"We were having luncheon together." Charles was conciliatory and as polite as he knew how to be, but it had no effect.

"Why?"

"Mr. Pope has received some wonderful news," announced James. "He's managed to get all the investment he needs for his company. And I had just heard I've been accepted as a member of this club, and so we came here to celebrate."

"More investment?" Oliver looked from one man to the other.

"Your father has been wonderfully kind and encouraging," said Charles. But if this was meant to stem the tide of Oliver's rage, it didn't work.

"But you were already sure of my father's money. That wasn't what you were celebrating today."

"No. Today I had the welcome news that another investor is willing to advance everything I need and more."

Oliver stared at him. "You seem very adept at getting people to put their hands in their pockets, Mr. Pope. What does it take to inspire such enthusiasm? I suppose we only have to remember the Countess of Brockenhurst leading you around her drawing room like a prize heifer. If I had your gifts, Mr. Pope, I can see my troubles would be at an end."

"That's enough." James was in an agony of guilt. The plain truth was he vastly preferred his bastard grandson to his legitimate son. He could only suppose that Oliver was jealous because he suspected his father's preference, but if so, he was right. He spoke sharply. "If Lady Brockenhurst chooses to support Mr. Pope, it is no business of ours—"

"Lady Brockenhurst?" This time Oliver's expression was simple astonishment. "So one minute Lady Brockenhurst is expressing a slight interest in your affairs, and the next she is giving you 'all the investment you need'? Heavens, what a sea change." His voice was dripping with venom.

James cursed himself. He'd let the cat out of the bag without meaning to in the slightest. Oh well. It was too late now. He could not unsay it.

"She believes in my business, yes," corrected Charles. "She has faith in it and she is expecting a return."

"It is a very good project," confirmed James. "She has made a wise decision."

"Really?" Oliver's eyes narrowed.

There was a pause. Charles shifted uncomfortably from one foot to the other. "Thank you for luncheon, Mr. Trenchard," he said eventually. "But now I must leave you, gentlemen." He nodded briefly to Oliver and walked out of the club.

Oliver turned to face his father. "Will you please enlighten me as to the appeal of that man?" He raised his eyebrows in mock surprise. "I simply don't understand why my own father and now the Countess of Brockenhurst would give money to some pushy bumpkin from nowhere. What's behind it? There is some element to this business you have left unsaid."

"You're quite wrong. He is talented, and his business is a good one." Even as he spoke, James knew he had not answered the question. "And his late father, the Reverend Mr. Pope, was an old friend of mine—"

"So old I've never heard of him."

"Have you not?" James smiled tightly. "Well, he was, and he asked me to look out for his son when Charles first came up to London and found employment in the cotton trade. Naturally, when I heard that his father had died, I felt the responsibility all the more, and I wanted to help him as much as I could."

"Well, you have certainly managed it, haven't you?" Oliver's voice was bordering on the shrill. "You've helped 'Charles' a great deal." His sneering tone was making James uncomfortable. "In fact, you've helped him rather more than you've helped your son. Here," he said, shoving a bundle of papers at his father. "I came to give you these." He did not trouble to wait until James had hold of them but withdrew his hand too soon, so they cascaded to the floor, surrounding James in a sea of paper.

"Mr. Trenchard." James's nemesis in black walked swiftly over. "Do let me help you." Together they squatted, gathering up the sheets of numbers and figures, to the evident disapproval of two elderly members on their way out to the street.

James didn't return to the office. He was too shaken by Oliver's rudeness. But by the time he got back to Eaton Square, he had gone through the initial fury provoked by his son's unacceptable behavior and come instead to a kind of sorrow. If only he'd managed everything differently, he thought. If they had never given up Sophia's boy, wouldn't any interest in his birth have faded long ago? Could he not have enjoyed a luncheon like today's without fear of exposure, with all the pleasure of any grandparent seeing their descendants flourish? But would Charles have become the gentlemanly figure he was now if the Trenchards had brought him up? That thought gave him pause and even pain. Might the Popes have made a better job of it than the boy's own grandparents could have managed?

"You look very serious." Anne was sitting at her dressing table as he passed her open door.

"Do I?" He stopped in the passage. "I had lunch with Mr. Pope today. He sends you his regards." If Anne was surprised, she made no comment. James could not see that Ellis was working in the room, behind her mistress. Before Anne could warn him, he continued. "It will not perhaps surprise you that Lady Brockenhurst has provided the last of the investment he needs to proceed with his business."

Rather than answer him, Anne turned to the maid. "Thank you, Ellis. That will be all, but take the pink with you. See if you can get the mark out."

James was going back over his own words in his head as the maid emerged from the room with a dress over her arm and walked toward the back stairs. Had he said anything to incriminate them? He didn't think so. He entered Anne's room and closed the door. "We should have some password for when the coast isn't clear," he said.

Anne nodded. "How sad to think we have so many secrets that we need one." She stooped to pick up Agnes and began to play with her ears. "Tell me more about your luncheon."

"He arrived at the office, full of the news. I took him to the Athenaeum."

"Have you been accepted? Why didn't you tell me?"

"I only heard this morning. Anyway, she's given him the rest of the money he needs."

"I see."

"Do you?" His tone made it quite clear that this was a serious moment for both of them.

"I see it will be hard to explain if it gets out."

"It won't need an explanation. Not by her, at any rate. People will guess the truth and she will confirm it."

Anne frowned. She knew, more even than James, that Lady

Brockenhurst was eager for the news to break, so that she and her husband might enjoy their grandson without subterfuge. She'd given her word not to tell the world, but she would not deny it if the world told her.

"I suppose there's a chance they won't make the link with Sophia." James was clutching at straws.

Anne shook her head. "Your own attentions to the young man will provide that link. And there's bound to be someone who remembers them together in Brussels. No. Once the news is out that he's the son of Lord Bellasis, it won't take long before they know who the mother was." She stood, the dog still held in her arms. "I'll speak to her. I'll go now and speak to her myself."

"What good will that do?"

"I don't know. But it can't do any harm. And since all this is my fault, it behooves me to try to avoid disaster."

James did not comment on her admission of guilt, but his anger had passed. This was where they were. Even he could see there was no point in going over and over it. And he hadn't considered how his interest in the young man might be used against him before this moment. "Should I send a message to Quirk not to unhitch the horses, if he hasn't already?"

"I'll walk. It's no distance."

"Shall I come with you?"

"No. And don't worry. Nobody will challenge the virtue of a matron in her early sixties." She put on her own bonnet, took up a shawl, and set off before he had time for further comment.

The short walk to Belgrave Square was too short a distance for Anne to change her mind, but now that she was actually on the pavement outside Brockenhurst House, she wondered what exactly she was going to ask. Anne was not a rash person as a rule; normally she thought things through, carefully weighing the positives and negatives. But there was something about Lady Brockenhurst that made her impulsive. The woman's high-handedness was infuriating.

By the time she knocked on the door, Anne no longer cared how unusual her arrival might seem. She was vexed, and her vexation was well and truly justified. And if Lady Brockenhurst was not at home, she would find some bench to sit on and wait. She glanced across at the gardens in the middle of the square. Given her own passion for gardening, it annoyed her slightly that neither her husband nor Mr. Cubitt had thought to ask for her opinion when they were being laid out, but still, the gardens were well enough. Then the front door was opened by a footman who was plainly puzzled to see her on the step. He had not been told to expect anyone.

"Is her ladyship in the house?" asked Anne, walking straight into the hall.

"Who shall I say is calling?"

"Mrs. James Trenchard."

"Very well, Mrs. Trenchard." The footman bowed and turned to walk up the stairs. "Please wait here. I'll see if she's at home."

Anne smiled at his choice of words. What he meant was that he would see if Lady Brockenhurst was prepared to receive her. She sat down on one of the gilt sofas for a second, only to stand up again. She realized, to her surprise, that she was quite excited at the prospect of a showdown with the Countess. Her blood was up, especially after the brisk walk. She looked toward the broad staircase, her eyes on the closed double doors of the above. There was clearly a discussion going on behind them. She saw the handle move, and she immediately turned her back, pretending to study a portrait of one of Lord Brockenhurst's ancestors by Lely. He looked rather smug in his high periwig, and a small King Charles spaniel was lying prone at his feet.

"Mrs. Trenchard?" asked the footman, appearing beside her. Anne turned, a small smile on her lips. "Will you come this way, please?"

Anne handed him her shawl and gloves and followed him up the stairs.

"Mrs. Trenchard." The Countess's voice sang out as soon as the door was opened. "I am afraid you have just missed tea. Would you bring some tea for Mrs. Trenchard, Simon?" The footman made a slight bow.

"No, please don't bother," said Anne. "I don't want anything." Again the man bowed and retreated. She started once more across the pink Savonnerie carpet. "You are very good to receive me, Lady Brockenhurst," she continued, as breezy and as confident as she could be. "I promise I won't take up too much of your time. I'm here—"

Caroline Brockenhurst did not need to be told that her unexpected visitor was in a fighting mood, so she cut her off before she could spell it out. "Mrs. Trenchard, do sit down." She indicated a small damask-covered armchair. "Do you remember Lady Maria Grey from my little supper?"

Anne looked toward the window at the pretty blonde girl, dressed in pale green, who was standing there. She had thought they were alone. She felt a moment of fleeting gratitude toward the Countess for silencing her before she spilled their secrets.

The girl smiled. "I remember you from the party, but I don't believe we were ever introduced."

"No," said Anne. "I don't think we were."

"I'm so pleased you felt you could look in," said Lady Brockenhurst, sounding rather the opposite.

"I was passing the house," replied Anne, perching opposite her. "And I wanted to talk to you about something, but it can wait."

"I'll go and leave you alone," said Maria.

"No need." Anne smiled. "It really doesn't matter." Actually, she felt uncomfortable. Now that she could not admonish the Countess for her foolish generosity toward Charles, there was no reason for her to be there. She wondered how soon she could leave without its seeming strange.

"Lady Maria was just telling me she had chanced on my young protégé, Charles Pope, the day before yesterday. He was crossing the square. I think he must have been coming away from this house. Do you remember him from my gathering?" She looked directly into Anne's eyes as she spoke. What on earth was she playing at?

"Charles Pope? I think so. Yes." Anne watched her hostess draw her closed fan through her hand and open and shut it twice.

Was she waiting to see Anne's reaction? Was she poking her feelings for sport? If so, Anne was determined to disappoint her. "He was very charming."

"I agree," enthused Maria, quite unaware of the game being played across her. "Charming and entertaining. We ended up walking together toward the London Library. I don't think my maid approved. And when Mama heard, she *certainly* didn't approve, but it was too late, by then." She laughed merrily. "Who is he? How did you come across him?"

"I forget now." Caroline must be a good card player, thought Anne. She gives nothing away. "But Lord Brockenhurst and I have taken an interest in him. We think him a coming man."

Maria nodded eagerly. "He told me about his plans and the proposed voyage to India. Have you ever been to India, Mrs. Trenchard?" Anne shook her head as Maria burbled on. "I should love to go. All that color. All that chaos. My uncle tells me it is quite beautiful. But then, I've never traveled anywhere," she declared wistfully. "Well, I've spent a lot of time in Ireland, we have an estate there, but that's hardly abroad, is it?" She smiled at the others. Neither of them said anything. In the face of their lack of comment, the girl kept going. "I'd love to visit Italy, too. The truth is, I should so like to do the grand tour that the young men take, to see Michelangelo's *David* and wander the corridors of the Uffizi. You must be fond of art, Lady Brockenhurst. Mama says you paint beautifully."

"Do you?" Anne was surprised, and she spoke the words before considering how they would sound.

"Is it so amazing?" said Lady Brockenhurst.

"But you still haven't explained why you first took an interest in Mr. Pope," said Maria. Anne wondered if this young woman knew how much she was giving herself away.

"I cannot remember now who first introduced him to us," said Caroline carefully, "but Lord Brockenhurst and I like to encourage young talent where we can. We have no living children, as you know, but we like to help the children of others." Anne looked at her. There was probably some truth in this, she thought. Even if, in this case, her words concealed more than they explained.

"He did suggest I might like to visit his office," ventured Maria.

"Did he? That was rather forward of him." Lady Brockenhurst's face was quite opaque. Something was going through her mind as she looked at this young woman. Was she hatching a plan, Anne wondered? But if so, what was it?

"Well." Maria blushed slightly. "I may have been the one to make the suggestion, but he said nothing to discourage me." Her head was cocked to one side as she lowered her gaze. Her long eyelashes fluttered a little and her cheeks glowed pink. She knew she was not behaving wisely. She was spoken for. Her mother had been quite clear that her future lay with John Bellasis. The land in Ireland that she had boasted of earlier was encumbered, and although her brother was doing the best he could with what their father had left, she'd been told in no uncertain terms that it was her job to keep their mother in her old age. She hesitated, on the brink of admitting what she really wanted, but if Lady Brockenhurst had taken an interest in Charles, and if she could be persuaded...

Anne looked at the Countess. Had she noticed the girl's color and the way she kept fiddling with her fan? She was certainly quite bold. Anne rather liked her.

"Well." Lady Brockenhurst paused. Maria Grey was engaged to her husband's nephew, and obviously convention dictated that she should not be encouraging any such meeting. But Anne was right. Caroline Brockenhurst had her own agenda. Or at any rate, she did now. "If you'd like to go, I don't see why not. I have already been to see him there, but we have more to discuss since my previous visit."

Maria could hardly believe her ears. "Really?" This was extraordinary. John Bellasis's aunt was suggesting a trip to see Mr. Pope in the City?

"I don't think we should make a formal plan," said Lady Brockenhurst smoothly. "Mr. Pope would only feel he had to make a special effort for you, my dear." She glanced at Maria. "I think it might be easier if it were just a spur-of-the-moment thing." They all knew what she meant. A spontaneous visit would be much easier to explain to Lady Templemore if it came to it.

"May I join you?" said Anne, her voice as innocent as a rose.

Caroline looked at her. How odd it was to have this shared secret, shared with a woman with whom she would have said she had nothing else in common. Still, it *was* a shared secret; at least it was until now. Anne was right that Caroline was tired of the deception. She would much rather have it out in the open. Society would find it amusing, talk of what a rogue Edmund had been as they laughed over their newspapers, and there would be no further price to pay. But as she grew to love Charles, she did have some slight conscience about the posthumous ruin of the slut who had borne him, even a trace of pity for her mother. "Of course," she said. "If you'd like to."

Anne sat quite still. She was going to call on her grandson, to have another opportunity to speak to him. When she had met him at the party, she had been bowled over by joy, but James's rage had meant that she did not dare engage him in anything like a conversation. Now they could get to know him, as James's involvement in his business would be a perfectly adequate explanation for the acquaintance. Of course, when the truth was out, their connection was bound to come under the heaviest scrutiny, but here was a chance to see him and talk to him once more, at least, before the storm broke. She could not resist. "I'd like to very much," she heard herself say. "Perhaps we can do some shopping while we're there, and make the day into a proper outing." And so the matter was settled. Anne felt herself warmed by the prospect as she walked home in the chill of the early evening. Even if it was another secret she would have to keep from her husband.

That evening, the atmosphere around the dinner table in the Trenchard household was fractious. James was tired and thoughtful, and Oliver was equally low. Today should have been a triumph, father and son lunching together at James's new club. Instead his father had chosen to take Charles Pope, a fellow from nowhere who was consuming James's attention as well as his money. Pope seemed to be quite the man of the moment, garnering the support of Lady Brockenhurst, invited to intimate gatherings at Brockenhurst House—it was enough to make anyone jealous. And Oliver was very jealous indeed.

Susan was not so much depressed as anxious. She hadn't heard a word from John Bellasis since their assignation in Isleworth. She'd expected a letter at least. He had spoken to Speer once in the street, her maid had informed her, under the pretext that he was keen to arrange another rendezvous, yet no invitation or suggestion had been forthcoming. She'd forced Speer to accompany her to Albany, and they had spent the best part of an afternoon strolling up and down Piccadilly like a pair of streetwalkers, all in the hope of bumping into him, but she had not been lucky. Her cheeks grew hot at the memory. She could not taste the food she chewed as she wondered if she'd made a mistake, tumbling into bed so readily with him. Had she given in too easily? She frowned. The problem was that she actually liked John Bellasis. He was handsome and dashing, not to mention the fact that he was due to inherit a great name and a substantial fortune. All in all, he was the perfect man with whom to effect her escape from the dreary family in which she found herself trapped. She looked across at her husband, picking at his food. In comparison to Oliver, John had been a generous, vigorous lover. Susan gave an involuntary sigh.

"Are you all right, my dear?" inquired Anne.

"Yes, Mother," replied Susan. "Of course."

"You seem rather distant."

"I'm afraid I haven't been quite well since my day in Isleworth. I must have picked something up from one of the people I met there." She shivered to make her words seem more authentic.

"I'm sorry," replied Anne, scrutinizing her daughter-in-law. There was something different about her, something new in her demeanor, but Anne could not quite pinpoint what it was.

"How did you get on with Lady Brockenhurst?" asked James, flicking his crayfish around the plate. He wasn't hungry either.

Anne glanced at the glacial faces of Billy and Morris who were standing on either side of the fireplace. "Very well, thank you."

"And she didn't mind you arriving unannounced?" he asked.

"You went to see Lady Brockenhurst?" Susan was clearly put out that she had missed such an opportunity. Anne nodded. "Was her nephew there, by any chance?"

"Mr. Bellasis?" Anne frowned. "No." What an odd question for Susan to ask. "He wasn't there, but his fiancée was."

"His fiancée? Really?" Susan's tone hardened slightly.

"Lady Maria Grey," said Anne. "She's a pretty little thing. I liked her."

"She was at the supper," said Oliver, as he nodded to Billy for some more soup. "She didn't seem very remarkable to me."

"And did you speak to the Countess?" asked James.

"We spoke," replied Anne, smiling at her husband's gaucheness. Why was he asking her these questions in front of the servants, or indeed Susan and Oliver?

The truth was that his eagerness had made him forget for the moment the need for discretion. Anne's look brought him back into line. "Good," he said. "We'll talk about it later."

Anne smiled.

Ellis was crouched on the floor by Anne's feet with a buttonhook in her right hand, unfastening the leather boots. She had heard from the garrulous Billy that her mistress had been to see Lady Brockenhurst, and she was intrigued.

"Did you have a pleasant afternoon, my lady?"

Ellis wasn't really sure what information Mr. Bellasis had paid her to gather or what Mrs. Trenchard knew about this man, Charles Pope. However, what she did know was that there was some secret between the master and his wife that they did not want the world to share. Ellis's banishment earlier that afternoon had told her as much. And as a result of their being alone to discuss it, Mrs. Trenchard had left the house with no warning. Now Ellis knew where she'd gone.

"I did," replied Anne as she slipped her right foot out of its casing. "Thank you," she added, wriggling her toes inside the silk stocking. "Do you know, they don't seem to be easing at all."

Clearly Anne was not being as free with information as Ellis had hoped. She tried again. "I'm not sure they were made for long walks, my lady."

"I didn't go far," replied Anne, taking off her earrings and looking at herself in the glass. "Only to Belgrave Square." She noticed Agnes sitting by her chair and scooped her up into her arms.

"Oh?" Ellis paused between buttons, hook in hand.

"Yes," said Anne. She wasn't so much talking to Ellis as thinking out loud. In truth, she was excited about the planned visit to Charles's office. Obviously, she couldn't talk about it to James, but she wanted to discuss it with someone. "What do you know about Bishopsgate?"

"Bishopsgate, ma'am?" Ellis looked up. "Why ever would you want to go to Bishopsgate?" She slipped off the second boot.

"No reason." Anne had woken up before she started giving all sorts of information to the curious maid. "I'm just calling on someone who has an office there. But I haven't been in years. I wondered if there was anywhere in particular that I should visit while I'm in the area."

"There might be some warehouses where you could buy material cheap," said Ellis. "Let me ask around. When is this trip?"

"I'm not sure. In a day or two." Anne didn't want to answer any more questions. She was conscious she'd said enough as it was. "Tomorrow, can we take out the old bombazine mourning dress? I want to see if it can be rescued or if I should order another. One should always have wearable mourning in the wardrobe." Ellis nodded. She knew enough to be fully aware that the conversation about Bishopsgate was over.

John Bellasis rewarded Ellis very well for her information. It was not often a maid received a sovereign for something heard while unbuttoning her mistress's shoes. But as he listened to how her employers had had a discussion in private that led to Mrs. Trenchard visiting

Lady Brockenhurst and finally to the plan of a trip to Bishopsgate, John almost laughed. He was getting somewhere. He knew well enough who worked in Bishopsgate; at least, who worked there and held the interest of both Lady Brockenhurst and the Trenchards. His own father's account of his visit to Brockenhurst House had made John eager to learn everything he could about young Mr. Charles Pope. "But she never mentioned Mr. Pope by name?"

"Not that I recall, sir. Not this time."

"Even so, there must be something going on between Pope and the Countess," he said as he stood, drinking the last of a small tot of gin outside the Horse and Groom. "Besides her investment, I mean."

"Do you think so, sir? I'd find that very hard to believe," said Ellis from under her shawl, which she had carefully draped to keep her face in shadow. She'd put it on at the last minute in case she was seen talking to Mr. Bellasis. She had her own reputation to think about.

"Don't misunderstand me. I don't pretend to know quite what is going on between them, but something is." He nodded fiercely, as if the point were proven. "And I can guarantee it'll be something that will surprise us all."

"If you say so, sir." Ellis sucked her teeth and folded her arms. She liked a good story, but she wasn't sure she'd like this one.

"Mark my words," said John. "He's an ambitious upstart, and in some way he's taking advantage of her."

"How 'taking advantage,' sir?"

"That's what we have to find out," John stated firmly. "And when we do know, I am pretty sure she will pay a fortune to keep it secret."

Ellis's mouth hung open. "A fortune?"

"And you can help me get it."

The following afternoon, Ellis stood outside the basement entrance of Brockenhurst House. She was nervous and she didn't mind admitting it. Mr. Bellasis had suggested she contact Lady Brockenhurst's maid to see what she could learn about her mistress's activities, and quite why she was entertaining a handsome young man like Charles Pope in her private sitting room, with the doors closed, in the afternoon. Mr. Bellasis had suggested she might open proceedings by asking if Mrs. Trenchard had left her fan behind after the supper. Not that she had, of course. In fact, Ellis had the fan in her pocket in case it proved necessary to "find" it.

She straightened her shawl and adjusted her bonnet, steeling herself to knock on the door. "Yes?" A young hall boy stood there in the dark green Brockenhurst livery.

"My name is Miss Ellis," she began. "I am lady's maid to Mrs. James Trenchard."

"Who?" the boy asked.

Ellis bit the side of her mouth in irritation. Had she been working for a duchess, she would not still be standing on the threshold.

"Mrs. James Trenchard," she persisted. "She came to her ladyship's supper the other day and she fears she may have left her fan."

"You'd better speak to Mr. Jenkins."

The basement of Brockenhurst House was bristling with activity. The rooms and passages were wider than they were in Eaton Square, so there was more space and natural light. It was impressive, and Ellis felt a mild pang of envy as she sat down on a hard wooden chair outside the downstairs pantry.

No one paid her much attention. They all had their jobs to do. Through the open door opposite her, she could see three footmen polishing the plate. In front of them on a table covered with a cloth of soft gray felt was an impressive collection of silver. Entrée dishes, serving dishes, salvers, sauceboats, soup tureens, teapots, kettles, and at least two dozen dining plates were heaped in piles as the men worked their way through them. It was not a job Ellis envied. You had to dip your fingers in bowls of rouge—a soft red powder mixed with ammonia—and rub the silver until it shone or your fingers blistered, or both. Yet they seemed to be enjoying the task, perhaps because it gave them the chance to talk.

"If you wait here," confirmed the hall boy, "I'll fetch Mr. Jenkins."

Ellis nodded. Through an internal window to her right, she

could see the cook hard at work in the kitchen. Bent over a pastry board and beneath a large collection of copper pans hanging from the walls or stacked up on the shelves, she was kneading dough. The cook picked it up and hurled it down, clapping her hands together as she did so in a cloud of flour. The dust hung in the air around her, illuminated by a shaft of sunlight that shone through the window.

"Miss Ellis?"

Ellis jumped. She had been so hypnotized by the cook, she'd failed to hear Mr. Jenkins's soft approach.

"Mr. Jenkins, sir." She got to her feet.

"I gather you are looking for something?"

"Yes, sir, my mistress's fan. She thinks she may have left it here after the Countess's reception the other night. I was wondering if it might have been muddled with one of her ladyship's. If I might just talk to her maid—"

"I'm afraid nobody's found a fan of any description. I'm sorry." Jenkins turned toward the back door, ready to usher her out.

"Oh..." For a moment, Ellis was flummoxed. She needed to have a word with Lady Brockenhurst's maid or the visit would have been pointless. "Mrs. Trenchard did also ask if I might talk to her ladyship's maid about her hair."

"Her hair?" Both of Jenkins's wide gray eyebrows rose slowly.

"Yes, sir. She was very impressed with her ladyship's hair at the party, and she was wondering if I might ask how to achieve such an effect." She smiled, as she thought, winningly.

Jenkins frowned. It was not the first time he'd heard this kind of request. Maids shared tips and fashions all the time. "Very well, I'll see if Miss Dawson is busy," he replied. "Would you kindly wait here? She may be with her ladyship, in which case there'd be nothing I could do."

Ten minutes later, the maid Dawson appeared. Privately she thought the request a little impertinent, but she was flattered, too, as she prided herself on her hairdressing skills. She'd spend hours combing out the false hair for her mistress, always keeping an eye in case the color had faded to make sure of a perfect match, and secretly she was delighted someone else had noticed. Ellis soon found herself being escorted up the back stairs and along passages until they went through a baize-covered door near the entrance to Lady Brockenhurst's private apartment.

On the second floor of the building and with large sash windows affording a generous view of the gardens and the square, Lady Brockenhurst's rooms were airy and comfortable. Not only did she have a huge bedroom, with a four-poster bed, some pretty gilt chairs and a table, she also had a second private sitting room and, of course, her own dressing room.

"Do you like the watercolors?" said Dawson, glancing back at Ellis as she led her through the bedroom. "Most of them were painted by her ladyship. This is their house." She indicated one picture with a short finger. "Lymington Park. It's been in the family since 1600."

"Think of that. Doesn't look old enough." Ellis could not have cared less about the house or the paintings.

"It's been rebuilt twice. The estate is more than ten thousand acres." Dawson clearly took an illogical pride in her employers' possessions, as if somehow they reflected glory onto herself. Which, in Dawson's mind, they did.

"Very impressive, I'm sure," said Ellis. "It must be wonderful to work for such a noble family." She paused. "If only I'd been so lucky."

Almost as soon as she'd walked into the dressing room, Ellis knew that her task would be difficult, if it was achievable at all. Dawson was one of the old-fashioned sort who make their employer's life their own. Sturdy, with a broad face and a slow gait, she had a friendly manner, but she was obviously not a gossip, at least not beyond her confidants in the servants' hall, nor would she be disloyal. She'd been in service there for too long, her eyes already on the small salary she would receive in her dotage. She had nothing to gain from being indiscreet with an outsider.

"I used to work for the Dowager," she said.

"Two generations of Countesses, how fortunate is that?" Ellis gushed, trying to be charming. "And you must have traveled a lot, far more than I, and seen so many interesting things."

Dawson nodded. "I can't complain. I've had a good life with this family." Ellis looked at her. Dawson was that rare beast, the happy servant. She didn't want revenge for a thousand slights. She didn't think the gods had turned away from her by leaving her in servitude. She was content. It was a hard concept for Ellis to grasp. It wasn't exactly that she disliked Mrs. Trenchard. She simply didn't consider her as belonging to the same race as Ellis. Despite their many years together, the injustice implicit in their relative positions meant that Ellis would have little conscience about betraying her employer. Whatever money she might have made from Anne, she'd earned. Earned with years of unremitting toil and lying and groveling and being forced to pretend that she was glad to be in service, when all the time she wished her employers at the bottom of the sea. She could lie to Anne's face without blanching. She would steal from her if she thought she could do so without getting caught. She had hoped to find something similar in the bosom of Lady Brockenhurst's maid, that the prospect of doing harm to the Countess would be snapped up by a grateful fellow captive. But faced with Dawson's loyalty, Ellis was hard put to decide what to do.

"No wonder you know so much about hairdressing," said Ellis with a bright smile. "You are the sort of person I can really learn from, even at my age." She laughed as she spoke and Dawson joined in. "My mistress really was so terribly taken by the Countess's hair." Ellis knew she was a convincing liar. She had trained in a hard school.

"Was she really?" Dawson touched her chest, tickled in spite of herself.

"Oh yes," continued Ellis. "Tell me. Do you do those very fine little ringlets in front of the ears?"

"That's a bit of a secret." Dawson opened the drawer of the dressing table to reveal a large collection of hair irons and curling papers. "I found this in Paris a long time ago and I've used it ever since." She held up a very narrow, delicate-looking iron. "I heat it on the fire here."

"How?" Ellis's voice was all reverent wonder.

"I have this contraption that fixes into the grate." She brought out a brass heating tray.

"What will they think of next?" said Ellis, wondering how long it would be before she had some tidbit worth taking home.

"It's wonderful when you think how we used to manage thirty years ago. Although," Dawson added, "perhaps the most important thing is a good supply of hair. I favor Madame Gabriel just off Bond Street. She has good sources. She says most of her hair comes from nuns rather than poor girls, and I feel that makes for better quality. The hair is thicker and has more of a shine to it."

As Dawson carried on explaining the technique of heating the hair without destroying it, and that the scented papers were also important to prevent scalding accidents, Ellis allowed her eyes to scan the room. On the dressing table between the tall windows there was a small enamel portrait of an officer, dressed in a uniform dating back twenty years at least.

"Who's that?" she said.

Dawson followed her eyes. "That's poor Lord Bellasis, her ladyship's son. He died at Waterloo. That was a terrible thing in this house. Her ladyship never recovered. Not really. He was her only child, you see."

"How tragic." Ellis studied the picture more closely. Dawson's answer had given her the excuse to go over and look at it properly.

"It's a good one. It was painted by Henry Bone." Again, Dawson's pride in the family possessions was asserting itself.

Ellis narrowed her eyes. The face appeared curiously familiar. There was something about the dark curls and those blue eyes that reminded her of someone who used to visit their house a long time ago. Was it in Brussels? That would make sense if he died at Waterloo . . . then she remembered. He was a friend of Miss Sophia's. She could recall how handsome he was. How strange to see his picture sitting on Lady Brockenhurst's dressing table. But she said nothing. Ellis never released information unless she was obliged to.

"Did her ladyship enjoy her party the other day?" asked Ellis.

"Oh, I think so." Dawson nodded.

"My mistress did. Very much. She said she met so many nice people."

"Not everyone gets into Brockenhurst House," said Dawson happily, forgetting for the moment that she herself would never be a guest there.

"There was one young man who struck her most favorably. What was his name now? Was it Mr. Pope?" Ellis waited.

"Mr. Pope? Oh yes," confirmed Dawson. "A very nice young gentleman. He's a great favorite of her ladyship's. A recent favorite, but he comes here often now."

"Does he, indeed?" Ellis smiled.

Dawson looked puzzled. What on earth was this woman suggesting? She picked up the curling equipment and started packing it away. "Yes," she said firmly. "My mistress and Lord Brockenhurst have taken an interest in his business. They like to encourage young people. They are very generous that way." This last wasn't really true—or not until this moment—but Dawson was not going to allow this stranger to infer that anything untoward was going on. She can find out her own hairdressing tips if that's the way she wants to carry on, she thought as she closed the drawer with a bang.

"How admirable." Ellis knew she had put a foot wrong and was anxious to remedy the situation. "I never heard of that. A great lady taking an interest in a promising young man's business. Mrs. Trenchard manages things well enough, but I don't believe she could be called a woman of business, or anything like."

"It may be unusual but it's quite true." Dawson was calmer now. Ellis had succeeded in soothing her indignation. "She's going into the City in a day or two to pay a call on him. At his office. She won't go through with the investment without being quite clear about what she is investing in. I know that for definite."

"She's actually giving him money? He must be charming." Ellis could not contain herself, and as a result Dawson's face began to cloud again.

"I don't know what that has to do with it. Her ladyship has a lot of interests." For a moment she had been going to mention that she was taking Lady Maria, to show there was nothing untoward, but then she asked herself why was she plying this stranger with family information. Her face tightened. "And that is all there is to be said on the matter. Now, I think it's time for you to leave, Miss Ellis. I am very busy and I'm sure you are, too. Good day to you." She stood. "I assume you can find your own way to the back stairs?"

"Of course." Ellis tried to take the other woman's hand. "How very kind and generous you have been. Thank you."

But this time she was less successful in gaining lost ground. "Never mind all that," said Dawson, pulling away. "I must get on."

Out in the passage, Ellis knew it would be hard to regain entry to Brockenhurst House, but she wasn't too worried. Miss Dawson was never going to give away any secrets if she could help it. That much was clear. Besides, Ellis had some real information to take back to Mr. Bellasis, and he should pay well for it. The question was, what would he do next?

·7·

A Man of Business

As Lady Brockenhurst's carriage pulled up outside the house in Eaton Square, Ellis could barely contain her curiosity. Standing at the window of Mrs. Trenchard's dressing room, her breath fogging the pane, she strained to see the activity in the street below. The Countess, in an elegant plumed hat and carrying a parasol, was leaning forward to give instructions to her coachman. Next to her in the barouche, also protected from the warm sunshine by a delicate fringed parasol, was Lady Maria Grey. She wore a pale blue and white striped skirt, finished with a tight, military-style navy jacket. Her face was framed in a matching blue bonnet edged with cream lace. In short, Maria looked, as she had fully intended, ravishing. They did not climb down onto the pavement. Instead, one of the postilions advanced toward the door and rang the bell.

Ellis knew they had come to collect her mistress, and so she headed for the stairs as quickly as she could manage, carrying everything she'd need. Mrs. Trenchard was already waiting in the hall.

"Will you require me any further this morning, ma'am?" asked the maid, holding up a green pelisse.

"I won't, thank you."

"I expect you're going somewhere nice, ma'am."

"Nice enough." Anne was too taken up with the prospect ahead of her to pay much attention to the question. And she had, after all, managed to conceal her destination from James, so she was hardly likely to give it away to her lady's maid.

Of course Ellis had a good idea where they were going, but she would have liked confirmation. Still, if she was frustrated, she did not show it. "Very good, ma'am. I hope you enjoy yourself."

"Thank you." Anne nodded to the footman, who opened the door. She also had a parasol, just in case. She was quite ready.

Lady Brockenhurst and Maria both smiled as she climbed in. Maria had moved so that she sat with her back to the horses, a real courtesy to someone of inferior rank, and Anne appreciated it. In short, nothing was going to spoil this day. Lady Brockenhurst was not her favorite companion on earth, but they had something in common—neither would deny that—and today they were, in a way, going to celebrate it.

"Are you sure you're quite comfortable, my dear?" Anne nodded. "Then we'll go." The coachman took up the reins and the carriage moved off.

Caroline Brockenhurst had decided to be pleasant with Mrs. Trenchard today. Like Anne, she was looking forward to seeing the young man again, and she found out that her pity for this woman, whose world would soon be, if not completely destroyed, then certainly holed below the waterline. She did not think it would take much longer for the story to come out, after which Edmund's memory would be, if anything, enhanced and Sophia Trenchard's would be ruined. It really was very sad. Even she could see that.

Anne looked at the wall of the gardens of Buckingham Palace as they drove by. How strange it was, the composition of their world. A young woman in her early twenties was at the pinnacle of social ambition; to be in her presence was the very peak that men like James, clever men, talented men, high-achieving men, strove for, as a crowning glory after a lifetime of success, and yet what had she done, this girl? Nothing. Just been born. Anne was not a revolutionary. She had no desire for the country to be overturned. She didn't like republics, and she would be content to curtsy low before the Queen should the chance ever arise, but she could still wonder at the illogic of the system that surrounded her.

"Oh, look. She's in London." Maria's eyes were staring upward. It was true. The Royal Standard was fluttering above the roof of the Palace, at the back of the open courtyard. Anne stared at the huge, columned portico with its glazed porte-cochère designed to shield the royal family as they climbed in and out of their coaches. It was rather public, when you thought about it. But then, they must be used to being objects of curiosity.

The carriage continued down the Mall, and soon Anne was admiring the splendors of Carlton House Terrace, which still impressed her with the novelty and magnificence of its design, even ten years after it was finished.

"I hear that Lord Palmerston has taken number five," said Maria. "Do you know the houses at all?"

"I've never been inside one," said Anne.

But nothing could silence Maria. She was as excited as a child in a toy shop, and they all knew why. "Oh, I do like the look of the grand old Duke of York. I don't quite know why he is commemorated so vividly, but I am so glad that he is." They had reached the break in the terraces, where a wide flight of steps led to a tall column holding a statue of the second son of King George III. "I wonder how big the statue really is."

"I can tell you that," said Anne. "I was here on this very spot five years ago, when they were erecting it. He was more than double the height of a man. Twelve feet or more, thirteen maybe." Anne smiled at Maria. She liked the girl, no question. She liked her for liking Charles, when there could be no happy outcome, but she liked her for herself as well. Maria had spirit and daring, and in any other walk of life she might have done things, interesting things. Of course, for the daughter of an earl with limited funds, the opportunities were not numerous, but that wasn't the fault of Maria Grey.

For a moment, Anne felt a pang of shame that James was missing it all. He might say how busy he was every waking moment, but he would have come for this. He enjoyed the company of his grandson—the grandson he knew so much better than she did— and he didn't bother to hide it from anyone. Not even from Oliver.

But still she hadn't told him about the proposed trip. The truth was, she'd allowed him to think that her visit to Lady Brockenhurst had persuaded the Countess to back away and be more discreet in her attentions to Charles, so this visit to Charles's place of work, *en pleine vue*, in a spanking carriage, with his own wife and a young Society beauty in tow, would have horrified him. Anne was only too aware that Caroline Brockenhurst had no interest in keeping their secret, that it must come out, and this exhibition would only hasten the exposure, for which James would ultimately blame her. Was that why she'd said nothing to him? And did she feel guilty if it were? After all, he'd lied to her for years—or if not lied, at least not told the truth. Now it was her turn. But more than anything, she simply wanted to see her grandson again.

The three women chatted as they traveled through the streets of London toward the City and Charles Pope's office in Bishopsgate. "Did you find your fan?" Lady Brockenhurst asked Anne as they drove down Whitehall.

"My fan?"

"That very pretty Duvelleroy you had at the supper. I particularly noticed how fine it was. Such a shame to lose it."

"But I haven't lost it," replied Anne, touched that the Countess had any memory of her fan.

"I don't understand." Lady Brockenhurst looked puzzled. "Your maid came to the house the other day to look for it. Or so my maid told me."

"She did? Ellis? How odd. I'll ask her when I get home." Ellis had been behaving rather oddly, Anne reflected. How little one knew about the servants, even the ladies' maids and valets who ministered to their employers. They talked and laughed as much as they were encouraged to do, and sometimes one could become friends with them. Or so it seemed. But then, what did one really know about any of them?

Soon the carriage had left fashionable London behind, and they were traveling through the old, twisting, overbuilt streets of the ancient City, whose layout had hardly altered since the Plantagenets were on the throne. Anne was struck by how squalid some areas were, even when they were quite close to main thoroughfares. The coachman had tried his best to steer clear of the less salubrious parts of the town, but the farther in they traveled, the stronger the smell of open drains, and the narrower and more unpleasant the streets became.

They were nearing the end of their journey, passing through a ramshackle market of stalls outside St. Helen's Church. The pavements and alleyways seemed to be crammed with market traders, all shouting from their loaded wooden carts, their cries drowning out the conversation in the barouche. "Peas! Sixpence a peck!" "Yarmouth bloaters, three a penny!" "Tasty young rabbits!" yelled one fellow as he walked alongside the carriage and held up a fistful of the furry wretches, wriggling in misery as they were swung by their feet.

"Why must they be kept alive, poor things?" Maria said with a sigh, more to herself than to him. But he looked back, straight into her eyes.

"How else would we keep 'em fresh, miss?" He kept staring at Maria—perhaps in surprise at this visitation by a lovely creature from a distant planet—before slowly wiping his nose on the back of his hand and turning away, only to pick on another carriage behind them.

There were boys and girls everywhere, mostly without shoes, playing with anything that came to hand: old boxes, bricks, the empty oyster shells that littered the cobbles. One even had an ancient hoop, cast out by some son of privilege, no doubt, but these children at play were the lucky ones. Others had no time to enjoy themselves. They were too busy trying to sell anything they could lay their hands on. Anne watched a scruffy-looking lad who could not have been more than six as he listlessly wove his way through the crowds and held up a string of dirty onions, hoping for a sale. On one corner she noticed an old woman sitting on some stone steps, a basket of heather and eggs in front of her. Despite the sunshine, her thick black cloak was pulled tightly around her, and she rested her graying head against the rough wall. By the time they reached Charles Pope's office, their senses were muted by the misery and hunger they had witnessed.

Maria was the first to break the silence. "I hate to see barefoot children, poor little things. They must be so cold." She shook her head.

"I agree," replied Anne, touching Maria's knee in sympathy.

This was altogether too sentimental for Caroline Brockenhurst. "But what can we do? No amount of charity seems to make any difference."

"They need more than our charity," said Maria. "They need things to be different." And while Anne was silent, she nodded gently in agreement.

Charles Pope's office was on the second floor of a rambling and fairly ancient building that must once have been a private house but that had long since been surrendered to the serious business of making money. His rooms were high enough above the street to dissipate the noise from the road below. After climbing several flights of the steep staircase, they entered and had hardly made an inquiry before an inner door burst open and Charles appeared. "Lady Brockenhurst," he said with a broad smile as he advanced to greet them. "This is a wonderful surprise." It was. He could scarcely believe it.

Caroline was pleased at his obvious joy. She had toyed with the idea of warning him, but she wanted to gauge the tone of the place, and if she had given him time he would no doubt have wanted to create a good, and perhaps misleading, impression. She'd written to prepare him for her first visit, but this time she had not. Of course there was always a risk he would be out, but she had decided to chance it. She could not know that Anne Trenchard had been less willing to find they'd chosen the wrong day for their excursion and had sent the footman, Billy, the day before to inquire if Mr. Pope would be in the office the following afternoon, but without revealing any names. So Charles had been told that someone was coming, just not who it was. Ellis learned all this from Billy after they had left, so now she had another snippet to report to Mr. Bellasis, though Anne, naturally, was quite unaware of the subterfuge swirling around her.

Back in Bishopsgate, Caroline was most interested in Charles's response to the presence of Maria Grey. "I can't believe you're here," he said without thinking. And then, to cover himself, "All of you." After this, if Caroline had suspected there was something going on between them, she now knew it. At least she knew that something *could* go on, if only they would let it.

"Lady Brockenhurst told me she would be passing by, and I thought I would invite myself to join her. I hope you don't mind," said Maria.

"Not at all. Not a bit. Quite the reverse."

Maria nodded, her hand outstretched. He stared at it. Should he shake it? Should he kiss it? Her crisp blue-and-white skirt appeared out of place in the drab confines of his workplace. Her blonde curls, her pretty lips; Charles could hardly look her in the eye.

"You're very kind if you really don't mind our pushing in," said Caroline quickly. Is Lady Brockenhurst trying to cover my awkwardness? he wondered. Am I being too obvious? He was painfully aware that Maria was engaged to Lady Brockenhurst's nephew. But then, she didn't appear too disapproving.

Maria recovered her nerve first. "We're on our way to a silk merchant's," she gabbled cheerfully, "Nicholson and Company." She had her own reasons for blurring their motives in coming. "We simply couldn't resist the chance to inspect you on the way."

He was blushing as he took her parasol and laid it to one side.

"What may I offer you? Some tea? Some wine?" He cast his eyes around the room as if he might find some alluring bottle poised miraculously on a shelf, tucked away and forgotten but just the thing to entertain great ladies on an afternoon like this. Then he saw Anne, who was standing at the back behind the others.

Lady Brockenhurst stepped forward. "May I present Charles Pope? Mrs. Trenchard is the wife of that Mr. Trenchard who has been helpful to you." The Countess smiled. How the pendulum of power swings back and forth. Less than a month ago she didn't even know she had a grandson. Anne Trenchard had kept him a secret for a quarter of a century. Now, here she was, introducing him to her. The irony was delightful.

Charles looked at Mrs. Trenchard. She had a pleasant, kind

face and benevolent eyes that seemed to be studying him from underneath her bonnet. There was something about her that gave him the impression they'd already met, but he could not place her. Then it came to him. "We talked briefly at Lady Brockenhurst's house the other night," he said.

Anne smiled pleasantly. "Of course we did." In reality, she wanted to cry out, to seize him and hold him to her bosom. But even though she couldn't, she did feel happy. The smile wasn't a lie.

"You met so many people that night." The Countess laughed gently. Anne shot her a look. Lady Brockenhurst seemed to be enjoying the awkwardness of the situation a little too much.

"I know of you from your husband," continued Charles. "Mr. Trenchard has been my benefactor to a flattering—to an incredible—degree. I am so very grateful to him for all the help he has given me, and it is a pleasure to receive his wife here." Charles's smile was also quite genuine. "Won't you come into my office?"

He led the way into the inner room, where they found a sofa and some chairs that they sat on after Charles had gathered up the papers and drawings that covered almost every surface.

"I seem to remember our conversation was interrupted when my husband dropped his glass," Anne said, and smiled. She had played that moment over and over again in her mind.

"Your husband has been very kind to me, Mrs. Trenchard," continued Charles. "Truly. He has shown exceptional generosity. And faith." He nodded. "In fact, I could not have dreamed of running my own cotton mill were it not for him. He has literally changed my life."

It was not that Lady Brockenhurst objected to any of this, but there was a trace of unexpressed indignation in her face that Charles recognized at once. She did not care to share the role of benefactor with that tiresome little man. "I owe an equal debt to you, Lady Brockenhurst," said Charles quickly. "You and Lord Brockenhurst have thrown a bridge across the torrent that divided me from my future. Now, thanks to you, I can begin in earnest." As he spoke the words, he thought they were rather good.

"What a lathering," said Maria. "If I didn't know better, I would think you were trying to sell us some brushes."

This was not the response he had been seeking, but then she laughed and clapped her hands at his expression just as the door opened and his assistant brought in a tray of tea things, and the moment had passed. None of which was lost on Caroline.

"Is that India?" asked Maria as she glanced at a large framed map that took up almost a whole wall of the room.

"It is." Charles was glad to take the conversation back to safer territory.

She stood to examine it more closely. "Is it new?"

Charles joined her. "The very latest," he said. "They are being updated all the time. The more provinces that are mapped, the more detailed the maps become."

"How marvelous."

"Do you really like it?" Charles beamed. He was almost annoyed at himself. He was only too conscious of his desire to impress this young woman with his gravitas and sense of purpose, but instead, whenever she spoke to him, he started grinning like a clown in a circus. "I used to have one where the territories were marked out according to rule. The native principalities were shaded in green and the parts run by the East India Company were pink. But this map is based more on the geographical features. As you can see, they've made a great play of the rivers and mountains and deserts."

"It's hard to imagine such a huge country," said Maria, running her cream kid glove over the surface of the glass. "Bengal," she read. "Punjab. Kashmir..." She sighed. "What a wild and romantic place it must be."

"Parts of the country certainly are very wild and uncultivated. There are tigers," said Charles sagely, hoping he sounded like an expert. "And elephants and snakes and monkeys, too. Then there are so many different religions and languages. It is a world in itself, really."

"I should adore to see a tiger in the jungle," said Maria, turning to face him. She was standing so close he thought he could feel the warmth of her breath on his cheek.

"When you do, ensure you're on the back of an elephant."

She gasped. "Is that how they travel?"

"They use elephants just as we might use a carriage," he continued. He knew he should move away, but he didn't want to. If she felt uncomfortable, he thought, she can be the one to take a step back. But she didn't either. Her skirts, resting on their stiff petticoats, were pushing against his knees. He steadied himself. "Apparently they are intelligent and very biddable, but riding them is like being on a boat at sea, and you must rock with each wave."

"I can imagine," she replied, half closing her eyes.

"And up here"—Charles swept his hand across the top of the map—"is part of the Silk Road, which starts in China and then goes through these mountains and on into Europe."

"And now it is the turn of cotton." Maria was having a wonderful time, even better than she had anticipated. Why, she asked herself silently? Is it just the presence of this man? Could it be as little as that?

"I have a feeling the cotton trade has been going for quite some time," Anne commented, moving toward the map.

"It has indeed, Mrs. Trenchard," confirmed Charles. "And India must come to dominate it, in time."

"I gather that the plantations in the southern states of America are the leading producers now." Maria had clearly come fully armed with information.

"Where did you read that?"

She blushed. "I forget. Somewhere." The truth was, she had scoured every book or publication she could lay her hands on. She just wanted to have something to say when she met him next.

"I prefer to find my suppliers in India," said Charles.

"Why?" Anne was genuinely interested. She was so used to Oliver's permanent grudge against the world and to Susan's complaining that she had almost forgotten the kind of conversation one might have with the young when they were at the very start of the serious business of being grown up. Unlike her son, this man had a sense of purpose and a determination to succeed. It was refreshing.

"The Americans keep their prices down through the use of slaves, while I am a follower of Wilberforce and Clarkson. I do not believe in profiting from slavery in any form." As the others nodded their approval, he held up his hand. "And before you commend my virtue, there is self-interest in my decision, too. I don't believe slavery can last in the modern world, and when it is abolished, America will not be able to compete with India. The day that happens, I would prefer my own business to be firmly established so that we are ahead of the game."

Anne caught Lady Brockenhurst's eye. How fine he was. She could not blame the other woman for wanting to acknowledge him publicly. And seeing Maria Grey's interest in him—was a good marriage really out of the question? She could tell Lady Brockenhurst was already making plans for the young couple, never mind her husband's nephew, and after all, the old King's daughters by that actress had married well: the Countess of Erroll, Viscountess Falkland, Lady De L'Isle... and didn't the Duke of Norfolk's illegitimate son marry Lady Mary Keppel ten years after she and James got back from Brussels? She was sure she'd read that. Wouldn't it serve as a template? What would Sophia want them to do? That was the question they had to ask themselves. She noticed Charles was watching her, so she asked him brightly, "Do you know which areas of India you will be visiting, Mr. Pope? What is the potential for development out there? A young man such as you must be full of ideas."

"He is," enthused Maria, cupping her hands together. "And to have managed this at such a young age..." She gestured around the office with one tiny gloved hand. She had no awareness of how much she was giving herself away.

"I am curious about you, Mr. Pope," said Lady Brockenhurst, walking over to his desk. It was cluttered with piles of paper, documents, and a selection of brown boxes tied up with red string. "You are a model of dynamism and industry and yet, unlike most people in your way of life, you were not born to it. In the normal way of things, the son of a country vicar—you are a vicar's son, I think—might have joined the Army or the Navy, but he would more probably be preaching as a curate, waiting for someone to find him a living."

Anne wondered what Lady Brockenhurst was fishing for. If Charles was demonstrating some quality in his blood, it was surely James's influence they could trace, not the Bellasis side of his ancestry. No Bellasis would have troubled himself to balance the books since the Crusades. For a moment, she felt rather proud of her husband. He could be tiresome in his eagerness to better himself socially, but he was a clever man nonetheless, with a real flair for business.

"How did you know I was the son of a vicar?"

A good question. The Countess floundered, but only for a fraction of a second. "You told me. When I was here last."

"Ah," Charles said, and nodded. "Well, he wasn't the average vicar, which probably explains it. He was an exceptional fellow."

"Was?"

"He died not long ago."

Of course he'd died. Anne had forgotten that. When James told her, he'd suggested he had read it in the *Times*, but now she wondered. Would James have missed their correspondence? she asked herself. Twenty-five years' worth of letters, reporting Charles's progress all that time. Although once James was in contact with Charles himself, the role of Mr. Pope in passing on information must have diminished almost to nothing. Still, he seemed to have been a good man. "He sounds like an excellent person," she said.

"I have been very fortunate." Charles glanced up at a pastel that hung behind his desk. The sitter was elderly, with a sprinkling of gray hair and dressed entirely in black. The white bands of a cleric set off his finely boned face, which was almost in profile, his mind perhaps on higher things. In his right hand he carried a book, which, on closer inspection, turned out to be the Bible. The chalk highlights were well done, and the whole thing put Anne in mind of the work of George Richmond. In truth, she was grateful to the Reverend Mr. Pope, when all was said and done. Maybe the increase in his income had been the initial incentive to take in a stray and unwanted fledgling, but clearly he had grown fond of the boy and given him a good grounding with which to take on life.

"It's an attractive picture." Lady Brockenhurst stared at it. "At least, it is the sort of picture that suggests it is a fine likeness, even though I did not know the sitter. He looks clever and kind. I hope he was."

"He was both those things and more. I think I told you about him when we first met."

"Tell me again." What a cool liar she was. Anne almost admired her for it. That is the problem of a situation such as ours, she thought. It makes liars of us all. In this very room, she and Lady Brockenhurst were liars incarnate, both parading as innocents before their ignorant grandson. Even Maria was a liar, if she still pretended she was going to marry John Bellasis when it must be clear that she was not—not willingly, anyway. Only Charles was not lying, unless he was hoping to hide that he was head over heels in love with Maria Grey.

"I was not their blood child." Charles was quite easy in his manner. But then, why should he feel uncomfortable? "My mother died in childbirth and my father in battle not long before, or so I was told. My father was Mr. Pope's cousin, and he and his wife—or my mother, as I think of her now—felt they should take me in. They were childless, and so perhaps there was something to be gained on both sides, but the fact is, they were very good to me, and she is kind and loving to this day."

"What about Mr. Trenchard? What was his role in all this?" Anne was curious how the first link was made.

"I had originally been intended for the Church, as Lady Brockenhurst suggested. But as I grew older my father could see that my gifts lay elsewhere, and so he managed to get me apprenticed to a banking house. But when I first came to London I saw at once that it was not a world I would easily understand. So my father asked Mr. Trenchard if he would be my guide until I found my feet. He and my father had been friends for many years."

Anne watched Lady Brockenhurst. She was clearly enjoying herself as she learned the secret history of her grandchild. "How fortunate that the Reverend Mr. Pope had friends in business."

"He had friends in all walks of life. Fortunately, Mr. Trenchard took an interest in me and has kept an eye on me ever since. When I decided to leave the bank, I came to him with the idea of purchasing a mill, and he agreed to back my instinct, which made it possible, and now Lord and Lady Brockenhurst have been kind enough to give me what I need to establish the operation fully."

"Is the mill already working?" Maria felt she had been silent long enough.

"Yes, but in a rather haphazard way, using what raw cotton I can find. Now I want to put in place a more stable arrangement that will allow me to expand. That is what Lady Brockenhurst has made possible. Shall I ring for some more tea?"

"I don't think so. Thank you." Anne was sitting with Maria on the sofa as sunlight streamed in through the large shuttered windows, creating a striped pattern across the wooden floor. Charles gathered up the tea things and placed them on the tray. Anne watched his fluid, even graceful, movements. How incredible that the fat, mewling baby she'd briefly held in her arms a quarter of a century ago had grown into such a handsome and self-assured man.

By her side, Maria was also watching Charles Pope. His father a soldier, she was thinking, and the cousin of a churchman . . . what was wrong with that? He might not be a catch, but he was at least a gentleman. Of course John Bellasis had a great fortune coming, but wouldn't Charles make a great fortune himself? And might it not come sooner? Lord Brockenhurst looked good for many years yet. And as she thought this, she talked, asking question after question about Charles's business and his schemes, hanging on his every word. How long would it take him to get to India? Would he be traveling alone? How would he know if his sources were reliable when he got there?

"It's not the reliability that matters most, initially, it's the quality," he explained, pacing the office in his enthusiasm. "The situation in India is difficult, and most of the cotton is currently low grade, but when one finds the right supplier one needs to commit to them. Only then can we start to improve the business. The weather is perfect, so it must be possible."

"Hear, hear!" came a voice from the door, accompanied by a slow, loud handclap. "Well said, that, man!"

John Bellasis was lounging against the door frame of the office. Charles stared at him in surprise. "Sir?" he said. "May I help you?" The man looked familiar to him, but his manner was proud and somehow hostile, as if he and Charles were already enemies. John's eyes were narrowed, his mouth hard. He was the very picture of arrogance.

"John?" said Lady Brockenhurst. "What are you doing here?"

"I might ask the same of you, my dear aunt." But he did not wait for an answer. "Lady Maria, as I live and breathe. Good day to you," John continued, ignoring Charles entirely as he strode across the office toward Maria, who was frozen with shock.

As if voicing her thoughts, Lady Brockenhurst spoke again. "How did you know where we were to be found?"

"I didn't. That is, not all of you. I expected to see you here, Aunt, but not...?" He stared vacantly at Anne. "I'm so sorry."

Charles spoke. "Mrs. Trenchard."

"Mrs. Trenchard, of course. I know just who you are." The irony being that he really did know—he had sat at a table with her at his aunt's soirée, after all—but he didn't want to show it. "And to discover Lady Maria here is a positive blessing from above." He did not sound as if he thought Maria's presence in Charles's office was much of a blessing. He did not sound like that one bit.

At first, when he'd received Ellis's note asking him to come to Piccadilly, he had been infuriated at her impertinence in sending for him, but when he heard what Billy had told her, that today was the date of the planned trip to Bishopsgate, he admitted she'd acted sensibly. Who was Mr. Pope, this figure from nowhere who had so mysteriously caught their attention? He needed to get to the bottom of what the fellow's hold over them was. Could it be blackmail, for some earlier misdemeanor buried in his uncle's past? But how would that explain the interest of the Trenchards? He had given Ellis a coin and thanked her. "Mrs. Trenchard said nothing more that would explain her reasons for the visit?"

"She made no mention of it, sir. It was the footman who told me. She keeps her own counsel as a rule."

"Does she? Well, we'll see if she'll keep it when I beard them in the lion cub's den, Mrs. Trenchard and my beloved aunt."

"You won't give me away, sir?" Ellis was not yet ready to lose her position. She would go when it suited her and not before.

"Don't worry. If you were sacked, you'd be no more use to me."

His problem, of course, was how to explain his following Anne Trenchard, a woman he barely knew, to an appointment he would have no information about.

Quickly he made his way to Brockenhurst House, and by good fortune Lord Brockenhurst was at home. It did not take John long to prompt his uncle into telling him that Caroline had gone to Bishopsgate to call on young Mr. Pope. John nodded.

"You are both taking such an interest in that man, sir."

"Caroline finds him promising, and he seems nice enough to me." Peregrine would never challenge any enthusiasm of his wife. Since Edmund's death, she had so few of them.

"That's very strange," said John. "I'm on my way to Bishops-gate this instant. How is that for a coincidence? I might look in and see if I can find her there." He knew the address of Pope's office. His research had already yielded that, and Lord Brocken-hurst would never remember that he hadn't asked for it. His alibi established, he hailed a cab and set off.

And now here he was, facing his nemesis with Mrs. Trenchard, Maria Grey and his aunt thrown into the mix.

"I'm afraid we've finished tea, unless you'd like me to ring for some more, Mr.....?'

Charles's inability to recognize John irritated him profoundly. How dare this young upstart not remember him from the supper? Who was this odious fellow who seemed to have the ladies so entranced? That was normally John's territory. His father had been right about this: There was something very odd—and deeply unattractive—about the way his aunt was carrying on with this insignificant nobody. More to the point, money was being diverted from him and his father, and he didn't care for it. Until now, his future had seemed comparatively easy to envisage. He simply had to borrow until his uncle's death, and then his father's inheritance—or more probably his own—would set everything straight, and all would be as merry as a marriage bell. Except that now the arrival of Mr. Charles Pope threatened to overturn the cart.

"You have already met Lord Brockenhurst's nephew, Mr. Bellasis, at the soirée," said the Countess, getting out of her seat. She was annoyed by John's intrusion. That was clear. And subtly undermined. She caught Anne's eye. This episode was over. It was time for them to leave.

"Mr. Bellasis, of course," said Charles, nodding briefly as his heart sank. So this was Maria's fiancé. "I do apologize. There were so many people, I was quite overwhelmed."

"You didn't look it." John stared at Charles from the chaise. The man had nothing to recommend him, and yet his aunt had crossed London to drink tea in this nondescript office. "So here we all are," he said, lightly tapping his fingertips together.

"That's what we'd like to know," said Maria. "Why are *you* here?" She smiled as she spoke, but it did not reach her eyes.

Lady Brockenhurst nodded. "Yes, John. Why are you here?"

"I was at your house this morning, and my uncle told me you had gone to Bishopsgate. I had an appointment in the area and was curious to see Mr. Pope again. He is quite the man of mystery. To me, anyway. Half my family and now the wife of one of the most famous builders of London together beat a path to this modest door, and I wanted to know why. I may call it modest without offense, I hope, sir?" he said with mock servility.

Charles forced a smile. "By all means."

John continued. "When I heard you were on your way here, Aunt, it seemed the perfect opportunity."

Charles felt it was time to join in, to make things smooth again. "Don't worry, Mr. Bellasis. It's a mystery to me, too. Why everyone seems to have taken such an interest in my welfare."

This time Charles's smile was more genuine. "You may be sure of that."

"I was wondering." John turned to Maria. "I'm going down to Epsom on Thursday. A cousin of mine has a horse running, and I thought you and Lady Templemore might like to accompany me."

"I'll ask Mama, of course, but I'm afraid she's not very fond of racing."

"What about you, Pope? Are you a man for the horses?"

"Not too much," replied Charles. His heart was singing because Maria had turned down the chance of spending a day with this man. Could he take it as a sign?

"No, I suppose not," said John, moving to stand in front of the map of India with his hands behind his back. "Your head is probably too full of cotton." He laughed to disguise the insult as a joke.

Lady Brockenhurst started moving toward the door. "It's time to leave Mr. Pope to his business. And we ladies have some business of our own. Will you come shopping with us, John?"

"I don't think so, Aunt. Unless you don't trust yourselves to make the right decisions." But he smiled as he said it. "As I said, I have something I need to attend to." Lady Brockenhurst nodded. Clearly he had no desire to spend the rest of the day trailing round some silk merchant's warehouse, but she did not blame him for that.

As it happened, John Bellasis really had made other plans. He'd arranged to meet Susan Trenchard later that day at Morley's Hotel in Trafalgar Square. In the final analysis, he had to admit there was nothing that staved off humiliation and irritation more effectively than sleeping with someone else's wife.

He had reserved the room in a woman's name, albeit a false one, and he found Susan waiting when he pushed open the door of number twenty-seven on the first floor. He'd seen her maid, Speer, waiting patiently in the hall downstairs, so he knew she was there. She'd said she didn't have the time to travel to Isleworth, and they both knew he would not invite her to Albany. Not yet. His set of rooms was not quite right for the lazy, luxurious aristocratic image he liked to project. Comfort in Isleworth was achievable on his budget, comfort in Piccadilly was not. Or barely. He would mention his address as often as he could, reminding the listener that Lord Byron used to inhabit Set A2, but he never entertained there, not even fellows. So instead, this time, he had paid for a room in the Morley. The expense was an annoyance, but he was forced to conclude that Susan was worth it as he lay on the bed later that afternoon, naked and content. Rarely had he come across a more enthusiastic lover. Most of the women he slept with were boringly concerned about the dangers of conception and the inevitable scandal that would engulf them, but Susan Trenchard did not appear to be troubled by any such thoughts. She was compliant and completely obliging, and John liked that, and her, very much.

"Susan, my dear," he murmured as he rolled over in the bed toward her, edging himself closer and beginning to kiss her arm.

"This is very nice." Susan could feel a request was on its way, a favor, perhaps a command. She knew him by now. She knew his selfishness. She knew his greed. And yet, with all that, when she was on her way to see him, she could feel her heart pounding in her chest. She wasn't sure if it was love or lust, but it was more than she had ever felt with Oliver. So she waited for her orders. She would oblige him if she could.

He was watching her. "I must be careful. I'm getting quite fond of you."

It wasn't overwhelming as a compliment, but Susan took it as such. "I'm glad."

"I need you to do something for me," said John.

"Of course. If I can."

"I need you to find out more about Charles Pope."

"What?" She sat up, the mood broken. "Not you as well? Everyone seems to be obsessed with that wretched man! It's driving Oliver mad."

"I hesitate to agree with your husband on anything, but that is exactly the point," said John, sitting up alongside her. "I don't know what it is, but there is something about him I don't trust.

He seems to have a kind of hold over my aunt, and when I called at his office this afternoon, I found your mother-in-law there. As well as Ma—"

"As well as?"

"Never mind."

This made her smile, which was not the reaction he was looking for. The fact was, she knew the name he had nearly spoken. In a way, she was even pleased to see he was so considerate of her feelings. One day she might need to use it against him. "Why did you call at his office?" she said. "Does he have a hold over you, too?"

"I wanted to know why they are all pursuing him. Why have they selected him as their protégé?"

"Instead of you?" Susan laughed.

"I'm not joking." John's voice was hard and cold. He could turn in an instant.

"No," she agreed. But she was not his creature. Already she was asking herself whether this situation might not be switched to her advantage.

"What bothers me most," he spoke as he turned his back on her to sit on the edge of the bed, "is why they have both given him so much money."

Studying his profile, she could easily see that this bothered him very much indeed. "How is Lady Maria?"

"Why?"

"No reason, particularly. But if you saw her this afternoon..." She dared him to deny it but he was silent. They both knew it annoyed him when she strayed into the territory of his own life, but he had given away that the girl had been at Charles's office, and she liked to jerk his chain. Susan could make trouble for him if she chose to do so, and it pleased her to remind him of the fact every now and then.

"She's very well, as it happens. Shouldn't you be getting back?"

But Maria Grey was not very well at that moment, or at least she was not getting the better of her mother in the argument that had been caused, deliberately, by John. He'd found time, on his way to meet Susan, to drop into his club in St. James's and scribble a note to Lady Templemore lamenting that she did not care for racing. He finished by asking that they might arrange some other outing soon.

"Why did you say I don't like racing?" Lady Templemore sat very still as she spoke. She was not a clever woman, but she had an instinct for people, and she was fairly sure that something was happening that she would not have approved of if she only knew what it was.

Maria almost wriggled under her mother's gaze. "Do you?"

"I like it as much as I like any other of the pointless activities we have to spend our time on."

Maria stared at her mother. "Then write back and accept his invitation."

"For us both?"

"No, not for us both. For you."

They both knew what they were discussing, even though neither had yet admitted it. "I hope you don't imagine you can go back on your word," said Lady Templemore, and waited for her daughter's answer. But Maria said nothing. She simply sat there, in her mother's pretty drawing room, hands clasped, silent. She would neither confirm nor deny her mother's suggestion, which was ominous. Lady Templemore had been afraid of this, and for a while she had been tempted to bring the girl's brother across from Ireland, but she was by no means sure that Reggie would take her side and not his sister's. When all was said and done, he had nothing to gain from John's fortune. It was she, Corinne Templemore, who intended to profit from the security of a son-in-law with money and position, to give her the comfort in her declining years that she felt she fully deserved. "Haven't I protected you since you were a child? Don't I deserve a little security at the end? You will not have long to wait to see the last of me." She swallowed a sob and leaned back in the damask-covered *bergère*, waiting to see if her words had their desired effect. They didn't.

"Mama, you are as strong as a horse and will bury us all. As for being looked after, I will certainly look after you as well as I possibly can, so you have nothing to fear."

Corinne dabbed her eyes. "You will look after me by marrying John Bellasis. That is all I ask. What's the matter with him?"

"I am not sure how much I like him or whether he likes me." This seemed like a perfectly reasonable argument to Maria, but her mother was having none of it.

"Pshaw. Fiddle-faddle!" The tears were done with as Lady Templemore got back to business. "A young couple must learn to like each other as they get to know each other. I hardly knew your father when I married him. How would I? When we were never allowed to meet unchaperoned before the engagement? Even then we might sit together on a sofa, but never out of earshot of our companions. No young girl of our kind knows her husband before she marries him."

Maria stared at her mother. "And is your marriage to dear Papa to be the model that encourages me to accept the situation with John?" This was rather a low blow, which Maria regretted in a way. But the time was coming when they would have to face the fact that she was not going to marry John Bellasis. She may have doubted it before today, but after this afternoon she knew it beyond any doubt, so she may as well start laying the ground now.

Of course she had no proof of Charles's intentions toward her. That was true. No spoken proof, that is. But she was quite certain it was her engagement and her rank that were holding him back. She was not so sheltered that she could not see when a man was attracted to her, and she was confident she could bring Charles up to the mark when she wanted to. She was not worried about her brother. Reggie might have liked the idea of his sister as a countess, but he would not force her into it against her will. And he would like Charles. She felt quite confident of it. No, the main task that faced her was persuading her mother to allow her to entertain the suit of a Manchester mill owner instead of an earl, and it would not be easy, she was well aware of that. But first things first.

"You have given your word."

Actually, as she listened to her mother's arguments, Maria found it quite strange that she *had* given her word to John Bellasis. What could she have been thinking? Might the reason be that she was never in love before and did not know what the word meant? Was she in love now? She supposed she must be. "I would not be the first woman to change her mind," she said.

"You will not throw away a great future. I won't let you. I forbid it." Lady Templemore sat back in exasperation. Watching this, Maria decided to let the matter drop. For the moment. She must allow her mother to understand gradually that the desired marriage would never take place, but there was no need to rush. As she silently said these words to herself, Maria found she was smiling. She had admitted for the first time that she was planning a true *mésalliance* for herself. Her heart was thumping at the enormity of the scheme, but the fact remained that this was what she intended, and she meant to see it through.

Susan wouldn't normally have accepted Anne's invitation to accompany them on a trip to Glanville. She despised the place. There was nothing about the great Elizabethan house and its beautiful gardens in the heart of Somerset that she found interesting or even comfortable.

First, there was the arduous journey to get there, which involved careful planning and endless amounts of bed linen, as Quirk steered the vast traveling carriage, stopping at coaching houses along the route to take luncheon, or to dine, sleep and change the horses for the next leg. It was a two-day journey at the very least, but Anne Trenchard preferred to take three. She said she was too old to have her bones shaken about by traveling at speed, and she liked to keep stopping to let Agnes have a run. No doubt a new railway would soon change things, but they were not changed yet. So Susan would be stuck in a carriage, discussing the finer points of gardening, for three whole days at a time—sometimes more, if it was raining and the coach got stuck in the mud.

But the main reason for her resistance to Glanville was that she didn't see the point of making the journey at all. Once you got there, what was there to do? Except engage in yet more discussions about gardening, walk around those very gardens, and eat endlessly at the long dining table. Occasionally these dinners would be attended by various local dignitaries, keen to make the acquaintance of James Trenchard in the hope that they could persuade him to part with some of his money and fund their worthy causes. Of the county's gentry they saw almost nothing. As everyone knows, thought Susan wryly, social climbing is notoriously harder in the country. In London people care less who you are as long as you dress properly and say the right things. In the country they are less forgiving. It made her yawn just thinking about it.

But this time John had persuaded her that it would be a good idea. As they spent the rest of the afternoon in bed together, he'd outlined his plan. She was to find out exactly who Charles was, and why James Trenchard was so interested in funding him, not to mention the curious alliance growing between John's aunt and Susan's mother-in-law. There might be something in all this that she could make use of. At any rate, it suited Susan's own agenda to put John Bellasis into her debt.

Oliver was perhaps the most surprised when Susan accepted the invitation to spend a month in the country with his parents. There would normally be tantrums and tears. He might even have had to go shopping and buy her a little something from his jeweler as a further argument for her compliance. But not this time.

Her reaction had pleased him. Truth be told, lately he'd found he rather preferred life at Glanville to that in London. He had made a real effort, or so he thought, to take an interest in his father's business, but the truth was he felt more cut out for the traditional life of a country squire. Why shouldn't he? They'd brought him up as a gentleman and this was the result. He liked hunting and shooting, in fact all the traditions, and the easy conviviality of country life, much more than the hours spent poring over plans and accounts in his father's or William Cubitt's office. He would walk about the estate, conversing with the tenants, listening to their concerns. It made him feel busy and valued and able. At one time he had accepted that they would not live at Glanville when his parents died, that Susan would insist on something bigger and grander and closer to London, but lately, as he and his wife had gone their separate ways, he'd begun to wonder if some accommodation might be possible. Then again, he had no heir, and life at a house like Glanville was all about continuity.

His heart soared as the carriage finally turned through the tall, honey-colored gates. At the end of the long drive stood a fine, three-story house that was in a significantly better state than when his mother had first found it in 1825. On a rather grandiose whim, James had instructed his wife to "find a seat" in the country for the family. Of course he'd expected her to buy somewhere impressive but convenient, a decent pile in Hertfordshire or Surrey, or at least somewhere relatively close to London. But Anne had had other ideas. When she'd chanced upon Glanville, a fine example of transition architecture as the fashion moved from Mediaeval Gothic to Renaissance Classical, with its gardens and park surrounded by thousands of acres of farmland, she knew it was what she was searching for. What she had always been searching for, in a way. That said, it also had a large and leaking roof as well as almost every kind of rot and beetle, and James had initially refused. It was not what he'd had in mind at all. He had no desire to live in Somerset, and he'd imagined a house that did not need to be almost entirely rebuilt. However, for one of the few times in her life, Anne had insisted.

Now, almost twenty years later, they both regarded it as her greatest achievement. She had painstakingly restored the house, falling in love with its little quirks: the stone monkeys that clambered up the Dutch gables, the Nine Worthies in their niches on the East Front. Sometimes James thought this labor of love was compensation for something else—if Anne had not been able to save her own daughter, then at least she might save this glorious old house. And the more she strove, the more enthusiasm and life she breathed into it, the more the place shone.

Her real triumph was the creation of the gardens, shaped from an expanse of nothing, and, as the carriage pulled up outside the house, the head gardener, Hooper, was already waiting for her. But before she could greet him, the rituals had to be observed, and Turton, who had traveled down ahead of them, stepped forward to open the door.

"Madam," said the butler as Anne climbed down the steps, her dog under her arm, "I trust you had a pleasant journey?" His voice was a little jaded. To tell the truth, he felt much the same as Mrs. Oliver when it came to Glanville. He too hated the journey down, but what he disliked even more was the quality of the local servants he had to deal with during these time-wasting stays in the country. Unlike most aristocrats, whose main residence would be on their estates, the Trenchards based themselves in London. So their principal staff remained there, and only a skeleton group traveled back and forth to Somerset. Turton, Ellis, Speer, and Billy the footman, who was also required to dress Oliver, were the only ones who accompanied the family to Glanville. The cook, Mrs. Babbage, had originally made the journey, but the tension and arguments that her arrival created in the kitchens became too disruptive and Anne had decided to employ a local woman, Mrs. Adams, who was much more convivial and less likely to demand ingredients that must be sent down from the capital. The result being that the food was significantly simpler in the country, the service a little slower, and Turton always wore a look of purgatory about him.

"Thank you, Turton. I hope everyone's managed to settle in."

"We're doing what we can, all things considered," he replied mournfully, but Anne was not going to be drawn into staffing problems as soon as she arrived. She was well aware of Turton's feelings, but she was of the opinion that if Glanville was going to survive, it needed the support of the local community, and that meant, first and foremost, employing the sons and daughters of the tenant farmers and those who worked on the estate. Where else were the young to go? They needed jobs, and it was the estate's duty to provide them, and if Turton chose to be irritated by that then it must be his problem and not hers.

"Oh, Hooper," she declared, rubbing her hands together, as she approached the gardener. "What news do you have for me?"

"My dear," James Trenchard called after his wife. "Won't you come inside? You must be tired."

"In a moment. I just want to hear what's happened in the garden while we've been away. Besides, Agnes needs a walk."

"Don't wear yourself out," said James as he went in with the others. But he didn't really mind. He loved to see his wife happy, and she was always happy at Glanville.

Later that evening they would sit down to dinner in what used to be the "pannetry" and the "buttery." The house was too old to boast a proper dining room, since its original inhabitants would have eaten with their household in the great hall. But Anne decided that her commitment to the Elizabethan era had its limits, and while they fixed the roof, they had also knocked out the wall between these two rooms to create a much-needed private eating space for the family. The walls were paneled, and a substantial fireplace was added to complement the large windows that overlooked the East Terrace. In a way, she loved the room all the more because she had invented it when she took possession of the house.

She was walking along the gallery toward the staircase when Ellis came after her, carrying a shawl. "You might need this, m'lady."

Ellis was in a good mood. She always perked up in the country. Unlike Turton, Ellis enjoyed being Queen of the May. It was rare that she managed to enjoy a sense of superiority, but out here, in the depths of Somerset, she became the fount of all knowledge when it came to the *beau monde*. She could recount the goings-on in London, describe the new shops, detail the fashion trends. Indeed, there was nothing she liked more than being able to share the latest stories about Lord So-and-So and Lady Such and Such as the staff settled around the table in the servants' hall below stairs. The workload was also lighter in the country. There was less entertaining and fewer evenings out, so there were scarcely any late nights and she spent far less time waiting into the small hours, sitting in Mrs. Trenchard's dressing room longing for her mistress to come home.

When Anne entered the drawing room, James was fidgeting by the fire. She knew what that meant. "Ring for Turton, why don't you? See if we can go straight in. I'd like an early night, if it can be managed."

"Would you mind?" He jumped up eagerly and tugged at the bell pull. Susan and Oliver were already down, and she understood without being told that Susan's chatter was driving her husband mad. He was probably hoping to find some relief in a decent glass of claret. Anne looked at her daughter-in-law. She certainly did seem very animated. She was normally so sullen at Glanville, but this evening she had made a special effort. Speer had pinned up her hair in a chignon, and she was wearing pale yellow silk, with some prettily set emeralds in her ears.

As soon as she felt she had Anne's attention, Susan began. "You'll never guess whom I saw in Piccadilly the other day." She hadn't wanted to have the conversation while they were rocking about in the coach, but there was no point in delaying it any further.

"I won't try." Anne smiled pleasantly, stroking Agnes, who was begging beside her chair.

"Mr. Bellasis."

"Oh? Lord Brockenhurst's nephew?"

"The very one. We met him at Brockenhurst House that time. Anyway, I was walking along with Speer, on my way to my glove-maker, and he suddenly appeared."

"Fancy that." Anne was starting to understand that this was leading somewhere, and she wasn't convinced it was somewhere she wanted to go. Happily, the butler entered at just that moment, and it was not long before they were seated around the table in the dining room.

Susan held her peace until the first course had been brought and they'd helped themselves, but no longer than that. As soon as the footmen had stepped back from the table, she began. "Mr. Bellasis told me he'd seen you and his aunt at Mr. Pope's offices in the city."

"*What?*" said James, putting down his knife and fork.

"Oh"—Susan's hand flew to her mouth in pretended alarm—"have I said something I shouldn't?'

"Of course not." Anne was very calm. "Mr. Trenchard has taken an interest in this young man, and so when Lady Brockenhurst suggested we pay him a call, I agreed. I was curious."

"Not half as curious as I am," said Oliver, and Anne saw with a sinking heart that he must have been drinking for some time before her arrival downstairs. "Why is it that my dear father takes twice the interest in the activities of this Mr. Pope than he does in our own work at Cubitt Town?"

"I do not." James had been preparing to reprimand Anne, but suddenly he found himself fighting his son and on the defensive. "I like Mr. Pope. I think his business plans are sensible and good, and I expect to make money out of them. I have investments in many different areas. You must know that by now."

"I daresay," said Oliver. "But I wonder if you take all the managers of these new businesses out to lunch at your club. Or if Lady Brockenhurst parades every investment opportunity around her drawing room."

This was making James angry. "I like and admire Mr. Pope," he said. "I wish you could boast half his industry."

"Don't worry, Father." Oliver had given up trying to control himself. "I am well aware that Mr. Pope has all the virtues you find lacking in your own child."

Susan decided to refrain from adding any more tinder to the fire. She had established without question that Mr. Pope was an extremely important, if mystifying, figure in this argument, but she did not think she would push it any further here. Instead she might as well sit back and let her ridiculous husband make a fool of himself.

"Sit down, Oliver," said Anne, for her son was on his feet, wagging a finger at his father like some itinerant preacher at a country fair.

"I will not! Turton! Have my dinner taken up to my room. I would rather not stay here and disappoint my father." So saying, he stormed out, slamming the door behind him.

There was a silence before Anne spoke. "Better do as Mr. Oliver says, Turton. Please ask Mrs. Adams if she can make up a tray." She turned to her daughter-in-law, determined to change the tone. "Now, Susan, do you have anything you want to do while you're down here, or shall we just plan our entertainment as each new day dawns?"

Susan knew what was happening, but she was happy to play along, launching into how they might amuse themselves until they returned to London.

That night James couldn't sleep. He could hear from Anne's easy, even breathing that she had not been kept awake by Oliver's outburst, but it wasn't only that. Anne had retired early and had made sure she was asleep before he arrived in the room so that he would have no chance to question her about her visit to Bishopsgate. He suspected this, but he could hardly shake her awake. What could she have imagined she was doing? Was he the only member of this family who was not trying to destroy their world? And as for Oliver, he was so spoiled. Now he was jealous of Charles, but if it hadn't been Charles, it would have been something else. What did he want? What did he expect? For his father to hand everything over to him on a silver platter?

James shook his head. He remembered how his own father had worked when he was a child. He remembered how hard he himself had worked. How low down the pecking order all those officers had made him feel as he found them their bread, their flour, their wine, their munitions on the grubby streets of Brussels. He also remembered the risks he'd taken when he returned. He'd gambled his resources on the Cubitt brothers and the development of the new Belgravia, and what a terrifying journey that had been. Sleepless nights, anxious days, and now here they were, sitting in their beautiful house in Somerset with an ungrateful wretch of a son and his equally spoiled wife, both of them expecting him, James Trenchard, to keep them in the manner to which they were determined to become accustomed. How he wished Sophia were here, beside him. In his mind he saw her as his true child, ignoring the barriers that held her back, pushing them down and step-ping over them, not whining or complaining but simply taking what was hers. In truth, she had never left him. There could not have been more than a few waking minutes since she was taken from them when she had not been in his mind, laughing, making fun of him, but always with love. Not for the first time he could feel his cheeks wet with tears at the loss of his darling daughter.

The rest of the time at Glanville passed without too much inci-dent, although relations between father and son remained strained. James had questioned Anne about the visit to Charles's place of work and she had justified it, saying that she knew Lady Brockenhurst was going and it felt wise to her to be one of the party. She would then be able to contain any awkwardness if the Countess was indiscreet, but in the event, she had not been. James was forced to admit this seemed sensible enough and he did not press the point, although he sensed that Anne was becoming accustomed to the idea that the day would come, before too long, when the truth would be free. In the meantime, she walked her dog in the park, discussed the coming season with her gardener, and retired early.

Susan tried to winkle out some information, but Anne was made of much sterner stuff than she appreciated and had no intention of giving away the least scintilla. "But there must be some reason for Father's interest in Mr. Pope?" Susan ventured once as they strolled together down the long lime avenue, Agnes trotting in their wake. "Especially as Lord and Lady Brockenhurst obviously feel the same. I am curious."

"Then you must stay curious, for I cannot help you. They like the young man, and they think he will reward their patronage. That is all."

Susan was clever enough to know that that was not all, or any-thing like all, but she could not think of a way to learn more. She did try to get something out of Ellis but was firmly rebuffed. Ellis had her pride. She was not about to be bought by the likes of Mrs. Oliver.

By the time they returned to London, son and father were talking again, although the wound clearly festered. For her part, Susan had survived her pastoral month and was trying to decide how to make the little she had learned sound like more when she told it to John.

She didn't have long to wait before she received a note suggesting that she and John should meet by chance in the Green Park, and so she set off with Speer in tow.

"But when you say important, how important?" said John impatiently. "I know he is important to Mr. Trenchard, but I want to know why."

"It must have something to do with his business, I suppose."

"Nonsense." He shook his head. "Anyone can see there is more invested in this than just money."

Susan knew he was right. "Oliver's furious about the whole thing. He thinks he is being pushed into second place by this nonentity."

John was at his most sardonic. "I am always sympathetic to your husband, of course, my dear, but his anger doesn't help me now."

"No." Susan was aware that she was not delivering what she had been summoned for, the reason why she had endured the endless weeks at Glanville, but there was something else that had begun to trouble her since their last encounter at Morley's Hotel. She had been planning to bring it up here and now, but seeing John's annoyance she thought it might be better to leave it. Except she couldn't leave it indefinitely.

He glanced down at her. "What's the matter? You look preoccupied."

"Do I?" she shook her head girlishly. "It's nothing."

But it wasn't really nothing. As she knew very well.

John followed Susan home to Eaton Square. Not that she realized. She was too busy talking to Speer, ordering her to pick up some ribbon, some trimming, anything, so they might give Oliver a good reason why they had been out all afternoon.

He waited on the corner, standing underneath a streetlight, in the hope that Ellis might manage to slip away for a minute. He was frustrated by the scant information Susan had managed to glean while in Somerset, but he had not been expecting much more and he had given Ellis the task of talking to his aunt's maid, Dawson. She must know most of the secrets of that household. He had told Ellis where and when he would be in the square, and finally, just as the sun was beginning to fade, Ellis appeared. She saw John waiting at the next corner and walked toward him. "Well?" he asked. There was no need for pleasantries.

"Oh, sir," she said, wringing her hands with carefully judged obsequiousness. "I'm not sure I have anything very useful to report."

"You must have something."

"I'm afraid not, sir," continued Ellis. "Miss Dawson isn't really the sort of woman we thought she might be."

"You mean, she is loyal to her employers?"

John sounded so incredulous that Ellis nearly laughed. She swallowed it, in time. "It appears so, sir."

John sighed loudly. Someone, somewhere must know something about this young man. He had to think. "I have a task for you."

"Of course, sir." Ellis always liked to sound helpful, even if there wasn't much she could do to make things better. It increased the tips.

"Ask Turton to meet me again. Usual place. At seven tomorrow evening."

"Mr. Turton likes to be back by seven, to get ready for dinner."

"Six, then." He had tried the ladies' way, of gossiping maids and curious daughters-in-law, and it hadn't worked. It was time for a rethink. "And don't forget." Before she could protest that she would not, he was striding away along the pavement.

Charles Pope was in a quandary as he stood near the Round Pond in Kensington Gardens. In his hand was a letter that had been delivered to his office. He turned it over and over, staring down at the light, precise writing. Was there any point in his being here? What could he achieve beyond more trouble? Maria Grey had written, asking him to call on her at her mother's house in Chesham Street, but he had refused. A man in his position could not call on a young woman of her standing, especially as she was already betrothed. Instead, he'd sent a note suggesting they should meet at the Round Pond at three in the afternoon. It was a public enough place, and there would be no sense of impropriety should they happen to bump into each other while out for a walk. Would there?

Except that, now it was nearly the appointed time, his nerve was failing. How could he claim to love her if he was prepared to risk her good name like this? But even as he asked himself the question, he knew that he had to see her again.

A stiff wind was blowing when he arrived at the pond. The water was choppy, with small waves lapping against the sides and splashing at his feet. Despite the breeze, there were plenty of ladies taking a stroll, some in groups of two or three, and small children were running around, zigzagging between them. Some older boys were struggling to get a scarlet kite off the ground, and behind them was a gathering of their anxious nurses, a few pushing the new basket-weave baby carriages, while others carried their charges.

He sat down on a park bench and stared at the ducks bobbing about on the surface of the water, all the time glancing anxiously around him, scanning the faces of passersby. Where was she? Perhaps she had decided not to come. It was already twenty minutes after the hour. Of course she had decided against the whole thing. She had discussed it with someone, her mother or her maid, and they had seen it for the mad plan that it was. He stood up. He was clearly making a fool of himself. This fine and beautiful girl was a thousand miles out of his league. What was he doing but wasting his time?

"I am so sorry!" He spun around and there she was, wearing a simple light tweed suit and clutching onto her bonnet. "I had to run." She smiled. Her eyes were bright and her cheeks flushed as she stood catching her breath. "It was much harder to escape Ryan than I thought." Then she laughed, because he was there waiting, and she hadn't missed him as she feared, and everything was wonderful again. She sat down on a bench and he sat with her.

"You've come alone?" Charles did not intend to sound as shocked as he felt, but she was playing with her reputation.

"Of course I've come alone. You don't think my mother would have let me out if she'd had the slightest idea where I was going, and I can't trust Ryan. She reports every move I make back to Mama. You are so lucky, Mr. Pope, to have been born a man."

"I'm rather glad you were not born a man." It was the most daring thing he had said to her, and he fell silent at his own courage.

She laughed again. "Perhaps. But I'm rather proud of myself today. I lost my maid and hailed a cab, for the first time in my life. How's that?"

He could not rid himself of the sense that he was luring her into danger. "But I don't see what good can come of our meeting. Certainly not for you. You have taken a great risk in coming here."

"Surely you admire people who take risks, Mr. Pope?" she asked, watching the ducks.

"I would not admire a man who allowed his beloved to sacrifice her reputation." He'd failed to notice that he referred to her, by implication, as his beloved.

But she had. "Because I'm engaged?" said Maria softly.

"Yes, you are engaged. But even if you weren't." He sighed. It was time for some reality to break into fairyland. "I am not the sort of man Lady Templemore would ever entertain as a possible suitor for your hand."

He had meant by this to bring things to a halt, but instead his words released a thousand possibilities. "Are you a suitor for my hand?" she said, looking him directly in the eye.

He returned her gaze. What was the point of lying now? "Lady Maria, I would fight dragons, I would walk over flaming coals, I would enter the Valley of the Dead, if I thought I might have a chance of your heart."

For a moment she was silenced by this declaration. She had grown up in a different world from his, and she was used to flowery speeches but not great passion. She understood now that she had inflamed a love in this straightforward man that was completely out of his control. He loved her with his whole being. "Heavens," she said. "We seem to have covered quite a distance in a few short sentences. Please call me Maria."

"I can't. And I have told you the truth because I believe you deserve the truth, but I do not think we have the power to make it happen, even supposing you should want to."

"I do want to make it happen, Mr. Pope. Charles. Be easy in that." She remembered the stiff and stilted conversation with John Bellasis she'd had in her mother's morning room and compared the two scenes with wonder. This is what love is like, she thought, not that absurd mixture of polite anecdotes and feeble, unfelt compliments.

Charles did not reply. He simply did not dare to look into her beautiful, hopeful, proud face for fear of losing himself completely. And whatever she said, she would surely break his heart. Even if she had no desire to, even if she was determined to stick to him through thick and thin, it must come to that in the end. She might bemoan her fate at being born a woman, but he was ruing the day he had been born the orphan cousin of a country parson.

A figure striding up the Broad Walk caught his attention. "Isn't that your mother?" he said suddenly, jumping to his feet. There was something about the shape of the woman's silhouette, the brisk air of impatience, that he recognized from that moment on the balcony at the Brockenhursts' party. He remembered how she had stood in the doorway, reeking of disapproval. Even then he had known that Lady Maria Grey was beyond his grasp.

She paled. "Ryan must have gone straight home and told her I'd given her the slip. I suppose she heard where I directed the cab. You must go, now."

"I can't," he said. "I can't leave you to take the blame."

She shook her head briskly. "Why not? The blame is mine. And don't worry. She won't eat me. But this is not the right moment for you to be introduced as my lover. You know I'm right. So, go."

She took his hand and squeezed it, then Charles drifted back across the graveled paths and lost himself in the shrubbery beyond.

Lady Templemore had arrived. "Who was that man?"

"He was lost. He needed to find the Queen's Gate."

She was very convincing. Lady Templemore sat on the bench. "My dear, I think it's time you and I had a little talk."

Charles heard none of this exchange, although he might have guessed its content. He didn't care. As he quickened his pace and walked back toward Kensington Gore, his chest was close to bursting. Nothing else really mattered, not any more. She loved him. And he loved her back. She had acknowledged him as her lover. That was all he really needed to know. If she did break his heart, it would be worth it for this moment. What came next he couldn't guess at, but he loved and was loved in return. For now, that was enough.

.8.

An Income for Life

John Bellasis braced himself before he crossed the threshold of his parents' house in Harley Street. He wasn't sure why he disliked it so much. Maybe because the place was so shabby in comparison to his aunt's splendid palace in Belgrave Square. Maybe because it reminded him that his origins were not quite as smart as they should have been. Or perhaps it was simpler. Maybe it was just that his parents bored him. They were dull people, weighed down with problems of their own making, and, to be honest, he sometimes felt a creeping impatience for his father to quit the scene, leaving John as his uncle's direct heir. Whatever the truth of the matter, he experienced a certain weariness as the door was opened and he stepped inside.

Luncheon at home with his parents was not an invitation he would normally accept with much enthusiasm. He'd usually concoct some excuse: an urgent, pressing engagement that sadly could not be delayed. But today he was—once more—in need of funds, so he had little choice but to be courteous to his mother, who always indulged her son and rarely refused him anything. It was not a fortune, but he needed something to tide him over until Christmas, and there was the question of Ellis and Turton to attend to. But that was an investment, he told himself confidently. A small outlay for a large reward, or so he hoped.

He wasn't sure what the butler and the maid would come up with, but his instincts told him that the Trenchards were hiding something. And at that point, any illuminating fact about Charles Pope and his connections would be helpful. John was banking on the butler. He recognized a venal soul when he saw one, and a butler enjoyed greater freedom of access within a private house than a lady's maid. Turton had carte blanche to wander where he chose and could lay his hands on keys that would be withheld from servants of a lower rank; the maid's territory was more circumscribed. Of course Turton had feigned surprise and consternation at their meeting when it was suggested he might investigate Mr. Trenchard's papers, but then again, it was amazing how persuasive the offer of six months' wages could be.

Walking into the small sitting room at the front of the house, John found his father in a high-backed chair by the window, reading a copy of the *Times*. "Mother not here?" asked John, looking around the room. If she were about, perhaps he could dispense with luncheon altogether and go straight to the essential question of finances.

It was an oddly decorated room. Most of the furniture, and indeed the portraits, with their heavy gilt frames and elaborate subjects, looked far too grand for their surroundings. The scale was wrong; it was clear these tables and chairs had previously occupied a larger setting. Even the lamps seemed bulky. It all generated a sense of claustrophobia, a feeling that permeated the entire house.

"Your mother is at a committee meeting." Stephen put down his newspaper. "Something to do with the slums in the Old Nichol."

"The Old Nichol? Why is she wasting her time on that stinking bunch of cockfighters and thieves?" John wrinkled his nose.

"I don't know. Saving them from themselves, no doubt. You know what she's like." Stephen sighed and then scratched his smooth head. "Before she gets back, I think I should tell you..." He hesitated. It was not like him to be embarrassed, but he was embarrassed now. "That Schmitt debt is still troubling me."

"I thought you'd paid him."

"I did. Count Sikorsky was generous and lent me some money at the beginning of the summer, and I borrowed the rest from the bank. But it's been six weeks, and Sikorsky is asking questions. He wants his money back."

"What did you think would happen?"

Stephen ignored his son's question. "You spoke once of a Polish moneylender."

"Who charges fifty percent. And to borrow from one moneylender to pay off another..." John sat down. Of course this moment had to come. His father had borrowed an enormous sum with no means of returning it. Somehow he had tried to put it out of his mind, but it must be faced. He shook his head. John thought himself irresponsible, but surely women were a safer addiction than gambling.

Stephen gazed rather hopelessly out the window. He was up to his neck in debt, and it would only be a matter of time before he would join those filthy beggars and vagrants on the street outside. Or would he simply be dragged off to the Marshalsea and imprisoned until he paid? It was laughable, really; there was his wife, busily helping the poor, when in reality her services were required a little closer to home.

For the first time in his life John actually felt quite sorry for his father as he watched him sink back forlornly into his chair. It wasn't Stephen's fault he was born second. John had always, consciously or unconsciously, decided that everything was the fault of one or other of his parents. Somehow it was their fault that they didn't live at Lymington Park, that they didn't have a large house in Belgrave Square, and even their fault that he, John, had been born the eldest son of the second son and not the first. He'd been a child when it happened but now, if he was honest, he felt it was only justice that Edmund Bellasis had died and made him heir. At least a solution was on its way. Otherwise there would be no hope for any of them.

"Aunt Caroline might be some help," said John, flicking a little dust off his trousers.

"Do you think so? You surprise me." His father turned and looked at him, hands clasped together, eyes imploring. "I thought we'd given up on that."

"We'll see." John rubbed his hands together. "I have a man on the case, as they say."

"You mean you're still looking into that Mr. Pope?"

"I am."

"There's definitely something going on. His hold over her is very strange, even improper." Stephen's lightly sweating face gleamed in the sunlight, dark eyes darting around the room. "Mark my words, Caroline is hiding something."

"I agree." John nodded, getting out of his chair. There was something about his father's desperation that was disconcerting. "And when I have some information, I shall challenge her with it, and at the same time I'll bring up our shortage of funds and remind her that we are a family, and families ought to pull together."

"You must be careful."

John nodded. "I will be."

Stephen was thinking aloud. "If Peregrine had only helped us out when I asked, then we would not be in this situation in the first place."

This was a little too much for his son to let pass. "If you hadn't gambled with money you do not have, my dear Father, we would not be in this situation. And anyway, *we* are not in any situation. You're in the situation. I'm not aware that I am in debt to one of the most unpleasant moneylenders in London."

Stephen was past defending himself. "You have to help me."

"John," declared Grace as she walked through the door. "How lovely to see you."

John looked at his mother. She was dressed in a simple dark-gray dress, with long, tight sleeves and a plain white frill at the neck. Grace had a wardrobe that looked as if it had been designed for serious meetings and charity functions. As a matter of fact, she would have thought it vulgar to wear the latest fashions to such events, and she always disapproved of those women who sighed with concern over the sufferings of the poor while wearing clothes that cost more than the average annual income. In her case, of course, she could not have afforded the latter anyway.

"How are you?" she asked, pushing up her hair, which had been flattened by her bonnet. She walked over and kissed her son. "We hardly saw anything of you this summer."

"I am very well." He shot his father a look as he kissed his mother back. John could always turn on the charm when he wanted something. "How was your meeting?"

"Disheartening," she said, her narrow lips pursed. "We spent most of the morning talking about Black Monday."

"What's that?"

"The day when the rent is due. They say the queues at the pawnbrokers go the length of the street."

"Pawnbrokers? What do they have to pawn?" asked John.

"I agree." Grace nodded, sitting down in the chair opposite Stephen. "Heaven knows, is all I can say. Incidentally, I was wondering if you have any news?" She looked inquisitively into her son's eyes.

"What sort of news?"

"Well, not to put too fine a point on it, we don't understand the delay in announcing the engagement." She nodded at her husband so he would back her up, but Stephen was too buried in his own woes to oblige her.

John shrugged. "I don't know anything about it. Why don't you ask Lady Templemore?"

Grace said nothing, but John could not help pondering his mother's words. Why hadn't they made the announcement? Then again, how eager was he for the marriage to take place? Mind you, eager or not, he certainly didn't intend to be turned down.

As a matter of fact, a very similar conversation was happening in the drawing room of Lady Templemore's London house in Chesham Place. It was a charming room in the French taste, more of a boudoir than a reception room, really, since it had originally been decorated by Lady Templemore's widowed mother. She'd left the house to her daughter, and since the late Lord Templemore had never shown much interest in London, it had remained pretty much as it was. At this moment, though, there was clearly some topic that was irritating both Lady Templemore and Maria, who sat grimly opposite each other, like chess champions preparing for a match.

"I say again, I do not understand the delay when the thing is settled." Lady Templemore's words may have been simple enough, but her tone suggested that she knew well enough things were *not* settled at all.

"And I say again, what is the point of pretending that I will marry John Bellasis when you know very well I will not?" Maria would never have described herself as a rebel. She was perfectly happy to conform with most customs and traditions, but she had seen a marriage between two people who were not suited to each other from very close quarters, and she did not intend to let any such thing happen to her.

"Then why did you accept him?"

Maria was forced to admit that her mother had a point. Why on earth had she accepted John? The more she considered it, the less she understood what could have been in her mind. It had been presented to her as an escape from their predicament, a safe haven. She knew her mother was running out of money and her brother would not have much to spare. She had been told these things often enough. And of course John was very good-looking, there was no denying that. But was she really so feeble, so trivial a person? She could only suppose that, never having been in love before, she had not realized the force of the emotion when it happened. And now it had.

"I hope you are not suggesting you have met someone else— someone who is not known to me—whom you prefer?" Corinne Templemore spoke the words as if they actually tasted unpleasant.

"I'm not suggesting anything. I'm just telling you that I won't marry John Bellasis."

Lady Templemore shook her head. "You're not thinking properly. Once he has inherited from his uncle, you will have a position from which you can do many interesting things. It will be a good and rewarding life."

"For someone, but not for me."

Lady Templemore stood. "I won't let you throw away your chance. I would be a bad mother if I allowed it." She started to leave the room.

"What are you going to do?" Maria's voice suggested that she realized her mother was undefeated and the situation was anything but resolved.

"You'll see." Lady Templemore swept out and Maria was left alone.

Turton was already seated at his usual table in the Horse and Groom, a small glass of gin in front of him, when John Bellasis arrived. He looked up as John entered the bar and nodded briefly in acknowledgment, but he did not stand, which, given their relative positions, might have alerted John as to what was coming.

John sat down at the table. He was slightly out of breath and, unusually for him, he was feeling guilty.

The luncheon in Harley Street had become more complicated than he had anticipated, and it had taken him some time to recover. His mother hadn't been able to help him in the end, not because she would not but because she could not. There was no money to spare and she had none to give. Bruised by this, he had gone upstairs to collect some things from his old room, only to see that a box had been placed on top of his wardrobe. Further investigation revealed that it contained a large and solid silver punch bowl, wrapped in a green baize cloth and buried under some books. He suspected his desperate mother might have hidden it, saving it for Emma, perhaps? At any rate, saving it from both her husband and her son, whose unused bedroom seemed the safest spot in the house. John felt some pity for her when he thought about it, but he took the punch bowl all the same. He needed ready cash, and so, with difficulty, he smuggled it out into the street, hailed a cab, and, following the example of the dwellers of Old Nichol, he went directly to a pawnshop he knew in Shepherd Market. They paid him well, a hundred pounds, and naturally he told himself that it was only temporary and he would soon be back to retrieve it. But still, it was the first time he had actually stolen from his parents, and he needed a moment to adjust to the idea.

"So," he said at last. "Do you have anything for me?"

"Good afternoon, sir," began Turton. Although he was used

to cutting deals and bargaining over bacon, venison, and hock, somehow he felt this type of contract required more stateliness. "May I offer you something to drink?"

"Thank you. I'll have some brandy," replied John, fidgeting in his chair, the money in his pocket almost seeming to weigh him down. He hoped this pompous man had come up with something worth having. He had better things to do than to waste his Thursday afternoon sitting in an unprepossessing public house with a servant.

Turton nodded across the room. The barman picked up a large brown bottle of brandy and a small glass and headed over to the table. He poured out a shot and left the bottle, with the cork half in, before shuffling away. John drank it in one. It made him feel a bit better, alleviating the irritation of the luncheon and the guilt of its sequel. To make matters worse, his parents would not let go of the subject of Maria Grey. But what could he do? The date of the wedding and the announcement in the papers were up to Lady Templemore. The girl was pretty enough, he thought, pouring himself another drink, but was he sure he couldn't do better? Breaking into his reverie, Turton gave a slight cough. It was time to return to the business in hand.

"So?" John asked again.

"Well," replied Turton, with a quick glance at the door.

The man was nervous, that much was obvious. And he had reason to be. They might have repealed the so-called "Bloody Code" twenty years before, and crimes committed by servants against their masters were no longer classed as petty treason and punishable by death. But it was still a common paranoia among the propertied classes that servants were strangers given permission to roam free in their houses on trust, and any breach of that trust was a serious offense and demanded extreme consequences. Turton might not be facing the noose but he was certainly risking prison. In order to gain access to Mr. Trenchard's private papers, he had "borrowed" a set of keys from Mrs. Frant and gone from drawer to drawer in the master's main desk, riffling through endless boxes before he found the bronze key Mr. Trenchard used for his private *secrétaire*. If discovered, his crime would not be easily forgiven.

In truth, Amos Turton wasn't devoid of conscience. He had worked hard for the family for many years and he felt a certain loyalty to them. The petty pilfering he indulged in, courtesy of Mrs. Babbage, did not belie that. He simply viewed it as a legitimate perk of the job. Unlocking desks and riffling through his master's things was another matter entirely. Yet as he grew older, Turton began to have an eye on his retirement, and his savings were nowhere near what he'd hoped to accumulate by this stage of his life. He had grown used to a degree of comfort, and he intended to enjoy that comfort for years to come. So when John had approached him once more, he had been ready to listen to his proposal.

"I haven't got much time." John was growing impatient. The man either had something or he did not.

"What about the money?"

"Don't worry." John rolled his eyes, as if to show that this was the easiest part. "It is here." He patted the pocket of his black coat. He did not mention that he had only acquired the money on the way to the pub that afternoon.

"Well, I did find something," began Turton, reaching into his pocket. John leaned forward as the man pulled out an old brown envelope. "It was locked away in one of the smaller drawers, which had its own key." John didn't say anything. What did he care about the details? "It's a letter that mentions a child, called Charles." John sat up. He was listening now. "The letter says the child is doing very well in his Bible studies, which Mr. Trenchard will be pleased to hear."

"His Bible studies?"

"Yes," said Turton. "And his guardian hopes that he will be suited to a career in the Church. The boy seems to have an aptitude for study. At any rate, he's a hard worker. And the writer expects to call on Mr. Trenchard for advice on the next step for his charge, as the need arises."

"Right," said John, scratching his head, trying to think.

Turton waited a moment to extract the full effect. "The letter is signed by the Reverend Benjamin Pope, but the boy is not his son."

"Why do you say that?"

"Something in his manner of outlining the news of the boy's progress for Mr. Trenchard's benefit. He writes as an employee filling out a report."

"But I thought Mr. Trenchard's advice was only sought when Charles Pope was first in London, attempting to get a foothold in business. Isn't that the story of how they first met? Now you're telling me that Trenchard has taken an interest in him—has received information about him—from his childhood?"

Turton nodded. "That appears to be the case, sir."

"Show me." John made a grab for the letter, but Turton was too quick. His slim hands held on tightly to the envelope. He was not a man to be duped, and he would not have trusted Mr. Bellasis any farther than he could throw him. He wanted his money and he wanted it now.

"If you put the letter on the table, then I shall put down the money," replied John.

"Of course, sir." Turton smiled as he laid the envelope down with his hand still placed firmly on top of it. He watched as John pulled a large wad of notes out of his pocket and counted them under the table. The Horse and Groom was hardly a place for the ladies, and twenty pounds, the agreed price for any substantive information regarding Charles Pope, was not something one would flash around in any establishment. Men would kill for a lot less.

John discreetly pushed the money across the table.

"Thank you very much, sir," replied Turton, releasing the letter at the same time.

John opened the envelope and began to scan its contents, his lips moving slightly as he checked the information that Turton had given him. This was proof that Charles Pope had a connection with Trenchard that started years before their business arrangement; proof that Charles was not telling the whole story, assuming he knew the truth. It was only now that John began to suspect that Charles Pope was Trenchard's son, but already it seemed odd that the idea had not occurred to him earlier. He turned the sheet of paper over, then looked in the envelope.

"Where's the other page?" he asked, looking at Turton.

"The other page, sir?"

"Don't get smart with me!" John's earlier shame had mixed with the brandy and he was perilously close to fury. "The first page. The one with the address of the writer? Where does Reverend Benjamin Pope live?"

"Oh, that page, sir." Turton smiled, almost apologetically. "I am afraid that page will cost another twenty pounds."

"Another twenty pounds!" John almost leapt from his seat. His voice was so loud that half the pub turned and stared at him.

"If you could keep your voice down, sir," said Turton.

"You're a scoundrel!" spat John. "A scoundrel—pure and simple!"

"That's as may be, sir, but my offer remains the same."

"To hell with your offer!" barked John.

"Then if you will excuse me, Mr. Bellasis," the butler replied, getting up from the table. "I have things to see to. Good day, sir."

It was not only John and Stephen Bellasis who were on the trail of Charles Pope. Oliver Trenchard was doing his share of investigating as well. As he lay in bed at night, he fretted. Why was this cuckoo taking over his life? Who was this man that his father so favored? In truth, although he thought he resented every penny that had gone Charles's way, it was really his father's attention that hurt, his obvious interest in and affection for Charles Pope that was driving Oliver mad. He knew he was a disappointment. But he told himself that his father would have been disappointed in any son. Now he knew that for a lie.

He might have expected it. He had never shown any interest in his father's achievements. He wanted everything his father wanted—money and a place in Society—but he was not prepared to work for it. He had no care for the company's activities, no desire to see the Cubitt Town project come to fruition. He went through the motions, but he was aware of the looks William Cubitt gave him when they were there together. Even the knowledge that his father had gone out on a limb to get him more interesting work did not spur him into any kind of enthusiasm. To start with, he'd always planned to sell his father's business assets as soon as the final breath left the man's body. But his emotions must have been more involved than he gave himself credit for, because there could be no question. He was jealous. Jealous of Charles Pope and his father's affection for this interloper. He told himself it was about money, about protecting what was his, but it wasn't. Not really. It was, in some twisted way, about love, although he would never have recognized it as such. Oliver Trenchard, for the first time in his life, was motivated. He was determined to find out who this upstart was, and if he could, destroy him.

James never gave much away about his various investments, and his role in Charles Pope's business affairs was no exception. Pope had bought a mill. James was trying to help him set it up. That was all Oliver could get out of him. In the end it was a chance remark of his mother's while they were walking with Agnes in the gardens at Glanville that caught Oliver's attention. Indeed, she seemed to know rather more about Charles Pope than he'd thought. They were talking, for some reason, about the new version of football that had been invented at Rugby School during the headmastership of the great Thomas Arnold.

"Although I've never played it, nor wanted to," said Oliver. "It seems a scrappy, violent game to me."

"You should ask Mr. Pope. He was at Rugby under Dr. Arnold." Anne could not see there was anything very dangerous in revealing such a thing, and on an afternoon like this it pleased her to talk about Charles. The revelation of his connection to the Brockenhursts was coming soon, anyway, and Oliver would have to learn the truth.

"How do you know?"

"Your father told me. He's taken an interest in Mr. Pope."

Oliver sighed. "Don't I know it."

But Anne did not respond to this, merely stooping to pick up a short stick, which she threw ahead of them for the dachshund to fetch. They were approaching the wonderful curving peach wall she had restored. It was winter and there was no fruit, but still it looked beautiful in the early evening light. She glanced down to check that Agnes was still with them. "They call this a crinkle crankle wall. I love that."

Oliver was not to be distracted. "And where else did Mr. Pope conduct his studies?"

"At Oxford. Lincoln College, I believe."

"And then?" Oliver was careful to modulate his tone, hiding the rage he felt inside.

"They had intended him for the Church, but his gifts were more suited to the world of commerce and so he applied for a job at Schroders bank, where he did well. It was then that his father asked James for some advice, and that was when your father first took an interest in him."

"He obviously liked what he found." Oliver struggled to keep the bitterness from his voice. The more Oliver heard about the meteoric rise of this young man, the more he disliked him. Charles Pope appeared to be so lucky, with a real head for figures, loving his work. "I suppose that was how he made the money for the mill."

"He made some money, yes. And when he wanted to go out on his own and he'd found a mill in Manchester that was for sale, James stepped in as his mentor."

"I'm sure Mr. Pope was very grateful to my father."

"I think he was." Anne wondered what Oliver would say when he discovered he had a nephew. It would be awkward at first. There was no point in denying that. Not least because she was sure he would feel protective about Sophia's memory. But in the end she knew they would adjust. That's if they were to be included. Or would it simply be the Brockenhursts' show from first to last?

It was true that Anne enjoyed talking about those details, for she'd only just learned them herself. Over a few quiet evenings in Glanville, when they had retired to her rooms, she'd spoken to James, asking him to tell her everything he knew about their grandson. And James, by way of finally apologizing to his wife, had agreed. He wanted to make up for having deceived her during all those years. He was not by nature a devious man, and it was a relief to unburden himself. So she heard how he'd been in contact with the vicar throughout Charles's childhood, learning about his schooling, his strengths and weaknesses, generally getting to know the boy, even at one remove. And now Anne was able to feel she knew him, too.

She looked up at the sky. "I think it's going to rain. Shall we go in? Agnes hates the rain. All dachshunds hate rain." And they trailed along the gravel paths toward the house, with Anne chattering about her new schemes in the garden. The little dog scuttled along behind them, and as they talked, Oliver was thinking how he could use what he'd heard to help him in his scheme to ruin Charles.

It didn't rain, and later that day Oliver went out riding. There was something about the rhythm of the horse that seemed to unravel any problem. And sure enough, as he trotted back to the house in the twilight, he decided that it might be a good idea to visit Manchester. If there was anything to be found out about Charles Pope, the place to look for it would be in the town where he had made his first inroads into investing in a real business. What was his reputation there? The man seemed to be too good to be true.

"Manchester?" said Anne as they gathered for dinner that night.

"Why do you want to go to Manchester?" asked James.

Oliver smiled at their incredulity. "I have some people to see. I've got a couple of ideas that I'd like to investigate further before I talk about them."

"Even to us?" Anne was quite intrigued.

"Even to you."

"You're not planning to abandon Cubitt Town?" James could hardly bear to think he had gone through the embarrassment of getting Oliver a job for nothing.

"Certainly not. Don't worry."

But they were all the more interested because he would not give them anything to go on. That night in bed, Susan spoke as she blew out her candle.

"What are you really doing in Manchester?"

"Minding my own business," he said, and rolled over to go to sleep.

He traveled on the new London to Birmingham railway, which had opened three years before and departed from Euston Station. He knew it well enough, as the magnificent glass and wrought-iron structure had been built by William Cubitt, and Oliver had been present at its opening in July 1837. But the five-and-a-half-hour journey had been exhausting as he had rattled around in the carriage with sooty smuts blowing in whenever he opened a window.

He took a branch line from Birmingham to Derby, which was, if anything, even more uncomfortable, and a coach from there the rest of the way. By the time he stumbled into the Queen's Arms on Sackville Street, he felt as if he had crossed a continent, but there was a certain satisfaction in the fact that he had made it.

Pope's mill was easier to find than he had feared it might be. The following morning he took himself to Portland Street, which he had been told was the center of cotton production, and there, among the smart and newly built warehouses and mills, he asked and was directed to David Street and a large, redbrick building, signed as Girton's Mill. He walked in and waited for the manager, a small man in a coat that was shiny from overuse, who introduced himself as Arthur Swift. Yes, this was Mr. Pope's mill. No, Mr. Pope was in London. Could he help?

Oliver explained that he was a friend of Charles Pope's and had hoped to look around the mill while he was in Manchester. This did not disturb Mr. Swift, who offered to give him a tour. Together they strolled through the various work spaces, all full, all busy. "Things seem to be going well," said Oliver.

Swift nodded enthusiastically. "Very well, as long as we can settle our supplies of cotton. You probably know that Mr. Pope has long-term plans for a fixed supplier in the Indian subcontinent."

"So he told me." Oliver looked up at the men working the looms in the clouded, dusty atmosphere. "Are you all content here?" He spoke loudly, above the noise of the machinery, and the men, hearing his words, ceased their work and brought the looms to a halt.

The question had come as a surprise, and at first there was a silence, then a sort of grudging acknowledgment. Swift looked at him. "Why should you ask that?" he said. "Why wouldn't they be content?"

Oliver nodded. "No reason. I was just curious."

But Mr. Swift was suddenly made uncomfortably aware that he had no written instructions to be hospitable to this Mr. Trenchard, and he had welcomed him in with no evidence to prove his friendly relationship with Swift's employer. "If you've seen enough, sir, I had better get on with my day." His voice was quite firm as he nodded for the work to start again and Oliver knew his visit was drawing to a close, but he had made his point and would now await the results.

Smiling, he thanked his guide for the time he had given so generously, and before long he was back out on David Street. He bought a newspaper and took up a position within sight of the mill. He did not have long to wait. Oliver had deliberately paid his call shortly before the dinner bell would give the men and women a half-hour break, and to avoid the dust that filled the factory air and clogged their lungs, many would come outside to eat whatever they had been able to set aside from their family's meager rations. Sure enough they emerged, blinking in the daylight, and looked around for somewhere to take their rest. Some carried stools, which they set down on the pavement. But one man broke away from the others and came across the road to where Oliver leaned against a wall, reading his paper. He looked up.

"Why did you ask that in there? Are we content?" said the new arrival. He was short in stature, as they all seemed to be, with dark stubble and the pale skin of one who spends little time in the sunlight.

"Well, are you?"

"No, we bloody well are not." The man stared at Oliver. "Are you here to make trouble for Mr. Pope?"

They were fencing with each other, of course. But Oliver had come a long way to find out what he could, and he did not feel there was any point in being too careful. "What sort of trouble could I make?" he said.

"Come to the King's Head Tavern in the Market Square at eight and you'll find out," said the man fiercely.

"May I know your name?"

"Don't worry about that. I'll be there. But I'm not the one you need to speak to."

Oliver nodded. Clearly he was not going to get a name, but why did he need one? He had connected with someone who disliked Charles Pope, and that was why he'd made the journey. So far, things were going according to plan.

That evening, he found the public house easily enough, but it was crowded and filled with smoke and it took a while for him to focus his eyes and look around. Before he had discovered anything he felt a hand on his elbow, and there was his companion of the factory visit. He beckoned, and Oliver followed him to a table in the corner where two older men were sitting. "How do you do. I am Oliver Trenchard." This time he was determined on names, and they could hardly refuse to reveal theirs after he had introduced himself.

The first man nodded. "William Brent." He was plump and seemingly prosperous, but there was a slight sheen over his red face that was off-putting.

The second man spoke. "Jacob Astley." He was thinner than his companion, older and bonier.

Neither of them looked like good candidates to spend Christmas with, thought Oliver as he took his seat opposite them. There was a glass waiting for him and a large jug of ale so he helped himself. "Very well, gentlemen." He smiled. "What have you got for me?"

"What is your connection to Pope?" This was Mr. Astley. He did not seem to feel the need to smile back and normalize their exchange, as Oliver had. He was here for some sort of business or, more likely, to settle old scores.

"If you must know, a close friend of mine has invested heavily in Pope's business, and I am anxious that he might have opened himself up to serious losses."

Brent nodded. "You are right to worry. He should withdraw his investment at the first opportunity."

"But that would ruin Mr. Pope. If he withdrew completely." Oliver was not quite sure this was true because he knew that Lady Brockenhurst might easily step in to avoid calamity, but he wanted to gauge these men's dislike. He was not disappointed.

"He deserves to be ruined." Astley raised his glass to his thin lips.

"May I know why?"

"You know he bought the mill from the widow of old Samuel Girton?"

"I do now."

"We had a deal with the old lady, but he came at night and frightened her out of her wits with tales of imminent ruin and dangers that only he could save her from, until she agreed to set aside the contract with us and sell to him."

"I see." Oliver thought of that smiling young man walking around Lady Brockenhurst's drawing room. Did this seem likely?

"That's not all," said Brent. "He cheats the customs men out of their duties when he imports cotton. He pays to have it undervalued when it is being shipped and so avoids half the tax when the shipments are unloaded here."

"He's not to be trusted," said Astley. "Tell your friend to get his money out while he still can."

Oliver looked at the man who had brought him there. "What is your connection to this?" he asked.

The fellow grimaced. "I was all set to be a manager at the mill if Mr. Brent and Mr. Astley had taken over. Pope knew it, but he hired me to work at a loom, along with the other poor fools who know no better."

"Why did you take the job?" said Oliver.

"What else could I do? I've a wife and four bairns to feed." The muscles of his jaw tightened in anger. "He told me it was to soften the blow of the other job falling through."

"But you think that was not his motive?"

The man shook his head. "Pope has no kindness in him. It was to humiliate me when I had no choice but to let him."

Oliver looked at them. The last point was unproven, of course, he was forced to admit that, but there was something he could work with in the frightening of the old woman and cheating the taxmen, which was the charge that would offend his father most of all. "How much of this are you prepared to write down?" he said.

Brent glanced at his companion. "We would not testify in a court of law. I'm not going back to the law for any man."

Oliver nodded. "That's understood. I need the information to convince my friend. But it will not come to court. If the worst comes to the worst, he can afford to lose what has already gone. As much as anything, I want him to back out now and give no more."

Brent made up his mind. "We can help with that." He looked at Astley to make sure he spoke for them both. "We want him out of business, but until then, we'd like as few men as possible to be taken in by his tricks."

"Because he's very charming," said Oliver. "People seem to like him."

"They like him until they know him," said Brent.

The journey home seemed less trying, maybe because Oliver had got what he wanted. Two letters had been delivered to him at the Queen's Arms earlier that morning, and he'd set off with them safe in his pocket. Whatever he lost of his luggage en route, he would not lose them. By the time he boarded the London train in Birmingham, he was feeling quite optimistic, and rather to the disapproval of his fellow passengers he found himself humming a tune.

Lady Templemore had not gone into her daughter's bedroom with any intention of searching it. Or so she said to herself as she pushed the door open. It was just to see that everything was tidy and as it should be. Maria was out walking with Ryan and the servants were downstairs, so it felt right that she should check.

This position was harder to maintain once she had seen Maria's closed traveling desk on the table beneath the window. It would be locked, but Corinne knew where the girl kept the key. She had never told Maria that she knew where the key was hidden in case the knowledge ever came in useful, and she had looked through her daughter's letters before now, more than once. Almost without admitting to herself what she was doing, she opened the concealed drawer in the bureau, removed the key, and unlocked the traveling desk. The leather writing surface was fastened shut by a small brass latch that slipped easily at the touch of her finger—and there were Maria's letters. She flicked through them. She knew the writers for the most part—her son, cousins, friends of Maria's from her first two Seasons—but there was one small crested envelope that surprised her. Although she recognized it well enough.

The letter was short. "My dear," it read. "If you will call on me on Friday afternoon at four, I think we might arrange another visit to Bishopsgate. Caroline Brockenhurst." Corinne stared at the small cream square of paper. "Another visit." What did that mean? *Another* visit to Bishopsgate? She knew who worked in Bishopsgate. When Charles Pope had walked with Maria and the maid, Ryan, as far as the London Library, Ryan had reported back everything he'd said. Had she stumbled on the reason why her plans were beginning to come apart in her hands? And why was Lady Brockenhurst arranging anything for Maria without first applying to her mother for permission? Then Corinne thought of Lady Brockenhurst taking Mr. Pope around the rooms at her party. Was this a conspiracy? If not, why had Maria said nothing about the invitation? She was silent for a few minutes. The day was Thursday. The visit was scheduled for the following afternoon. She had twenty-four hours. Very carefully she replaced the letter, locked the desk, and put the key back in its place. During this time she made two decisions. The first was to pay a call on the Countess to coincide with her daughter's, and the second took her to her charming *bonheur du jour* in the pale blue back drawing room on the first floor. An hour after she sat down to write, she rang the bell and gave the footman two envelopes to carry by hand to their separate destinations.

Oliver chose to tell his father of his discoveries at the office and not at home. They had questioned him about his visit north at dinner after he returned the night before, but he said nothing of any substance beyond voicing surprise at the size and prosperity of the new Manchester he had witnessed.

He'd thought the shock of his revelations might catch his father unawares, and it would be kinder to give him the privacy of his workplace as a shelter while he was off guard. But the next morning, when the clerk showed him in and his father stood up to greet him, James did not seem very put out to see his son there.

"Is this about Manchester?" he said.

"Why do you say that?" asked Oliver.

"Because you make a mysterious trip north, telling no one your purpose in going there. Then you make a special request for me to put aside some time for you with no interruptions. Obviously you have something to tell me, and I think it must be connected to the trip."

Oliver nodded. He might as well begin. "It is."

He was so solemn that James almost laughed. "You look very grave."

"I am grave," Oliver replied, walking toward his father's desk. He glanced around the paneled room, taking in the large map of Cubitt Town and his sister's portrait hanging above the fireplace. There was no such image of himself, he noted. They'd never even asked for one to be painted, not since he was a child. He sat in the chair opposite his father. "I have news," he said. "Which I am not sure you will be pleased to hear."

"Oh?" James sat back in his chair. "What sort of news?"

"It concerns Mr. Pope."

James was not unduly surprised by this. He had long suspected

Oliver's antagonism toward his grandson. The sour memory of that afternoon at the Athenaeum was enough to confirm it. So it was clear that Oliver had gone to Manchester to rummage through Charles's past. It was with the trace of a sigh that James nodded. "Go on."

"My journey north was useful. I believe I can say that. At least, I hope it will be useful to you." James wondered how long it was going to take him to get to the point. "I went to see Mr. Pope's mill."

James nodded. "Girton's Mill? It's a fine place, isn't it?" He waited patiently for the reveal.

"The point is, by accident, I came across two men who'd had dealings with our Mr. Pope a while back. Mr. Brent and Mr. Astley."

"By accident?"

"Not quite. They heard I knew Mr. Pope and they sought me out."

"I have the feeling you are going to tell me something I don't want to hear."

"I'm afraid so." Oliver nodded sorrowfully. "According to them, he frightened the poor widow he bought the mill from into making a deal with him, when she had already agreed to sell it elsewhere."

"To these men, presumably."

"Does that mean the story is not true?" James was silent. Oliver started again. "He also makes a habit of cheating the customs men. He has his cotton undervalued before it is loaded and falsely labeled, and then avoids half the tax that is due when it arrives in England."

"We pay too much tax."

"Does that mean it's right to lie and steal?" Oliver could see that his father was disturbed by what he was hearing. "Do you really want to invest with a bully and a liar?"

"I don't believe it." James stood. He saw that Oliver's whole purpose in traveling north had simply been to displace Charles in his affections. What was making him uncomfortable was not the news about Charles but the bitter realization that relations between himself and his son were even worse than he had feared. "I'll ask him about it," he said.

"I have here two letters, one from Brent and one from Astley. I shall leave them on this table. Don't worry. They have no wish to testify against Pope in court. They've made that clear. But they agree that you should know the truth."

"No doubt they were very reluctant to tell their stories in court." James's tone was impatient and angry. Who were these faceless men to come into his life and attempt to destroy his trust in the man he loved most on earth?

"I know it's very unpleasant for you, Father. I'm sorry."

"Are you really?" James looked down at the busy street below. "I'll go and see him."

"I should read the letters first."

"I'll go and see him."

His tone told Oliver that it would be better to leave it there. Oliver had no real conviction, one way or the other, about the allegations he had transmitted. Maybe the charges were true, maybe not. But he was sure Pope would recognize the names and that, in itself, would be damning. He only had to make his father doubt, after all. But he had misunderstood his father's response to the news.

James Trenchard did not wait long before going to see his grandson. He needed to confirm his innocence. "How did your son meet these men?" Charles asked, trying to keep his voice calm. James was sitting but Charles moved about the office, digesting what he had been told.

"I don't know."

"But he went to see my mill?" Actually, he already knew this as his manager, Swift, had sent him a telegram informing him of it. "Why?"

James shrugged. "I don't know that either. He must have had some reason." He knew the reason. His son hated Charles and the attention James had lavished on him, and for that James was responsible, in part at least.

Charles was angry. He had not asked for James's patronage. He appreciated it but he had not asked for it, and now he was being punished for James's interest in him. "He must have had more than 'some reason' to make such a journey," he said. "Clearly he had a very real purpose for going to Manchester. Was it to meet these men?"

"I'm not sure. He says he came across them while he was up there. I assume there's no truth in these allegations."

But Charles was in a quandary. He knew Brent and Astley well. They had almost succeeded in buying the mill from old Mrs. Girton for a fraction of its value, and Charles had stepped in just in time to save her from losing a great deal of money. Then he had negotiated to buy the mill himself, but at a market price. Naturally, they resented him as they had so nearly brought it off. The customs cheating was more complicated, and he was not certain how they could have known about it. The truth was, he'd ordered and paid for a cargo of raw cotton, received from India. He had assumed the quality was the same as the previous order he had made from the same source, and all the papers were filled out to this effect. When it was opened, however, there had been a mix-up of some kind and the cotton was considerably finer. He'd declared the change to the customs officers and a payment had been made, but the incident had taken place. It was not a lie. What was obvious was that Brent and Astley knew Oliver had gone to Manchester to make trouble for Charles, and they were eager to give him some weaponry with which to do so. Obviously, he could explain all this to James, but here was his problem. Did he really want to set Mr. Trenchard against his own son when it was obvious that he, Charles, was already coming between them? Did he want to reward Trenchard's kindness and support by destroying his family? He had the Brockenhursts as backers now, and while it would slow things down to lose the Trenchard investment, still it could be managed even if it would all take longer. Clearly, Brent and Astley thought that if Trenchard's money was pulled out, the mill would cease to trade and they could move in and snap it up from the bailiffs, again at a fraction of what they should pay, but they would be disappointed in that, whatever happened now.

"I wish you would either say that Oliver is talking nonsense or there is some truth in what he has told me." James was growing impatient.

Charles looked at the letters once more, the allegations spelled out in black and white. "And these were given to Oliver to show to you?"

"Apparently. Although they'd never testify in court."

"No. I should think not." For a moment, Charles's anger was very near the surface.

"Does that mean you know them of old? That we should not take their word for anything? Just say it, and I will report back to Oliver that their accusations are false."

"Don't do that." Charles turned to face his champion. "These things did happen. Not quite as they have been relayed to you, but there is some truth in the stories. I would not have you quarrel with your only son over me. I assume we should think about removing your money from the business. It cannot be done at once."

But James had stood and he hovered near the door. "I'm not taking my money out," he said firmly. "What made you think such a thing?"

"You should. If your son is not happy about our association."

James was silent. It was a conundrum. He could hardly pretend Oliver *was* happy when the very sight of Charles made him as angry as a tiger with a sore tooth. James had no wish to break with Charles, but nor did he want to live in enmity with his only surviving child. Maybe he should let Oliver think his words had had some effect, but not disturb the business of his grandson. Then, after a while, things might settle down. How complicated it was. Would they all be less confused if Lady Brockenhurst just spoke out? Charles took his silence for agreement.

"I will manage it in stages and add ten percent for all the nuisance I have put you through."

James shook his head. "I am not aware of any nuisance. Nor will I take out the money." Once again, he was assailed by the thought that he might as well tell the boy now about his real identity. Weren't they nearly at that point, whether he liked it or not? But he remained silent.

James Trenchard was on edge for the rest of the day, but it was not because he'd doubted Charles. The man was strong-headed, yes, he was certainly that, and probably stubborn and determined to get his own way. His mother had been the same in that. But dishonest? Never. He smiled. Thinking like this had brought the image of Sophia back again. He remembered her determination to be invited to the Duchess of Richmond's ball, all those years ago. Nothing could have stopped her and nothing did. How beautiful she'd looked that night, how confident, how glowing, how in love....He sighed as he sat at his desk. Of course Charles had had a father, too. Could Charles have taken after him? They may not have seen it while he was alive, but Edmund Bellasis must have been a snake to seduce an innocent young girl, pretending a marriage, inventing a priest. He must have been odious, and yet they were deceived by him. Was there a chance that Charles took after him? But he shook his head. No. That was not the Charles Pope he knew.

That evening, Anne found her husband very quiet. He sat at dinner in complete silence, playing with his food, listening to Oliver and Susan discuss the state of modern Manchester, contributing nothing. Actually, Oliver had a lot to say about the Capital of Cotton. He had been impressed by what he'd seen and he spoke animatedly.

"Your visit was a success, then?" said Anne.

"I think so." His tone was suddenly more guarded and he glanced at his father.

Susan was contributing almost as little as James. She seemed thoroughly preoccupied this evening, although there was no very obvious reason why. She hardly touched her food or her wine. She was listening to Oliver, but more as an excuse not to have to talk herself than because of any real interest in what he was saying.

Later, as James stood in his dressing room, his arms outstretched while Miles, his valet, undid the cuffs on his shirt, his wife gently knocked on the door and came in.

"Would you excuse us, Miles," she said as she crossed the room and sat on a buttoned chair in the corner, Agnes curled up snugly in her lap.

"Of course, madam," replied Miles, bowing deeply.

Miles had a tendency to be obsequious. He had not been working long for the Trenchard family, having left the drafty castle of Lord Glenair in the Scottish Borders to move to the capital just over a year before. Despite being paid twice his previous salary, he still regarded his position in Eaton Square as a stopgap before he moved on to more refined surroundings. Still, he performed his duties efficiently.

"Would you like me to come back, sir?" he asked.

"No. That will be all. Good night," replied James.

As soon as the valet had left, Anne wasted no time in asking her husband what was wrong. She stood to help him with his buttons, leaving the grumbling dog in possession of the seat. "You've barely said a word the whole evening. What's happened?"

"You don't want to know."

"But I do. I want to know very much."

James recounted his visit to Charles.

"What did he say?"

James shook his head. "He said there was some truth in the account, although not in every detail. Then he offered to return my investment with interest. I know what's happened. Charles didn't want to come between Oliver and me. I'm sure that was at the bottom of it." He took up a brush from his dressing table and passed it over his scalp.

"He's done nothing wrong. Of that I'm certain," declared Anne. But she shared James's desire to resolve things. Maybe it was time to tell Oliver. She didn't quite trust Susan to keep a secret, in which she wronged her daughter-in-law, who had plenty of secrets of her own, but Anne thought it might be necessary to take the risk. As she considered it, on her way back to her bedroom, it occurred to her that she might, with profit, employ the services of an ally.

The footman's voice rang out across the drawing room. "The Countess of Templemore."

Caroline Brockenhurst looked up. "What?" she said, which was not the most welcoming sound, as Lady Templemore walked toward her. Caroline had of course been expecting Lady Templemore's daughter, and she was annoyed and a little uncomfortable at the substitution. She wondered briefly if she could get a messenger to tell Maria not to come, but it didn't seem a very realistic proposition. She stood to receive her unwanted guest. "How nice," she said to bury her initial reaction. "They've just brought tea. Can I give you some?"

"Thank you," said Corinne as she sat down on a pretty Louis Quinze chair. "I'd love a cup of tea, just as soon as you tell me what this means." So saying, she removed the letter to Maria from her reticule and handed it to the Countess.

Lady Brockenhurst stared at it. Of course she knew what it was even before it was in her hands. "I've invited Maria for tea," she said, without batting an eyelid. "She should be here at any moment."

"To plan your visit to Bishopsgate. Or should I say *another* visit?"

"She is an excellent companion on a drive. You know that better than I. You have brought her up very well." By now she had poured the tea and a cup was safe in Corinne Templemore's hands.

"Whom do you visit in Bishopsgate?"

"Do we visit anyone in particular?" Lady Brockenhurst's tone was very light.

Lady Templemore's was not. "You tell me."

"My dear, something is troubling you. I hope you will allow me to know what it is."

At this, Corinne started to laugh. The change of mood was disconcerting, and Caroline found herself wondering if her guest might be ill. Corinne reached into her reticule and took out a piece of folded newsprint. "On the contrary," she said. "I'm not in the least troubled. I have cause for celebration in which I hope you'll join me. Did you see the *Times* this morning? Or the *Gazette*?"

"We don't get the *Gazette,* and I didn't read the *Times.* Why? What is it?"

She smoothed the paper out and handed it to Caroline. There it was. "The engagement is announced between John Bellasis, Esq., son of the Hon. and Rev. Stephen Bellasis and Mrs. Bellasis, and Lady Mary Grey, daughter of the Dowager Countess of Templemore and the late Earl of Templemore." Caroline studied it hard. For a second, the sense of crushing disappointment almost took her breath away. "Aren't you going to congratulate me?" Caroline looked up. Corinne was staring at her.

"Of course. Many congratulations. Has a date been set?"

"Not yet. But I hate long engagements."

Before Caroline could say more, the footman was back with them. "Lady Maria Grey."

The young woman walked into the room but stopped dead when she saw her mother. "I thought you were going to see Lady Stafford this afternoon." She was very composed by the time she had spoken.

The mother looked back, quite as cool as the daughter. "As you can see, I changed my plans. I wanted to talk to Lady Brockenhurst about the announcement."

Maria was silent.

"Congratulations," said Lady Brockenhurst.

Still Maria said nothing.

Corinne was growing impatient. "Don't sulk."

"I'm not sulking. I'm not saying anything because I have nothing to say."

Before the mother could add to this, the footman returned. "Mrs. Trenchard," he said, and Anne walked into the room.

Caroline stood. "Good heavens. What an afternoon this is turning out to be."

Anne was as taken aback as her hostess when she saw the other women in the room. "If I'd known you had people here, I'd have left you alone. They brought me straight up."

"And I am delighted that they did." Caroline was actually quite glad to see Anne, for once, as the tension between the mother and daughter was increasingly uncomfortable. "May I present Mrs. Trenchard?" she said. "This is Lady Templemore."

"I think we saw each other at the soirée here a while ago," said Anne pleasantly.

"Did we? It may be so." Lady Templemore was trying to work out how to leave and take her daughter with her before any more trips to Bishopsgate were arranged.

"Hello, Mrs. Trenchard," said Maria, for the first time employing a friendly voice.

"Hello to you, my dear. I hope everything is well." Anne took the girl's hand in hers.

Lady Templemore found herself bridling at their familiarity. How could Maria know these people, do these things, without her knowledge? Was this woman here to arrange another visit to Bishopsgate, too? She felt as if she had let slip the traces of her daughter's life. "We are celebrating the announcement of Lady Maria's engagement."

"Oh?" Anne was as surprised as she was sorry. She really had not believed this would ever happen.

"It was in the papers this morning," said Corinne.

"I must have missed it. I shall look when I get home." But Anne glanced at Maria, and nothing in the young woman's face indicated that anything out of the ordinary had happened. She simply stared ahead, took a cup of tea from Lady Brockenhurst, and drank it.

"I'm going to leave you," said Anne. "I'll come back another time."

"No, don't." Lady Templemore was standing. "We're going now. We have a great deal to talk about. Maria?"

But the girl did not move. Instead she said calmly, "You go, Mama. I want the chance to catch up with Lady Brockenhurst's news. She will be my aunt, you know."

Caroline nodded. "That's right, my dear. And you will be my niece. You go, Corinne, and we'll send Maria back in the carriage later on. She will be quite safe with us."

"I can stay," said Lady Templemore.

"I wouldn't hear of it. You have much more important things to do. William, please escort Lady Templemore down to her carriage." She spoke like a tsar issuing a ukase, and it was clear she would brook no further argument. For a moment it looked as if Lady Templemore might put up a fight even so, but in the end she thought better of it and left. The footman had accompanied her and the other women were alone.

"I'm not going to marry him, if that's what you're thinking." Maria spoke as if she were defending her position, but of course she was among friends.

"Am I allowed to say I'm glad?" Anne sat down again.

"And me," added Caroline. "Although I dread the conversation with my brother and sister-in-law. John would have offered you a great position, but position isn't everything, and if *I* say that, it must be true." They laughed, Maria with relief as much as anything else.

Then she spoke. "How is he?" she asked, her cheeks flushing.

None of them needed to inquire as to whom they were discussing. "Very well, I think," said Caroline. "At least, I haven't seen him since I saw him with you. Mrs. Trenchard?"

"I haven't seen him either." She hesitated. Should she discuss her grandson in front of Maria, even if the girl was in love with him? That much was clearer than ever after the exchange she had just witnessed.

"Go on," said Caroline. "It is vulgar to be mysterious."

"No, it wouldn't interest Lady Maria."

The young woman protested at once. "Anything to do with Mr. Pope interests me a great deal."

But before she could go further, the footman returned. "What is it, William?"

"The Countess of Templemore is outside in her carriage, m'lady. She is waiting for Lady Maria."

"Thank you, William," said Caroline. "Lady Maria will be down in a moment." The man knew he'd been dismissed and he left. The three women looked at one another. "You'd better go, my dear. There's no point in antagonizing her any more than we need to."

"If you see him, give him my love." Maria had clearly accepted that her mother would win this round. "And tell him not to believe what he reads in the papers." In another moment, she had gone.

"Now, tell me," said Caroline, settling back in her chair.

"Very well." Anne nodded. "My son recently paid a visit to Manchester. I think he went for the sole purpose of finding something to Charles's discredit. While he was there he met some men who'd been involved with Charles in business. They accused him of obtaining the mill in an underhand way, and of cheating Customs and Excise."

"I don't believe it," said the Countess.

"Nor do I, and nor does Mr. Trenchard. But what disturbs my husband is that he believes Oliver's motive for traveling north and delving into Charles's history is because he is jealous of the attention James has paid our grandchild. Now Charles does not want to come between father and son."

Caroline thought for a moment. "In other words, the deceit is getting out of hand and threatening the unity of your family. I think," she said slowly, as if still ruminating over an idea, "I think I should like to acknowledge Charles."

"What do you mean?" Anne's heart was in her mouth.

"Let me speak. I know there is nothing to this nonsense, but your son is obviously determined to show Charles in the worst possible light. For some reason he has taken against him, and that will only get worse. Now Maria Grey will be harassed by her mama in an effort to force her up the aisle with my worthless nephew. All of this can be resolved if you will only allow us to give him a name and a position and publicly include him in our family. You know Henry Stephenson? The bastard son of a duke, but he married the daughter of an earl and they are to be seen everywhere. We already know that Maria will kick and scratch until she's allowed to be with Charles. Lady Templemore will not be pleased, of course, but she will fight less furiously once she knows we are behind the match and her daughter will always be welcome in this house. My dear, please think. A good life is waiting for Charles if you will allow me to give it to him. Let this business be the crisis that takes us to a resolution."

It was quite a speech, and every fiber of Anne's being was crying out against it, but as she listened, she was forced to acknowledge that there was logic in the Countess's words. James would not agree, but what could her argument be here and now? "Do you intend to make some kind of announcement?"

Lady Brockenhurst almost laughed. "Certainly not. I shall simply let the news slip out. I shall privately acknowledge that Charles is Edmund's son, and that will be that." Caroline smiled, delighted with her decision. "Of course, we have a little time. I shall have to inform Lord Brockenhurst, and there is the question of how we break the news to Charles...." She tapped her fingers together and walked toward the open door of the balcony.

"What about Sophia?" asked Anne.

"Yes." The Countess nodded. "We have to think what we do about Sophia."

"When you tell him Edmund was his father, he's bound to ask questions about his mother."

"Might it be better not to tell him anything? Wouldn't you prefer to keep her name away from public knowledge?"

Anne looked at her. "You mean, to wipe her out of the story altogether?"

"I am only thinking of her son. He can have a good, rich life, with an excellent marriage and the best Society. Of course, you'll say these things would not have mattered to her—"

"No." Some impulse was forcing Anne to be honest. "No, they were important to her. She would have appreciated what you want to do for Charles."

Lady Brockenhurst smiled, but more gently than usual. "That is kind of you. And I am touched. Are we agreed, then?"

"I must talk to James," said Anne. But she already knew that nothing either of them might say would make a difference.

Quirk took her back to Eaton Square. He told the others downstairs later how silent she was, how thoughtful, as they made the short journey. She spent the entire time sitting in silence, staring ahead of her, lost in thought.

When they arrived at the house, Anne went straight to James's library and found him reading at his desk. "She's going to tell him," she said, almost wringing her hands in misery. "Lady Brockenhurst is going to acknowledge Charles as her grandson. She says they can survive his being illegitimate. Society will still accept him if they see that he is part of the Brockenhurst family. She's already chosen his bride."

"Charles would never put up with that."

"No." She held up her hand, forced to be honest again. "He loves her. So do I, if it comes to that. She's charming. But she will take him further out of our reach."

He stared into the fire. "And Sophia? What part does she play in this happy story?"

"Lady Brockenhurst thinks she should play no part. He will be Edmund Bellasis's son and his mother will be a mystery love, vanished into the mists of time. In that way, Sophia's reputation will be safe and we will pay no price."

James stared at his wife. "Then he is lost."

She couldn't understand him. "What do you mean, he is lost? Charles? It's Sophia who will be lost."

"No." James shook his head. How could his wife, his normally very clever wife, not see the truth? "He is lost *to us*."

"In what way?"

"If he is acknowledged as a Bellasis, then, for the sake of our daughter, and indeed for all concerned, we must fade into the background and no longer try to include him in our lives."

"No." Anne found that tears were coursing down her cheeks.

James continued. Anne might as well be clear about it. "It's true. If the Countess keeps her word and does not name her, then we owe it to Sophia to protect her memory. The more we see of him, the more we risk someone making the connection. If we love our daughter, we must give up our grandson."

The wave of grief was overwhelming. To Anne it felt as if her beautiful, determined child were dying all over again.

James took her hand in his, trying to give her strength to bear the blow. "We have lost Charles to the Brockenhurst family for good. Let us wish him well and go on our way."

John Bellasis was furious. He hated being backed into a corner, but most of all he hated the fact that a servant, a *butler*, had got the better of him. John considered himself to be a man of the world; he was smart, knowledgeable, sophisticated, and yet he had not seen the man's treachery coming. He shivered with annoyance as he sat in the back of his carriage on the way to the Reverend Mr. Pope's village of Buckland in Surrey. In the end, he'd paid the extra twenty pounds to the odious Turton to see the first page of the letter and, crucially, learn the address. It had occurred to him that he could probably have found out which parish Pope presided over, but how long would it have taken? He blamed himself. He should have started the process sooner. Because if he were really going to make this situation pay, for him and his father, he needed to confront the Reverend Mr. Pope and harvest all the facts before he tackled his aunt.

As he drove through the village, past the duck pond and a flock of scratching hens and screeching geese, John was reminded why he lived at Albany. Some would call the village a rural idyll—there was the blacksmith hard at work and, on the other side of the green, a wheelwright bent double, forcing spokes into a hub—but John cared nothing for such bucolic charms. The country bored him and fresh air made him cough.

Next to a sturdy Saxon church, with a large and well-populated graveyard, John found the rectory. It was pretty enough with its rose-filled garden and mellow stone façade although, he noted thankfully, smaller and less grand than his father's house in Lymington. He should have been reluctant to admit that Charles's upbringing had been on a par with his own. He instructed his coachman to wait before he marched up the garden path.

"Sir?" An elderly housekeeper answered the door. Bent over, with her gray hair scraped back under a cap and a long beak of a nose, the woman had the appearance of a vulture John had once seen when a friend took him on a private visit to the new scientific zoo in Regent's Park. Having explained his business and given his name as Mr. Sanderson, John was escorted to a modest parlor. It was warm and comfortable, with a fire in the grate, and over the chimneypiece was a pastel he recognized at once as a portrait of a younger Charles Pope, perhaps by the same artist who had fashioned that picture of the Reverend Mr. Pope in Charles's office. It was rather a romantic image, with the sitter posed in an open shirt and his hair arranged in becoming, tangled curls, but there was a hint of strength in the blue eyes. John felt slightly uncomfortable looking at it, considering his motives for being there.

"Good afternoon, sir," came a female voice.

John turned. A middle-aged woman, perhaps in her early fifties, stood in the doorway in a simple, undecorated black dress. She was plump, with kind eyes, her hair neatly arranged with a small widow's cap pinned on her head and tidy ringlets framing her face. "Good afternoon to you, madam," he said.

She waved him to a chair by the fire, sitting herself. "How may I help you?"

"I was rather hoping to speak to your husband."

"Then I'm afraid you have had a wasted journey. The Reverend Mr. Pope is no longer with us. He has been dead a year this coming Tuesday. In fact, you were lucky to find me here. I must be out soon to make way for the next incumbent."

"That's very hard." John was all concern.

"Oh, no. He gave me twelve months to go and that was generous. You have no need to worry about me. My son is carrying me up to London to live there with him, so I shall have a whole new adventure, which is a privilege at my time of life." She blushed with pleasure at the thought of it.

John was annoyed with himself. Why hadn't he found all this out? There was movement at the door, and the old woman who had admitted him staggered into the room with a tray of tea things and laid it on a table in the corner. Mrs. Pope stood and started to pour as soon as they were alone again. "Was it something I could help with?"

"Well, in a way it is of your son that I wish to speak."

She smiled. "Do you know my son, Mr. Sanderson?"

"We've met." John couldn't decide how much to lie right at the outset. "I've been to his offices in the City."

"And there you have the advantage of me." But her gentle eyes were bursting with pride.

"He's doing so well," said John. Clearly, he would get a lot more out of her as Charles's friend than as his enemy.

She almost laughed with pleasure. "I know. And in the cotton trade, too. It's so far from anything his father had expected at the start but, thank the Lord, he lived long enough to take pride in Charles's achievements."

"You say he had expected something different at the start?"

"We both did. In those days the best idea for his future seemed to be the cloth, but as he grew older it was clear that his true talents lay elsewhere." She ran on happily, remembering those dear days of long ago.

John sipped his tea. "Why did you say 'at the start'?"

This was disconcerting, but she did not yet guess anything was amiss. "Well, I mean, when he first—when we first—that is, when he was a baby and we began to plan his education. He was such a good pupil." She obviously felt she had regained the shore, and she reached for a biscuit as a reward.

John decided to take the plunge. "Do you have any children of your own, Mrs. Pope, or is Charles your sole charge?" She stared at him. He raised his hand in a deprecatory manner. "I should have explained myself. I am a friend of James Trenchard. That is really how I know Charles."

She relaxed, her momentary concern smoothed away. "Oh, I see."

"It's a wonderful thing that Trenchard should have taken such a responsibility for the boy from the very beginning. He's been so generous."

"Oh, very generous. Always."

"Was he the only person to watch over young Charles once he had been taken in by you and your husband? I suppose what

I mean is, was anyone else involved? Did you receive any other income for the child?"

But now, at last, Mrs. Pope seemed to sense that all was not quite as it seemed. Her brow clouded and she put down her cup. "What exactly is it that you want from me, sir?"

"Nothing, really." In a way John had what he wanted already, so he wasn't too worried that the situation might be dissolving. "I have heard so much of you from James that I was curious to meet you when I was passing this way."

But she had been running over their conversation in her head, and she heard it differently from before. "If that is so, why did you not know that my husband was dead?" She stood. "I do not believe you, sir. I do not believe you know Charles, or, if you do, I do not believe you wish him well. And now that I think of it, I do not believe that Mr. Trenchard has ever spoken of us to you or of you to us. I shall however certainly report to him that you have called on me."

Since John had given a false name, this did not concern him. "I am sorry to have upset you, Mrs. Pope, but if you'll just—"

"Will you please go, sir?" She strode across the room to seize the bellpull and, giving it a stern yank, she waited in silence until the old woman appeared. "Janet, Mr. Sanderson is leaving."

John stood. "I am sorry to have offended you, madam. Thank you for my tea." But she did not say another word, only waiting until he had left the room. Then she sat down at her desk and began to scribble furiously on a sheet of writing paper.

Susan Trenchard had come to Isleworth to have it out with John, or at least to confide her fears to him. But he hadn't listened. He was too preoccupied, even as she gave herself to him in the lovers' nest she had come to know so well. Now he'd told her why.

"Are you serious?" Susan rolled over to see his face. She hadn't been feeling all that well when she arrived, but the news he'd just told her drove any such considerations from her mind. She was astonished.

"Quite serious. He's a man, isn't he?" John looked at the clock.

He really should be getting dressed. There was a dinner to get back for, but he was loath to leave. This woman really was becoming something of a habit. He ran his hand over her warm, soft skin, and it was a habit he was finding increasingly difficult to break.

"Mr. Trenchard with a bastard son?" Susan started to laugh, and her eyes glinted in the light in a way he could not stop looking at. "But he's so dull."

"Even dull people make love."

"Don't I know it!" Susan groaned, as she remembered Oliver's unrewarding efforts. "So what happened to this boy? Do we know where he is now?"

"He's quite grown up these days. It all happened twenty-six years ago. And yes, we know exactly where he is now." John smiled at her. He felt quite optimistic suddenly.

"You're teasing me. Why? Have I met him? Do I know him?"

"That depends. How well do you know Charles Pope?"

Susan sat up sharply, with a gasp. "Charles Pope?"

"I believe so."

Susan threw herself back against the pillows. "Well, I suppose it does make sense. Oliver has been going nearly mad with Mr. Trenchard's doing everything he can for the young man. He's been sponsoring the fellow ever since he came to London, and now he's invested heavily in Pope's project in Manchester. He showers the man with favors, and Oliver had found them lunching together at his father's club. And to hear Mr. Trenchard talk about the fellow! He cannot mention him without smiling. If I didn't know my father-in-law too well, I would think he might be in love with Mr. Pope. He certainly couldn't like him more."

John's forehead wrinkled in distaste. "What a horrid thought. Does Mrs. Trenchard suspect anything, do you think?"

Susan frowned. "I couldn't say. She likes Mr. Pope, and you saw her when she went to visit his place of work. But her husband's interest in the Manchester mill might explain that. She is quite opaque, my mother-in-law. It's hard to guess what she's thinking."

"Are you fond of her?"

She thought for a moment. "As a matter of fact, I am quite. More than she is of me. If I had to take any of them with me into my next life, it would be her."

"Your next life? When does that begin?"

"I'm not sure." She ran her tongue over her lower lip, making it glisten.

John started to dress. "I'm interested that he kept it secret from his own family. Most men would have admitted it long ago. Half the great families in England have acknowledged illegitimate relations. Why not the Trenchards?"

Susan shook her head. "He doesn't have the confidence. He probably thinks he's kept it secret to spare his wife's feelings or to spare Oliver, who will not take kindly to the news, I can assure you. But it isn't that. He'll have worried about his position in Society."

John laughed. "He doesn't have a position in Society."

"Well, he thinks he does. Or at least, he hopes so." She was laughing, too, by this stage. But suddenly she grew serious. "Wait a minute. If Pope is Trenchard's bastard, why is the Countess of Brockenhurst so taken with him? You can't have forgotten her parading him around her drawing room that night."

John nodded, fastening his shirt and patting at his hair in the glass. "I know. How old would she have been when Charles was born? Forty-one?"

Susan stared at him. What could he possibly be suggesting? She shook her head. "Don't be ridiculous."

"Why were they at her party? Why does Lady Brockenhurst know the Trenchards? She doesn't know anyone else like them."

"I'm not listening to you." Susan climbed off the bed and went in search of her underclothes, strewn about the floor. She gathered them up one by one.

But John had started to explore the idea and he couldn't let go of it. "Why is it so impossible? Wouldn't that explain everything? Including the secrecy?"

She came to him for help with her corset and stood patiently as he fastened the hooks. "Twenty-five or twenty-six years ago, the Countess of Brockenhurst must have been one of the most glamorous women in England, daughter of a duke, sister of a duchess, at the peak of her powers and at the peak of Society. James Trenchard, on the other hand, was a supplier of food for the Duke of Wellington's troops in Brussels, a victualler. He was a fat, dumpy little man, with a working-class background and the face of a butcher, and in those days he had no money to speak of. Certainly nothing like the riches that came later. With his looks, to get Lady Brockenhurst into bed he'd have to have been the Tsar of Russia."

John was not convinced. "But I bet he was pushy, even then; keen to take any advantage that was open to him, keen to get on. And what better ladder could he find than my dear aunt?"

Susan was wearing her dress now, and she turned to let him fasten her up. "You mustn't talk like that, John. It's dangerous to say such things."

"It may be dangerous. But it doesn't mean it's not true. And what better explanation do you have that fits all the details and every circumstance?"

She said nothing as she watched him pull on his boots. He straightened up, reaching for his cape. He was ready to go.

·9·

The Past Is a Foreign Country

Anne Trenchard was sitting at the breakfast table, eating scrambled eggs. She and James had been up half the night, trying to work out what they could do when Lady Brockenhurst acknowledged Charles. But in the end Anne was forced to admit that James was right. They would lose Charles the instant the Countess welcomed him into her family. They could never explain to him who they were, or how they were connected, not if they wanted to protect the memory of Sophia. It would have to be enough that James had invested in Charles's business and been his benefactor. They must try to maintain some sort of link through that. Although they would have to be careful even there so that no one guessed the truth.

Turton leaned in. "Would you like some more toast, ma'am?"

"Not for me, but maybe for Mrs. Oliver."

He nodded and left to give the order. Anne knew that Turton shared James's opinion that it was eccentric for married women to come down for breakfast. They would have preferred them both to have trays in their bedrooms like the other women of their kind, but there was something in the habit that struck Anne as indolent and she had never succumbed. James had given up suggesting it. She stirred the eggs on the plate without lifting the fork to her mouth. It all seemed terribly unfair, but hadn't she brought this whole situation upon herself? Hadn't she and James sent the child away and kept him a secret? Wasn't she the one who had told Lady Brockenhurst in the first place? Anne wondered, as she had countless times before, if there was more she could have done to save Sophia. Why had her beautiful girl died? What if they'd stayed in

London? If they'd had a London doctor? She didn't know whether to rage at God or at herself.

She was so full of such thoughts, thinking of things she might have done differently, that Anne barely noticed Susan enter the dining room.

"Good morning, Mother."

Anne looked up and nodded. "Good morning, my dear."

Susan was wearing a pretty gray morning dress. Speer must have spent a good half an hour on her hair, pinning it up at the back and creating two sets of tight curls on either side of Susan's face, offset by a straight middle parting. "Your hair looks very nice."

"Thank you," replied Susan. She stood before the chafing dishes, then turned and went to her seat. "Turton," she said as the butler reentered the room. "I think I'll just have some toast and a cup of coffee."

"The toast is on its way, ma'am."

"Thank you." She glanced at her mother-in-law with a bright smile.

Anne smiled back. "Busy morning?"

Susan nodded. "Quite busy. Shopping, then a fitting and luncheon with a friend." Her tone was as bright as her smile. In truth, Susan did not feel particularly bright. In fact she felt anything but bright. However, she was a good actress, and she knew that until she had made some decisions she must give away no clue as to what was worrying her.

"Where's Oliver?"

"He's gone for a ride. He's trying out that new horse of his. He left at dawn, which was rather hard on the groom. He wanted to show the beast off in the park," she added, before nodding at Turton who had arrived with a rack of hot toast.

"Thank you," she said, and she took a piece, but she only played with it.

Anne sat and watched her daughter-in-law. "You seem distracted, my dear. Is it something I could help with?"

Susan shook her head playfully. "I don't think so. It's nothing.

I'm just running through lists in my head. And I'm nervous about my dressmaker. The skirt was quite wrong when I went for the last fitting, and I'm praying she's got it right this time."

"Well, if that's all it is." Anne smiled. And yet there was something. Anne didn't know what, but she could see the young woman was preoccupied. As she looked at Susan, it occurred to her that there was a slight softening of the lines of her jaw, and her cheekbones were not as prominent as they had been. I wonder if she's putting on weight, thought Anne. That would explain her not eating. She decided to make no comment. If there is anything more tedious than being told you've grown heavier, she couldn't imagine what it might be. Susan looked up, as if aware that her mother-in-law was studying her. But before she could say anything, Turton came back into the room with an envelope on a silver salver. "Excuse me, ma'am," he said, clearing his throat as he walked toward her. "This has just arrived for you."

"Thank you, Turton," said Anne, retrieving it from the tray. She looked at the new Penny Red stamp, so sensible an innovation, and checked the postmark—Faversham, Kent—but she could not remember anyone who lived in the town.

"I shall leave you to your letter," said Susan, standing up from the table. The truth was, she sensed that she was about to suffer a bout of nausea, and she wanted to be alone in her room if her instincts were correct. Lies are so complicated, she thought. And not for the first time.

Anne glanced up from the envelope. "Enjoy your luncheon. Who did you say you were meeting?"

But Susan had already left the room.

The letter was from Jane Croft, the woman who had been Sophia's maid all those years ago in Brussels. Jane had been a nice girl, as far as Anne could recall, and Sophia had been fond of her. They didn't discuss the matter at the time but, as a lady's maid, Croft must almost certainly have guessed at Sophia's pregnancy although she'd never said anything about it, as far as Anne knew, either before or after Sophia's death. When they withdrew to

Derbyshire, the plan was for Croft to remain in London on board wages until her mistress returned. Of course, that return never took place, and Croft had moved on to another job outside the city. But there was no ill feeling, only sorrow to see her go, and she'd left with a bonus and excellent references. These seemed to have done their work, and when Anne last heard, Croft had been hired as a housekeeper for a family in Kent, the Longworths of Sydenham Park. Presumably the house was near Faversham. Anne started to read, then stopped and took a breath. If she'd been surprised to hear from the maid after so many years, she was astonished by the contents of the letter.

Croft wrote how she and Ellis had remained in contact, exchanging notes every few months. However, Croft had been troubled by some gossip Ellis had included in her most recent epistle, about a young man called Charles Pope. "I would welcome the chance to discuss this with you in person, madam. But I would not care to write any more on the subject." Anne stared at the words on the page, with a hollow feeling beginning to trouble her in the pit of her stomach.

At first she was simply furious with Ellis. Why on earth was she writing to Jane Croft about Charles? What would she have to say about him? He was a young businessman who was supported by Mr. Trenchard. Why would one maid write that to another? Then it struck her that Ellis might have been eavesdropping, spying on her mistress, listening to her private conversations with her husband. At the thought, a fist of ice closed around her heart. Ellis had certainly been behaving strangely over the past few months, that was clear—and what was that peculiar business about the lost fan that wasn't lost at all? Anne looked up. Turton had resumed his position by the fireplace.

"Could you ask Ellis to join me in the drawing room?"

Turton received the request with his usual opaque stare. "Certainly, ma'am," he said.

When Ellis came in, she could tell at once that this was not a simple meeting to discuss a frock or a new trimming for a hat.

"Will you please close the door?" Anne's voice was cold and formal. As she turned away to carry out the instruction, Ellis tried to run through what might have given her away. Had she been seen talking to Mr. Bellasis? Was there someone in the pub who knew them both? She desperately raked her brain to come up with a believable story that would place them together without blame, but she couldn't think of anything. She turned back to face her mistress.

"Ellis," began Anne. "I have had a letter from Ellen Croft."

"Oh, yes, ma'am?" Ellis allowed herself to relax slightly. She didn't know what this would be about but it could not involve Mr. Bellasis, since she had definitely never written anything about him.

"Why were you writing to her about Mr. Pope?"

For a moment, her mind was a blank. Why had she written about Mr. Pope to Jane? Surely it could only have been that the master was taking an interest in him. What else would she have had to say about him? "I think I may have mentioned that the master was very kind to a new young protégé, ma'am. I don't think it can have been more than that. I'm sorry if you're displeased. I certainly had no wish to offend you."

Her flustered loss of dignity was very effective. Anne stared at her. Maybe there was nothing to it, after all. James *had* taken an unusual interest in Charles's business. That would be common knowledge downstairs, and what of it? She began to feel a little easier. But there were still matters to resolve.

"While I have you here," said Anne, "why did you go to Brockenhurst House to find a fan that was never lost?"

Ellis looked at her. How had Mrs. Trenchard found out? Presumably that happy slave, Dawson, had given her away. She composed her features. "That's not quite how it was, ma'am."

"Oh? Then how was it?"

"You'd commented on the Countess's hair on the night of her party. I went to see her lady's maid, so I might ask how it had been arranged."

Anne frowned. "I don't remember saying anything about Lady Brockenhurst's hair."

"Oh, you did, ma'am. And I wanted to please you." Ellis was now trying an expression of wounded affection. It worked quite well.

"And the fan?"

"That was a muddle of my own making, ma'am. I couldn't find the fan after you got back from the party, and I assumed you must have left it there."

"Why didn't you ask me?"

Ellis smiled. She could sense she was winning. "I didn't want to bother you, and I knew I was going there anyway, to talk about the hair."

"Where was the fan in the end?"

"I'd put it in the wrong drawer, ma'am. I suppose I was so tired by the time you came home, I wasn't thinking straight."

This was well aimed. Anne could not rid herself of a feeling of guilt when she kept her maid up until the small hours simply to help her undress. And Ellis knew that.

"Very well. But in future, think twice before you start writing about the activities of this family to your friends." Anne was convinced that she had overreacted. "You may go." Ellis started toward the door. "One thing." The maid stopped. "Croft will be coming to see me. I would like her to stay the night if she wishes. Can you please tell Mrs. Frant?"

"When will she be coming, ma'am?"

"I'm not quite sure. In the next few days. She's on her way to join her brother in America."

"Very good, ma'am." Ellis nodded and left.

She closed the drawing room door with a slight sigh of relief. She had contained the problem. But the exchange had presented more questions than answers. She had hardly mentioned Pope in her letter to Jane, yet her friend had felt impelled to write to her mistress of a quarter of a century previously at the mere mention of his name. Why? And why had the mistress been incandescent when there was nothing in the contents of her own letter that was worthy of comment? Here was something to report back to

Mr. Bellasis. If it wasn't worth another sovereign, her name wasn't Mary Ellis.

"Mr. Turton," Ellis hissed as she came down the basement stairs. "I need to have a word."

Turton did not enjoy being bossed around in his own household by a woman, but there was something about Ellis's expression that forced him to comply. The fact was, he and this woman were both in the pay of John Bellasis, and she could put him in prison if she wished. He beckoned her into his pantry and shut the door.

"Jane Croft has written to the mistress and now she's coming here."

"Who is Jane Croft?"

"She was lady's maid to their daughter in the old days. She left after Miss Sophia died."

Turton looked rather impatient. "I don't understand what all this has to do with me."

"I've always kept in touch with Jane, and the other day I mentioned Mr. Pope in a letter to her."

Now the butler seemed quite shocked. "Why ever would you do that?"

Ellis shook her head. "There was nothing to it. I just wrote about Mr. Trenchard having a new favorite. But it was enough to make Jane write to the mistress, and that was enough for the mistress to summon Jane up to London."

Turton absorbed this. Of course he knew more than Ellis about Charles Pope's connection to the family. That letter he'd stolen for Mr. Bellasis had made it clear young Mr. Pope was Mr. Trenchard's son, but even he could not see what place the ex-maid of a dead daughter had to play.

The maid interrupted his reveries. "We should tell Mr. Bellasis."

He nodded. "Yes," he said. But he did not know what Mr. Bellasis would make of it. Still, it might be a way for Turton to worm his way back into Mr. Bellasis's good graces. He knew he had not been forgiven for the double charge on the letter from Charles Pope's adopted father. "You're right. I'll go."

"No, I'll go," said Ellis. If there was a tip coming, she wanted to be there in person to receive it. "I'm the one to tell him what the mistress said, since she said it to me. You'll have to think of an excuse if she rings for me while I'm gone."

Turton nodded. "Tell him I told you to go."

Ellis nodded. If she had suspected before that things were not entirely well between the butler and their joint employer, she knew it now.

Maria Grey was reading on a bench in Belgrave Square when she looked up to see her mother walking toward her. They did not live in the square, but since Chesham Street was so near, they had contrived to be given a key to the gardens, and it was a privilege they valued. Ryan, her maid, was sitting a little way off, knitting. The girl was so used to feeling like a prisoner under guard, she hardly noticed it any more. Lady Templemore paused for a moment to enjoy the sight of her daughter. Maria was dressed in a dark red dress with a tight waist and long sleeves. She looked like a medieval princess waiting for her lover to return from the Crusades. She was very pretty. There could be no question about it, and everything could still be well if only she, Corinne Templemore, could control her for just a little while longer.

"What are you doing?"

"Reading." Maria held the book up for her mother to see.

"Not a novel, I hope." But she was smiling as she said it.

"Poetry. Shelley's "Adonais: An Elegy on the Death of John Keats."

"How impressive." Lady Templemore sat down next to the young woman. She was conscious of a need to hold her nerve, not to shout, not to criticize, just to hold her nerve until the situation had been managed. "I have some good news."

"What's that?"

"Louisa has written to ask you to Northumberland."

"Northumberland?"

Lady Templemore nodded eagerly. "I envy you. Belford will be wonderful at this time of year."

Maria looked at her mother. "What would I do in Northumberland?"

"What do you do here? Walk, ride, read—which you always enjoy." She chattered on, as if the proposed trip were a marvelous bonus, one to be envied. "I long to get away from London, with all the dirt and fog. Just think. You'll be walking along the cliffs, looking out to sea..." She trailed off, as if almost overcome by the power of this seductive image.

Of course her daughter knew what was going on. "But I don't really want to leave London, Mama. Not at the moment."

"Of course you do."

"No." Maria shook her head firmly. "I don't."

"My dear." Corinne reached over and took hold of her daughter's hand. "Won't you allow me to know what is best? Just this once?" Her words were accompanied by a sweet and poignant smile. "I'll have everything ready for you when you get back. How jealous the other girls will be."

"What will be ready?"

"Why, your marriage. We'll take you for a fitting before you go. Then, when the dress is made up in calico, someone can travel to Belford and try it on you there. And we can have a final fitting when you get back. There'll be a day or two to make sure everything is just right."

Maria closed her book carefully. "Have you settled on a date?"

Lady Templemore was chuckling inside. Her daughter seemed to be accepting it. She had been poised for tears and a struggle, but quite the opposite was happening. "We have. I've exchanged letters with the Reverend Mr. Bellasis, and we've settled on a Wednesday in early December. That way, you can spend the autumn in the north, and come back relaxed and happy and ready to take on a new adventure."

"And John Bellasis is my new adventure?"

"Marriage for a young girl is always an adventure."

Maria nodded solemnly. "And where is the adventure to begin?"

"They wanted it to be at Lymington, but unless you object I'm inclined to ask for Brockenhurst House instead. We really can't traipse over to Ireland, and there's no other place on our side with a stronger case. But I enjoy London weddings, and they are so much less trouble for everyone else. A nice Belgravia marriage. I like the sound of it." She glanced through the trees to the line of windows on the first floor of the house as she spoke. There was the ballroom that would soon be the scene of the wedding that would ensure both their futures.

"That's very kind of Lord Brockenhurst," said Maria.

Lady Templemore nodded dreamily. "Apparently he is content to host it at either house. He's pleased with John's choice, they tell me, and he is more than glad to welcome you into the family." The tone of this conversation was so normal that Corinne was beginning to allow herself to think that everything would be resolved satisfactorily, after all.

"What about Lady Brockenhurst? What does she say on the subject?"

Corinne glanced at the girl but she was looking straight ahead, without any signs of temper or stress. It was just a question. There was nothing more to it than that.

"I'm sure she'll be delighted."

"But you haven't spoken about it yet?"

"Not yet, no." She sighed with happiness at the prospect before her. "I'll send a note and we can go for a fitting tomorrow morning. We might as well get the business *en train*."

Maria was numb with dread as she followed her mother back across the road on their way to Chesham Street. She might be used to living under surveillance, but she was not used to the feeling of terror that gripped her now. The noise of children playing in the square, the birds, the wind, and the chatter of passersby faded into the background, until all she could hear was the sound of her own heartbeat drumming in her ears. She sank her teeth into her bottom lip and forced her nails into her fingertips. She had to think, and think quickly. She could not marry that man. She would rather die. It had seemed like some distant, nebulous idea until this moment, a mad scheme of her mother's that would never come to pass. But now it was on the brink of becoming a reality. She just couldn't bear to think about it. But she must. Because one thing she knew absolutely: She must act before it was too late.

John Bellasis knew what Jane Croft's secret must be. Ellis had hardly begun to sketch out the incidents of that morning before he realized that he had come upon the final missing piece of the puzzle. Jane Croft was the mother of Charles Pope. It had to be. While they were in Brussels, twenty-five years before, she and James Trenchard . . .

"Was she good-looking, this Jane Croft?" he said, catching Ellis by surprise. "When she was young?"

"Good-looking enough, I suppose. Yes. Why?" Ellis had lost her own train of thought. What could Mr. Bellasis be talking about?

From knowing who Jane was, John quickly moved to a clear and vivid understanding of why she was coming to London. She wants to see her son, he thought. She wants to see her son before she goes to America. She won't be back and she knows it. She wants to see him, as a grown man, before she leaves England forever.

He turned to the waiting maid. "And before Miss Sophia died, this Jane Croft was kept on board wages for weeks, doing no work, waiting out her time? Is that right?"

"She did no work because the young mistress was away in the north."

John nodded, the thoughts whirling through his brain. They kept her on, feeding her, letting her rest, until her time was almost come, and then she was sent somewhere for the baby to be born. James Trenchard arranged the whole thing, but he must have had his wife's compliance. She must have known. Was she enraged? Or forgiving? Maybe the latter, if Croft wanted to see her old mistress now, twenty-five years after she had betrayed her. But these thoughts were unspoken and, for Ellis, his silence was becoming oppressive.

"I ought to get back, sir. Or I'll be missed." Ellis did not move. She was hoping for the tip that she would not be sharing with Turton.

"Report back to me when she gets to London. Bring me anything you learn. Engage her in conversation. Go through her things. Find out everything she knows about Mr. Pope." He was almost excited. Of course there was still one clue that had to be solved, and in many ways it was the most important. What was the link to Lady Brockenhurst? It wasn't surprising to learn that she was not Charles Pope's mother. Susan was right about that. How would she and Trenchard ever have got together? But there was still some connection that held her fast. And Jane Croft might be the key to the puzzle. It was this particular link that would yield dividends. He was ready to bet his last penny on it. "Go. Let me know the moment you have anything." But still Ellis did not move, and they both knew why. At last he felt in his trousers and produced a guinea. She took it and moved off, past the figure who ducked into a doorway at the sight of her.

Susan Trenchard hurried toward the entrance to John's set. He was still at the bottom of the staircase when she appeared. "That was a narrow squeak," she said. "I just missed my mother-in-law's maid."

"You should have told me when you were coming."

"I did. You're supposed to have luncheon ready for me."

"Don't worry. We can send my man to fetch something." He started up the staircase. He hated entertaining at his home. He felt these modest rooms gave no impression of who he really was. "Why are you here? What's the urgency?"

Susan looked up at him. "Well, I'm not going to tell you on the stairs."

But she was going to tell him when they were safely in his rooms. Heaven only knew what would happen then.

Ellis had never considered herself a lucky woman. By her reckoning, being born into service was not to be envied, and she'd generally always found that she had to fight every step of the way through life. But just for a moment, on that day when Jane Croft arrived at Eaton Square for the meeting with Mrs. Trenchard, Ellis felt that, at long last, she had been dealt a winning card.

She'd been turning over John Bellasis's plan in her head ever since their meeting. On the afternoon Croft was expected, Ellis was to get some time alone with her old friend to discover what Croft knew on the subject of Charles Pope, and preferably to find a chance to go through her things. She was to do all this before Croft had an opportunity to speak to Anne Trenchard. It was something of a tall order, but Mr. Bellasis had been insistent and there would be a good tip in it, that she knew for certain.

In the end, Ellis was lucky. Croft arrived only a few moments after Mrs. Trenchard had left the house to attend a charity gathering somewhere on Park Lane, and she was not expected back for at least two hours.

The passing years had been kind to Jane Croft, Ellis thought as she looked her old friend up and down. The former lady's maid had been attractive enough to turn soldiers' heads all those years ago in Brussels, when she and young Miss Sophia would gad about town, seemingly without a care in the world. The odd thing about war, Ellis was not alone in observing, was the way it made everyone so reckless and impetuous, as if the smell of approaching death encouraged the living to make as much of their time on earth as they could.

"You're looking well. You hardly seem a day older," she said.

"Thank you," Croft replied, tidying her brown hair that had only grayed slightly at the temples. "You, too," she lied politely.

"Mrs. Trenchard won't be back for a few hours," said Ellis. "Let's ask Mrs. Babbage for some bread and cheese, and then we can have a good old chin-wag." She signaled for her to take a seat in the corner of the servants' hall while she went to give the order.

"Thank you. That's kind of you," said Croft, suspecting nothing.

So over bread and cheese and a glass of cider, they caught up on each other's news. Croft's life since she left the Trenchards' service had worked out well, and it seemed she had enjoyed her time as a housekeeper, with all the responsibility and extra money that entailed.

"Then what's this I hear about your going to America?"

Croft smiled. It was exciting. "My brother emigrated to America years ago now, not long after we got back from Brussels, and he has prospered in the building industry."

"What part of America has he settled in?"

"New York. There's been a lot of development since the turn of the century, and he has risen on that wave. Now he is building a new house for himself on a street they call Fifth Avenue, and he wants me to come over and run it for him."

"As a servant?"

"As his sister. He never married."

Ellis raised her eyebrows. "He might marry now if he's as rich as you say."

"He's thought of that. He wants me to live with him, whether or not he takes a wife."

Ellis found herself becoming rather jealous. Croft was to leave service and run a fine house in a new country. How fair was that, when Ellis still had to bow and curtsy and try to eke out a living by spying and stealing? There didn't seem to be any justice in it. "I hope you can adjust to the different climate," she said sourly. "I believe the extremes of heat and cold can be very trying to the spirit."

"I think I'll manage," said Croft, well aware of what was going through her friend's mind. "Of course I'll have to decide what to do with my spare time. It's not something I've ever known before."

"What a problem to have," said Ellis, giving a rare smile. "When do you sail?"

"Thursday. I'll make the journey to Liverpool in the morning, which I am not looking forward to, but I've sent all but one bag ahead to my hotel, so that's something. Then I'll spend the night there and go on board the following morning."

Ellis felt a strong desire to talk this adventure down and spoil Croft's obvious pleasure, but she resisted it. There were more important things at stake. "What was it you wanted to see Mrs. Trenchard about?" she said.

Croft gave a slight shrug. "It's something or nothing." She hesitated, unsure whether she should say anything more.

"You know you got me into trouble by mentioning that I'd written about Mr. Pope." Ellis looked wounded rather than severe.

"No, I didn't know that. I'm ever so sorry."

"So I think you owe me an explanation."

Croft nodded. She had no idea that the woman before her was anything but a slightly envious friend. "I was tidying everything up when I was packing, going through old letters and the like and throwing out what I did not want to keep forever. You know the sort of thing."

"Of course."

"Well, I came upon some papers of Miss Sophia's that I wanted to pass on. I don't know if the mistress will keep them, but I just didn't feel I had the right to destroy them. So I thought, why not deliver the bundle in person before I go? I daresay she'll throw them on the fire the moment I'm out of the room."

"It seems a long way to come for that."

"Not really. I was in Kent, so it just breaks the journey to Liverpool. Besides, I've not been to London in years. I've heard about the master's building work and read descriptions in the papers, but I wanted to see for myself what the city's become, before I left. I don't know that I'll be back this way, if you know what I mean."

Ellis knew at once that this was her chance. "Of course I understand, and I'll tell you what. If you go now, you'll have plenty of time before the mistress gets home. She won't be back for at least two hours. Let me give you a list of the streets and squares you ought to visit, make an outing of it, enjoy yourself."

Croft nodded, but there was something nervous in the movement. "I don't suppose you could come with me? Only it's been a while since I was out walking in London."

Ellis gave a light laugh. "The chance'd be a fine thing! I've got work up to my ears. But don't worry. I'll give you some money if you like, for a cab to take you around."

Croft shook her head. "No, I've got money."

"Then you mustn't miss this chance. It won't come again."

"Well, that's true. What shall I do with my bag?"

"I'll have one of the hall boys take it upstairs to your room. You're sharing with me tonight." At this, Croft stood and went to reach for her cape, which was hanging in the passage outside.

It was not much more than five minutes before Ellis had taken her bag into Turton's room and the two of them were searching the contents.

In even less time they found what they were looking for. Inside a large leather envelope there was a bundle of letters, together with other papers.

"We need to be quick," she said, watching the butler as he scanned the papers carefully.

But Turton was thinking. "What will he give us for them?"

"We can't steal these, or we'd be discovered as soon as the mistress gets home and asks to see them. We must make copies now, at once, before she returns."

He did not seem quite convinced. "But how do we know he'll pay enough?"

Ellis was becoming impatient. "Mr. Turton, I don't know why, but you've fallen out with Mr. Bellasis and it is clouding your judgment. I have not. This is our chance to have something worth selling that he will want to buy. We can haggle later, but right now we must make copies so he can buy them if he wishes, which he will. Then the mistress is given the originals and nobody is any the wiser."

"Why don't you make the copies?"

"Because I—" Ellis was silent for a moment. She was going to say she couldn't write, but that wasn't true. She could. But not well enough for Mr. Bellasis's eyes. What annoyed her was that Turton knew it.

Turton stared at her, enjoying her discomfort. "Very well. I will copy the papers as quickly as I can, and then you can take them over to Mr. Bellasis. But you are not to put them into his hand until you have decided on the price. Unless you want me to go."

"No. If he's angry with you, it may make him less inclined to pay." Turton nodded. There was logic in this.

Having resolved to do it, he was quick. He sat down at his desk with a steel-nibbed pen and ink while Ellis stood guard. He barely spoke as he scratched and scribbled on the thick white paper, copying down the information. He nodded gruffly to Ellis as soon as he'd finished. "Put the real ones back and then take these to him."

"Are they worth something?"

Turton thought for a moment. "They are either worth a great deal to Mr. Bellasis or nothing at all."

Ellis didn't understand him. "How's that?" she said, but he did not elaborate. Instead he handed her the leather envelope of papers so that she could place them back in the bag and carry it upstairs to her bedroom on the women's side of the servants' attics.

Half an hour later, Ellis was standing in the entrance courtyard at Albany as a servant came out of the porch to tell her that Mr. Bellasis was indeed in residence and would receive her.

John's reaction to the papers was not quite as she had expected. He read them through, in absolute silence, while she waited by the door. Then he read one of them again and his face was so still that he could have been a statue. She could not tell if he was delighted or fascinated or horrified. At last he looked up. "Where are the originals?"

"Back in the case where Miss Croft left them. Up in my room."

"Fetch them." His tone was as stern as a commander in chief giving the order to charge.

Ellis shook her head. "I can't. She'll know who took them. And then what?"

"Do you think I care? Fetch them at once. I will give you a thousand pounds to compensate you if you should lose your place."

Ellis could not believe her ears. How much? A thousand pounds, more money than she'd ever dreamed of, for some papers that Croft had described as "something and nothing"? She stared at him.

"Have I made myself clear?" he barked, and she nodded, still rooted to the spot. "Then go!" His shouting seemed to wake her from a dream, and she flung open the door of his set and started to hurry down the stairs. She was running by the time she reached the pavement, careering down Piccadilly, so that people stopped and turned to watch her hurtle by.

When she reached the basement door of number 110, she was panting, drawing in her breath in gasps. Turton was still in his pantry. He looked up. "How well did we do?"

She ignored the question. "Is Jane Croft back?"

"She's been back for twenty minutes. She was only a quarter of an hour ahead of the mistress."

Ellis's heart was pounding in her chest. "The mistress is back?"

"She is. She asked after you, but I said you'd gone out and she didn't seem to mind. She went upstairs, took off her cape and bonnet, and went straight into the drawing room."

"So Jane...?" Ellis's voice trailed off.

"She's in there with her now. The mistress rang for her as soon as she was settled and Miss Croft has just gone up."

There was a moment of hope. If Croft had gone straight in, maybe the papers would still be in her case. Without a word, Ellis turned on her heel and started to race up the stairs, on and on, two at a time, past the drawing room floor, past two floors of family bedrooms, until at last she had reached the attics. She raced to her own room, but the case was on the bed, open, and the leather envelope was gone.

It was the nearest Mary Ellis would ever come to owning a thousand pounds. Or anything like it.

Anne could not have been more delighted to see Sophia's former maid. The sight of the woman, older of course but not so changed as to be unrecognizable, reminded Anne that she had always liked her. And talking together seemed to take them both back to happier times. She invited the maid who was no longer a maid to sit in her presence. She had asked for some cordial to be brought up, and now she offered her visitor a glass.

"Do you remember the Duchess's famous ball?" asked Anne.

"I should, madam. I've been asked about it often enough in the years since." She took the cordial and sipped it. She found it a little sharp, but the honor of being invited to take a glass with the mistress was reward enough. It didn't have to taste nice. "And I remember how beautiful Miss Sophia looked in her dress." Croft smiled.

"Her hair was so pretty." Anne was in her own reverie.

"I took some trouble over it, I can tell you," said Croft, and they laughed.

It was good to laugh and not cry for once, thought Anne; to share their happy memories of Sophia before they parted. But then that same memory forced her to change the tone. "She was very upset that night, when we got home."

"Yes," said the maid, but she did not dare elaborate.

Anne stared at her. "It's a long time ago now, and I'm glad to hear you've prospered. I'm sure your life in America will be rewarding and full. But since we may not meet again..." She hesitated.

"We won't meet again, madam," said Croft softly.

"No." Anne looked at the fire burning in the grate. "So I wonder if we may be honest with each other for this last moment together?"

"Certainly, madam."

"Do you know what happened that night at the ball?"

Croft nodded. It was odd to be having this conversation with a woman she would once have curtsied to. It was almost as if they were equals. Which in a way, when it came to this business, they were. "I know that Lord Bellasis, him that we'd all thought such a proper gentleman, had tricked and betrayed her, and she learned it that night."

"Did you know about the wedding charade before then?"

"No." The maid was anxious to show that she had not been party to hiding secrets until Sophia forced her to be. "She never told me anything about it until it was found to be false. And of course it was only later that she..." Croft sipped her cordial and looked at the floor.

"That she discovered she was pregnant." It was odd for Anne, too, to be able to talk about the subject with another human being who was not her husband or Lady Brockenhurst. She had never done such a thing before.

"I asked her to tell you, ma'am. Right away. Straight off. But it was as if she was in a daze and somehow couldn't think."

"She told me in the end."

"Yes," said Croft.

They stared at each other. They knew so much that no one else knew. No one else except James. Even Lady Brockenhurst, who thought she knew everything, had never met Sophia, so she was missing half the story. Anne spoke again. "She told me in time to make our plans for traveling north. And all might have been well, if only..."

"If only she hadn't died." Croft's eyes were full of tears and, as Anne watched, one brimmed over and ran down the former maid's cheek. Anne loved her for crying over her lost child. "I suppose the baby's grown up by now. Is he still living with the Reverend Mr. Pope? Or is he in London now? I assume he's the young Mr. Pope that Miss Ellis told me about?"

"But how did you know about the Reverend Mr. Pope?"

Croft looked at her. "I'm sorry, ma'am. I don't know as you'll want to hear it." She stopped.

"Go on," said Anne. "Please."

Her visitor's tone was apologetic when she spoke again, revealing the secrets of long ago. "You see, Miss Sophia used to write to me, ma'am. Up until the end. We talked about the baby and what would happen, and she wrote that he or she was to go and live with the Popes in Surrey. I seem to remember that Mrs. Pope was childless, although I've lost the letter where she said it."

Anne was astonished. "So you know everything."

"I haven't told a soul, I swear. Hand on my heart," said Croft, doing just that. "I won't ever discuss it with anyone, either."

"Don't worry," replied Anne. "I find it comforting. That she had someone else to talk to."

And now Croft took up the leather envelope and placed it on

her lap. "I have some papers here, madam." She hesitated. "One of them testifies to the false marriage. It's signed by the man who said he was a priest. He names himself Bouverie. I suppose you'd call it the marriage certificate, if it weren't a lie. Then there's a letter from Bouverie describing how the young couple came to marry in Brussels so far from home." She paused as she pulled out the two sheets of paper. "She gave them to me that night in Brussels, when she got home from the ball, and told me to burn them, but I never did. I didn't have the nerve. I didn't feel they were mine to destroy."

"I see that." Anne took the papers and glanced through their contents.

"But I'm leaving the country now, and especially as Miss Ellis mentioned Mr. Pope in her letter to me, I thought it would be best to give you everything. I don't know if you'll want to keep them safe. You might want to burn them yourself. But that's for you to decide, not me." With that, she handed the leather satchel over.

"Thank you, Croft—I should call you *Miss* Croft now—that is generous and thoughtful." Anne took it and looked inside. "What are the rest?"

"Some letters from Miss Sophia about the plans for the baby coming, describing the doctor and the midwife and suchlike. I didn't want to risk my dropping dead and some stranger coming upon all that information. Again, it's best with you. I've kept one of her letters to remember her by, but there's nothing in it that a stranger might not read."

Anne smiled at this, her eyes starting to fill again, and then she looked at the writing on the envelopes. She slowly ran her fingertips over the curls of each letter. Darling Sophia—even now, the mere sight of her handwriting was enough to make the tears flow. How young the writing looked, with its loops and swirls. Sophia's hand had always been flamboyant. Anne imagined her, sitting at her desk, quill in hand. "Thank you," she said again, looking directly at her visitor. "I am very touched. We have so little left of Miss Sophia, you see. Not enough memories. It's wonderful to have something of her returned to us after so many years."

That night, alone in her bedroom, Anne read them through again and again. She couldn't stop the tears, but the love she felt for this lost child, hearing her voice again as she read the phrases Sophia had chosen, was so fierce it almost felt uplifting. She would not tell James yet. She wanted to keep the letters to herself for a while. She rose and locked them in a small cupboard in her room, before her husband made his appearance.

Oliver was looking forward to having luncheon with his father at the Athenaeum. The uncovering of Pope's dubious past had been tiring and expensive, but it was done, and he hoped that now there could be a new rapprochement between his demanding parent and himself. After all, he'd done James a favor, enabled him to withdraw before he made a fool of himself over Pope and his wretched cotton. James had told him that Charles had not denied the accusations, which had interested Oliver. The letters confirmed Pope's guilt, of course, but still, Oliver had expected him to try to weasel his way out in some way, and he had not. So be it. It was time for Oliver and James to move forward with their lives, in a new and enriched spirit of familial love and cooperation.

"Good day, sir," said the club servant as he collected Oliver's silver-topped cane, gloves, and silk hat. Oliver smiled. He liked it here; it was civilized. It was where he should be. Following the man through the hall and past the sweeping staircase, he walked into the large dining room with its tall windows reaching almost from ceiling to floor. The dark wood paneling on the walls and the deep maroon patterned carpet gave the room an intimate, discreet feeling.

"Father." He waved with a slight gesture at James, who was waiting at a round table in the corner. The older man stood in welcome.

"Oliver," he said, with a jovial smile. "I'm glad to see you here. I hope you're hungry." James was in the mood to humor his son. The previous few months had been fraught and uncomfortable, and he was eager to mend bridges and defuse the tense atmosphere they had been living with for some time. But on this day he was not confident his goal could be achieved, given what he knew he would have to say.

"Excellent," replied Oliver, rubbing his hands together as he sat down. James could see his son's optimism and confidence, and he was only too aware of what they probably stemmed from. Still, he thought, let Oliver be the one to introduce the subject.

They picked up their menus. "Where were you this morning?" said James.

"Riding," Oliver replied. "It was a beautiful day and Rotten Row was very crowded, but I'm pleased with that new gelding."

"I thought I might see you at the meeting in Gray's Inn Road."

"What meeting?" Oliver squinted at the list before him. "What's hogget?"

"Older than lamb, younger than mutton." James sighed gently. "We were discussing the different stages of the new development. Didn't they tell you it was happening?"

"They might have done." Oliver caught the eye of a waiter. "Shall we get something to drink?"

James watched him as he ordered a bottle of Chablis to start with, and then a bottle of claret. Why was his son so endlessly disappointing? He'd managed to secure him a position on one of the most exciting projects in the country, and the boy could barely raise even a flicker of interest. Granted the development was not at its most fascinating stage—dredging vast tracts of marshland in the East End—but the problem was deeper than that. Oliver did not seem to understand that the only real fulfilment on this earth was to be gained through hard work. Life as a series of momentary pleasures satisfied no one. He needed to make an investment in it, an investment of himself.

If Oliver had heard these thoughts spoken aloud, he would have been incensed. He was willing to make an investment in life, just not the life his father had planned for him. He wanted to live at Glanville and come to London for the Season. He wanted to watch over his acres and talk to his tenants and play a role in the county. Was that wrong? Was it dishonorable? No. His father could never appreciate a set of values different from his own. That is what he would have said and, to be fair to Oliver, there was some truth in it. But as they sat nursing glasses of the wine he had ordered, they both knew that the figure of Charles Pope was looming over their conversation, standing behind their chairs, and the subject would have to be addressed before much more time had passed. Eventually, Oliver could resist no longer.

"So," he said, slicing into his meat. "Did you let Mr. Pope down lightly?"

"What do you mean?"

"What do you think I mean? You've always been such a stickler for honest dealings. Don't tell me you've dropped your standards?"

"It's true that I have kept my money in his company," said James carefully. "It remains a good investment."

Oliver leaned forward. "What about the letters I gave you?" His voice was low and aggressive. "You said you'd charged Pope with them and he didn't deny a thing."

"That's true." James had chosen partridge and he was regretting it.

"Well, then."

When James replied, his voice was as smooth as silk. If he had been talking down a wild animal, he could not have been more subtle. "I did not believe the whole thing was quite . . . right."

"I don't understand." Oliver's mouth was set. "Are you saying it was all a lie? In which case, am I the liar? Is that it?"

"No," said James, trying to appease his son, "I don't think anyone was lying. Or at least, not you—"

"If the men who wrote the letters had not been telling the truth, Pope would have denied it."

"I'm not so sure. And besides, when you're in trade . . ." Oliver winced. Why wouldn't his father let the family move on from their trading roots? Was it so much to ask? "When you are in trade," his father repeated firmly and on purpose, "you get an instinct for people. Charles Pope would never try to cheat the customs men. It's not in him."

"I say again, why didn't he deny it?" Oliver screwed up his napkin.

"Keep your voice down." James looked around him. A few of the other diners were beginning to glance over at their table.

"Must I ask you again?" Oliver spoke, if anything, more loudly than before. He also tossed his knife and fork as noisily as possible onto his plate. James didn't need to look about them to be aware that they had become the chosen spectacle of the dining room and would be the subject of excited conversation afterward in the library. It was so exactly what he didn't want.

"Very well. If you insist. I believe that Charles Pope was reluctant to be the cause of a quarrel between you and me. He did not defend himself because he did not want to come between us."

"Well, he has come between us, hasn't he, Father? This Mr. Pope? He's been standing between us for some time!" Oliver pushed his chair back and stood, boiling with fury. "Of course you'd take his side. Why did I think for one moment you would not! Good day to you, Father. I wish you well of your Mr. Pope!" He spat the words out as if they were poisonous. "Let him comfort you. For you have no son in me!"

The room was silent. When Oliver turned he saw at least a dozen pairs of eyes trained on him. "To hell with the lot of you!" he declared, and with a toss of his head he marched out of the club.

At that precise moment, Charles was sitting in his office, staring at the portrait of his adopted father. He should be feeling excited, he told himself. This was a key stage of his career. His business was funded, including his proposed trip to India, and everything was set fair. But somehow he didn't want to leave London now, and his prospects had lost their luster. The truth was, when he thought about it, it was Maria Grey he did not want to leave. He picked up his pen. Was he really prepared to sacrifice everything he had worked for to stay near a woman who could never be his wife? Why must life be so impossible. How could it have happened? He was in love with a woman who was betrothed to someone else. Worse. Who was entirely out of his reach. Only misery and humiliation could lie ahead. He stared up again at the pastel. What advice would that wise man have given him?

"Excuse me, sir?" A clerk rapped quietly on the open door, holding an envelope.

"Yes?"

"This came for you, sir," said the clerk. "It arrived just now by messenger. He said it was urgent."

"Thank you." Charles nodded, holding out his hand and taking the letter. He glanced at the writing. "Is the messenger still here?"

"No, sir."

"Thank you," said Charles again, waiting until the man had left before opening it.

"My dear Charles." He could hear her voice as he read. "I need to see you at once. I shall be in Hatchards bookshop until four o'clock this afternoon. Please come. Yours affectionately, Maria Grey."

He stared at the letter for a moment, then snatched his watch out of his pocket, his heart beating wildly. It was already a quarter past three. There was very little time. He grabbed his hat and coat and ran out of the office past his startled clerks.

He had three quarters of an hour to get to Piccadilly. He sprinted down the stairs and ran out into the street, staring anxiously up and down Bishopsgate for a hackney carriage. But there was none to be seen. He stood on the pavement, surrounded by a melée of people, workingmen and women shuffling along, going about their business. Which was the quickest way to Piccadilly? If he started to run, could he make it in time? His palms were sweating and his chest was heaving. He felt tears of frustration welling up in his eyes. He raced down the pavement, then changed his mind and hurried out into the road again, frantically searching for a cab.

"Oi!" yelled a large man driving a dray. "Get out of the way!"

"Please God," Charles prayed as he ran toward Leadenhall Market. "I'll never ask anything from you again. If you will just help me to a cab." And then, just as he turned the corner of Threadneedle Street, he spotted a hackney carriage. "Here! Here!" he shouted, waving his arms.

"Where to, sir?" asked the driver, coming to a halt.

"Hatchards in Piccadilly, please," said Charles as he collapsed onto the black leather seat, his heart still pounding in his chest. "And please be as quick as you can." He closed his eyes. "Thank you, God," he mumbled under this breath. But of course, he would ask his maker for other favors, and he knew it.

It was five minutes to four when Charles finally arrived outside the bookshop. He leapt out of the cab, paid, and tipped the driver before bursting through the double doors of the bay-windowed emporium, where he came to an abrupt halt. Where was she? The shop was enormous. He had not remembered it to be so large, and at this hour of the day it was crowded with women, all wearing bonnets that shaded their faces. He checked his watch again. Surely she'd wait; surely she knew he was bound to come?

But where would he find her? He looked among the shelves displaying works of fiction, weaving his way through a sea of wide skirts held out by the heavy petticoats beneath. He strained to glimpse under the brims of bonnets as their owners perused the books in their hands, gently calling her name as he went. "Maria? Maria?" One girl smiled at him but most gave him circumspect glances and, avoiding his eyes, attempted to move away. He picked up a copy of *Mansfield Park* by Jane Austen and pretended to read it as he searched up and down the aisles. Where would she be? What did she like? What subject might interest her?

Suddenly, he spoke aloud. "India!" he said, and the customers near him edged away. "Excuse me!" He hurried over to a man who was stacking shelves nearby. "Where would I find a book about India?"

"Travel and Empire." The shop assistant sniffed at his ignorance. "Second floor."

Charles bounded up the staircase as if he were a hurdler on a sprint, and then, suddenly, there she was, standing in an alcove, leafing through a book. She had not noticed his arrival, and for a moment, now that he had found her, he allowed himself the luxury of enjoying the sight. She was dressed in a fawn skirt and jacket with a matching bonnet trimmed in leaves of lime-green silk. Her face, intent on what she was reading, was even lovelier than he remembered it. That's true, he thought with a kind of wonder, no matter how beautiful she is in my imaginings, when I see her again, she is more beautiful still.

Then she looked up as if aware of his eyes trained upon her. "Charles," she said, clutching the book to her chest. "I thought you'd never come."

"I only got your message at a quarter past three. I've been running ever since."

"He must have stopped on the way, the wicked man." But she was smiling. Charles was here. Everything was well again. She had put her hand in his at their greeting but he had not surrendered it. Now she remembered why she had summoned him and drew it back. Her expression grew serious. "You have to help me," she said.

She spoke with a kind of urgency that told him at once that he had not been called for frivolous reasons. "Of course I will."

Maria wanted him to know the full truth. "Mother means to send me away, to her cousin in Northumberland, to get me out of London while she plans my wedding to John Bellasis. She has already set the date." Much to her annoyance she started to cry, but she wiped her eyes on her glove and shook her head to rid herself of any weakness.

Against his better judgment, Charles allowed himself to slip an arm around her shoulders. "I'm here now," he said, quite simply, as if that fact would make all the difference, as he intended that it should.

She looked up at him fiercely, with the face of a warrior. "Let's run away together," she whispered. "Let's leave everyone and everything."

"Oh, Maria!" His emotions were in turmoil. With every fiber of his body he wanted to say that he'd loved her ever since he first saw her on the balcony at Lady Brockenhurst's soirée. He wanted to tell her that there was nothing more in the world he'd rather do than run away with her. Run away and never come back. He touched her soft cheek with his hand. "We can't. You must know that."

She took a step back as if she'd been slapped. "Why not?"

He sighed. Some of the other customers were watching them, these two lovers, with the woman on the brink of tears. He had a sinking feeling that they were enjoying the spectacle.

"I won't be the person responsible for your ruin. If you ran off with a merchant from the East End, every door in London would be slammed in your face. How could I do that to you? If I loved you?"

"If you loved me?"

"Because I love you. I will not be the instrument of your downfall," he said, shaking his head sadly. He looked around again. "Even this meeting is asking for trouble. How did you get rid of your maid?"

"I shook her off. I'm getting rather good at it." But her tone was more sad than playful. "So what are you saying? That I must die an old maid? For I will not marry John Bellasis, not if Mama locks me in a tower and feeds me on bread and water to the end of my days."

He could not resist a smile at her fighting spirit. "We should go," he said. "We're beginning to attract attention."

"Who cares?" Her sorrow was gone. Now she was defiant.

"I do." Charles was thinking furiously. What could they do that would protect Maria and not ruin her? Then, suddenly, he realized where they should go next. "Come with me," he said, more determined now. "I have an idea."

"Is it a good one?" asked Maria. She was starting to recover her spirits. Charles might not be willing to elope with her, but he clearly was not going to abandon her, either.

"I think so. I hope so. We'll find out soon enough."

And he drew her gently toward the staircase.

It was half past four when the vehicle came to a halt outside Brockenhurst House in Belgrave Square. Maria and Charles got out, paid, and walked quickly toward the door. "The Countess will have an idea of what we should do," Charles assured Maria as they stood on the steps. "I don't pretend to know her well, but she is fond of you and she is fond of me. She'll have something to say on the matter."

Maria was less convinced. "All that may be true, but John is her husband's nephew, and in our world blood trumps friendship every time."

At that moment the door was opened by a footman in dress livery, and as they stepped inside it was at once obvious that the house was full of activity, with maids waiting to take the ladies' cloaks and other footmen standing by the staircase.

"What's happening?" said Charles.

"Her ladyship is giving a tea party, sir. Are you not invited?" He frowned. He had only admitted them on the assumption that they were.

"She will be pleased to see us, I'm sure," said Charles smoothly.

The footman received this information but it made him nervous. What if they had not been invited for a reason? He was trying to weigh which action—turning them away when they were wanted, or letting them in when they were not—would get him into the most trouble. In the end, he knew he had seen both of them at other gatherings given by his employer, and so he thought it was probably better to send them up. He nodded to a man at the base of the stairs. "Take Mr. Pope and Lady Maria Grey to the drawing room."

They started toward the steps. "I'm rather impressed he should remember our names," said Charles.

"It's his job," replied Maria. "But are we right to do this?"

When they reached the entrance, the principal drawing rooms of Brockenhurst House, for there were two of them, linked by double doors, seemed to be entirely filled with women. At least, there were few men in their midst, chattering and laughing, their black morning coats in sharp contrast to the sea of color surrounding them, as the vast skirts of the ladies' costumes billowed about like water lilies on a lake. Servants walked among the guests carrying plates of sandwiches and cakes and filling cups from teapots. One or two of the ladies looked up, curiously.

"Where will we find her?" said Maria, but the answer came quickly from behind them.

"Here," said Lady Brockenhurst.

They turned and there she was, smiling, perhaps a little surprised. "We're very sorry to have forced our way into your party, Lady Brockenhurst—" But Charles got no further.

"Nonsense. I'm delighted to see you." The Countess allowed herself a moment to enjoy the sight of him. "I would have invited you both if I had thought you'd find it in the least bit amusing." She was wearing a dress of pale pink damask edged in lace, with a little ruff at her neck, a stiff costume in its way but still becoming. Only Maria knew it was not a color the Countess would have worn until recently.

"We need your advice," said Charles.

"I'm flattered."

"But it may not be advice you're willing to give." Clearly, Maria was altogether less optimistic about the outcome. "You might feel you must support the other side."

"Are we to take sides?" Caroline Brockenhurst's right eyebrow rose in an ironic arch. "How interesting. Would you like to come with me to my boudoir, my dear? It is only across the landing."

Maria was slightly taken aback. "Can we leave your guests?"

"Oh, I think so." Lady Brockenhurst already knew what was coming, since she had been expecting it for some time. She also knew how she intended to deal with it.

"And Charles?"

"Mr. Pope can stay here. It won't be for long. He will not mind that."

"No, indeed," said Charles. He was delighted that their hostess seemed so willing to get involved in their troubles.

The women walked toward a door that was different from the one they had come in by. Then they stopped. "I should warn you, Mr. Pope," said Lady Brockenhurst. "I am expecting Lady Templemore."

Maria caught Charles's eye. This was not what they wanted to hear. "Consider me warned," said Charles.

In fact, at that moment Lady Templemore was standing in the doorway at the other end of the double drawing room. She had been told downstairs that her daughter had already arrived, accompanied by Mr. Pope, news she had received in complete silence. She'd suspected something of the sort when Ryan had told her that Maria had given them the slip. But to find them here and together was a shock. It must mean that they believed Lady Brockenhurst would be their friend, and yet how could she be? Corinne Templemore was reluctant to think such evil of her old ally. Until, that is, she witnessed Maria leaving the room with a smiling Caroline, and Mr. Pope left to look after himself, surrounded by the elderly beauties on the guest list. As she stood there, some of the ladies nodded to her, but she approached none of them. Among the crowd, sitting on a damask *bergère* opposite her, was a distinguished-looking woman in her late fifties. Dressed in blue silk trimmed with gilded braid, she wore a heavy rope of gleaming pearls around her neck and pearl earrings. Her hair was curled and pinned up at the back and on her lap lay a feathered fan.

"Lady Templemore," she said. "Good day to you." She had seen that Corinne's eyes had never left that young man sitting on the other side of the drawing room and she was curious. There was something fascinating in the other woman's stillness. Was this an unlikely liaison? A May-September romance in reverse? Whatever the truth, it was clear that some sort of intrigue was being played out before her, and she was enthralled.

Corinne stared at her for a moment, brought out of her daze by the question. "Duchess," she said. "How pleased you must be by the success of the fashion you invented. Afternoon tea will clearly outlast us all."

The Duchess of Bedford accepted the compliment modestly. "You're kind, but we never know what will last," she said, allowing her eyes to follow Lady Templemore's to the distant seated figure of that handsome young man.

Corinne smiled coldly. "Maybe not." She spoke in a voice so hard that the Duchess knew at once that her seeming obsession with the dark stranger was anything but a concealed passion. "But we sometimes know what will *not* last. Not if I have anything to do with it." With that, she moved forward, gliding through the throng, managing her skirts, looking neither to left nor right until she faced the figure of Charles Pope.

He was talking to a woman at his side and did not notice her at first. Then she spoke. "Mr. Pope," she said. He turned.

"Lady Templemore. Good afternoon." In his mind, he thanked Lady Brockenhurst for giving him a warning, or the shock might have shown on his face.

"I might have known you'd be involved." Lady Templemore's face was implacable.

"Involved in what?"

"Don't lie to me."

Charles felt a strange calm spreading through his whole being. He had always known the day would dawn when he would have to fight it out with Maria's mother. Even when he told himself Maria was beyond his reach and tried to accept it, still, at the back of his mind was the sense that this battle would be joined. "I am not a liar," he said as pleasantly as he could manage. "I will tell you anything you wish. I found her in Hatchards. She was distressed and so I brought her here. She is with Lady Brockenhurst now."

"I know you have been meeting in secret. Don't think I don't. I know everything about you." Corinne had dropped her voice, but even so, a woman near them rose and moved to a different seat, aware that something more important than tea-party gossip was happening and it would behoove any listener to give the couple space.

It was not, of course, entirely true that Corinne knew everything about him, but she did know quite a lot. After that first encounter, the maid, Ryan, had reported back with enough information for her to make further enquiries. It did not take long to establish that he was a country vicar's son starting out on a career in trade. The idea that he should imagine he could court her daughter offended Corinne Templemore to the very core of her being.

Charles, aware of the curious looks they were receiving, had also dropped his volume, but he hoped he was speaking firmly. He did not intend to be bullied by this woman, whoever she might be. "We have met a few times, it is true, but not really in secret," he said. Of course he was being a little jejune and he knew it. That meeting in Kensington Gardens, for instance, might have been in a public place, but it was still a secret. Or why had he scuttled away through the bushes like a runaway convict at Lady Templemore's approach? Still, he justified his words to himself by the thought that it was not for him to reveal their love to her mother. That was for Maria to do, in her own time. She might, after all, decide against such a revelation, although he did not now think she would. If she was prepared to elope, surely she was strong enough to face her parent.

Corinne had some justification. Born pretty and well-bred, if not rich, she might have achieved an enjoyable life if she had not been married off at sixteen to a man seemingly in a permanent rage from the moment they left the Church. As a result, she had spent almost thirty years in a freezing house in the middle of nowhere dodging her husband's insults. He had even died angry. Out hunting, his horse refused a gate, and he whipped it with such fury that it reared and threw him. His skull was dashed against a rock, and that was the end of the fifth Earl of Templemore. After her release from the storm of her marriage, she saw in John Bellasis a haven of peace and comfort that was surely earned, and she looked forward to it. At least until this outsider from nowhere overturned the cart.

But Corinne's decision to confront Charles was ill judged. Had she been more moderate, had she chosen to woo Charles and appeal to his sense of honor, she might have hoped to send him packing. But a direct attack was bound to be counterproductive. As Charles studied the angry, flushing face of the woman before him, he was struck by the irony that Lady Templemore had changed his mind. The thought would have enraged her, but it was true. He'd refused Maria's plea in the bookshop because he believed it his duty to make her give him up rather than live her life in the shadow of a scandal, but this imperious, arrogant woman had altered his view of the matter. In fact, if Maria had returned at that moment and asked him again to elope, there and then, he would probably have agreed.

At all events, Corinne Templemore had not come here to bandy words with this impertinent nonentity. She was only frightened that her rage was so great it would run away with her tongue and she would create a scene that would be all around Belgravia before it grew dark. In an effort to compose herself, she smoothed the violet silk of her skirts. Then, when she was sure she was in command of her temper, she looked at his face once more. "Mr. Pope," she said. "I am sorry I was rude just now."

"Please." He lifted his hand in a gesture of dismissal. "Don't think of it."

"You misunderstand me. I am only sorry because it may lead you to ignore what I am saying. The fact is, to indulge the notion of any connection between you and my daughter is either criminal or unbelievably stupid. You will know which." She waited for his answer.

Charles stared at her. "Maria and I—"

"*Lady* Maria," she said, waiting for him to continue.

He took a breath and tried again. "Lady Maria and I—"

But she cut him off once more. "Mr. Pope, there is no 'Lady Maria and I.' It is an absurd concept. You must understand just this: My daughter is a jewel as far above you as the stars. For your own sake as much as for hers, forget her. Leave her alone if you have a shred of honor in you." So saying, she walked back to a seat near the Duchess, took a plate and a cup from a passing footman, and began to chatter to her neighbor without so much as a glance at the man whose life she had attempted to grind into the dust.

As soon as they were in her boudoir, Caroline shut the door and waved the girl to a seat. "I suppose this is about my husband's nephew?"

Maria nodded. "In part. I will not marry him, whatever Mama says."

It was Caroline's turn to nod. "You made that clear enough when we heard about the announcement of your engagement in the newspapers."

"Things have gotten worse since then." As Maria spoke, she allowed her eyes to wander around this pretty room with its delicate furniture and fire twinkling in the grate. Some invitations were jammed into the gilded looking glass. A half-finished piece of embroidery, stretched across a round frame, lay on the worktable. Books, flowers, letters all contributed to the charming, relaxed jumble. How untroubled Lady Brockenhurst's life must be, she thought; how easy, how enviable. And then she remembered that her hostess's only son was dead.

Caroline stared at her. "You're making me impatient," she said.

"Of course." Maria cleared her throat. It was time to tell the story. "Mama is ordering me to leave London and stay with her cousin, Mrs. Meredith, in Northumberland."

"Which would be disagreeable to you?"

"It's not that. I like her. But Mama wants to make the preparations for my marriage while I'm away, so that I would come home and be married a few days later."

Caroline thought for a moment. So she was right. The whole situation was coming to a crisis. The moment she had imagined for so long was almost here. Still, she knew what she must do. She felt a slight pang as she prepared to break her promise to Anne Trenchard, but in all honesty, could it be avoided? The other woman would forgive her when she knew the facts. "Maria," she said, "I have something to tell you that I had rather we keep a secret from Charles Pope. It will not be for long, and he will know the whole truth in the end, I promise."

"Why can you not tell him now?"

"Because the secret is about him, and naturally it will be more traumatic for him than for you. And I must explain it in front of Lord Brockenhurst, who is away. You will be there when I tell him, but you must give nothing away until I do. I must have your word on it."

This was probably the most intriguing thing Maria had ever heard anyone say in her entire life. "Very well," she said carefully, adding, "if he will learn it eventually."

"I am telling you now because I think you will see that it affects your own position. It will change things, not so much as your mother would have liked, but it will definitely make your position different, and it is possible that she may be brought around." Lady Brockenhurst had declared her side in no uncertain terms.

"What should I do in the interim?"

"You will stay with me, here, in this house."

There was something almost unsettling in the unhesitating conviction behind every word Lady Brockenhurst spoke. She was in no doubt whatsoever about the desirability of the lovers' preferred outcome, nor did she seem to question that she could bring it about.

Maria shook her head, as if to clear it of the glistening dreams that were finding their way into her mind and her heart. "Mama will not be brought around to Charles. I would love to believe she could be, but she won't. If we are to be together, we must break away and make our own life, apart from her."

"What does Charles say to that?"

"He won't do it." Maria stood and went to the window, looking down on the carriages of the guests standing in the square. "He says he will not be the cause of any scandal that would harm me."

"I should have expected no less of him."

Maria turned back into the room. "Maybe. But you must see that my situation is hopeless."

Lady Brockenhurst smiled. She did not appear to understand that this conclusion was final at all. "Sit down, my dear, and listen." And when Maria was settled back on a little satin sofa next to her chair, she continued. "I think you will know that Lord Brockenhurst and I had a son, Edmund, who died at Waterloo."

"I did know that, and I am very sorry."

How strange, thought Caroline, that she could speak of Edmund again as part of a positive and life-affirming story, and not just from behind a veil of tears. She looked back at this young woman who she was determined would be a central part of her life from now on.

"Well, before he died..."

.10.

The Past Comes Back

John Bellasis was sitting in a large leather armchair in the library of the Army and Navy Club in St. James's Square drinking a cup of coffee and reading a copy of *Punch*, a new magazine he had heard of but never seen until then. Dressed in a pair of fashionable pale yellow trousers, a blue Valencia waistcoat, a white shirt, and a black frock coat, he had made something of an effort with his appearance. That afternoon, he was waiting for a friend, Hugo Wentworth, to arrive and he was very keen not to appear down on his luck.

Wentworth was a member of the club, which had opened only four years earlier, in 1837, the year that had seen the young Queen Victoria ascend the throne, and as an officer in the 52nd Light Infantry, Wentworth was eligible to belong to it, but John didn't envy him. With the membership confined to those in the forces, when John did visit the place he found the conversation rather flat, and the food... well, the food left a lot to be desired. It was not for nothing that Captain Higginson Duff had christened it "The Rag." The story went that, on returning from a tour, he'd described the unappetizing supper he'd been served as a "Rag and Famish affair." The Rag and Famish was a squalid gaming house, not unknown to John's own father, that was notorious for its filthy rooms and disgusting dinners, so the remark was clearly intended as an insult. But the members chose to be amused rather than offended, and the club had been known as The Rag ever since.

"Bellasis!" came the booming voice of Hugo Wentworth, who was standing in the doorway and pointing straight at John. "There you are!" He strode across the room, resplendent in his uniform, the noise of his heavy boots thudding on the Turkish carpet. "You look very dashing," he said. "You certainly know how to show a man up."

John shook his head. "Nonsense. There is no civilian dress that can compete with a uniform, as we all know."

Hugo coughed. "Is it too early for a glass of Madeira?"

"It's never too early for a glass of Madeira," said John. But he wondered how much longer they would have to go on with this small talk. He was impatient to start the business that had brought him here.

"Good, good." Hugo looked around and caught the eye of a club servant. "Madeira, please," he said as the man approached. "For both of us."

"What is your news?" said John. Evidently they were going to have to wade through a certain amount of idle chatter before Wentworth would begin.

Hugo's tone became serious. "I've just been told I'm off to Barbados. I must say I don't fancy it one bit. Can't stand the heat."

"No. I can imagine."

"Anyway, what will be, will be," he said. "By the way, I saw the notice of your engagement in the *Times*. Congratulations. She's a lovely young woman."

"I'm very lucky," said John, without meaning it.

"When's the wedding?"

"Soon, I think."

His leaden tone told Captain Wentworth it was time to move on, and at last he did. "Now"—he took out a packet and removed some papers from it—"I have done a little digging, as you asked."

"And?" John sat up in his chair. This was what he'd come for.

He had not been himself since he'd read the copied material that Ellis had brought him. And when she'd failed to return with the originals later that day, he had been forced to acknowledge that the information they bore witness to could not be destroyed or even contained. In the first of Sophia's letters she'd told her maid of the child she had conceived. A child who was to be sent to live with a family named Pope as soon as it was born. That much he had absorbed easily. He'd long realized that Charles Pope was in some way connected by blood to one of the major players in this game. John had suspected him of being James Trenchard's son. Now it turned out he was the son of Trenchard's daughter. All this was fair enough. Trenchard had been anxious to keep the secret to protect his daughter's good name, and John understood why. The letters had also allowed him to fill in the missing piece of the jigsaw. The father of Sophia Trenchard's baby was Edmund Bellasis, John's own cousin. It all made sense—Trenchard's patronage of Charles Pope, Lady Brockenhurst's obvious affection for him. There was nothing to surprise in this revelation. On the contrary, for the first time since Charles Pope had come into their lives, everything was clear.

Then he had read the remaining sheets. The first was apparently proof of a wedding in Brussels. This was when he'd barked to Ellis that he would give her the ludicrous sum of a thousand pounds if she could retrieve the originals. The maid had run off as John settled down to read the rest. But suddenly he was faced with a conundrum. If there really had been a marriage, if Sophia and Edmund had been husband and wife, then why was it necessary to keep the child a secret, to place him with the Popes? Why was the boy not brought up by his grandparents amid the splendors of Lymington Park? Why had he not been acknowledged as Viscount Bellasis in his turn, the heir to his grandfather, superseding Stephen and John in the line of succession? He picked up the final letters in the package, and there was his answer. In them, Sophia Trenchard spoke of her horror and her shame at being "tricked." Was this the case? That there had been no true wedding? That the marriage lines were false and Bellasis had deceived the girl into believing there had been one? It must be so. There was no other explanation that would fit the facts. Who, then, was the Richard Bouverie who'd signed the false certificate of marriage and who had written the letter of explanation as to why the ceremony had been performed in Brussels? Might he have been a fellow officer, a regimental friend of Edmund's? Why else would he have been out there? One thing was clear. Sophia believed Bouverie had impersonated a clergyman so that Edmund might succeed in getting her into bed.

But before John could celebrate—indeed, before he could decide what he should do next, if anything—he had to be quite sure of the truth. He needed proof that Bouverie was an impostor. Only then would he be able to think straight. Only then would he be safe. When Ellis had failed to reappear and it dawned on him that he would not, as he had hoped, be able to throw the originals onto the flames flickering in the grate of his modest drawing room, he had flung himself down on the sofa, clutching a bottle of brandy, and racked his brains. In the small hours, he'd remembered his friend Hugo Wentworth, a captain in the 52nd Light Infantry and a self-appointed military historian. Bellasis had been in the 52nd Light Infantry when he died, and surely it must be possible for Wentworth to review the evidence in their records and discover if Bouverie was a fellow officer. And so he had written to Hugo, supplying him with what information John was prepared to commit to paper, asking him to indulge his old friend for a moment and do "a little digging."

And now here they were.

"Right." Hugo tapped his chest. "I've brought your letter asking about this Richard Bouverie." He paused. "He was in fact the Honorable Richard Bouverie, a younger son of Lord Tidworth, and he was indeed a captain in the Fifty-Second Light Infantry alongside your cousin, Lord Bellasis. They died together at Waterloo."

At his words, John felt a wave of relief. Edmund had behaved like a scoundrel, his brother officer was no better, and Sophia had been seduced. Charles Pope was the result, and he, John, could still claim his inheritance. He smiled at Wentworth. "I don't suppose we could have another glass?" he said.

"I wouldn't mind. But before we do, there's more." Hugo started to unfold a sheet covered in his own small writing.

John felt the touch of an icy finger on his spine. "What sort of more?"

Hugo cleared his throat and began to read from his notes. "Captain Bouverie retired from the army in 1802, after the Treaty of Amiens was signed with Napoléon, and then he went on to take holy orders."

John stared at him. "But you said he fought at Waterloo."

"Well, now, this is the thing." Hugo smoothed out the paper. He was enjoying himself. Clearly he felt he had turned up something fascinating.

"Go on," said John, but his voice was as cold as the grave.

"It seems that he made the decision to return to his regiment, the Fifty-Second Light Infantry, just after Napoléon escaped from Elba in February 1815."

"But was that allowed? For a member of the Church?"

"All I can say is that, in this case, it was. Maybe strings were pulled by his father. Who can tell? But he was readmitted to his regiment. An example of the Church Militant, I suppose you could say." Hugo laughed, pleased with his joke. "I think he must have been a brave chap. When old Boney marched back to Paris without a shot being fired, he would have known the Powers couldn't tolerate his return and that a battle was coming. Obviously, Bouverie felt his duty was to fight for his country."

John's heart was pounding. He paused for a moment to catch his breath. "But did he have the power to perform a marriage when he was an officer again?"

"Oh yes. He was a clergyman before the fighting started, and he was a clergyman when he died."

"So any wedding he conducted in Brussels before the battle was legal?"

"Yes, so there's nothing to worry about. Whomever he married were definitely husband and wife. So I hope it's soothed any concerns you had on that score." He waited for John to say something, but his friend just stared blankly back. "As I said, the news is good." He waved at the club servant, pointing at their glasses, and the man soon returned with the decanter. "I know you'll want to thank me, but please don't. I really enjoyed it. I've been thinking that I might like to write something about that time. The question is, would I have the discipline?" But still John said nothing. Hugo tried again, wondering at his friend's silence. "Might I know the parties in the wedding you were worried about? Was there a story behind the request?"

At this, John woke up. "Oh no. It was just a relation of mine. The wife died in childbirth and the father was killed in the battle. Their son was a little nervous about his own status." John raised his eyebrows humorously and his companion laughed.

"Well, you can tell him he has nothing to worry about. He's as legal and legitimate as the little Princess."

Caroline was in her private sitting room at Brockenhurst House, cleaning her brushes. In front of her was an easel, a large canvas, and a wooden palette covered in curls of paint that went in a circle of colors from browns, blues, and greens to various shades of yellow, pink, and white. On the tray next to her was a collection of cloths, palette knives, and paintbrushes varying in width, shape, and thickness.

"Don't move," she said, looking around the canvas at Maria, who was sitting on a pale peach divan. "I'm afraid I haven't used oils in too long and I'm a little rusty."

The truth was, Caroline liked having Maria in the house. She had initially offered the girl shelter because she was determined to protect her for her grandson, but, as time wore on, Caroline had to admit she enjoyed her company. She placed a well-judged stroke on the pretty, pale face that was beginning to emerge from the canvas. She supposed she had been lonely without knowing it. That must be the truth. She'd been lonely since Edmund's death, but, like all her kind, she would never have admitted it. Still, sitting here now with Maria, she felt as if the weight of the last twenty-five years had been lifted slightly, as if the world were coming alive again.

That said, her plans had gone awry. When Maria had first begged for her help she'd intended to take the girl to Lymington, invite Charles to join them, and then she would tell her husband and her grandson the truth in one sitting. But the day after her tea party she'd received a letter from Peregrine, who had stayed in the country, to say that he was going shooting in Yorkshire and he would return via London. So she and Maria had lingered on in Belgrave Square, waiting for Lord Brockenhurst to come home.

"Have you had any news from your mama?" she said.

Maria shook her head. "Nothing. She'll arrive one of these days with Reggie or someone to drag me away."

"Then we shall take hold of your other arm and prevent it. Anyway, would Reggie pull on her team or yours?"

Maria smiled. It was true that she thought she could count on her brother if it came to a fight.

There was a sound at the door and Lady Brockenhurst looked up. "What is it, Jenkins?"

"Your ladyship, Lady Templemore is in the hall." The butler knew enough to be sure that he was right not to have shown the Countess straight into the drawing room.

Caroline looked at Maria. "Talk of the devil."

"Indeed," said the girl. "But we must face her sooner or later, so it might as well be now." She stood, arranging her skirts as she did so.

Her hostess considered this for a moment and then nodded. "Please bring Lady Templemore up to the drawing room."

The butler gave a slight bow and left.

"Perhaps you'd better stay here." Caroline stood to remove her painting apron and check her appearance in the glass above the chimneypiece.

"No," said Maria. "This is my battle, not yours. I'll see her."

"Well, you're not going in there alone," said Caroline, and the two women walked across the gallery together to face the enemy. The green marble columns that linked the balustrade of the staircase with the decorated plaster ceiling seemed to lend a certain formality to their progress—as if we're going into court, thought Maria.

Lady Templemore was already sitting on a damask Louis XV *bergère* when Caroline walked into the room. She looked rather stately and, somehow, very much alone, which gave Caroline a slight twinge of guilt. "Can I offer you anything?" she said, as pleasantly as she could manage.

"My daughter," said Lady Templemore, without a trace of a smile.

At that moment, Maria entered. She had stopped by a looking glass on the gallery to tidy her hair before she faced her parent's stern gaze. "Here I am, Mama."

"I've come to take you home."

"No, Mama." She was as definite as she knew how to be.

The words were unexpected, even shocking. It had never occurred to Lady Templemore that she could not reclaim her own child when she wanted. For a moment nobody said anything.

Lady Templemore was the first to break the silence. "My dear—"

"No, Mama. I am not coming home. Not yet, at any rate."

Corinne Templemore struggled to maintain her equilibrium. "But if word leaks out—which it is bound to—what will people think?"

Maria was very calm. Lady Brockenhurst's opinion of her was rising by the minute. "They will think I am staying with the aunt of my fiancé, which they will find perfectly normal. Soon, however, we will announce that the marriage will not now take place. And that I am going to be married instead to a Mr. Charles Pope. This they will find very interesting indeed, and they will no doubt discuss it a great deal. Who is this Mr. Pope, they will say, and that will keep them happy until there is news of an elopement or some great man in the City fails, and then they will talk about that and we will fade away into the background and get on with our lives." She was sitting on a sofa, and as she finished speaking she clasped her hands with resolve and let them rest in her lap.

Lady Templemore stared at her daughter, or rather at the faery changeling that had stolen her true daughter and was now sitting in her place. But she did not answer. Instead she turned to Lady Brockenhurst. "You've done this," she said. "You have corrupted my child."

"I do hope so," said Lady Brockenhurst, "if this is the result."

But Corinne Templemore had not finished. "Why are you doing this? Are you jealous of me? I have living children, while your son is dead? Is that it?" Her calm, even pleasant, voice as she spoke was, if anything, more startling than if she had shouted and torn out her hair by its roots.

It took a moment for Caroline Brockenhurst to catch her breath. At last she spoke. "Corinne—," she said, but Lady Templemore silenced her with a gesture of her open hand.

"Please. My Christian name is only for the use of my friends."

"Mama," Maria said. "We must not be at odds, like ruffians fighting in the street."

"I should prefer to be attacked by a ruffian than by my own daughter."

Maria stood. She needed to use this moment to move things forward. Otherwise she and her mother would be caught in a dead end. "Please, Mama," she said as reasonably as she could, "I will not come home until you have had time to accept that your plans for me to marry John Bellasis will not come to fruition. When you are able to grasp this fact, I'm sure we can soon repair matters between us."

"So that you can marry Mr. Pope?" Her mother's tone was not encouraging.

"Yes, Mama." Maria sighed. "But even there, things are not perhaps quite as bad as you think." She glanced at Caroline in the hope that her hostess would take over the argument. She was not sure how much, or how little, she should say.

Lady Brockenhurst nodded. "Maria is right. Mr. Pope is less obscure than he might at first have appeared."

Lady Templemore looked at her. "Oh?" she said.

"It seems that his father was the son of an earl."

There was a silence as Corinne absorbed these surprising words. Then, when she had thought for a moment, she spoke. "Was the father illegitimate? Or is Mr. Pope himself a bastard? Since clearly there can be no third explanation for your statement, if it is true."

Lady Brockenhurst took a deep breath. She was not quite ready to play all her cards. "I might remind you that, fifteen years ago, the illegitimate son of the Duke of Norfolk married the daughter of the Earl of Albemarle, and today they are welcomed everywhere."

"And you think because the Stephensons have gotten away with it, Charles Pope would, too?" Lady Templemore did not sound as if she agreed.

"But why wouldn't he?" Caroline's voice was as soft and as pleading as Maria had ever heard it. The woman was begging, and of course Maria knew why.

But Corinne Templemore was unrepentant. "For a start, because the Duke brought up Henry Stephenson as his son and he was recognized as such from his birth. And secondly, because I am not aware that Lady Mary Keppel broke off an engagement to an earl in order to marry him. Your meddling has cheated my daughter of a position that would have allowed her to do some good in the world. I hope you're proud of yourself."

"I think I could also do good if I were married to Charles." Maria was growing irritated with her mother's intransigence.

At this, the Countess of Templemore finally got to her feet. Caroline was forced to admit there was something impressive in the woman's stance; well dressed, her back as straight as a poker, she was unbendingly severe and all the more imposing for that. "Then you must manage it without your mother's help, my dear, for I will have no more of you. I'll send Ryan around with your things as soon as I get back. You are welcome to keep her on as your maid, but it must be at your own expense. Otherwise, I will give her notice. I'll ask Mr. Smyth at Hoare's to write and explain your income under your father's trust, my dear, and in future you will communicate with him but not with me. Henceforth, I cast you off. You are adrift and you must sail your own barque. As for you," she turned to Caroline, hatred shining from her eyes, "you have stolen my daughter and ruined my life. I curse you for it." With that, she swept out of the room and down the great stair-case, leaving Maria and Lady Brockenhurst alone and silent.

Susan Trenchard couldn't tell precisely what her mood was. Sometimes she felt hopeful, as if her life were about to change for the better. Sometimes things seemed darker, as if she were trembling on the brink of an abyss.

She had told John she thought she was pregnant the last time she'd gone around to Albany. She spoke almost as soon as they had climbed the stairs to reach his little drawing room. He was puzzled as he listened, surprised even, although not at first hostile. "I thought you were unable to conceive," he said. "I thought that was the whole point."

It was an odd choice of phrase. "What does that mean? The whole point?"

He covered himself by ignoring her question. "I suppose you're sure?"

"Quite sure. Although I haven't had it confirmed by a doctor."

He nodded. "Perhaps you should. Do you have one you can trust?"

She looked at him. "I'm a married woman. Why do I need one I can 'trust'?"

"True enough. But go to a doctor who'll know what to do." Again, his wording was odd, but she could see he was distracted. She knew her mother-in-law's maid had just walked away when she arrived, and Susan could only suppose he'd learned something, presumably about the mysterious Mr. Pope, which was taking up his attention.

At any rate, they'd made the decision that Susan would arrange an appointment on a certain day to see her physician, and she would then report back to his rooms where he would be waiting for her. Except now she was here, he was nowhere to be seen. His silent servant had let her in, and she'd been shown to a chair in the sitting room where she'd waited, crouched over a meager fire. The master had kept an appointment in St. James's, and it must have run longer than he expected. But he would be back shortly. How long was shortly? The servant couldn't tell and nor could she, since she'd been waiting for almost an hour.

John's absence gave Susan time to review her situation. Did she hope they would marry and she would be rescued from the dreariness of the Trenchard household? In her dreams, yes; but now that the first flush of infatuation had passed, she was too clever a woman to believe she was the chosen candidate to be the next

Countess of Brockenhurst. A merchant's divorced daughter? She would not fit easily into the history of the Bellasis dynasty. And anyway, how long would a divorce take? Could they find a tame Member of Parliament to usher through a private bill dissolving her marriage, and would it be in time for them to wed before the baby was born? Almost certainly not.

What, then, did she want? To be John's mistress in perpetuity? To take a house somewhere and bring up the child as his? Once his uncle was dead, there would be plenty of money for this sort of arrangement, and yet...and yet...Susan was not certain it would suit her, to live outside the boundaries of Society, even the dull and ordinary level of Society that she had succeeded in penetrating. But could she stand to stay with Oliver, and would she even have that option? Oliver Trenchard might not be a genius, but he would know the child was not his. They hadn't made love for months. There was a certain irony in the realization that for years she had lived as a barren woman, pitied on every side, when she had not been barren at all. The fault must have been Oliver's, but of course he would not see matters in that light. Maybe to accept the post as John's kept woman was the best choice available. Finally, the door opened.

"Well?" John said as he entered the room.

"I've been waiting for the best part of an hour."

"And now I am back. What happened?"

She nodded, knowing perfectly well that there was no point in even trying to make John Bellasis feel guilty. "I've done what you asked. I've seen a doctor and I am pregnant. Three months or more."

He took off his hat and threw it down impatiently. "But will he see to it? Or has he done so already?"

His words cut her like a knife. *Will he see to it?* In all her thoughts, Susan had included the child as part of her calculations. Not once had she entertained the notion that she might get rid of it. She'd waited ten years to become pregnant, and now that she was, John wanted her to risk her life, to flush it out and away? Indeed, he did not even appear to understand there was an issue to be discussed.

She shook her head impatiently. "Of course not!" Then she paused, staying silent until she could breathe more easily. "I don't want to be rid of it. Did you think that I would? Have you no feelings for the child?"

John looked at her, seemingly puzzled. "Why would I have feelings?"

"Because you're the father."

"Who says? What proof do I have? You fell into bed with me at the first opportunity. Am I to take from your behavior that you're a new Madame Walewska, untouched and pure until you caught the eye of the Emperor?" He laughed harshly as he poured himself some brandy from a waiting decanter and threw it down his throat.

"You know it's yours."

"I don't know anything." He filled his glass again. "This is your problem, not mine. I will, as a friend, pay for you to solve it, but if you refuse, then that is the end of my responsibility." He dropped into a chair.

Susan looked at him. For a second, her rage was so great that she felt as if she had swallowed fire, but she knew enough to keep control of her feelings. If she shouted, she would get nothing from him. But might there still not be a way to bring him around, if she played her hand carefully?

"Are you quite well?" she said, moving away from the subject. "You seem preoccupied."

He looked at her, surprised by the gentleness in her tone. "Do you care?"

Susan was nothing if not resourceful. "John, I can't answer for you," she smiled winningly, "but I have been in love with you for many months. Your happiness means more to me than anything else on earth. Of course I care." Even as she spoke the words, she marveled at her own dishonesty. But she could see they'd had an effect. How weak men were. Like dogs, one pat and they're yours for life. "Now won't you tell me what's the matter?"

He sighed, leaning back, putting his hands behind his head. "Only that I've lost everything."

"It can't be as bad as all that."

"Can't it? I have nothing. I am nothing. I will always be nothing." He stood and walked to the window. His rooms looked over the courtyard in front of the building, and he stared down at the activity below, at the people hurrying about their daily lives, while his life seemed to have vanished in a puff of smoke.

Susan was beginning to understand that she was dealing with something more than petulance. "What has happened?" she said.

"I've discovered that I will not, after all, be the next Earl of Brockenhurst. I will not inherit my uncle's fortune. Or Lymington Park. Or Brockenhurst House. Or any of it. I am heir to nothing." He did not care that she knew. Anne and James Trenchard would have seen Sophia's papers by now, and sooner or later they would have them looked into. They must, and when they did they would learn the truth and publish it for the whole world to read.

"I don't understand." This extraordinary revelation had for the moment taken Susan's mind off her own predicament.

"That man, Charles Pope, is the heir. My nemesis. It seems he is the grandson of my uncle and aunt."

"Isn't he supposed to be the son of my father-in-law? That's what you told me before."

"That's what I thought before. But he's not. He is my cousin Edmund's son."

"But then why has he not been recognized as such? Why does he bear the name Pope? Shouldn't he be...what is the courtesy title?"

"Viscount Bellasis."

"Very well. Why isn't he Viscount Bellasis?"

"He is." John laughed, but the sound was harsh. "He just doesn't know it."

"Why not?"

"They all thought he was illegitimate. That was why he was put away, given a false name, brought up far from London."

Susan was genuinely interested. Her mind was working like one of the new railway engines. "When did they find out the truth?"

"*I* found out the truth. They don't know it yet. There was a marriage between Edmund and the Trenchards' daughter. In Brussels. Before Waterloo. But they think it was false. They think it was a trick to seduce her."

Susan blinked. So many revelations at once. Oliver's sister, Sophia, of sacred memory in that household, had been seduced. Except, no, she had not. At least, not without a wedding first. It was almost too much to take in. "So you say they don't yet know the truth?"

"I don't believe so. You see, I had a friend of mine look into the marriage, and it was legal." He pulled a sheaf of papers from his inner pocket. "They think the clergyman who presided at the ceremony was in reality a soldier, and so it wasn't valid. When the facts are that he *was* a soldier, and an Anglican priest as well. And I have the proof right here."

"I'm impressed you haven't burned the papers. If they don't yet know."

At this, he laughed again. "Don't be. I would have done, but there's no point. I only have copies of the proof of the marriage. They have the originals."

"But if they haven't seen your friend's evidence—"

"They'll find out the truth. They're bound to."

And now Susan saw her chance. Far from his loss ruining her hopes, she realized almost at once that it gave her a real option for the future. A realistic ambition. "John," she said carefully. "If all this is true and the title is gone—"

"And the money."

She nodded. "And the money. Then why shouldn't we marry? I know you would not have chosen me if you'd been the head of your family, but now you will be the son of a younger son. It's not so much. I can divorce Oliver and go to my father. He has money of his own, lots of it, and I'm an only child. I'll inherit everything. We could have a good life together. We'd be comfortable. We could have more children. You might take up a commission in the army, or we could buy land. There may be better-bred women on offer, but few who could provide for you as well as I can." She paused. She had made what sounded to her own ears like a good case. She would have a husband in Society, and he would have the means to live like a gentleman. Surely, given his situation, he had nothing to lose and everything to gain?

John stared at her for what seemed like an age.

Then he threw back his head and laughed. Except he didn't just laugh. He roared with laughter. He laughed until the tears rolled down his cheeks. Then he stopped and turned to face her. "Do you imagine that I, John Bellasis, the grandson of the Earl of Brockenhurst, whose ancestors fought in the Crusades and on almost every major European battlefield since, would ever—" He stared at her with malice, his eyes as hard and cold as stone. "Do you seriously imagine that I would *ever* marry the divorced daughter of a dirty tradesman?"

Susan recoiled with a gasp, as if she had been drenched with icy water. He had started to laugh again now, almost hysterically. As if all his own misery at his fall were finding its expression in his cruel, savage humor.

It was a hard and vicious slap across her face. Susan stood, her hands on her cheeks, her heart racing.

He hadn't finished. "Don't you understand? I need to make a brilliant marriage. Now more than ever. Not Maria Grey, with her downcast looks and her empty purse. A *brilliant* marriage, do you hear me? And I am sorry, my dear, but that scenario could never include you." He shook his head. "Poor little Susan Trenchard. A grubby little tradesman's tart. What a joke."

She was quite silent and still for a moment, not speaking, not moving, until she felt she once more had mastery of her body and her voice. Then she spoke. "I wonder if you would ask your man to call me a hackney carriage? I will follow him down directly."

"Can't you go down now and hail one yourself?" He spoke to her as if they had never met before this day.

"Please, John. There is no need for us to part so badly."

Was it some tiny shred of decency, a last trace of honor, that made him grumble "very well" and leave the room to give the order? No sooner was he gone than she'd seized the papers abandoned near his chair, stuffed them into her reticule, and hurried out. She was halfway down the stairs before she heard him call her name, but she quickened her pace and ran through the court-yard into the street. A minute later, she was in a hackney cab and on her way home. As John rushed out onto the pavement, looking furiously up and down Piccadilly, she shrank from the window and leaned back in her seat.

Oliver Trenchard was in James's library in Eaton Square, drinking a glass of brandy and leafing through a copy of the *Times*. By his own standards, if not his father's, he'd had a busy day, although the office and his work for the Cubitt brothers had played no part in it. He'd been riding in Hyde Park for most of the morning, visited his tailor's in Savile Row to approve the design of a pair of shooting breeches, then a luncheon party in Wilton Crescent, after which he joined a group of friends for a game of whist. Although Oliver wasn't a gambler. He disliked losing too much for his wins to offset it. In fact, while his lack of industry may not have pleased his father, Oliver's vices weren't great. It was true that he drank when he was unhappy, but his real sin would have been women, if only he could have shaken off the image of his wife whenever he had an assignation. There she would be in his mind, with her superior smile and her eyes looking for someone to flirt with, someone other than her husband...and he would abandon his plans and go home. If he could just learn to forget her, he knew he could be content. Or so he told himself as he settled into his chair and raised his glass to his lips, hoping to avoid both his father and Susan.

Despite living in the same house, Oliver had successfully managed not to speak to his father since that unpleasant luncheon at James's club. He had deliberately left the house late every morning long after James had gone to work, and he often returned home in the small hours, hoping his parents would both be safely tucked up in bed. However, that day he'd miscalculated, thinking James was out to dinner, and just as he put down his glass and folded the paper in half, his father walked into the room.

James stopped in his tracks. He was evidently not expecting to see his son there, either. "Are you still reading the *Times*?" he asked, slightly awkwardly after such a long silence between them.

"Unless you would like it, Father?" Oliver replied, politely enough.

"No, no. Carry on. I just came in to find a book. Do you know where your mother is?"

"Upstairs. She was tired after a long walk this afternoon. She wanted a rest before dinner."

James nodded. "You have no trouble speaking to her, then?"

"I have no quarrel with her," said Oliver calmly.

"Just with me." James was beginning to sense that the tensions between them were coming to some sort of climax. Were he and Oliver at last to join battle when they had delayed it for so long?

"You and Charles Pope."

This was the mystery that James could not fathom. "And you dislike him so much that you were prepared to travel the length of England just to try to ruin his good name?"

"Did he have a good name to ruin?" Oliver snorted, and returned to his paper.

"Did you give those men money? In Manchester? To write the letters?" James demanded.

"I had no need to. They wanted him destroyed as much as I."

"But why?" James shook his head in disbelief and stared at his son. It was so hard to understand. Here was Oliver, a passenger in life, reading in this pleasant library which was fitted up like the best gentlemen's libraries that James had seen, gilded spines gleaming in the light from the oil lamps. A portrait of King George III hung over the chimneypiece, and an inlaid desk sat between the bookshelves on the long wall. What could be nicer? An oasis of civilization in the city. How different from the ragged, crumbling, threadbare setting of his own youth. And what had Oliver done to earn it? Nothing. But was he ever satisfied, ever happy, ever even content? "So you deliberately went all the way to Manchester just to find something, anything, that would damage Mr. Pope in my eyes?"

"Yes." Oliver did not see much point in obfuscating now.

James was bewildered. "Why would you want to ruin a man who has never done anything to you?"

"Never done anything to me?" Oliver repeated the words in a tone of wonder. "He has stolen my father and is in the process of stealing my fortune. Is that nothing?"

James snorted with indignation. "It's nonsense."

But this time Oliver had decided to say it all. His father wanted to know what was behind his hatred of Pope. Very well. He would tell him. "You lavish him with your attention, this newcomer, this outsider, this upstart! You give him your money and your praise without stinting!"

"I believe in him."

"That may be." Oliver was almost sobbing. He felt himself starting to shake. "But, by God, you don't believe in me, and you never have! You've never supported me, never cared for me, never listened to anything I've said—"

James could feel a fist of anger forming in his chest. "May I remind you that I have gone out on a limb, endangering my friendship with the Cubitts, men I respect more than anyone living, in order to make a career for you? And what is my reward? To see you miss every meeting, cut every appointment, to go riding, to go shooting, to go walking in the park! Am I not allowed to be disappointed? Am I not allowed to feel that my son is not worthy of the trouble I have taken?"

Oliver stared at his father, this undignified, insignificant man, with his red face and his tight coats, who knew so little of the finer things in life. It was odd. In one way he despised the man. In another he craved his respect. Oliver could not really understand the situation or himself, but he knew he could not keep silent anymore about what troubled him most. "I am sorry, Father, but I cannot change places with Sophia, which we both know is what you would have wished. I cannot place myself in the grave and set her free. It is out of my hands."

So saying, he wrenched the door open and left James alone in the flickering light from the grate.

Susan was unusually quiet as Speer dressed her hair before dinner. The maid had some inkling that things had not been smooth between her mistress and Mr. Bellasis, but of course she could only guess what had gone wrong. Naturally, she knew that Mrs. Oliver was pregnant—something no one can hide from a lady's maid—and she was equally sure Mr. Bellasis was the father, since eleven years with Mr. Oliver had not produced even a miscarriage. But if Mr. Bellasis and her mistress had been discussing the matter that afternoon, and if Mrs. Oliver had dreams for the future that included Mr. Bellasis, they had obviously been dashed.

"Are you ready to dress, ma'am?" asked the maid.

"A little later. I have something I want to do first. And can you find me a piece of paper and a ribbon?" Susan waited patiently until the maid returned, carrying what she had been asked for. Then her mistress took out a bundle of papers from her reticule, rolled them in the sheet of white paper, tied the ribbon, and sealed it with some wax from her writing desk in the corner. She turned to Speer. "I need you to write on this. Just write James Trenchard, Esquire."

"But why, ma'am?"

"Never mind why. Mr. Trenchard does not know your handwriting. He does know mine. I won't ask for your secrecy. You already know enough to hang me."

The maid was not entirely reassured, but she sat at the desk and did as she was told. Susan thanked her, took up the bundle, and left the room.

James was almost dressed when he heard the knock on his dressing room door. "Who is it?"

"Me, Father."

He could not remember Susan ever visiting his dressing room before. But he was decent and needed only his topcoat to complete his toilet, so he opened the door and asked her in, dismissing his valet as he did so.

"How can I help?" he said.

"This bundle was handed to me outside on the street, as I came toward our front door." She held out the packet and he took it.

Her manner was subdued, which was quite unlike her, and for a moment James wondered if there was more to this than she was saying. He stared at the packet she had placed in his hands. "Handed to you by whom?"

"I don't know. A boy. He ran off."

"How odd." But he had opened the packet and now he started to look through its contents. The blood seemed to drain from his face as he read through page after page. At last he looked back at Susan. "This boy, was he a servant? A page?"

"I don't know. He was just a boy."

James stood quite still for another long moment. "I must go and see Mrs. Trenchard."

"Before you do, there is something else I want you to know." Susan summoned up her courage. She was placing everything she had on the next roll of the dice. She'd assumed a modest, almost blushing manner, which seemed appropriate, but she had to gauge it just right. She took a deep breath. This was the moment. "I'm going to have a child," she said.

And suddenly James's happiness was doubled, trebled, quadrupled. In one flash, his daughter's name was rescued from shame, his grandson would inherit a great position, and his son, the next Trenchard in the line, would also have an heir. For a second, he thought he would literally explode with joy. In the two or three minutes since his daughter-in-law had joined him in the room, his life had entirely changed. "Oh, my dear. Are you certain?"

"Quite. But now you must go to Mother."

"May I tell her?"

"Of course."

On the whole, Susan was relieved when she returned to her bedroom to find Speer laying out her clothes for the evening. She had ensured the ruin of John Bellasis, which had been her principal purpose. If the Trenchards had not known the truth before tonight, they would know it now. That done, she had embarked on a plan to save her own reputation, and while the outcome of her gamble was uncertain, she was still glad that the end was in sight.

John Bellasis was cursing himself for not having burned the proof of Bouverie's appointment to the ministry. Why had he kept it? What good was it to him? And if he'd destroyed it, then Susan would only have had papers to show them that were copies of the ones already in Anne Trenchard's possession. Who knows how long the Trenchards would have continued in their belief that the marriage was a sham? But now, thanks to his stupidity, he was lost, and everything was beyond his control, thanks to that ridiculous woman. If he could have strangled her then and there he would have done it.

Impulsively, John took a cab to Eaton Square, but when he got out of the vehicle, he hesitated. If he rang the doorbell, what would happen? He would be shown in and eventually someone—probably not Susan but someone—would see him, and then what would he say? After a few more minutes, he decided not to wait and be spotted by a member of the family or a servant as he lounged against the railing protecting the gardens of the square. Instead, he went round the corner to the Horse and Groom, where he always met Turton. If the butler were there, he might prevail on him to...what? Steal back the papers? What good would that do? He assumed Susan would have shown the documents to the family, and by now they would know Bouverie was genuine. They could easily find more proof to back up the claim. Very well. He would just have a drink to calm himself down and then he might walk back to Albany. Perhaps twenty minutes outside in the cool of the evening would dampen his fury. He pushed the door open and looked around.

But it was not Turton leaning against the long, scarred, and stained wooden bar that ran almost the length of the low and smoky room. It was Oliver Trenchard, nursing a glass of what looked like whisky. And, as he saw him, John Bellasis had an idea. It was a desperate one, maybe, but desperate times breed desperate measures. He knew from Susan that Oliver hated Charles Pope, that he blamed his own estrangement from his father on the newcomer, and that he would do anything to be rid of him. He knew, too, from his erstwhile mistress that Pope was aware he'd caused Oliver and his father to quarrel, and Pope was sorry for it. Oliver had told his wife that the man hadn't denied the charges he'd brought against him, but that James had never believed they were true. Susan had more than enough cleverness in her to solve this puzzle, as she'd confided in John. Obviously, Charles Pope was uncomfortable that he had pushed father and son apart and was trying not to make things worse. John frowned. Couldn't he use the quarrel? Wouldn't Pope do anything he could to patch it up? Couldn't he, John, make Oliver his instrument?

The plan continued to form in his mind. Oliver wanted Pope out of the way; he'd made no secret of it. He had denounced Pope in front of many people, including his own wife. If anything happened to Charles Pope, wouldn't Oliver Trenchard be the first suspect? And if they could find proof that Oliver and Pope had arranged to meet...

Oliver looked up. He saw the figure of John watching him and almost blinked in case it was an illusion. "Mr. Bellasis? Is that you? What on earth are you doing in this stinking hole?"

"I was going to have a drink to calm myself." It was an odd answer.

"Do you need calming?" asked Oliver.

John moved closer, casually leaning against the bar alongside the other man. "You know who I mean by Charles Pope?" He smiled, but inwardly, as he saw Oliver's face flush with rage.

"If I hear that name one more time—"

John signaled to the barman for two more glasses of whisky. "I should like to teach him a lesson he'll never forget," he said.

Oliver nodded. "And I'd like to help you."

"Would you?" said John, taking hold of his glass and downing the contents in one. "Because you could help me, if you've a mind to."

The owner looked along the bar at the two men, heads bent, muttering into each other's ear. He wondered what it could be about, this urgent conference. He'd seen them both in here before, but never together.

James walked into his wife's bedroom while Ellis was still tidying her hair. "May I see you alone for a moment?" said James.

Anne thanked the maid. "Come back in ten minutes," she said. Then, when the door was closed, she turned to her husband. "What is it? What's happened?"

"Look at these." He placed the papers in front of her.

She looked through the first two or three. "Where did you get them?"

"Some boy pushed them into Susan's hands as she was walking into the house. What do you make of them? They're copies, of course."

"I know they are copies," said Anne, standing. "I have the originals." She bent to unlock the cupboard and retrieved the papers that Jane Croft had given her. She said nothing as she handed them to him.

She could see at once that James was hurt. "Why didn't you say anything to me about them?" he said.

She wouldn't give him the real reason—that she'd wanted to keep a part of Sophia for herself. It was only for a little while, she'd told herself. She had planned to show them to him eventually. Whether she would have kept to this, Anne would never now know. "They're Sophia's false marriage papers. She told her maid to burn them when we were in Brussels, but the woman never did. Croft came here to put them into my keeping when she was on her way to America. They change nothing." James looked at his wife for a moment before he spoke. The enormity of what he had to say silenced him. Anne was puzzled. "If I'm missing something, please tell me what it is." She sat, waiting patiently.

"This is what you're missing." James removed one paper from the others. "It is not a copy, and you will not have seen it." Anne took the sheet from his hand. "Someone has looked into the man who faked the marriage. Richard Bouverie, or the Honorable and Reverend Richard Bouverie, to be precise. Because it seems he was a clergyman before he rejoined the army and was therefore fully qualified to perform the marriage service. In other words, the wedding was not a sham. Sophia *was* Lady Bellasis when she died, and Charles is legitimate."

"And Edmund was an honorable man." Anne's eyes filled with tears as she thought of how they had traduced and turned against this brave young man who may have been impetuous and even foolish, but who had truly loved their daughter and wanted only the best for her. She would go to church the next day and have prayers said in his name.

"How like you to think of that." But James, too, was happy that his judgment of his daughter's suitor had not been so wide of the mark. He'd spent the last quarter of a century blaming himself for Sophia's ruin, but now he wondered why he'd allowed himself to be so easily convinced and not looked further into it at the time. Why had they all simply accepted Sophia's horrified verdict, when she saw Bouverie outside the Richmonds' house, that the man was a charlatan? But then, how easy it is to do things better with the benefit of hindsight.

Anne was still staring at the papers laid out before her on her dressing table. "How did you say Susan got them?" she asked.

"A boy pushed them into her hands in the street."

"But I know this writing—"

Anne could not finish the thought before the door opened and Ellis reappeared. "Are you ready for me, ma'am?"

Anne nodded and James started to gather up the bundle as Ellis crossed the room to join her mistress. Then she stopped with a gasp and her hand flew to her mouth. She was quite unprepared for the sight of the papers in Anne's hands, and she'd spoken before she could regain control of her senses. "Where did you get those?" she said, only hearing the words after she had spoken them. Then, faced by their stares, Ellis made a desperate bid to save herself. "I mean, what interesting-looking papers, ma'am."

Anne was the next to speak. There were not too many candidates, after all, if the papers had been copied by someone whose writing was familiar to her. And it was Ellis who had welcomed

Croft when she first arrived. "Would you like to tell me about them, Ellis?" She studied the floundering maid, this woman who had helped her and served her for thirty years and yet about whom she knew so little. Could she, Anne, have betrayed her employer of thirty years if their roles had been reversed? She doubted it, but then she'd never had to endure the bitter tests of humiliation and survival that were so often the hallmarks of a servant's life.

James was becoming impatient. "If there is anything you can tell us to diminish your guilt, now is the time to say it."

Ellis's mind was in turmoil. Of course she should have insisted Mr. Bellasis read the copies and then burn them in front of her eyes. But would he have obeyed her? Probably not. She was thinking fast. Her job was gone, she could not save it, but she might at least manage to stay out of prison. "It was Mr. Turton, sir. It was him what found them in Miss Croft's bag, and he made the copies."

"On whose orders?"

Ellis thought. She'd lied about Turton searching for the papers, but was there any point in lying further? Would it benefit her to save Mr. Bellasis? No. He wouldn't pay her any more now. What would he have to gain by it? But then, there were her references to consider. How was she to get another job without good references? And Mrs. Trenchard wouldn't want to give them, that was certain. Ellis started to weep. She had always been quite good at weeping when it was required. "I'm ever so sorry, ma'am. If I'd known it might hurt you, I'd never have gone near the whole business."

"You watched Turton copy out Miss Sophia's letters, yet you never thought it might hurt me?" Anne's tone had become hard.

James was fidgeting. "The point is, who were they copied for?"

Ellis decided some direct talk might save time. "I know I've lost my place, sir. But I'm not a bad woman."

"You're not a good one," said Anne with some asperity.

"I've been weak. I know that. But if I have no references, I'll starve."

"I see." James was in command of the situation at once. He understood what they were being told sooner than his wife.

"You're saying that if we will give you some sort of reference, you will tell us who asked for the copies to be made. Is that it?"

Of course that was exactly it, so Ellis was silent. She stood there before them, staring down at her hands.

"Very well." James silenced his wife with a gesture when it looked as if she might intervene. "We will give you a reference, not a glowing one, but a reference that should make it possible for you to find gainful employment."

Ellis sighed with relief. She was glad she'd had the presence of mind to bargain with her last chip. "Mr. Turton made the copies for Mr. Bellasis, sir."

Anne looked up, startled. "Mr. John Bellasis? Lady Brocken-hurst's nephew?"

Ellis nodded. "That's the one, ma'am."

James was thinking. "Of course it was John Bellasis. And he'll have been the one to look into the man Bouverie. Which we should have done twenty years ago. If Bouverie was a fake, then John Bellasis would still be the next Earl. If Bouverie was genuine, then Bellasis would have nothing." He had forgotten Ellis's presence for a moment, but a discreet cough from Anne brought him back to the present.

"What was your role in all this, Ellis?" Anne said.

The woman hesitated. How much should she tell? She'd got her reference now, and she knew the Trenchards well enough to be sure they would not go back on their word. Still, there was no need to tell them more than was necessary. "Mr. Turton made me take the copies around to Mr. Bellasis's rooms."

Anne nodded. "Very well. You may go. You may stay the night here, but you will leave tomorrow. With your reference."

Ellis bobbed a curtsy and left the room, closing the door gently behind her. Things could be worse, she thought as she started down the stairs. She'd been paid well enough until the end, and she had some money saved, thanks to her tips from Mr. B. She'd find another job with someone too stupid and selfish to take the trouble to look into her past.

Back in the room, James Trenchard took his wife's hand. "We

mustn't tell anyone. Not Charles Pope, not the Brockenhursts, not the family. We must have this information on the clergyman checked and rechecked until we know for certain that Sophia's marriage was legal. Then we must investigate how we have it registered with the authorities. I do not want to raise anyone's hopes only to let them down."

Anne nodded. Of course she was happy. She was delirious with joy. But there were elements of the story that didn't quite seem logical. If John Bellasis had gone to the trouble of researching the marriage, why would he not guard the information closely? Surely he would have been praying that the validity of the marriage would remain a secret. Edmund was dead. Sophia was dead. Bouverie was dead. The only proof was the paper he'd commissioned, and if he'd burned it, no one would have been any the wiser. So why did he let it out of his hands so carelessly? And who was this boy who gave the bundle to Susan in the street?

"There's something else." James's voice brought her back into the present. "It was driven out of my mind for a moment, but you'll be very happy." He paused for effect. "Susan is pregnant."

It was like an answer to Anne's unspoken question. "Is she, really?" She arranged the expression on her face to one of delight.

James nodded, grinning from ear to ear. "She just told me. Over ten years with Oliver, and nothing. We'd all given up. And yet now she's going to have a baby. Isn't it extraordinary? What can have changed?"

"What indeed?" said Anne.

Oliver was late arriving home, and Susan was dressed and ready when he looked into her room.

"I think I'll go on down," she said.

"Do. Start dinner if you like."

She could see he was angry. Had he and James had another quarrel? He was swaying a little and held on to the door frame to steady himself. So he was drunk. Never mind. She would go down and use the time she had alone with his parents as best she could. She was guessing her way through this trial, but if she could only get it right, if she could only carry them with her, then disaster might be avoided. Oliver would be her greatest test, but there was no point in speaking to him while he was in this state. The key to it was courage, and while Susan might have been short of some of the other virtues, she did not lack that.

When she reached the drawing room, her parents-in-law were there and waiting. She approached Anne with a sinking stomach. Of all of them, Anne was the one with enough brains and enough understanding of human nature to guess the truth. "Has Father told you?" She waited, patiently, for the reaction.

"He has," said Anne. "Congratulations." But her tone was not delirious. She looked at her daughter-in-law through new eyes.

"Go on!" shouted James from across the room. "Give her a kiss!"

Anne leaned forward and planted a cool peck on Susan's cheek.

Susan dutifully kissed her back. "Oliver may be a while. He'd only just arrived home when I came down. He says we're to go in without him, if we want."

"Oh, I think we can wait," said Anne, coolly. "James? Have you spoken to Turton?"

Her husband shook his head. "I thought I'd leave it until after dinner. Or is that cowardly?"

"It's important that he hears it from you and not from Ellis, although we may already be too late."

"Quite right." Her husband nodded briskly. "I suppose we'd better give him some sort of reference as well, if she's to have one. I'll look out a couple of bottles of champagne while I'm down there." In another moment he was gone and the two women were alone.

Susan had dressed carefully but demurely for the evening. She wore a shirt of pale russet chiffon and a darker russet wide silk skirt. Her hair was arranged in a simple chignon with becoming curls in front of her ears. The effect she was striving for was well-bred simplicity, a good woman, pure, upright, a pillar of society. That was how she wanted to look, as Anne recognized well enough.

"Shall we sit down?' said Anne, and they did, choosing two pretty gilded chairs on either side of the marble chimneypiece. After a moment, Anne continued. "Why did John Bellasis give you those papers?"

Of course the question was a shock, catching Susan off guard for a moment. Her breath stuck in her throat, but she stopped herself from lying just in time. Her mother-in-law had guessed the truth, or at least some of it, and the younger woman had the sure sense that she might just possibly get through if she spoke boldly, but she knew she would not if she hid behind lies.

"He didn't. I took them."

Anne nodded. She almost liked Susan for not attempting to deceive her further. "May I ask why?"

"He told me they proved that Charles Pope was legitimate and the heir to his uncle, and that once they were shown to the right people, he, John, would lose everything. You couldn't have known any of that, or why was Mr. Pope left toiling away in some dirty mill in the north?"

"We knew there was a marriage, but we did not believe it was genuine."

"John seemed to think you'd have the facts investigated when you saw the original letters, and then you'd learn the truth."

Anne sighed. "And so we should have, a quarter of a century ago. But now Mr. Bellasis has done it for us. It's ironic, really. If he'd left well enough alone we would probably have been none the wiser." This thought had only just occurred to Anne. It made her dizzy. "Why did you want to harm him? If you were lovers?"

Again, the boldness of the question winded Susan for a second time, but she was in deep by now. Only the truth would suffice. "I wanted him to marry me, if I divorced Oliver. I never dreamed of such a thing when I thought he would become Lord Brockenhurst—or if I did, I knew it was just a dream. But when he was only the penniless son of a younger son, it did not seem outlandish. I shall have more money than him. Much more."

"I agree with you." Anne sounded as if they were discussing

the merits and demerits of a new cook. "I should have thought you might have been the answer to his prayers."

"Well, I wasn't," said Susan. "He laughed in my face at my presumption."

"I see." Anne did see. Susan had been dazzled by this handsome man with his style and his Society manner. They had met when she was lonely and barren and unloved. "So you aren't barren, after all," she added. "That must be a relief, albeit a complicated one."

Susan almost smiled. "If I'd known the fault lay with Oliver and not with me, I'd have been more careful." How strange this exchange felt. She looked around the room, with its pleasant colors and gleaming furniture and pictures, a room she knew so well but would never think of in the same way again. They were talking like two equals now, two friends even, which in one way was extraordinary when Susan thought about it, although she had always had a higher opinion of Anne than of any other member of the family.

"And this is the point." Her mother-in-law's voice became more serious again. "Oliver is unable to father children." There was real sorrow in her tone and so there should be, thought Susan. It is terrible for a mother to know that her son can never have an heir.

"It seems he cannot father them with me. But then, Napoléon couldn't have children with Josephine but had a son with Marie Louise."

"Oliver is not Napoléon," said Anne with a certain finality. She was thinking. There was a silence between them, interrupted only by the ticking clock on the mantel shelf and the burning coal shifting noisily in the grate. Then she looked at Susan directly. "I want to be sure about the deal you are offering."

"Deal?" Susan had not thought of it as a deal.

"You want to stay with Oliver now that your exit route with John Bellasis has been cut off?"

Susan's heart was thudding in her chest. The next few minutes would decide her fate. "I would like to stay in this family, yes."

There was a sudden yapping that made them both jump. Agnes had woken from her place on the hearthrug and was pushing against Anne's skirts, begging to be lifted. Once the dog had been settled in her lap, Anne continued. "How will you handle Oliver? I assume he must know the child is not his."

Susan nodded. "Yes, he will know. But leave Oliver to me."

"What do you want of us, then, James and me?" Anne was curious to see how much of this was planned. In fact, Susan was making it up as she went along, but she had enough style to make the whole business sound premeditated.

"I want Oliver to see how pleased Father is by the news, how overjoyed, how proud of his son, how happy. It is a long time since Oliver made his father happy."

Anne did not say anything for a while. The silence was long enough for Susan to wonder whether the surreal conversation had come to an end. But then Anne did speak. "You mean, you want Oliver to understand that he has a great deal to gain if he accepts the child as his?"

"He will be the winner by it." Susan was actually coming to believe this.

Anne nodded slowly. "I will do my best, and I will keep your secret, on one condition. If you will live at Glanville."

Susan stared at her. *Live in Somerset?* Two or even three days' journey from the capital? "Live there?" she said, as if it must have been a question intended for someone else.

"Yes. Live there. And I will keep your secret."

Susan was beginning to understand that she had no choice in the matter. Anne spoke as if she were asking a question when in fact she was giving an order.

She had not finished. "It's time for us to admit that Oliver will never be happy in the career James has mapped out for him. He will never make his mark in development or trade or any of it. Very well. Let him be a country gentleman. That's what he wants. Who knows? He might be a success." In truth, the loss of Glanville was a dagger to her heart. It was like the loss of a limb; worse, the loss of half her life. Glanville had been her love and her joy, but she knew it would be her child's redemption and so it must be. "I will continue to visit, but not as the mistress of the place. From now on, that would be your position. If you'll take it on. Will you?"

Susan already knew no other decision was possible. What contrasting fates lay ahead? On the one hand, to be a divorced, adulterous wife with a bastard child, living in exile, alone and rejected by anyone of even the smallest pretensions. On the other, to find herself the mistress of a great house in the West Country, with a husband and a son or daughter, playing her role in county society. It wasn't exactly difficult. But...

"Could I come up to London for the Season?"

Anne smiled for the first time since Susan had entered the room. "Yes. You will come here for two months every year."

"And I may make the occasional visit?"

"You may. Although I think you'll be surprised by how much you enjoy country life once you enter into it." Anne paused. "I have one other condition."

Susan tensed. So far, this was an arrangement she could live with if she had to. And she had to. "What is it?"

"James must never know. This baby will be his grandchild, and he must never even suspect anything else."

Susan nodded. "If it is left to me, he will never know a thing, and I will do my best to make sure Oliver never gives us away. But now I have a condition."

Anne was surprised. "Are you in a position to make conditions?"

"I think I can make this one. Oliver must never suspect that you know the truth. The child's beginnings will be our secret, Oliver's and mine. Only then will he be able to protect his dignity."

Anne nodded. "I see that. Yes. You have my word."

"Your word on what?" James's voice startled them, but Anne was always in control of her own reactions.

"That they will have Glanville for their use. A child should grow up in the country. Did you find the champagne?"

"I've asked for it at the end of dinner."

How easily she could distract him. Before James could make

any further comment, the door opened and Oliver came in. He had changed and splashed some water on his face, which seemed to have sobered him up, much to Susan's relief. Although strange thoughts assailed her as she looked at her husband. By the time she slept tonight, her future life would have been decided, one way or the other.

As his son entered the room, James let out a spontaneous cheer. "Hurrah! My dearest boy!" he shouted, grinning from ear to ear. "Many congratulations!" He was hugging the young man so tightly he couldn't see the look of bewilderment on his face.

Oliver looked over at his mother and opened his mouth, but before he could speak, she talked firmly across him. "This is wonderful news, Oliver. Susan and I have been discussing things, and I might as well say it now: You are to have Glanville. You must give up your London work and retire to Somerset."

"What's this? You never said he'd have to retire." James broke loose from the embrace, but Anne silenced him with a gesture of her hand.

"There's plenty of money. Why not? What are we trying to prove? Oliver was born to be a squire, not a businessman." Anne looked at her husband. She knew this was one of those moments in a marriage when a key decision is taken, almost by chance, that will change everything. James had wanted his son to follow in his footsteps ever since Oliver was a boy, and it had led to failure and resentment and to the pair of them falling out to the extent that they could barely speak. "Wouldn't you rather admire him than feel disappointed all the time?" she murmured into his ear. "Do your business with Charles. Let Oliver go his own way."

James looked at her and then nodded. It was faint, but he nodded.

Anne smiled. "Thank you, God," she whispered under her breath, though whether she was addressing her Maker or her husband she hardly knew.

"What is happening? Why are you talking like this?" Oliver was entirely bemused. It seemed that all his dreams were being made true in an instant, but why?

James sighed. He had accepted Anne's decision. "Perhaps your mother is right. A child should grow up in the country."

"A child?" Once again, Oliver could not believe that his ears were working properly.

"We don't have to keep it to ourselves any longer, my dearest one," said Susan. "I've told them." Her voice was calm and firm. "They're so happy for us, and Mother wants to give us Glanville. So we can live there as a family." Now she began to gush, like a girl on her way to a first ball, deliberately creating a wall of sound behind which Oliver could gather his thoughts. His face darkened, so she jabbered even more. "Isn't it wonderful? Isn't it what you've always wanted?" Her eyes were boring into his, holding him like Dr. Mesmer in a hypnotic trance. She drew close, taking him in her arms and bringing her lips to his ear. "Say nothing." She squeezed him as she spoke. "We'll talk later, but if you speak now we may lose everything, and we will never have another chance like this. Be silent now." His body stiffened, but for once he heard her words and he stayed quiet. He would think before he wielded the ax.

Mr. Turton was a very angry man. He'd served this family for more than two decades, and now he was to be turned out into the streets like a dog. He'd been told to leave in the morning by the master just before dinner was announced, and he'd been sitting in the servants' hall ever since. The rest of the staff were avoiding him, but Miss Ellis was there with her own tale of dismissal, and now they were sampling a bottle of the best Margaux he could find in the cellar. "Drink up," he said. "There's more if we want it."

Ellis sipped the delicious wine carefully. She enjoyed good wine, but she did not like to be drunk. Being drunk meant losing control, and that was something she would never allow if she could help it. "Where will you go?" she said.

"I've a cousin in Shoreditch. I can stay there. For a few days, anyway." Turton was seething. "While I look around and see what's going."

Ellis nodded. "We've Mrs. Oliver to blame for this. If she hadn't poked her nose in where it wasn't wanted, we'd be high and dry."

The butler was surprised. "I don't see what she's done. Miss Speer said a boy just pushed the papers into her hands in the street. What was she supposed to do?"

"Don't give me that." Ellis raised her eyes in exasperation. "Mrs. Oliver's no better than she ought to be. How do you think she's pregnant after ten years of sleeping with Mr. Oliver and nothing to show for it?"

Turton was astonished. "How do you know she's pregnant?"

"Never ask a lady's maid a question like that." Ellis finished her glass and reached for the bottle to refill it. "Just take my word. Mrs. Oliver and Mr. Bellasis have been playing games not fit for children."

"Mr. Bellasis?" Turton felt as if he must have been asleep and missed everything.

"I saw her. When I took the papers to him. Just as I was leaving. She dodged out of sight, but I knew it was her." Ellis nodded wisely. "There was no boy. She took those papers to punish him, I shouldn't wonder. She'll have wanted him to stand by her, but Mr. Bellasis wouldn't bother with a tradesman's daughter like her. Not him." She threw her head back with a harsh laugh.

"I see." Turton thought for a moment. "Is there anything there for us, Miss Ellis? Anything that might prove useful?"

She stared at him, the same thought gradually dawning. "I don't think we could get anything from him, Mr. Turton. What would he care if all the world knew her for a slut? But she might pay to keep it quiet. If we leave it a while, until the baby's born—"

"I don't think so." The voice made them start. They'd both thought themselves alone. Speer stepped into the doorway.

"What are you doing there, Miss Speer? Are you spying on us?" Turton's voice was sharp, as if he could take command of the situation, as he had always taken command for so many years.

"Excuse me, Mr. Turton, but you're not the butler here now. You've been sacked." Speer's voice rapped out the words so they almost seemed to echo around the walls. "And don't think I'll take your orders any more, 'cause I won't." This was a side of Speer neither of them had seen before. She came toward them and took a seat at the table. She was quite casual in her manner, more at home than they, and when she spoke again, her voice was like the soft purr of a cat.

"If you ever approach Mrs. Oliver again, either of you, by letter or by word, I will report you to the police for theft. I will testify against you and you will serve a term in prison. After which you will find no further work as servants, not for the rest of your lives."

For a moment, there was complete silence between them all. Then Ellis spoke. "What have I ever stolen?"

"Items from Mrs. Babbage's kitchen. The pair of you stole them together. Wine, meat, general supplies. Why, over the years you must have stolen hundreds of pounds' worth and sold them for your benefit."

"That's not true!" Ellis was angry now. She'd done enough bad things, she'd spied and even lied, but she was never a thief.

"Maybe," said Speer. "But Mrs. Babbage will testify against you. If they make inquiries they'll know that stuff went missing while you were both here, and do you think she'd testify against herself?" She smiled, eyeing her own fingernails. It was the first moment Turton fully realized that, along with his job, he had lost his power.

After a moment, he nodded. Of course the cook would never incriminate herself, he could see that, not to save him or to save Miss Ellis, who had always treated her as a lower species of being.

"I'm going to bed," said Turton, getting to his feet.

But Speer wasn't finished. "I must have your word, both of you. We will never hear from either of you again, once you have left this house."

Ellis stared at her, this taut, composed figure who was queening it over them from the security of her position. "She'll get rid of you, Miss Speer. You know too much. She won't want that hanging around her in years to come."

The maid thought for a moment. "Perhaps. But if she asks me to go, I'll only do it with the kind of references that would get me a job at Buckingham Palace." Of course this was true, so Ellis did not attempt a rejoinder. Miss Speer hadn't finished. "For the moment, she is my mistress, and my job is to protect her from the likes of you." Ellis glanced at Mr. Turton. How little attention they'd paid to her, this nobody who, all of a sudden, was telling them what to do.

The butler spoke first. "Rest easy, Miss Speer. You won't be hearing from me at any point in the future." With a slight bow, Turton left the room.

"You win, you bitch," said Ellis. And with that, she rose and followed him out. Speer didn't mind the insult. She was made of sterner stuff than that. She wondered how to let Mrs. Oliver know what she'd done for her. There must be a way. She knew there was truth in what Miss Ellis had said, and that Mrs. Oliver would want to see the back of her eventually, so she could hire a maid with no memories of Mr. Bellasis or of that time in her life. But, as she had said, whenever that hour came, she, Speer, would be the winner. For now, Mr. Turton and Miss Ellis had left the story, and she was in charge.

Susan came up to bed first. The evening had continued on a note of jollity, mainly driven by James since he was the only innocent in the room. The others—Susan, Oliver, and Anne—knew the truth, so it was rather a draining business to have to listen to James's ramblings while toasting each other with champagne, and Susan retired as soon as she decently could. She knew what was coming, and she did not have long to wait.

"Whose is it?" Oddly, dinner seemed to have sobered Oliver up even more, which was against all logic, but it was so.

Susan looked at her husband, who was standing half in, half out of the room. This was the final hurdle that faced her. If she could clear this one, then the road ahead was open. She had sent Speer downstairs earlier and was already in bed when he appeared. Now he shut the door carefully and approached her. Clearly, whatever he thought about the matter, he did not want to be overheard.

She was ready for him. "It doesn't matter whose it is. Your wife is pregnant. Your parents are happy. The life you have always wanted to live has been offered to you."

"You mean I'm to accept it?"

"Aren't you?"

He was restless, wandering about the chamber, looking at the books on her shelves, at ornaments on her desk, thinking aloud. "How do I know this mystical figure, the absent father, will not be part of our life from now on? Am I to tolerate that? Am I to be a *mari complaisant*?"

She shook her head. "No. I will not reveal his name because he is of no importance. I will never see him again—well, not if I can avoid it."

"I suppose I should have expected something like this. Sooner or later. You're always flirting, always making a fool of yourself. I've seen you. A dozen times."

Normally, she would have lashed him with her tongue for such an accusation. She was cleverer than Oliver and could always get the better of him. But this time she stayed silent, instinctively sensing the pace at which she should travel. After a few moments, Oliver sat down heavily by the fire, turning his chair to face the bed. The flames cast a flickering light over him, making him seem almost ethereal. "Aren't you at least going to say you're sorry?" he said.

Susan braced herself for the boldest part of her argument. She'd had time to think. She was ready. "I am not sorry, because I have done what I set out to do. I am pregnant with our child. That was my purpose, and that is what I have achieved."

Oliver snorted. "You're surely not telling me that this was deliberate?"

She stared at him. "Have you ever known me to do anything without a purpose? Have you ever known me to act impetuously?"

She knew from his expression that he was starting to listen to her in spite of himself. "You mean, you thought I could not make you pregnant?"

"You've been trying for almost eleven years."

"But we thought the fault was yours."

She nodded. "And now we know it was not." Had she succeeded in deflecting the jealous rage and tantrums that she had been dreading? She continued carefully. "You see, I wanted to be sure it was me and not you, because it had to be one of us."

"And this is the result." His face was quite opaque.

"Yes. This is the result. I am pregnant with our child. Whether it's a boy or a girl, you have an heir. Would you really want to devote your life to Glanville, to the house, to the estate, if you had no one to hand it over to? Is that your ambition?"

"I want my own child."

"And you shall have it. That is what I want, too. And that is what I shall give you. If I had not done what I've done, you would be childless to the end of your days."

At this, Oliver was silent. On either side of the chimney breast were two oval portraits in chalk of himself and Sophia as children. She must have been about six and he was three or four, wearing a frilly collar over the top of his little woolen jacket. He stared at his long-ago self. He had a vague memory of the artist and of being bribed with an orange to keep still. Susan continued to talk behind him. "We'll reopen the nurseries at Glanville that have been closed since your mother bought the house. You can teach the child to ride, to swim, to fish, to shoot, if it's a boy. If you ever want to be a parent, Oliver, this is the only way."

When he turned back to her, she was almost shocked to see that his eyes had filled with tears. "Are you saying you've done this for me?"

"I've done it for us." She felt she now had the reins of this exchange firmly in her hands, and she could steer it as she wished. "We were growing tired of each other, tired of our life together. Our childlessness made us sad every day. I knew it would only be a matter of time before we separated, and what would lie ahead then? For either of us?"

"Why didn't you tell me your plan?"

"For two reasons. I might truly have been barren, in which case nothing would have come of it, and it would have driven you further away."

"And the other reason?"

"You would have forbidden me. But, as it is, we are going to be parents."

He said nothing, but she saw that he reached up quickly to wipe his eyes. The truth was, she had found something buried in Oliver; she had released a man who had been hidden from her for half their marriage. She waited, almost motionless, her hands resting on the counterpane, as he walked back and forth, up and down the embroidered rug at the foot of her bed. There was a noise of a dogfight in the street below, and he went to the window to see if he could make it out.

He was going to forgive her. He knew it by then. He wasn't sure if she had done all this for him or for herself, but either way, he was now convinced she hadn't simply taken a lover and been caught out. That's what he couldn't have borne. And she was right. The life he had wanted for years was now within his grasp, and it was a good life...

"One thing." He did not move but spoke with his face still turned toward the windows.

"Name it," she said, starting to feel relief flooding through her.

"After tonight, we will never again mention that it is not my child. Not even between ourselves."

Susan felt her breath come more easily. Her shoulders loosened and she leaned back among the lace-edged pillows behind her. Then she spoke with the voice of a lover. "Why would I ever say otherwise? It is your child, my darling. Who else could have a claim to it?"

Then he came to her and took her hands, and bent to kiss her mouth. Initially, the idea was rather revolting to her, but Susan was nothing if not disciplined. She did not feel attracted to this man. Indeed, she wondered if she ever had been. She did not even like him, or enjoy his company. But his affection was essential if she were to make a success of this life on earth. Very well. She would learn to like him. She would even conquer her revulsion at the idea of their making love. After all, she must have liked him once, at least a bit. He was quite wrong, of course. She had absolutely taken a lover in John Bellasis and been caught out, just as her husband had suspected; but that version was gone now, lost in the ether, and she would learn to adopt her own story of personal sacrifice to bring about a child for them to love and bring up together. She reckoned that it would not take her much more than a year to believe it implicitly. If she tried hard enough, she knew she could forget the truth. And with that thought, she opened her mouth to kiss him as passionately as she knew how. His tongue felt unpleasantly large in her mouth at first, and it still tasted of sour wine, but Susan didn't care.

She was in the clear.

.11.

Inheritance

C aroline Brockenhurst stared at her visitor. She could hardly take in what she was saying. "I don't understand," she said at last.

Anne was not surprised. It was a great deal to digest. She had thought for some time how best to explain the situation, but in the end she'd come to the conclusion that she just had to say it. "We know now that your son, Edmund, was legally married to my daughter, Sophia, before he died. Charles Pope is legitimate, and in fact is not Charles Pope at all. He's Charles Bellasis, or to be exact, Viscount Bellasis, and the legal heir to his grandfather."

James Trenchard had come home that day bursting with joy. He held in his hand the proof he'd been waiting for. His lawyers had registered the marriage and it had been accepted by the Committee of Privileges. At least, this last would take some time to complete, but the lawyers had scanned the evidence and they could see no difficulty. In other words, there wasn't any further need to keep it secret. It was Anne who decided they must tell Lady Brockenhurst straightaway. So she'd walked round and found her alone. And now she had told her the news.

Caroline Brockenhurst sat in silence as a million different thoughts jostled for a place in her brain. Would Edmund really have married without telling them? And the daughter of Wellington's victualler? At first she was filled with indignation. How could this possibly have happened? The girl must have been a little minx. She knew Sophia had been pretty. Caroline's sister, the Duchess, had told her that much, but what a schemer she must have been into the bargain. Then the greater truth started to impress itself on her. They had a legitimate heir, she and Peregrine. And an heir who was industrious, talented, and clever. Of course he must abandon his trading at once, but he would. As soon as he knew the facts of the case. He could bring his abilities to bear at Lymington, or on their other estates. Then there were the London properties that no one had done much with in a century or more. There was such a lot for him to tackle. She concentrated again on the woman before her. They were not friends, exactly, even now, but they were not enemies. They had shared too much for that.

"And he knows nothing? Charles, I mean."

"Nothing. James wanted to be quite sure there would be no obstacles that might have disappointed him."

"I see. Well, we should send a message first thing in the morning. Come to dinner here tomorrow night, and we can tell him together."

"What about Lord Brockenhurst? Where is he now?"

"He's been shooting in Yorkshire. He'll be back tomorrow, or so he said. I'll send a telegram to confirm he's to come here and not go on to Hampshire." She thought for a moment. "If Mr. Trenchard was successful in getting the marriage accepted, how did he explain your daughter's surname on the registry of the birth?"

Anne smiled. "All husbands are the legal fathers of any children born during a marriage."

"Even when they're dead?"

"If a child is born within nine months of a husband's death, the legal assumption obtains that he is the father, whether or not the wife took his name, whether or not he is named as the father in the registry."

"Can a husband not repudiate a baby?"

Anne thought. "There must be some mechanism for that, but in this instance one look at Charles's face tells us all who his father was."

"True enough." And now, at last, the warm glow of relief and real joy was beginning to flood through the Countess. They had an heir, whom she already admired greatly, and he would soon have a family for her and Peregrine to love.

Anne must have been entertaining similar thoughts as she suddenly asked: "Where is Lady Maria? What does she know?"

Caroline nodded. "I've told her Charles is our grandson, as I thought then it might be enough to soothe the feelings of her mother. In fact, I was wrong, but that is what she knows." She smoothed her skirts, relishing the knowledge of the news she'd have to tell the girl when she came back.

"Where is she now?" said Anne.

"With Lady Templemore. Her brother arrived from Ireland last night, and a footman brought a summons this morning. She's gone there for dinner, partly to see him and partly to ask for his help in talking her mother around. I am tempted to send a note saying no such persuasion will now be necessary, but I suppose it must play itself out."

Reginald Grey, sixth Earl of Templemore, was a man of real principle, if a little less passionate about his beliefs than his sister. He was handsome in his way, and upright, if perhaps a shade dull. But he loved his sibling fiercely. They had gone through a lot together, Maria and he, crouching behind the landing balustrade to listen from the nursery floor to the battles being waged below, and those unsettling years had created a bond between them that would not be easily broken, as their mother gloomily acknowledged. The family was sitting together in Lady Templemore's drawing room, and it was easy to see that the mood in the room was not encouraging.

"How are things at home?" said Maria, in an attempt to move the talk along. She was wearing an evening frock in pale green silk, with embroidery around the low neck setting off her well-formed shoulders and bosom, even if the effect was wasted on her brother.

"Very good. We've lost two tenants recently, but I've taken their land in hand. I suppose I must be farming about a thousand acres directly. And I've decided to make more of the library. There's a man coming to see me when I get back about installing new bookcases and moving down the chimneypiece from the Blue Bedroom. I think it'll work well."

Maria was listening intently, as if to show she was an adult making adult choices. "I'm sure. Papa would have liked the idea of that."

"Your father never read a book in his life," said Lady Templemore. "Not if he could avoid it." She rose to rearrange the Meissen figures on the mantel shelf. She was not making things easy.

Reggie Templemore decided there was no point in avoiding the subject any longer. "I gather from your letters that you two have been at odds recently."

Lady Templemore ceased her attentions to the display on the chimneypiece. "You gather correctly," she said.

Maria decided to take the bull by the horns. "I have met the man I am going to marry. I hope this can be done with your permission and your blessing. I would like to walk down the aisle on your arm. But whether or not you approve, I will not marry anyone else."

Reggie held up his palms as if to calm a frightened horse. "Whoa." He smiled as he spoke, attempting to take the anger out of the situation. "There's no need for fighting talk, not when it's only the three of us here."

"Maria has thrown away a great opportunity that would have transformed both our lives. She can hardly expect me to approve of her decision." Corinne returned to her seat. If the moment for the discussion had arrived, she might as well involve herself in it.

Reggie waited for the ruffled feathers to settle back into place. "I do not know this man, of course. And I am sorry if Maria is not to wield the power to do good that was on offer, but I cannot pretend to any strong pangs of grief at the thought of losing John Bellasis as a brother-in-law. His personality was never as attractive as his position."

"Thank you," said Maria, as if her brother had already won the argument. "He didn't like me and I didn't like him. That's all there was to it."

"Then why did you accept him?" said her mother.

"Because you made me feel that, if I didn't, I was a bad daughter."

"That's right. Blame me. You always do."

She sighed and leaned back in her chair. Hard as it was to believe, Lady Templemore had the uncomfortable sensation that matters were sliding out of her control. She had hoped her son might talk some sense into his sister, but he seemed to have sided with Maria from the start. "I do not think you understand, Reggie. The man she has chosen as a husband is a bastard and a tradesman." It was hard to tell which she thought the worst insult.

"Strong talk, Mama." Reggie was not sure he was quite comfortable with the direction this conversation was taking. "Maria?"

Naturally, Maria was made uncomfortable by this since, as far as she knew, both her mother's accusations were quite true. Charles was a bastard, and he was a tradesman. She corrected the facts a little as she answered him, but she could not transform them. "It's true he is the illegitimate son of a nobleman, received and welcomed by his father's family. And he is a respected cotton mill owner in Manchester with plans to expand and develop his business." As she spoke her tone grew more confident. "You'll like him enormously," she added for good measure. "I know you will." To be fair, she was reasonably sure this was true.

Reggie was quite moved by his sister's enthusiasm. Clearly she thought this man weighed equally with John Bellasis in the great scales of life. He found himself wishing that it could be so. "May we know the name of the nobleman who is so pleased to have an illegitimate son?"

Maria hesitated. She didn't believe she had the right to name the Brockenhursts, not without their permission. "Actually, his father is dead," she said. "It's his grandparents who have welcomed him into their lives. But I'm not at liberty to name them just yet."

Witnessing her daughter's confidence that this nonentity could somehow be made to look the equal of her former suitor was driving Corinne to distraction. She turned to face them both, shrugging her shoulders as she did so. "But surely, when you match him against John Bellasis—"

"Mama." Even Reggie was beginning to resist his mother's obstinacy. "John Bellasis has gone and he will not be back. We couldn't revive that even if we wanted to."

"Which we do not!" added Maria, as forcefully as she dared.

"But a tradesman?" Corinne was not going to give in without a fight.

"Eight years ago—"

"Really, Maria. No more about the Stephensons."

"No, not this time. I just wanted to remind you that Lady Charlotte Bertie married John Guest, and he was an ironmaster." Maria had done her homework. She could probably list every mismatch in London's recent history. "They're received everywhere."

Her mother was not so easily defeated. "Mr. Guest was also very rich and a Member of Parliament. Mr. Pope is neither."

"But he will be both." Maria did not of course have any idea if Charles even wanted to be a Member of Parliament, but she was certainly not going to allow any Welsh iron man to have the advantage.

"And you say his grandparents welcome him, but his father is dead?"

Maria looked nervously at her mother. Had she revealed too much? Had Lady Templemore guessed the connection with the Brockenhursts? Why had she been so detailed in her description? But before she could add anything more to the discussion, the door opened and the butler appeared. Dinner, it seemed, was ready.

"Thank you, Stratton, we'll be there in just a moment." Reggie spoke with the conviction of the man of the house, even though he was almost never there.

His mother looked at him in surprise. She'd been adjusting a loose shawl around her shoulders in preparation for the chill of the dining room below and was not aware of any reason for them to linger. But the man had nodded and retreated and the three of them were alone once more.

Reggie spoke. "I will see this man, Mr. Pope. I will send a message in the morning, and I am sure he will make time for me—"

"Of course he will!" said Maria, making a mental note to send a message of her own to Bishopsgate. A message that would get there first.

Reggie continued. For a man of twenty, he really did have authority, and Maria felt proud to call him her brother. "I will listen to what he has to say, and, Mama, I cannot promise to support your stance. If the man is a gentleman, then I suggest we should talk instead about real conditions, real agreements, by which he would protect Maria's future and earn the right to join our family."

Corinne threw back her head in disgust. "So you are defeated."

Reggie was a match for her. "I am realistic. If Maria will not marry any other man, then let us at least try to see if we can come to terms with this one. In the end, Mama, I'm afraid your choice is going to be simple. You must decide whether you wish to get on with your children or live at war with them. Now, shall we go down?"

Susan Trenchard was checking her rooms. Everything they were taking was packed except for the clothes and things she would need on the journey. They were moving to Somerset. Anne had advised against traveling so far much later in the pregnancy, and so they had decided to go now. Susan did not relish it, either the journey or their future in the country, but she accepted both. They had a job ahead of them, to make the house and the estate their own, and she would like to get the nurseries into a respectable condition, even if superstition prevented her from redecorating them before the birth of the child. The only thing that concerned her was Oliver. True to their agreement, they had never mentioned the paternity of the baby since that night, and nor did she intend to, ever again. But he was still preoccupied, even maudlin, and she wondered if he was coming to regret his decision to go along with her plans. He could be difficult, as she knew well enough, and she prayed that he was not getting ready to be difficult now.

One case stood open in the corner, to take whatever was left. The rest had been carried out to the vast traveling carriage that had made its way up from Somerset and waited now in the mews behind the house. A hall boy would guard it overnight, and then they would leave as soon as they had breakfasted. Unlike her mother-in-law, she intended to make it to Glanville in two days, and for that they needed an early start. As she looked at the clothes she had retained for traveling, the door opened and Oliver came in.

"Are you ready to go down?"

She nodded. She was wearing a simple gray dress, which would be useful for the night they must spend at the coaching inn on the way. It was quite becoming but not as formal as James usually demanded. "I know this isn't very smart, but I've kept a silver necklace out that may raise its rank a bit. Speer took it down to clean, and she'll be back in a moment."

Oliver was hardly listening. He nodded without comment, glancing around the room. "Will you miss London?"

"We'll be back for the Season." She spoke happily, because that was what she had decided. To be a happy wife from here on in.

"It's a long way off." But Oliver was not sneering or angry or even drunk; he sounded more wistful. Maybe he was worried for her. He slumped into a chair near the fire, glancing around him as if he were looking for something, but she could not guess what it might be.

She smiled. "I wish you'd tell me what's wrong," she said.

He did not deny it, which confirmed that something was amiss. "You wouldn't understand."

"Try me."

But the door opened and the maid returned, holding the filigree necklace Susan had spoken of, and in another moment it had been fastened around her mistress's neck. Susan and Oliver were ready to descend.

Charles Pope was torn. He'd only recently welcomed his mother to London and installed her in the rooms he had taken for them both in High Holborn. She'd been in the City for less than a week, and, although she professed excitement at this new turn her life had taken, she was also nervous to find herself in the rattle and clatter of a modern city after a lifetime in a rural village. He felt he should go home and see to her comfort, for a few more days at least, but instead he stared at the note in his hand. It had been delivered not much more than an hour earlier.

Dear Mr. Pope,

I wonder if you will indulge me with your company this evening. Very possibly not, after the last time we met, when I allowed my anger to overtake my manners. But I believe it would add greatly to the happiness of a man we both hold dear if we could manage to settle our differences. I am sure they are of my making and not yours, but I would take it as a great compliment if you would indulge me in this. I will be at the Black Raven on Allhallows Lane at eleven. I cannot get there sooner as I have committed myself elsewhere, but I would prefer to get things settled sooner rather than later.

Yours, Oliver Trenchard

Charles had read it several times by this point. The letter was undated and did not bear an address, but he had no reason to question its authenticity. James had shown him some notes Oliver had submitted on the Isle of Dogs development and the writing certainly looked genuine. And he knew only too well that he had caused difficulties between James and his son. It would be a good thing if they could move past their troubles, since it was a poor return, after all James had done for him, to make trouble in the family. For a moment he thought he might carry the letter to James's house in Eaton Square, but then wouldn't that be defeating the object? To call James's attention to the quarrel before there was a solution? He did not know the public house named in the message, but he was familiar with Allhallows Lane, a narrow alleyway not far from Bishopsgate on the river's edge and walkable from his office. Why must it be so late? If Oliver was busy that evening, why not just leave it for another day? But then, if he objected to the time, might it not be interpreted as a refusal to patch things up, when the truth was that he wanted nothing more?

In the end, he decided to walk back to his rooms, settle his mother, eat something with her and, after that, keep the appointment. She would retire to bed as soon as he left, if not before, and there was both a landlady and his own servant to keep an eye on her. With that in mind, he called for his coat.

Maria, her brother, and her mother had spoken of little that was contentious at dinner. They were served by the butler and the solitary footman and Corinne did not care to advertise her family's difficulties to the servants. So they had discussed Reggie's plans for Balligrey and gossiped about their friends and relations in Ireland until it was almost possible to forget that Maria and her mother were engaged in a struggle that could only end in victory for one of them. "You're very secretive about your own life," said Maria playfully. "Is there anything you ought to tell us?"

Reggie smiled as he reached for his glass. "Experience has taught me to keep my cards close to my chest."

"That sounds promising. Doesn't it, Mama?"

But Lady Templemore was not prepared to be drawn into merry banter when she had such heavy thoughts weighing on her mind. "I'm sure Reggie will tell us when he's ready," she said, nodding to the footman that they had finished. The man stepped in to remove the plates.

"I don't want to wait," said Maria, but she did not succeed in getting much more out of her brother. Only that he "might" have found the daughter of some friends of their parents very "congenial," and it was "possible" that something could come of it.

"If her parents really are old friends, then that in itself is balm to this wounded soul," said Corinne when the servants were momentarily out of the room, but she did not attempt to elaborate.

Only later, when they were back in the drawing room and the servants had left them, did she speak to any purpose. "Very well," she said.

Maria was taken unawares, halfway through pouring a cup of coffee for herself. She looked up. "Very well what?"

"I will wait for Reggie's verdict. If he likes your Mr. Pope, if he approves the match, then I will try to follow suit. He is the head of the family now. It is he who will carry the burden of this man as a brother-in-law. I will be dead soon, so what does my opinion matter?" She sat back on the sofa with a sigh, suggesting a vaguely infirm condition, and picked up her fan from the table by her elbow.

For a moment, neither Maria nor Reggie moved. Then the girl threw herself on her knees before her mother and, seizing her hands, began to kiss them as tears coursed down her cheeks. "Thank you, dearest, most darling Mama. Thank you. You won't regret it."

"I am regretting it *now*," said Lady Templemore. "But I cannot fight both my children. I am too weak. I will try my best to like him, this man who has stolen my daughter's future."

Maria looked up at her. "He hasn't stolen it, Mama. I have given him my future quite freely." At least the mother did not pull her hands away, letting them rest in her daughter's, and although she shed a few tears that night as she lay in bed, over the loss of the paradise she had dreamed of, still, all things considered, Corinne Templemore preferred to be on good terms rather than bad when it came to her children. They had been down a difficult, rocky path together while their father was alive, and it did not suit her to fight with them now.

The fruit had come in, arranged on a silver epergne with little baskets held around a central bowl of roses all filled with plums and grapes and nectarines, glistening in the light of the candelabra at either end of the table. It looked like something from a painting by Caravaggio, thought Anne. Mrs. Babbage could be quite artistic when she put her mind to it. She had ordered a good dinner to send Oliver and Susan on their way, and, to be honest, she was pleased that Susan had somehow brought her son around. Anne intended to abide by the agreement and never mention the child's paternity again. For a second she had thought of telling Caroline Brockenhurst that now *all* of Anne's grandchildren would have Bellasis blood, but she knew that if she told even one person, eventually James would hear, and that she did not want. So Susan's secret was safe with her, and Anne was glad. She wasn't exactly fond of her daughter-in-law, but she thought Susan clever and competent when she put her mind to anything, and this latest fright, this brush with scandal, seemed to have brought her out of the selfish mist she moved around in and made her engage with the practicalities of their new life. Dr. Johnson wrote that if a man knows he is to be hanged the following morning, it concentrates the mind wonderfully, and maybe the same could be said of the threat of ruin. Anne was sorry to have surrendered Glanville. She would go there for visits, perhaps not much less than she did already, but it would no longer be her kingdom. Queen Susan would henceforth rule. Still, she knew it was a sacrifice worth making, to allow her son to live his own life instead of his father's.

But when Anne looked down the table at her son, she realized that something still appeared to be troubling Oliver. She'd tried once or twice over the past few days to ask him what it might be, but with no success. He'd answered her inquiries, insisting that there was nothing amiss, but still...

"Have you seen Mr. Pope lately, Father?" Oliver's words were a surprise, since they all knew he had no love for Charles Pope and would normally have preferred to steer clear of the subject. As far as Anne and James knew, he still had no idea of Charles's true identity, as James felt it only right that Charles should learn it first, or at least no later than everyone else. He was, of course, quite ignorant of Susan's role in the story, and Anne was not going to disabuse him. So she was content that Oliver should find out once Charles, Lord Brockenhurst and the Templemores had been told at dinner the following evening.

After pausing a moment to get over the strangeness of the question, James looked at his son. "What do you mean, 'lately'?"

"In the past week." Oliver was eating a peach and some of the juice dribbled down his chin. Susan noticed it and felt her jaw tightening with irritation, but she forced herself to let it go. If he wanted to have juice on his chin, then so be it. It was his chin, after all.

"No," said James. "He's moved lodgings to have some more space for his mother—" He caught Anne's glance and corrected himself. "For Mrs. Pope, who is coming to live with him. He knew he would need a while to settle her in."

Oliver nodded. "Do you know where those lodgings are?"

James shook his head as he began to peel a peach, puzzled as to where this conversation might be leading. "Somewhere in Holborn, I think. Why?"

"No reason," his son replied. Anne caught Billy glancing at Oliver in curiosity until he saw her watching him and blushed. She would have to call him Watson now that he was the butler. They all would.

"I think there is a reason." James's voice had an edge to it, and Anne supposed it was because he knew he would have to defend Charles against Oliver's criticism. But the younger man didn't seem aggressive or angry or even rude. If she'd had to put a name to his mood, she would have said he was worried. "Oliver, can you come with me?" James threw down his fruit knife and stood, discarding his crumpled napkin on the table. He led the way across the hall to the library.

They walked in silence, but once they were there James shut the door and spoke. "Now, what is going on? Why are you preoccupied, and what has this to do with Charles Pope?"

In a way, now the question had come, it was a relief for Oliver to unburden himself. How he'd gone to the Horse and Groom hot with anger; how John Bellasis had found him there. "He knew I was in a rage about Pope, though I don't know how, and he started to question me. He was curious about the man, and, as we know, Pope is a great favorite with Mr. Bellasis's aunt. Perhaps he was jealous. I know I was."

"But what happened? What did he do? What did you do?" Anxious for something to occupy his hands, James seized the poker and began to stir the dying fire back into life.

Oliver did not speak at once. He tried to think of ways to make what he had to say sound less serious. But he could not. "He said he wanted to teach Pope a lesson."

"What sort of lesson?"

"I don't know. I was pretty drunk before he arrived. And I was angry with Pope myself."

"You don't have to explain that you wished Charles Pope ill. I would expect nothing else from you. Go on." His tone was anything but conciliatory, but Oliver had begun, so now he might as well finish.

"He asked me to write a note to Mr. Pope. He said he couldn't write the note himself, as Pope didn't care for him and wouldn't respond to it. But if I wrote a message, saying that I was sorry we had fallen out, and that it would give you pleasure if we could be reconciled, then Pope might agree to meet me."

"It would give me pleasure?" James gave a derisive snort.

"Somehow Bellasis knew you were unhappy that I'd taken against your protégé. Anyway, I wrote the note and had a drink with him and left."

James stared in disbelief. "You wrote a letter to lure Charles Pope to a place where he...what? He would be beaten up? By thugs arranged by Mr. Bellasis? Was that it?"

"I told you, I was drunk."

"But not too drunk to hold a pen, by God." For Oliver, his father's fury was washing away the precious peace he had been reaching for since they had made the decision to let him escape to Glanville. Here he was, once again, a disappointment, a failure, a fool. "When was this meeting to take place?"

"He didn't say. He wouldn't let me date the note, so that he could choose when to send it. I suppose he had to arrange a reception committee, and make sure everything was prepared. That's why I asked if you'd heard from Pope."

"Where was he to meet you? Or rather, to meet Bellasis?"

For Oliver, it was as if he'd been carrying a dangerous, half-formed secret locked in a bottle for the days since he'd done this thing. He had not wanted to acknowledge that he'd been stupid and a dupe, but of course he had. Now it seemed the poisonous secret had escaped from the bottle and it had grown large enough to push everything else out of his mind. "I can't remember."

"Then try harder!" James strode to the bell rope and gave it a tug. When the footman hurried across the hall from the dining room, James shouted almost before he'd opened the door. "Send the boy to tell Quirk to get a carriage out! The brougham! We'll need to go fast!"

Oliver was bewildered. "But go where? You don't know his present address, and I can't recall where the note invited him. And why should it be tonight?"

James stared at him. "If it's already happened and he's seriously hurt, then I'll never forgive you. If it hasn't happened yet, then we'll warn him, even if we have to wait all night outside his office. Now where was the meeting place? In the City? In the country? You must know that, at least!"

Oliver thought. "I think it was in the City. Yes, because he said Pope would be able to walk there from his place of work."

"Then we'll start in Bishopsgate. Get your coat, while I speak to your mother." James walked toward the door.

"Father."

James stopped at the sound of his son's voice. He turned to look at him.

"I'm sorry." It was true. Oliver's face was white with regret.

"Not as sorry as you're going to be if anything's happened to him."

John Bellasis shivered, though whether from the cold or the prospect ahead of him it was hard to tell. He had dismissed his hansom some streets away from Allhallows Lane, as he did not want the cabby to have a clue as to his destination, so he was walking through the East End of London at night, unaccompanied, alone.

When Oliver Trenchard had left him that night at the Horse

and Groom, he'd put the note away, telling himself that he'd never use it. Thinking that he could somehow absolve himself of the guilt for having it written in the first place. Of course, he knew why he had made Oliver write it. He knew what he had intended from the moment he saw Oliver in the bar, and he was suddenly clear, in that second of seeing him, that it was within his reach to dispose of the obstacle to his own personal happiness. Yet still he hesitated.

He'd waited every day for the summons from his uncle. Would he and his father please come to Brockenhurst House, as there was some news that would have a bearing on their future? But it never came. There was no announcement in the newspapers, no letter from Aunt Caroline, nothing. The Trenchards must know the truth by now, since he himself had given them the proof, as it pained him to remember. Then it occurred to him that they must be waiting until everything could be vouchsafed as true and legal. That no one would be told, perhaps not even the Brockenhursts, until Charles Pope's claims could be validated and upheld in court. And from that followed the thought that if he could bring himself to do this deed, if he could find the courage—for it was a kind of courage that was required—then he must do it before the announcements had been made. The death of a viscount, the heir of an earl, would be splashed across every newspaper and journal in the land. But the death of a young cotton merchant, just starting to build his business . . . that would barely warrant a tiny column in the bottom corner of the page.

Still he delayed. He would sit alone in his rooms, staring at the note Oliver had written, until at last he began to suspect that he lacked the nerve to do what he must do if he was to correct the hideous injustice that fate had planned for him. Did he, after all, lack courage? Was he afraid of detection and the hangman's noose? But if he did not act, and every hope and dream were dashed to the ground and lay in pieces at his feet, was the life that awaited him any better than the noose?

Through these days, he stayed inside, locked in his rooms. He dined alone, waited on by his silent servant whose wages, he thought with a twinge of humor, were anything but safe. He drank alone and in some quantity, sure in the knowledge that even his simple life—and it was comparatively simple next to the lives of so many of his more fortunate contemporaries—would be at risk the moment the news broke that he was no longer an heir with a future but a man drowning in debt with no promise of an income. His debtors would close in like sharks, hoping to seize what little money remained, and his father could not save him. Indeed, Stephen's troubles were, if anything, worse than his son's. They would both be declared bankrupt, and what came next? A life of destitution in Paris or Calais, eking out the tiny pension that Charles Pope (he could not bring himself to think of his cousin as Charles Bellasis) might be persuaded to grant? Was that really preferable to seizing a chance, a challenge, that must end in triumph or the gallows?

And so, such thinking had brought him to the morning of that very day, after a sleepless night. He took out an envelope and, with the note open before him, imitated the writing well enough for one word, *Pope*, before he put the note inside and sealed it with wax. He carried it outside, waited until he was some distance from Albany, and hailed a hansom cab, giving the driver the address of Pope's office and a tip to deliver the letter.

As he walked away, he told himself the man might have been a rogue who would pocket the money, destroy the envelope, and take up another passenger as soon as he was hailed. Let it be, he thought. If that was what happened, then that was what was meant to happen. But still he knew he must prepare. He must go early to the Black Raven, he must scout the distance from the public house to the river, he must finalize a plan. Once more he spent all day in his rooms, lying on his bed or pacing the floor. From time to time he would toy with the idea of simply not going, of letting Charles arrive to find no one there to greet him. He would ask for Oliver Trenchard, of course, not John Bellasis, and the innkeeper would shrug, having no knowledge of the name, and Charles would go home and get up on the morrow, ready and able to steal every-thing that should have been John's. But as he considered this final thought, he knew he must act. Even if he failed, he would have tried. He would not have submitted to the cruelty of the gods without a struggle.

"I will be late tonight, Roger," he said to his servant as the man held his topcoat open for him. "Do not expect me before the small hours. But if I am not in my bed by eight o'clock tomorrow morning, then you may start to make inquiries as to my whereabouts."

"Where should I look, sir?" said the man, but John just shook his head and did not answer.

"Murder?" Oliver's shock at his father's suggestion was quite genuine. Even though James was in the grip of a rage so powerful it threatened to unhinge his mind, he could still see that.

Oliver had thought Charles Pope was threatened with violence but no more than that. He could see John Bellasis hated the man, if anything more than Oliver himself hated him, but that had seemed to indicate a beating was in order. And Bellasis would get away with it. He would no doubt hire men to do the dirty work. They would run off, leaving no clue for the Peelers to work with, and the matter would be soon forgotten. But murder? James's suspicions seemed outlandish to his son. John Bellasis, try to murder Charles Pope?

"But why?" he said.

They had a way to go to reach Bishopsgate, and James could see no reason to leave Oliver in the dark any longer. As they journeyed through the gaslit streets, he told the story: the marriage in Brussels, Sophia's mistake in thinking she had been betrayed, Charles's true identity. Most of all he spoke of the threat to John Bellasis's inheritance, which would only recede should Charles Pope disappear forever.

Oliver was silent for a moment. Then he sighed. "You should have told me, sir. Not now. Long ago, before you knew who Charles Pope really was. Whether well born or a bastard, he is still my nephew, and you should have told me."

"We worried about Sophia's reputation."

"Do you think I could not have kept silent to protect my sister's name?"

For once James did not snap back at Oliver's argument because it was a reasonable charge, which James was forced to concede. He had made the same mistake with Anne, and come to repent that. Why didn't he trust the members of his own family? It was his weakness, not theirs, that had kept him silent. He sat back in his seat as the carriage rolled on through the night.

Maria walked back to Belgrave Square from Chesham Street in the company of her mother's footman. There really was no need to get a coach out for a ten-minute journey, and she enjoyed the cool night air. She was lighthearted, with a spring in her step, and she would probably have dismissed the man if she wasn't aware that it would have annoyed her mother, which was the very last thing she wanted to do that evening. She'd always known that Reggie would make things better, and so it had proved. Now, of course, Charles had to pass her brother's test, but she was confident he would. He was a gentleman, after all. Not a great catch, but a gentleman, certainly. And hardworking and intelligent and everything else that Reggie valued. And the truth was, she was touched, very touched, by the way her mother had yielded to her son's decision.

Maria had been strong and determined in her struggle. She had moved out of her mother's house and, in a sense, made Corinne quarrel with her old friend Lady Brockenhurst. She had been cold and unyielding when her mother had tried to argue the case for John Bellasis, pointing out that if the man cared for her, why was he not there to argue the case for himself? But Maria did not like quarreling with her sole living parent. Her father had been a harsh man, with his children as much as his wife, and when he'd died, though they would not admit it, the three of them had a slight sense of having survived him, of relief that they were still going and he was out of the picture. She knew that Reggie felt, as she did, that their mother had earned her years of peace, and it pained Maria for them to be at odds. Now that was done. She had no doubt that once her mother got to know Charles she would like him, reluctantly at first, perhaps, but she would. And whether or not he came to like her, still he would protect Lady Templemore and see to her comfort, so that in the end the benefits of the marriage would be much the same as they would have been with John. They were, and would be from now on, a united family, and that was the way Maria liked it.

She had reached Brockenhurst House and the door was opened by the night watchman, who always sat in an arched, padded leather chair in a corner of the hall, wide awake, or so he said, until he was relieved by the butler at eight o'clock. She dismissed her mother's footman and started toward the stairs after bidding the watchman good night. But he had a message for her. "Her ladyship's waiting for you, m'lady. In the boudoir."

Maria was surprised. "She hasn't gone to bed?"

"No, m'lady." The man was quite sure. "She was most particular that I was to tell you she was waiting up to see you."

"Very well. Thank you." Maria had reached the stairs by this time, and she started to climb.

Charles came out of the front door of his new lodgings and took a deep breath. The chill of the air was refreshing after the slightly overheated sitting room he had passed the evening in with his mother. But he'd been glad to spend the time with her. She was excited at the idea of her new life, and there was something heartening in the confidence she always displayed as far as his future prospects were concerned. She knew his business would soon be expanding throughout the world, and that he would make a fortune. She was equally certain he would buy a house in the most fashionable part of London and she would be able to run it for him, until his wife arrived, of course. And apparently none of this was going to take any time at all.

Naturally, Charles had to tell her that he thought his wife had already arrived, but he wanted to play it carefully, as he did not want his mother to think she was surplus to requirements. He was determined to make her welcome and comfortable whatever direction his life took, and he was confident that Maria would feel the same. So he gave the gentlest of hints, that there was someone he wanted her to meet, and Mrs. Pope had taken it in good part. "Will you tell me her name?"

"Maria Grey. You'll like her very much."

"I'm sure I will, if you have chosen her."

"Things are not quite settled yet."

"Why not, if she's the one?"

The little sitting room allotted to their use was pretty, especially for rented rooms in Holborn, with patterned chintz curtains and a buttoned sofa where his mother sat, next to the worktable she had brought with her. She was half attending to a piece of embroidery, but his silence at her question made her stop and rest her needle. She waited.

He gave a slight grimace. "It's complicated. Her mother is a widow and naturally protective of her only daughter. She is not entirely convinced that I am all that she is seeking in a son-in-law."

Mrs. Pope laughed. "Then she is a very stupid widow. If she had any sense she would have bowed down and kissed the ground the moment you walked through her door."

Charles was reluctant to make his mother an enemy of his future bride's family. "Lady Templemore has her reasons. Another marriage had been arranged for Maria, and she can hardly be criticized for wanting her daughter to keep her word."

"I can criticize her, this *Lady Templemore*"—her disdainful emphasis of the name was another sign of trouble to come. Charles rather regretted letting his mother in on his difficulties—"if the girl can see that you have more worth in your little finger than her feeble suitor, she is displaying good sense. Her mama should listen." Now she continued her work, but with a touch of anger, stabbing at the cloth as if it had been playing up in some way. "Why is her name Templemore if the girl is called Grey?"

"Her late husband's title was Templemore. Grey is the family's surname."

"Lord Templemore?"

"The Earl of Templemore, to be precise."

The sewing began to assume an easier rhythm as his words sank in. So Charles was on the brink of a brilliant match. That was no surprise. He had always been brilliant in everything he did, as far as she was concerned. But the news was a source of particular pleasure to Mrs. Pope, although she would have felt guilty in admitting it. "I wouldn't care if he was the King of Templemore," she said firmly, pausing in her work for a moment. "They'd still be lucky to have you." Charles decided to leave it at that.

Now Charles was on his way to the appointment with Oliver Trenchard. He had decided to walk. There was no hurry. He meant to walk to his offices every morning unless there was a reason not to, and his destination was not so far from there.

It seemed to him that Oliver's note held out the hand of friendship and, if this were so, Charles was determined to take it. Ever since that luncheon at the Athenaeum, where Oliver's jealousy— for it was certainly jealousy—had been so overwhelming, Charles had felt his every meeting with James had somehow been poisoned. Then Oliver's attempts to ruin him in Mr. Trenchard's eyes, with the bogus accusations from those scoundrels Brent and Astley, had been proof that none of Oliver's fury had abated. James's faith in Charles and his refusal to believe in his wrongdoing could only have inflamed the situation. As to whether or not Oliver had reason for his anger, if James had indeed been guilty of neglecting his own son in favor of a young stranger, Charles would not pass judgment. At any rate, they would all be happier if they could learn to live in peace. Charles valued James Trenchard's support and help. He could see the ridiculous side of the man—his eager self-promotion, his needy scrambling up the greasy pole of social advancement, none of which interested Charles—but he could see the intelligence, too. James understood business, its eddies and currents and tides, as no man had ever understood it in Charles's experience. That he had come from nothing and scaled the ladder of nineteenth-century England was no surprise to his protégé. His teaching would shave years off Charles's own journey, and he meant to take full advantage of it. He was also genuinely grateful.

Charles was passing near his office now, on his way down to the river. During the day, Bishopsgate was a hive of activity, jammed with traffic, its pavements crowded with men and women all hurrying this way and that. But at night, it was a quiet place. There were some pedestrians, the occasional drunk, the occasional beggar, even the odd prostitute, although he would not have thought it busy enough to promise much trade, but for the most part it was an empty thoroughfare, its vast, dark buildings looming above him. For a moment he had a strange impulse to turn back, to miss the meeting and go home. It was like a sudden message, quite distinct but unexplained. With a shrug, he dismissed the thought, turned up his collar against the chill, and continued on his way.

Maria's heart was beating like a hammer. Not because of Charles's position and prospects—she'd had all that on offer from John Bellasis and turned her back on it—but because her mother had been reconciled to Charles before she even knew. If Reggie had not come over, if they had continued in enmity until tonight, then she would always have thought her mother had changed her mind because of Charles's altered circumstances. Now she knew Corinne had accepted Charles as he was, not because she'd wanted to, but because of her love for her children. Lady Brockenhurst was of the same opinion. "I knew she would come around to him. I told you so."

They were sitting together in the boudoir, in front of a warm fire. Caroline had sent for two glasses of sweet wine, a sauternes she was fond of, to toast the news. Neither of them wanted to go to bed.

"You told me, but I didn't believe it."

"Well, I'm glad she proved herself a true mother, and now she will have her reward. She must come to dinner tomorrow night. But don't tell her first. It'll spoil the surprise."

Maria sipped at the delicate gilded glass. "And Charles still knows nothing?"

"Mr. Trenchard would not allow him to be told until everything had been checked by lawyers. I daresay that was sensible." It was still hard for Caroline to say anything very charitable about James Trenchard, but the fact was, he and she were legally related now; at least, they shared a grandson, and so she had better get used to the idea.

Maria could read her hostess's disdain. "Charles assures me that Mr. Trenchard has many fine qualities. He admires him very much."

Caroline thought about this. "Then I will try to do the same."

"I like his wife," said Maria.

The Countess nodded. "Yes, I agree. I do quite like the wife." It was hardly the most gushing of testimonials, but it was a start. In truth, Caroline did approve of Anne, who, unlike her husband, seemed indifferent to social advancement and indeed to others' opinions of herself and her family. There was something instinctively well bred in her lack of interest in being well bred. If only her husband could learn from her. Caroline felt she would have to take a hand, or at least get Charles to take a hand, in bringing his grandfather forward.

"Were you surprised that your son would have married without first telling you?" The moment she had spoken, Maria regretted her words. Why open old wounds now? Of course her hostess must have felt surprise and, worse, shock, even betrayal, and while all this could be veiled by a happy ending, it could not be completely expunged.

But Caroline was thinking. "I don't know how to answer you," she said. "Obviously, we would not have thought the girl suitable, which he knew. He wanted to present us with a *fait accompli* rather than invite our opinion, which would have been negative. But maybe I should admire him for that. Edmund was our son, but we had not crushed his spirit. Then again, was the girl an adventuress, prodded and poked by her snobbish father to reach above her station and use her beauty to hook an innocent boy she was not worthy of?" She paused, staring into the flames.

There was a moment of silence, and her words seemed to hang in the air between them. Then Maria spoke. "What does it matter, really?" she said, and her voice seemed to wake Caroline out of the short trance into which she had fallen. And, as Lady Brockenhurst was forced to acknowledge, there was truth in the question.

What did it matter? John's mother, Grace, had been well enough born, but did that make him a more suitable heir than Charles? No. A thousand times no. And whatever Sophia Trenchard may have lacked, she clearly had spirit and drive, and many other qualities beside her beauty. Edmund would not have been caught—if she had been out to catch him—were she only a pretty face. Caroline was very fond of her husband, but Peregrine was not a driven man. He had been born to a place in life to which he had no objection, but he'd never had a goal that she was aware of. Charles had goals, and he would have goals for the estate and the family, of that she was certain, and when she looked at his two grandfathers, she knew which one had given him that determination to succeed. She turned to the girl beside her and smiled.

"You're right. It doesn't matter. What matters is the future you and Charles will have together."

"And you mean to tell him tomorrow?"

"That reminds me. I never sent the message. I'll write it tonight and have it taken to Bishopsgate first thing."

"And my mother?"

"I'll send a message around there, too. Then we shall have an evening of revelations."

The moment the carriage stopped outside the offices, James was out, banging on the door to be admitted until an upper window opened and a tousled head looked out. James knew him for Charles's clerk. A condition of his employment must have been that he should live above the shop. The young man recognized James's voice, and a few minutes later they were in the office as he struggled to light lamps and make them welcome in his nightshirt.

But he could not help them. "I know Mr. Pope had an engagement this evening. A message arrived earlier in the day. But I could not tell you where it was to be."

"This message," James's eagerness was making him sound angry and the clerk shrank back. "Did he say who it was from?"

"No, Mr. Trenchard. But he seemed glad of it. Something about mending what was broken. That's all."

"And he gave no clue as to where this engagement might take place?" Oliver was just as anxious, but his tone was more moderated. He knew there was no point in frightening the fellow. Although he wanted answers. If his father was right and there were plans for murder, then was he not complicit? Had he not been the lure to catch the victim? He did not know what he felt about Charles Pope now that the truth was out, but he was quite certain he did not want him hurt or dead. "Have you nothing at all that might help us find him? I think it was somewhere near here. So that Mr. Pope would be able to walk there from this office."

The clerk scratched his head. "But he went home to have dinner with his mother. She's just come up to London. Mind you, that's not so far." He thought for a minute. "I think you're right, sir. He said something about its being near the river—"

"My God!" gasped James.

"Wait a minute." Oliver was speaking now. "Is there a street... let me think. All Saints? All Fellows?"

"Allhallows Lane?" said the clerk, and Oliver let out a shout. "That's it! Allhallows Lane. And there's a tavern there. The Black...Swan?"

"The Black Raven. There's a public house called The Black Raven." The clerk was praying that these men had found what they were looking for and he could go back to sleep.

James nodded. "Come down and instruct our coachman."

"It's easy enough to explain—"

"Come down!" And he hurried out, with the others following in his wake.

A damp fog was rolling up the Thames by the time Charles arrived at the narrow, cobbled street that led to the tavern. It was thick and heavy and permeated his coat, making him shiver and pull the dense material around him. He knew Allhallows Lane but not well, and not at night, when the smells of the dirt and waste and refuse in the gutter seemed to be compounded by the odor of fish from nearby Billingsgate Market. He looked about. There was the sign, dimly lit by a hanging lamp but clear enough. The Black

Raven. The longer he stood there, the stranger it seemed that this dingy place should have been chosen by Oliver for their rendez-vous. Perhaps he had meant to be courteous and give himself the journey from Eaton Square, rather than make Charles travel half-way across London. But even so...

He opened the tavern door. It was a long, low-ceilinged, Eliza-bethan black-framed building, left over from earlier times and now encircled by the growing city. Time had not been kind, and it looked like the sort of haunt frequented by thieves and cutpurses rather than the socially ambitious son of a wealthy builder. Nor was it the sort of establishment anyone would travel across London to visit. Oliver must have heard the name and mistaken the standard. But after a moment, Charles released the door and walked farther in.

As he stared through the dense cloud of pipe smoke, he was hit by the acrid odor of spilled beer and stale sweat. His eyes watered a little as he pulled out his handkerchief and held it to his nose. The lighting was low, despite the numerous candles stuck to the top of old beer barrels and wedged in the necks of wine bottles, and the room was almost full. Most of the wooden seats were already taken by men wearing rough coats and workman's boots, their conversation muffled by the sawdust on the floor. But he didn't have long to wait. He had not been there for much more than a minute when a shape rose out of an alcove seat and came toward him. The man was wearing a cloak that covered him almost entirely and a hat pulled down low on his brow. "Pope?" he said as he passed. "Come with me."

For want of a better idea, Charles followed the stranger out into the street, but the man did not pause, walking on toward the river. Finally, Charles stopped. "I will go no farther, sir, unless you tell me who you are and what you want with me."

The other man turned. "My dear fellow," he said. "I am so sorry. I had to get out of that pit of iniquity. I couldn't breathe. I thought you would not care to linger there yourself."

Charles peered at him. "Mr. Bellasis?" He was astounded. Bel-lasis was the last man he was expecting. "What are you doing here? And where is Oliver Trenchard? It was him I came to meet."

"Me too." John was very smooth. He had made up his mind to do this thing and he found, to his surprise, that his determination was not diminished by Charles's presence. He had worried that the sight of his intended victim might drain away his purpose, but it had not. He was ready. He wanted to do it. He just had to get the man to the river's edge. He spoke again. "Oliver Trenchard sent me a message to meet him here. But why the devil did he choose such a hellhole?"

"Possibly he thought it was convenient for me," said Charles. "You remember that my offices are nearby."

"Of course. That must be it."

None of which answered any of the questions that were crowding Charles's brain. "I don't understand why you're here," he said. "Trenchard and I have a private matter to resolve. What is your part in it?"

John nodded, as if absorbing the information. "I can only assume that he wants us to reconcile, too."

Charles looked at him. Once his eyes had grown used to the light, or the lack of it, he could make out John's face. For all his friendly talk, the man's expression was as haughty and arrogant as ever, with his cold eyes and his curling lip. "I was not aware we had a quarrel, sir," he said.

What he did not notice was that Bellasis had been ambling slowly down the lane toward the river as he spoke, and without thinking, Charles had kept up with him, gradually falling into step as they made their way toward the water. They had only to cross the road to reach the edge. There was a long, low guardian wall along this stretch of the river, reaching down into the water, as they were standing on what must naturally have been a hill before it was built upon, and so the Thames was flowing at least ten feet below them. It was deep. John knew that from the fast-flowing current. He had chosen the tavern at this point on the river for exactly these reasons.

"I'm afraid we do have a quarrel, Mr. Pope. I only wish we did not," said John with a sigh.

Charles looked at him. There was something strange about

his voice, an almost strangled quality that distorted his words. Charles began to wish that there was some traffic passing, but there was nothing. "Then I hope we may resolve it, sir." He smiled as he spoke, trying to make it seem as if this were a normal conversation.

"Alas, we cannot," muttered John, "since the only resolution possible for me depends on your—"

"On my what?"

"On your death." And with that, in a sudden movement, John seized him and forced him back against the low wall. Taken by surprise, Charles fought like a tiger, kicking and pushing with all his might, but the other man had already confused his sense of balance, and the parapet of the wall was pressing into his knees. John Bellasis was only rendered stronger by the fight. He had made his decision now. If he failed to kill Charles, he would still hang for attempted murder, so he had nothing to lose by finishing the job. With a final massive effort, he hooked his foot around Charles's ankle, forcing his leg against the other man's thigh, while giving a sudden mighty push to his chest, then releasing his hold. Charles felt himself falling backward, over the wall and down and down, until he was in the icy water, choking on the filth, dragged under by his thick coat, which was already soaked through and as heavy as lead, trying and failing to kick off his shoes, reaching for something, anything, to grasp onto, anything to hold him above the surface. But there was nothing on the plain brick wall above him, and John knew there was nothing.

Bellasis peered down into the darkness. Was Charles gone already? Was that his head still above the water, or was it simply a ripple, a piece of flotsam? In his concentration, he did not hear the running feet, nor feel anything until two hands seized his shoulders and swung him around. He found himself staring into the faces of James Trenchard and his son.

"Where is he? What have you done?"

"Where is who? What are you talking about? What might I have done?" John never flinched. As long as Charles was dead, they had nothing on him. Even now, John could be saved. Every detail could be blamed on Oliver, and James's testimony would be worthless, or so John thought. Then they heard the cry.

"Help me!" The disembodied voice came out of the darkness like the call of a dead spirit speaking from beyond the grave.

Without a word, James wrenched off his coat and shoes and plunged into the river. As they heard the splashing and shouting below them, Oliver and John stared at each other. "Leave them," said John, his voice like warm oil. "Let them go. Your father's had a good life, but let him go now. Then you will have a great inheritance, and so will I. Let us be free of the pair of them." And Oliver hesitated. John saw it. He saw Oliver weaken for a moment, for Oliver Trenchard was a weak man. "Don't worry. He's an old man. It won't take long. You know it's for the best. For all of us."

For the rest of his life Oliver would struggle to understand how he could have entertained the notion even for a second, but he did. He never spoke of it again, but he knew that he did. The death of Charles Pope seemed no great loss to him in that moment, and to be spared his father's judgments and disapproval, to have the money but be free of the chastisement... "No!" he shouted, pulling off his own coat and jumping in after his father. He could hear that he'd been weakened by the cold of the water. James had gone in without thinking and John Bellasis was right. He couldn't hope to last long. But Oliver reached him before he went under. He took hold of him under his armpits and began to swim back to the river's edge, commanding Charles to follow them and hold on to his waist. How he got the three of them back to the wall he never knew; maybe it was guilt that spurred him on, remembering the notion he had entertained, if only for a fraction of a beat. The steep wall might have defeated them, as Oliver grappled vainly at the smooth and slippery surface of the bricks to find something, anything to hold onto, but the hubbub had brought a group of the drinkers from the pub to the scene, and one man came with a rope.

James was lifted out first, then Charles, then Oliver, until the three of them were sitting side by side, coughing up river water, almost dead to the world but not quite. When he saw that they were saved, John Bellasis slipped away. He'd moved farther back through the crowd as it gathered, and now he left it entirely. His victims might be in a daze, but if one of the men or women helping them had seen any part of what had happened, they would have no qualms in handing John over to the Peelers, who were no doubt on their way. He threw off the cloak and hat, kicking them into an open drain, and found his way back into Bishops-gate, where he hailed a cab and disappeared.

Anne could not remember her dream. Only that it had been happy until suddenly there was a disturbance and she opened her eyes to find she was being shaken awake by Mrs. Frant. "You must come at once, ma'am. There's been an accident."

After that, it was a relief to run into the library and find James, Oliver, and Charles, all soaked through but still alive. Charles seemed to have suffered the most. The servants were all awake by now, and she rang at once for Billy and her husband's valet, Miles, to help them all upstairs. While the other servants prepared baths, she ran down to the kitchens to supervise some hot soup. No one dared disturb Mrs. Babbage, so Anne and Mrs. Frant contrived to do their best, and Mrs. Frant carried up the tray.

Charles was in bed, washed and dried and wearing one of Oliver's shirts when Anne saw him next. He was groggy and tired, she could see that, but he was alive. James had given her enough of the story for her to understand what had happened.

"I still don't see why John Bellasis wanted to kill me. What am I to him, or he to me?" For Charles, the nightmare they had lived through seemed completely illogical.

For a moment, Anne thought of telling him the truth, there and then, but it seemed late, and he was confused. Surely it would be better to wait until he could absorb what they were saying. "We'll discuss all that tomorrow. The first decision we have to make is whether we report this to the Peelers. It has to be your choice."

"If I could understand why, then I think I would know better what to do," said Charles, so there they left it for the time being.

Later that night, Anne discussed it with James. "I don't believe we can turn Bellasis over to the law without telling the Brockenhursts," she said. "They would bear the brunt of the story when it became public knowledge."

But James was still enraged by what they had lived through. "You weren't there when he threw Charles to his death, for his death it would have been if we had not appeared at that moment."

"I know." She reached for her husband's hand and squeezed it. "You saved our grandson, and I shall follow your lead, whatever you and Charles decide."

"Oliver saved us both. I was going under for the third time."

Anne smiled. "Then God bless Oliver for a loyal son." Which was all she would ever know about the matter.

Oliver himself was in a very different state of mind at that moment. Susan had woken in time to see him being brought in by Billy, bathed, and put to bed, but he had been silent throughout, refusing to answer her questions. Indeed, it was the servant who told her what had happened. Then Billy left and they were alone. "I shall cancel the coach for tomorrow. We can wait another day until you are quite well." Still he said nothing. "Is there something you're not telling me?" Susan asked as gently as she knew how.

To her amazement, Oliver burst into tears, seizing her and holding her to him as fiercely as she had ever known, sobbing as if his heart must break. So she stroked his hair and spoke soft words of comfort and knew that her plan was coming together and that before too long she would have him back, completely under her control.

Lady Brockenhurst had chosen to receive them all in the main drawing room. She wanted to make a show of it, and the footmen were instructed to wear dress livery. The Trenchards had arrived first, predictably enough, with James almost dancing with excitement at the thought of the evening to come. Caroline was prepared for his elation, and Maria had been deputed to keep him happy until the gathering had properly begun.

Lord Brockenhurst had arrived, as promised, but he was quite bewildered by all the preparations. "What on earth are we celebrating?" he asked, time and again, but his wife wouldn't tell him. Since he had not been part of any of the process, he might as well hear the news at the same time as Charles and the others. She had written to Stephen and Grace, rather than invite them to witness their own humiliation and the dashing of their hopes. She did not admire anyone in that family, but she did feel sorry for them now. Their manner of living was finished, since, when the truth got out, their credit would be gone, and while Peregrine might bail them out from time to time, he would not give money to fund their bad habits indefinitely. In short, now that John would not inherit, it was time for them to learn to cut their cloth accordingly.

Lady Templemore was the next to present herself, along with her son, whom Caroline had hardly seen since he was a boy home from school. "Is Mr. Pope here yet?' he asked, curious.

"No," said James. "He stayed with us last night, and he had to go home to fetch his mother. She will join us for dinner."

Reggie received this information with more joy than his own mama, although she did concede that it was probably "better to know the worst now." When Charles himself came into the drawing room, with Mrs. Pope on his arm, the party was finally complete, and Caroline asked them all to come down into the dining room.

"You're stretching it out rather, aren't you?" said Peregrine, but he didn't object. The truth was his wife intended to stretch it out, for this would be one evening none of them would ever forget.

When Stephen Bellasis read Caroline's letter he felt physically sick. For a moment, he actually thought he was going to *be* sick, but the sensation passed and he simply sat there, staring into space, the sheet of paper in his trembling hands.

"What is it?" said Grace. As an answer, he handed the letter to her, watching as the blood drained from her face. At last she broke the silence. "So this is why he's gone. He must have known."

"Maybe they told him," said Stephen.

Grace nodded. "Peregrine might have written to him. It would be only fair."

"Fair!" Stephen snorted. "When did Peregrine ever do anything that was fair?" But although he tried to sound disdainful, inside he was terrified. Would he have anything like the hold on Peregrine he had enjoyed as father of the heir? Of course not. They were doomed to be a sideshow now, nearly-people, of no account. No wonder John had left.

They'd found the note pushed through the door, though whether John had brought it himself or sent a servant they would never know. He was leaving London, he said. He was leaving England. They could dispose of his rooms, keep what they wanted of his possessions, and sell the rest. He would not be coming back. When he was settled, he would let them know where he might be found. For Stephen, the news was as if someone had pulled the string out of a pearl necklace and sent the beads of their life flying in all directions. And now Caroline's letter had destroyed what little hope remained. Who was this Charles Pope? A sneaky little tradesman who had trespassed into their lives and stolen all their dreams.

"At least we now know why Caroline has always made such a fuss of him," he said.

"No, we don't," snapped Grace. "If he is the legitimate heir, why has he been hidden away since birth? We know nothing. Nothing. Except that John is gone and he won't be back." She was crying as she spoke, crying for the loss of her son, for the loss of her son's future, for the loss of everything they had been counting on, everything they held dear. As soon as the news reached the streets, the last of their credit would be gone and the money-lenders would engulf them. She supposed the Harley Street house must go, although she doubted the sale price would cover their debts. They would retreat to the rectory at Lymington, and she would try her best to keep Stephen away from temptation, but it would not be easy. The truth was they were beggars, and beggars are never choosers. It was a matter of survival, of getting by, of gathering what crumbs they could catch from Peregrine's table. That was all that lay ahead.

Grace stood. "I'm going up," she said. "Don't be too late. Try to sleep, and maybe things will look better in the morning." She didn't believe her own words, and nor did he. On her way to bed, she wanted to check on the silver wine cooler she had stored in John's old room years before. After all, she'd hidden it away in case of a rainy day, and now it was all set to pour. She would need to get it out of the house in the morning as the bailiffs could arrive at any moment. But when she entered the room, she could see the boxes on the wardrobe had been disturbed, and so, with a sinking heart, she knew it was gone, even before she had climbed onto the chair. She was not surprised. It was all of a piece with the rest of her luck. "Well," she thought, "I hope he spends it sensibly."

But Grace knew he would not as she made her weary way across the landing to the dark and ugly bedroom that awaited her.

Charles Pope's astonishment was the greatest, naturally. Although, as he listened, so many details seemed to fall into place. He wondered now why he had never asked himself if there was a blood link that would explain James's determination to help him succeed, or Caroline's *idée fixe* that she must invest a fortune in the activities of a young and obscure adventurer she barely knew. He could never have guessed the final discovery, that he was legitimate after all, but he did think he should have divined the blood connection long ago.

His wonder at his own transformation was matched by that of Lady Templemore, who could hardly believe that, just as she had brought herself to swallow the bitter pill, it had suddenly been converted into nectar. Naturally, she'd suspected—when Maria spoke of the Earl whose son was dead—that Charles must have Bellasis blood, but she'd given no sign of it in order to be able to punish Caroline, so angry was she to see her daughter foisted off with a bastard offshoot. Now all was changed. The very same position she had longed for, striven for, fought for on behalf of her cherished daughter had been given back, enhanced this time by love. She wanted to sing, she wanted to dance and throw her arms above her head and laugh, but instead she had to control her enthusiasm, lest she be mistaken for some greedy outsider, hungering for things that had no moral worth. So she smiled pleasantly and nodded and found herself chuckling at Charles's witticisms, because she had begun to see that Maria was right and the young man was attractive, even very attractive, which, strangely, she had not noticed before.

Reggie Templemore was delighted, too, but his happiness was less complicated and more tempered than his parent's. He had been called over to London by his mother and his sister to arbitrate in a family dispute, which of all things he detested the most, and lo and behold, the fight had evaporated in a sea of universal joy. Added to which he thought that Charles seemed a nice enough fellow, and he was happy that his sister had found so creditable a way forward. He had nothing much invested in the fight, which had only recently been made clear to him, so his gladness was of a calmer order than some of the reactions on display around the table, but he was glad all the same. Now he might return home with more confidence in the future. He had been particularly pleased when Charles had explained to his grandfathers (to the delight of one and the bewilderment of the other) that he would not be giving up his mill or his cotton business. He would appoint a competent manager, of course, but he felt he had an instinct for trade and he did not intend to neglect it. Naturally, Peregrine shook his head at this contrary ambition, as he saw it, but Caroline did not. After she had thought it through, she tended to side with James Trenchard on the matter, the first and probably the last time she would do such a thing. Reggie was only too happy to welcome someone with a head for business into the family. It was a gift that none of the Greys had possessed for centuries.

Mrs. Pope had not spoken much during the discussion, but she was perhaps the person most affected in the room. The daughter and wife of Church of England vicars, it was odd enough to find herself dining amid the splendors of Brockenhurst House, let alone to learn that her son would one day be the master of this very house and many others besides. But gradually, through the evening, it became clear that her status in Charles's life would remain quite unaffected. He wanted her to enjoy his elevation, not to feel undermined by it, and so she determined she would follow his lead and celebrate. Only once did she weigh into the talk in a forceful way, when Lord Brockenhurst attempted to suggest that now Charles should abandon his dealings with the cotton market. At this she shook her head. "Oh no," she said, and her voice was quite stern. "You'll never get Charles to stop working. You might as well tell a fish not to swim or a bird not to fly." Caroline had clapped her hands at this, and Charles raised a toast to Mrs. Pope's health.

It would be hard to say which of the two grandfathers was most delighted with the way things had turned out. James had a viscount for a grandson, with a head for business, too, who could share all that he'd never been able to share with Oliver. James's descendants would be in the forefront of British life, and he, in his imaginings, would walk with the great ones of the earth henceforth. Anne did not suffer from these delusions, but she saw no harm in indulging James for the time being. He could feel like a successful man at this moment. Why shouldn't he? He'd achieved everything he had set out to achieve. And she wanted him to enjoy that feeling for as long as he could. For herself, she was happy that Sophia's child was destined for a life of distinction. She liked Maria. She even quite liked Caroline, more than she ever thought she would, and she was content. She saw herself spending time at Glanville with Oliver and Susan, or at Lymington with Charles and Maria, and otherwise leading a quiet and pleasing life. She thought she might take a hand in shaping up some of the gardens in the squares of Belgravia. James could make that happen for her, and it would be a fulfilling use of her time. Her son and her grandson were settled happily, or, in Oliver's case, happily enough, and no one could ask for more than that.

Only Oliver, in all that high-spirited company, was rather muted. The truth was that when he reviewed his own actions, he felt ashamed and humiliated and even bewildered that he could have chosen to behave as he had done. Even his jealousy of Sophia's son seemed petty and unmanly when he looked back on it. The fact that he had not known Pope was his nephew was no excuse. It was hard, perhaps, to accept that James's grandson would give James more pleasure than his son, but now things had worked out for the best. And a few years of running Glanville might help Oliver to feel less of a failure. Still, he was haunted by his decision to help John Bellasis by writing the note and, worse, his moment of hesitation by the river's edge. That, at least, he could never share with anyone, and so he must carry the scar of guilt to his grave.

Oliver had gone around to John's lodgings earlier that day, but he was told that Mr. Bellasis had left. His trunks had been loaded in the small hours onto a cart that would accompany his cab to the station, although which station the doorman could not say. Oliver wasn't surprised, and when he told the facts to Charles later, back in Eaton Square, they'd agreed, against James's wishes, to let the matter drop. The scandal would be immense, John would be hanged, and none of them would ever be free of the shadow cast by that one terrible night. In fact, Charles, showing more forgiveness than either James or Oliver were capable of, suggested that he might have to find some sort of pension for John, as he'd lived his whole life in expectation of inheriting and had no skills with which to keep body and soul together. Clearly, the loss of his prospects had driven John mad, truly insane, and would they be right to hang a man for that? To this, when he had finally accepted the proposition, James added one condition. Any pension must be paid only as long as John remained out of Britain. "England, Scotland, Wales, and Ireland must all be free of him. Let him roam the Continent in search of a resting place, but he will not find one here." And so it was agreed between them: John Bellasis must spend the rest of his life as a wanderer, in exile, or come home to live as a pauper.

Susan had a complicated role to play during the festivities. She had known the truth about Charles before any of the rest of them, but she could not show that she knew, since she had learned it in bed with John Bellasis. And so she had to gasp and cheer and clap her hands in amazed delight, all the while knowing that Anne, seated across the table from her, was fully aware that Susan was pretending. But things would be easier from now on. They would not discuss the revelations of Susan's past, nor the true origins of the child she carried, nor anything else that endangered the happiness of the younger Trenchard couple. If Susan strayed again, if she made Oliver unhappy, then things might be different, but Susan would not stray. She had gone to the cliff edge once, and she did not intend to do so again. Her mother-in-law would not betray her, and she would not betray Oliver. She could make it work, and she would.

As for Peregrine Brockenhurst, the news had entirely remade him. He did not fully understand why Caroline had kept him in the dark when she'd first discovered this young man was Edmund's son, but he didn't care. He saw his wife through the eyes of reverence. He was in awe at her grasp of how the world worked, at her capacity to control and command. Now his life had a point again, managing the estates had a point again, and his family had a future once more. He could almost feel the energy come surging back through his body. He was eager—a sensation so strange that he had difficulty identifying it when it first began to manifest itself once more. He did feel a slight twinge of pity for John, who had banked everything on the card of his inheritance only to turn it over and find it was a joker. He would consult Charles and see what could be done. In fact, Charles would know what to do about everything. Of that he was quite confident. Yes. He would leave it up to Charles.

The evening was over and the party made its way down into the hall. There was some idea that James's carriage might take Charles and Mrs. Pope back to Holborn, but Charles wouldn't hear of it. He'd find a hansom cab easily enough, he said, and that would be more than sufficient. As they reached the bottom of the great staircase, Maria lingered near him, and when they were exchanging good-byes Caroline Brockenhurst spoke. "If he really means to travel home in a cab, then why not go outside with him, my dear, to look for one?"

The others were rather startled that this suggestion should come from one to whom appearances were all, but Maria stepped forward and took Charles's arm before his grandmother could change her mind. As they left the building, Lady Templemore aimed a slightly questioning look at her hostess, but Caroline was unrepentant. "Oh, I don't think anything too terrible will come of it," she said.

To which Anne replied, "Nothing terrible will come of it at all."

And that was more than enough to suggest to the assembled company the alliances and differences that were to determine the way the family would manage itself over the coming decades.

Out on the pavement, the lovers scanned the square, waiting for an empty vehicle. Maria broke the silence. "Can I put my hand in your pocket? I'm so cold. I shouldn't have come out without a wrap." And of course he stripped off his coat and wrapped her in it, and soon her hand, entwined with his, was warm inside the pocket.

"Does this mean I can come to India with you?" she asked.

He thought for a moment. "If you want. We can make it our wedding journey, if your mother won't object."

"If she tries to object, she'll have to deal with me."

He laughed. "You must think me very stupid. That I suspected nothing."

But Maria wouldn't have that. "Certainly not. To the pure in mind all things are pure. You have no taste for intrigue, so you wouldn't have suspected it in others."

He shook his head. "Mr. Trenchard's interest was perhaps explicable. He was a friend to my father, or so I thought; maybe I can be forgiven for accepting his help without questioning it. But Lady Brockenhurst? A countess suddenly feels the urge to invest in the business of a young man she hardly knows? Wasn't that a clue for someone less blind than I?" He sighed at his own inadequacy.

"Nonsense," said Maria. "All the world knows it is better to be gullible than suspicious." And with that she tilted her face up toward his, and he had the great pleasure of planting a kiss on her lips. They did not know it then, but he would love her with the same passion until he died. Which is quite enough to make a happy ending.

Later that night, Anne was seated at her dressing table while Mrs. Frant was brushing out her hair. James and Oliver were still downstairs in the library, enjoying a glass of brandy, and Charles had returned to Holborn with Mrs. Pope. Before they parted, the plan was made for them to move into Brockenhurst House as soon as they chose, and so this part of their story was almost settled. Anne did not entirely envy Mrs. Pope's probable future as a sort of unpaid companion to the Countess, but at least her life would not be lonely.

"I think we should start looking for a new lady's maid," Anne said. Mrs. Frant had been a lady's maid in the past and she knew what she was doing, but it was too much work for one person to combine the two roles, as they both knew.

"I'll make inquiries in the morning, ma'am. Leave it to me." Mrs. Frant had no intention of leaving it to Mrs. Trenchard, who had selected that nasty, dishonest Miss Ellis when she was left to her own devices. Nobody like that would get past Mrs. Frant. "And may I make a suggestion, ma'am?"

"Please."

"Might we confirm Billy in his post as butler? He's a little young, I suppose, but he knows the house and Mr. Trenchard's ways, and he's certainly eager to be allowed to try."

"If you think he could manage..." Anne was rather surprised that Mrs. Frant would want a man in his thirties in the position. "But wouldn't it place more responsibility on your shoulders?"

"Don't worry about that, ma'am." Mrs. Frant was fully aware that by obtaining the position for Billy, he would be forever in her debt. If she controlled the butler and chose the lady's maid, her life would be a good deal simpler. And that was what Mrs. Frant wanted. A simple life, with her own good self in control of it. "But of course, it's entirely up to you, ma'am," she added. And with that she placed the brush down on the dressing table. "Will that be all?"

"Yes," said Anne. "Thank you. Good night."

So the housekeeper closed the door behind her, leaving Anne to her thoughts. She would accept Mrs. Frant's suggestions, in the hope that things would settle down. Then they could just get on with their lives.

It was late, and a slight drizzle had started to fall as John Bellasis made his way from the dirty backstreet restaurant to his dreary, cheap hotel. He had left his man, Roger, to unpack and arrange his rooms as well as he was able, but they were a sad substitute for his set at Albany, modest as it had been. He doubted Roger would stay for long. He was too far from his old friends and haunts, and for what? What would exile in Dieppe ever bring him? What was John doing there, for that matter? He couldn't believe that he was safe. Just because they had not set anyone on him at once, as he had feared they might, did not mean they would let things rest forever. He must keep moving, that was the answer, and never stay too long in one place. But how was he to manage? What was he to live on? Idly, he found himself wondering what was the French for moneylender.

Then the drizzle turned to rain and he broke into a run.